A

R U T H   S U C K O w

O M N I B U S

A BUR OAK BOOK

A

RUTH SUCKOW

OMNIBUS

BY RUTH SUCKOW

WITH A NEW INTRODUCTION

BY CLARENCE A. ANDREWS

University of Iowa Press 𝚿 Iowa City

University of Iowa Press, Iowa City 52242

Copyright © 1988 by the University of Iowa

Printed in the United States of America

First edition, 1988

Book and cover design by Richard Hendel

Typesetting by G & S Typesetters, Inc., Austin, Texas

Printing and binding by Versa Press, East Peoria, Illinois

"Susan and the Doctor," "What Have I?" "A Great Mollie" (originally "Strong as a Man"), "Midwestern Primitive," and "The Little Girl from Town" originally appeared in *Harper's Monthly Magazine*. "Home-coming," "The Crick," and "Three, Counting the Cat" originally appeared in *Good Housekeeping*. "A Part of the Institution" originally appeared in the *Smart Set*, "Visiting" in the *Pictorial Review*, and "The Man of the Family" in the *American Mercury*.

Library of Congress Cataloging-in-Publication Data

Suckow, Ruth, 1892–1960.
    A Ruth Suckow omnibus / by Ruth Suckow; with a new introduction by Clarence A. Andrews.—1st ed.
        p.   cm.—(A Bur oak book)
    Short stories reprinted from various periodicals.
    Contents: Ruth Suckow / by Clarence A. Andrews—Susan and the doctor—Home-coming—A part of the institution—Visiting—The crick—What have I?—A great Mollie—Three, counting the cat—Midwest primitive—The little girl from town—The man of the family.
    ISBN 0-87745-207-5 (pbk.)
    I. Title.   II. Series.
PS3537.U34A6   1988
813'.52—dc19   88-15059
                                                            CIP

CONTENTS

RUTH SUCKOW

.   .   .   .   .   .

BY   CLARENCE   A.   ANDREWS

The small town, the family farm, and the close-knit family of several generations are disappearing from America. But once they were mainstays of a way of life that, along with our concept of democracy, helped our country's experiment in social and political organization work.

Ruth Suckow was the fictional delineator of that way of life—the transitional era between the initial settlement and development of the midwestern frontier, and the creation and development of social concepts and technological innovations that were to point the way to our present social state.

Short-story writer, essayist, and novelist, Suckow (1892–1960) was born in Hawarden, Iowa, a newly settled town in the northwest corner of the state. Through her parents' German immigrant ancestors, she got a glimpse of the Old World; in the town and countryside, she watched the transition from the frontier to an organized society. In the nine Iowa towns in which she grew up as her Congregational minister father took over successive pastorates, she saw other towns of varying sizes in various stages of growth and development. Author and editor Frank Luther Mott, one of the developers of the university's Iowa Writers' Workshop, commented, "Probably the three best vantage points from which one [might] observe life in midwestern small towns are the office of the local newspaper, the doctor's office and the parsonage; and so Miss Suckow (who must have had very sharp eyes from childhood) was advantageously placed."

But Suckow did not write from such a limited background. After high school, she was educated at Grinnell College (where James Norman Hall, another well-known Iowa writer, graduated the year Suckow matriculated there) and in Boston and Denver. She later lived near the campus of Iowa State Teachers College in Cedar Falls; in Chicago; in Greenwich Village; in Robert Frost's Vermont home; in Tucson, Arizona; in Yaddo, a New York writers' colony; and finally in Claremont, California. Thus she was able to bring to her fiction the viewpoint of one who had traveled much and had a great variety of social experiences.

At the University of Denver, where she earned an M.A. in English, and at the University of Iowa, where she spent a year under the tutelage of John Towner Frederick, Suckow was exposed to concepts about the nature and role of fiction which were to play an important part in twentieth-century fiction and literary criticism. Frederick, a novelist in his own right and an editor and critic as well, was instrumental in the development of a great many young midwestern writers. He taught them to base their fiction on their observations of the life around them—on farms or in towns and cities. Fiction was to consist of a slice of life with no formulaic beginnings, middles, and endings. Frederick published many stories by these writers in his *Midland*, a magazine he had founded in Iowa City in 1915.

Frederick's principles reinforced Suckow's own notions of what fiction should be. In a 1927 essay in *The Saturday Review of Literature*, she rejected Poe's classic definition (a short story is a story which can be read at one sitting) and *any* definitions which began, "*The* Short Story is . . ." Short stories, she wrote, should be "a running commentary upon life; fireflies in the dark; questions and answers; fragments, or small and finished bits of beauty; [with an] effect that is poignant, deep, and lasting; whatever, in fact, their author has the power to make of them. . . ."

Suckow's characters include boys and girls, men and women, the elderly, families, farmers, small-town and city dwellers. In her 1934 novel *The Folks*, her most ambitious work, she writes about a four-generation family from the ending of the horse-and-buggy era to the 1930s depression. Her settings in the novel include a farm, a small town, an apartment in Greenwich Village, and California. Suckow's characters are usually in some situation or stage which should have some solution, but the solution is not always found, and, if it is, it is often ambiguous.

Frederick published Suckow's first short stories in his *Midland*, then, characteristically, recognizing her talent and her potential for larger audiences than the *Midland*'s, introduced her to Henry Mencken and George Jean Nathan. They published Suckow's short stories first in their *Smart Set* and then in their *American Mercury*. Her three short novels, one of which is included here, were published in the *Smart Set*. But when she sent Mencken and Nathan the longer novel, *Country People*, they said it was too long and persuaded their financial backer, Alfred A. Knopf, to publish it in book form.

In all, Suckow was to publish eight novels, three volumes of short fiction, two anthologies of miscellaneous work, and numerous uncollected essays, short stories, and reviews. Her books were all published by major American publishers. A few were reprinted in foreign editions.

A Part of the Institution is "the best of the lot" of the short novels. Its setting, "Adams College—'the Pioneer College of the Prairies'"—could be any one of the small denominational colleges in the Midwest, but the college and Adamsville have many resemblances to Grinnell College and Grinnell, Iowa.

In Hester Harris, a girl who has grown up in Adamsville, and whose constant girlhood prayer has been to go to Adams and be taken into the Elizabeth Barrett Browning society, Suckow has created an original fictional portrait. In Jinny, one of three persons whose relationships with Hester last through the years, Suckow, while not creating an original type, as she admitted in a 1928 essay entitled "Literary Soubrettes," has created the prototype of those bohemian girls who are characters in *The Odyssey of a Nice Girl* (1925), in *The Kramer Girls* (1930), and in *The Folks* (1934):

> *She is not the princess of the fairy tale. She can never wear a crown [or] marry the prince. . . . [But] she has one privilege denied the heroine—she can afford to be herself. . . . she acts as a safety valve, a relief, a little fresh breath of actuality, without whom fiction . . . would have been almost totally unenlivened.*

Of the women in Suckow's novels and short stories, John T. Frederick wrote:

> *[They] are not magazine-cover heroines, not romantically virtuous or interestingly unprincipled; they are not such figures as middle-aged masculine [book] reviewers tend to fall in love with. But they are human beings of terrible veracity. And they are human beings related in their experience to the most critical contours of our times.*

Of the eleven stories in this collection, five are from the long-out-of-print *Children and Older People* (1931); three of these were honored by selection as annual "best-short-stories-of-the-year." (A number of other Suckow short stories were similarly selected.) Three of the others were first published in *Good Housekeeping* and one in the *Pictorial Review*—magazines appealing primarily to women. One appeared in *Harper's Monthly*, a magazine then appealing primarily to men, and one was published in the *Smart Set*.

The stories published here contain a number of themes and characters which have their analogies in other Suckow fiction. "The Little Girl from Town" contrasts the idealism of the town with the practicality of the country. "The Man of the Family" has a theme common enough in actual life in the early part of this century: a boy forced to go to work to help support his family. However, his decision creates a problem for a store owner and his wife. A quite different version of the theme is seen in "A Start in Life," which is not in this book. "A Great Mollie," a favorite of Suckow's, concerns a mannish type who can do anything men can do, often even better. Mollie, though, is quite different from the mannish Georgie in *The Kramer Girls* (1930). "Home-coming" offers another Suckow theme, the contrast between past and present, a theme also used in "What Have I?" "Visiting" involves another Suckow theme, that of generational conflict.

"The Crick" (a midwest pronunciation of *creek*, a small stream) is set in a small town which is both the Hawarden of Suckow's childhood and the New Hope of *New Hope* (1942). A central character in both is a minister's small daughter whose name is Delight. The "crick" is prominent in both story and novel. But Delight is a much different person in each. In the novel, which is idyllic in tone, Delight and a town boy her age are constant companions during the two years her father is a minister in New Hope. But it is Clarence, the town boy, who has adventures along the creek—a creek which never floods in the two years, although now and then there is talk of a possible "overflow."

The setting of "What Have I?" is not a small town or rural area, but rather the suburb of a city. The implicit theme of corruption or embezzlement looks toward *The John Wood Case* (1957), Suckow's final novel.

In a letter, Ferner Nuhn, Suckow's husband, wrote that his wife had a lifelong affection for cats. Some fictional spinoffs of that affection are the cat Washington Bonney in *The Bonney Family* (1928) and the story "Spinster and Cat" (not in this collection). A cat serves as the catalyst for an important decision in "Three, Counting the Cat" in this collection (originally titled by Suckow "The Next One after the Last"). Noting the importance of detail in Suckow's fiction, Ferner Nuhn commented that Washington Bonney is first of all a cat, but secondly he is important in his relationship to human beings, for if things-in-themselves were Suckow's first concern, their relation to other things and to people was her ultimate concern.

"Midwestern Primitive" has one of Suckow's favorite characters—a German mother—and a favorite theme: the place of the individualist in our society.

"Susan and the Doctor" is an unusual story for Suckow—and one which shows that the critic who said her work lacked a touch of the meretricious had not read all of it. For her time, Suckow took the situation in this book about as far as she could. One has only to turn on the television set any night of the week to see what a modern author would do with this theme!

For a time in the 1920s, Suckow spent her summers in the village of Earlville, Iowa, where her father had twice had a pastorate. There, living in a two-room cottage, now the site of a Ruth Suckow memorial park, she raised bees and produced honey (skills which she had learned while living in Denver), becoming a familiar sight to village residents as she bicycled in knee-length knickers between her apiary and her cottage. The proceeds from her work financed her residence in the wintertime in her Greenwich Village apartment, where she wrote her fiction. In later years, her stepmother, Opal Suckow, was the Earlville village librarian, and the Earlville library is now the Ruth Suckow Memorial Library.

Occasionally during those summers, Ferner Nuhn, a writer and book reviewer from Cedar Falls, some seventy miles to the west, would drive his Model T Ford across dusty or muddy roads to call on Suckow. They were married in 1929, just after publication of *The Bonney Family*.

Probably because short stories did not have the potential for enough income to support her while writing, beginning with the success of *Country People* (1924) and *The Odyssey of a Nice Girl* (1925), Suckow concentrated more and more on book-length works. During the decade after *The Folks* (1934) she wrote only three short stories, some essays and book reviews, and, finally, *New Hope* (1942), in which she returned to the past of her own childhood in Hawarden. The consequence of looking backward almost half a century, says Martin Mohr, was "a nostalgic realization of a simple happy time before the outside world intruded on the complacency of [rural and small-town] Iowa." A decade later, in 1952, she combined some previously uncollected stories and "A Memoir" in *Some Others and Myself*. "A Memoir" is a spiritual biography of her parents and herself, and some of the stories are equal to Suckow's best work done earlier—when she was much younger. (She was now sixty.)

In 1958, despite an illness which had plagued her for a long time and which had been responsible for the Nuhns' move to California, she published her last book, *The John Wood Case*, a novel of the consequences in and to a small town when one of its leading citizens and church members confesses to having embezzled a large sum of money over a period of years. By coincidence, just three years later, in a town located partly in the same county as Hawarden, Suckow's literary subject was revealed to have a close parallel. A woman who, like John Wood, was a prominent citizen and pillar of her Congregational church confessed to embezzling several million dollars from the bank of which her father was president and where she was employed.

The John Wood Case was a fitting conclusion to the career of a writer who, in the words of a professor of literature who knew her well, "left us as she came, an artist with incorrigible integrity whose moral and spiritual values were the foundation of her life and art."

A

·   ·   ·   ·   ·   ·

RUTH SUCKOW

·   ·   ·   ·   ·

OMNIBUS

SUSAN AND

· · · · · ·

THE DOCTOR

· · · · · ·

Susan started going with the boys early. Too early. Her mother had died, and there was no one to look after her. Her father had affairs of his own on his hands.

Susan's escapades, from the time she was thirteen, had been a source of talk in the town where she lived. But they seemed all to have happened in a past that was now incredible. People had almost forgotten that she had once gone with Buddie Merton and Carl Flannigan and Chuck Myers and Pat Dougherty— her affair had been going on for so many years with the Doctor.

And it had obscured not only her relations to other men, but almost everything else about Susan. People did not think about the long and steady efficiency of her position in the Farmers Bank, where she had risen from clerk to assistant cashier, and where she was actually a stand-by. When they went into the bank, and up to Susan's little barred window, they did not see her—slim, shining-haired, immaculate—as the cashier who dealt out nickels and dimes and bills with swift, experienced, white fingers. They did not recall how her present security was due to herself alone. She had never depended upon her father for a living. She had never depended upon any one. She had borrowed money and taken a business course and then asked old Henry Houghton for a place in the bank; and it was upon that first meager and grudging admission that she had lived and put money aside and paid for the always fashionable perfection of her tailored clothes and the smartness of her hats. They looked through the little window at her white hands and smooth hair, and thought:

"I wonder how her affair is coming on with the Doctor!"

Oh, yes! Susan was handy, and she was bright. She made some of those pretty clothes herself—knitted scarves when scarves were in fashion, and embroidered collar and cuff sets when they were the thing. She kept her two rooms and kitchenette at Mrs. Calverton's in exquisite order. Women did admit that. And there were men in town who said that no one in that bank knew as much about its business as Susan. But all that seemed irrelevant to the consistent interest of her love affair.

It obscured the rest of her life to Susan herself. There was never a moment when she was not aware of it. At the bank, when she was making up accounts with swift and practiced accuracy, it was there in her breast, something unsatisfied, an ache and a craving; it was there behind the businesslike rhythm of the adding machine; and when she sat at the big table in the back room where the sunshine lay slantwise in the morning its sweetness enveloped her in dreamy pain. She could never give herself up to the warmth of the sunshine. Her white fingers had to keep at work to ease the craving and subdue the thoughts that drew to their tight, inevitable center in her mind.

"Always at it!" old Tommy Munson, wealthy farmer and nominal vice president, said to her jovially when he came into the bank.

He was the only person in town who thought of Susan as cashier and seemed never to have heard of her affair with the Doctor.

It was with her when she went out on the street at noon. She frowned at the outdoor brightness. Suppose the Doctor should come past! The possibility of it blinded her for a moment, with a tense persistence of desire; and she would have liked—if she could have liked!—to stay in the shelter of the bank, where it was shaded and apart. She might be with Nita Allen, the stenographer; but her eyes could not be restrained from their restless, watching alertness. She must notice every car on the street. She must look down the narrowing vista to the building where the Doctor had his office on the fifth floor, and must strain for a brief and unsatisfying glimpse of the small and distant figure of a man who might be the Doctor himself coming out of the building. In Wessel's drugstore, where she had her tuna-fish sandwich and glass of malted milk at the shining new counter, she had to talk gay and brightly, in the usual ironic repartee, with the crowded line of stenographers and young business men, above her restless preoccupation and the constant small wear of pain.

"Hello, Susan! How are you?"

"Fine."

"Where do you keep yourself these days?"

In the busy street of the growing town she felt almost a stranger—she, Susan, who had lived here all her life and knew every window display in every store! But her affair with the Doctor had set her apart from the rest of the town—from the old crowd, her own crowd: Elsie Adams, who was married and had two babies; Letha Grove, who lived with her parents and hadn't changed since high school days; Mary Wilson, who came back now and then from her work in Chicago. Susan seemed never to have known another man than the Doctor; and at times, when she heard in the drugstore the animated chatter about dances, she would wonder if she could actually be Susan—the one whom the boys used to fall over one another to ask to dances, who chose this one or that with imperious freedom, who was the most popular girl of her day.

She was tense and defiant in her loyalty—and the thing had been going on, how many years?—but all the same, her eyes could not meet the curious or carefully incurious eyes of older women, her mother's friends, whom she might pass on this street and who would ask her, "Well, Susan, how are you getting along?" The consciousness of her affair with the Doctor hung between them, clouding the old neighborly relationship. Mrs. Andrews had tried to "speak to her" once about it. She had talked about Susan's mother while Susan stood with head up and lips haughtily closed. But it made Susan dread the street.

When she went into the bank again she would sometimes stand for a moment, humiliated and hurt through every nerve, because this one thing must claim her whole being. The spirit of independence, upright and narrow, that lived in her slim body rebelled. She thought of the time when she used to say airily to Carl Flannigan, "No, I can't go anywhere—I've got to do some work for the bank"; and of the later days when, after one of those excitingly perilous meetings with Pat Dougherty, who was just getting his divorce, she used to go back to the bank, and think with cool exultancy, "Well, here I'm by myself!" She, Susan, who had always been so sure, imperious, efficient, cool . . .

"I won't stand this. It's got to end."

But then the far more torturing fear that it might end shot through her in pain.

But when she went home after work—home? well, back to Mrs. Calverton's—at half-past-five, through smoky twilights of fall or the veiled tenderness of spring, resentful wonder would come over her again. Had there actually been a time when she was her own self, Susan, free and wild and belonging to herself; when she could walk swiftly through such a twilight, breathing the acrid smoke, or linger and lift her face to the damp spring air, with love left over for the little leaves and the tulips, with nothing to come between her and the night?

She went up the same gray-painted steps of the large, neat porch. She put her hand on the same bronze knob of the door. Inside, the house odor, orderly and slightly aging and remote, never quite that of home, enveloped her in dreariness. She could not stand the board that creaked on the stairs and the hot-water faucet that ran a meager and maddening trickle.

How could she endure this place a day longer? She had certainly never meant to spend all her life in a rooming house. Independence was all right. She wasn't going to have to ask anybody for things. But Susan had always planned, being methodical and worldly shrewd, that when the time came, when she was ready, she would marry and have a home of her own, the kind she wanted. And here she was, well along in the twenties, with nearly all the other girls in the crowd settled, and she still living in two rented rooms at Mrs. Calverton's! Sometimes it seemed as if her whole scheme of life were going astray.

But when she entered her room, with its waiting orderliness of cushions and reading lamp and cigarette trays placed here and there, the dreariness vanished. Her impatience sternly curbed itself. Mrs. Calverton was used to the whole thing. The Doctor could come, and she let them alone. A move—one little thing like that—and the whole perilous, precious status of the thing might be lost.

Besides, the Doctor would be here in a little while.

Susan went into the kitchenette. The shelves were filled with things of his own special choice—Mocha coffee, fig preserves, salted almonds. Susan saw these things, and they brought back the beloved and secret intimacy of a hundred little dinners. She used to love to put on her best clothes and go out to dinner with men, to the dining room of the Melrose, the most expensive place in town, where she would see people and be seen by them. But there was a painful kind of delight in giving up these old pleasures of hers—her own special pleasures. She wanted them again at times; but there was the same delight in sacrificing them to his demands for secrecy and seclusion.

Anyway, he would be here in a little while. She would be with him.

He came up the stairs, into the living room, into the doorway of the kitchenette. Susan felt the vital largeness of his presence, warming the whole place into life; although—with her old manner of cool concentration—she did not turn from her work at the small gas stove. His arms were around her, and she was drawn backward.

"Susan! Aren't you going to tell me you're glad to see me?"

Through his arms she felt the straining domination of his need.

The dinner was exciting and happy and cozy—one of their own little dinners, at the card table with the linen cloth that Susan had embroidered in her leisure time, with the favorite dishes she had kept from her own home, and with the orange candles and the green-glass candlesticks that he had brought her. The shades were down. Their voices were low, so that even Mrs. Calverton could not hear. He told her his professional troubles and leaned upon the cool practicality of her advice, even while he was demanding from her the sympathy that her pride would not seem to yield him. The old atmosphere of troubled splendor was about him, blinding her clearsightedness, and forcing devotion, that was half maternal, out of the independence she could not admit that she had lost.

And then, when dinner was over, he wouldn't permit her to wash the dishes, upset the precision of her routine to her anger and delight, and drew her to him.

But after he had left, Susan lay in her narrow bed aching and alone. Her tingling body was tense with resentment. No matter how they parted, her body was left tense and aching—for he went away, he left her alone, she could not stay warm and at ease in his arms and wake up beside him in the morning. She hated him.

Then she turned and tossed. Her sleep seemed always to be shallow and tense. She craved wildly to break away from him. Why must her own need be sacrificed to his? Her life was passing. But it was as if he had sown within her the seed of his trouble. She could not wrench it out of her. In the night, in the darkness, she could let her coolness be diffused with aching tenderness. This was the only way that it could be for him—so he thought; and she, Susan, was the only woman in town with courage to take him as he must be taken. She thrilled with pride of his largeness, handsomeness, and splendor; and she would rather have him secretly, equivocally hers than to have all the common, tame little men whom the other girls had married. The straight and narrow loyalty that made her a stand-by in the bank held her to him in tense, undeviating devotion.

The affair had begun in quite a different way.

Susan, for the time being, was free of all her men. In disgust she had broken the last frayed end of her brief but hotly melodramatic "case" with Pat Dougherty. And she didn't want to go with any one for a while. It seemed to her that she had tried nearly all the eligible men in this town, and that there was no interest in any of them. There wasn't a one whose silly devotion could make up for the loss of her position in the bank or who could give her anything that could surpass it.

"I'm hard-hearted," Susan said coolly and with a slightly malicious enjoyment of power, to the wistfully sentimental Letha Grove. "If I ever get married, I'll marry for money. I'll marry a man who can get more for me than I can get for myself. At present—I'll stay as I am."

In idleness and in revulsion from the extremely hot persistence of Pat Dougherty, Susan had looked up some of the old high-school crowd again. She took pleasure in going with Letha Grove and "the girls" to concerts and basket-ball games. There was in it a defiance of the men who admired her, and a challenge to them. Never had she enjoyed her work at the bank so much. She exulted in the rapid, ceaseless click of her adding machine. Whenever she thought of Pat Dougherty, it was with a wild, glad sense of escape. At this time Susan used to wake up and look out at the dew-wet grass of Mrs. Calverton's lawn, with a feeling as cool and free and fresh as the morning.

However, such a state of affairs could not last for any one used to as much excitement as Susan. She began to get restless and to make excuses when the girls wanted her to go somewhere with them. She wanted—what did she want?—she didn't know. But something.

"I'll tell you what's the matter with you," Mrs. Calverton said. Susan used to go downstairs sometimes and talk to Mrs. Calverton in the evening. "You've never been in love. That's what's the trouble."

"I!" Susan exclaimed. "This is about the first time I've been out of it."

"You think so," Mrs. Calverton said.

She rocked. She was mending curtains, while Susan embroidered a stamped pink nightgown that she had bought in the "art goods department" of Stephenson's store. She ducked her mouth and bit off a thread.

Susan laughed. It was funny to hear Mrs. Calverton talking to her!—Mrs. Calverton, shapeless and faded, whose husband (every one knew) had been good-for-nothing, never kept a job, went out with other women, and had left Mrs. Calverton to take in roomers and keep this old family home of hers going.

"That's so," Mrs. Calverton insisted. "I know what I'm talking about." She added, with that portentous mysteriousness in talking about men and marriage that older women affected, and that Susan had always laughed at, "You'll see some day!"

Susan laughed gleefully again. But when she went back upstairs to her room, that she had taken such delight in arranging and keeping just as she wanted it, she felt restless and lonely. She resented Mrs. Calverton. Old married women always pretended to know so much. Besides kindness, and a sad dwelling upon past mysterious events, it seemed to her that there had been resentment in Mrs. Calverton's tone, and a gloomy looking forward to seeing Susan leveled down at last with other women. But, superior as she felt, what Mrs. Calverton had said—her tone and her look of quiet, mysterious knowledge recurred sometimes to Susan; and again she felt that restlessness.

She began to look at men with a different eye, although she was scarcely aware of it. Town seemed all dull and too familiar to her, and she thought of going away somewhere. She was jealous of her present freedom, and tired of it. At any rate, she couldn't stand "the girls" any longer!—their twitterings, their secrets, their eager veiled interest in every man who appeared. They all seemed silly to her; and there was even more interest in the saddened, subdued, mysteriously completed presence of Mrs. Calverton.

Not that Susan thought much of Mrs. Calverton's great wisdom!

One day she happened to pass the Doctor on the street. She had never really thought, before, of how handsome he was— and interesting, too, and mysterious! Living in that big old brick house, in the great lawn that was dark with trees, and with the dimly romantic legend of the "not quite right" aunt and invalid mother. She hadn't really thought of his good looks or noticed them because she hadn't considered the Doctor within the realms of possibility. He had never gone with a woman in this town. He never appeared at dances. Susan began to amuse herself by wondering about him and speculating half idly about him. When she hurt her arm, in a fall from the rocks at a picnic, she wouldn't let Ross Crabtree take her to Doctor Bradley's office when they got to town; but the next day, in a spirit of mischief and daring, and she didn't know what else, Susan went to the Doctor's office.

She hadn't exactly meant anything at first—or nothing that could be put into words. She hadn't thought when she began it that it would be essentially different from her other wild and yet carefully controlled affairs that never went too far. . . . Or had she meant something more? Had she been restless, wearied, impatient, tired of her cold and narrow hardness, wishing to be forced somehow into change? . . . At any rate, she had meant nothing like this. She hadn't dreamed, seeing that handsome face upon the street one day and wondering what the Doctor would be like if she knew him, how the sullen humors, the regal gloom, and lordly gayety, the insistent warmth of his intimate presence could break into her shining hardness; and how at last her cool strength, at the appeal of his sudden childishness, could diffuse into a passion of tenderness. She had no idea when she started deftly, and with a subtly cool speculation, to draw him to her, that the thing could ever be real—that he would want more of her, and that she would give it, with the future—always so clear to Susan—lost in haze.

Dissatisfaction, certainly, hadn't come in at the start! There had been first—looking back, when she happened to be alone, over the long, half buried, only half comprehended course of the whole affair—first that subtle and slightly malicious pleasure, then amazement, fear, defiance, shame, and glory. She had grown closer and closer to him; and her first imperious overriding of difficulties had changed imperceptibly into defense, support, and compensation for his bonds.

It was a long while before dissatisfaction had actually begun—a tiny, gnawing restlessness at first, and then a never-ended craving, and now a mingled long resentment and sick tenderness. In the beginning she had found a dramatic pleasure in taking him and yielding to him in spite of difficulties. The impossibility had added to the intensity in a way that shook her with a wild, rapturous surprise, while at the same time that small, subtle, calculating part of her mind had kept thinking that the same impossibility left her ultimately free. Free! Well, she had learned something since then. Mrs. Calverton, had Susan admitted it to her, might well have been satisfied. Slowly, quite beyond reason, seemingly beyond her own desire, it began to enrage Susan that he did not simply burst the bonds, cast off those two old women, and be hers entirely. Always now, until his arms went round her, drowning her in rapture and tenderness, she was angry that he held her so, in this long suspension of living, that he would not finally take her or finally let her go.

But to her amazement, her shaken and furious incredulity, whenever she finally determined to bring the affair to some conclusion, she was stopped, in breathless terror, by the still more unbearable thought that she might lose him entirely. Beyond that she could not go.

Other girls in town, girls living at home and managing only a "date" now and then with an unattached man, envied Susan and the Doctor. They saw the two driving off in the Doctor's car, not to a dance—they never went to dances—but all by themselves for a long, mysterious ride. People had seen them sitting, or wandering slowly, under the trees in Dawsons Grove. The intimate apartness of the ambiguous couple, with the wonder and speculation that surrounded them, seemed to these girls so much more romantic than the open and inevitable companionship of the married couples in town. Letha Grove, if Susan had known it, looked at her with that furtive dubiousness not because she disapproved of her, but because she admired her, and because Letha felt herself humble and colorless beside Susan. The audacity and mystery of the unexplained relationship gave Susan a kind of glitter in the eyes of the town.

But Susan herself could scarcely realize how the situation and the relationship between them had slowly changed through the years.

She remembered, with brooding nostalgia now—a wonder if she could have made things end differently—what he used to tell her at first.

"You're the only thing I've got in this town. The only thing I've got in this damned, futile existence." And then his voice broke, and his big handsome body was twisted and crumpled in pain and longing before her awed, incredulous eyes. "Oh, God, Susan—give me some happiness! You're free. You can do as you please with yourself. And I'm held in this damned— oh no, God, I can't call it that!—but I can't live in it any longer, they never let me out of it."

Yes, that was true. It was she who had been the free one, the incalculable one, at first. He used to tell her that she lived in the open daylight and he always in shadow. She was the only ray of daylight that he had. Was it through a long, underground persistence of craving, then, to right the balance and assert his final necessity of domination, that he had slowly bound her to him and taken her freedom with her love? By the giving of a free gift she had bound herself. But that she, Susan, should be conquered and held at last by tenderness!—what an amazing overturning of nature and fate.

Gradually, what he said to her came to be:

"But how can I? You knew how things were in the beginning. Well, it's just the same. They're still alive. And you wouldn't live with them."

Even that was true. The old imperious Susan could not

even have contemplated being shut up for a night with those terrible women in that gloomy house.

But it was his contentment, she thought now, that made her resentment burn. (But wasn't it she who had made him so?) Nevertheless, it was his contentment, under the long habit of sacrifice to those women, with the unfailing, romantic comfort of Susan's love—no matter how he might burst out into terrible despair at times, and at times cry brokenly in her arms. She wondered if he had grown to enjoy the gloom of misanthropy, his dark and dramatic aspect of it, fostered by the shuttered gloom of the big brick house. Sometimes it seemed to Susan, bitterly, that that was all her love had done for him. He was content to live in the aging splendor of the old home and then to come for happiness to the bright, small orderliness of Susan's rooms, to eat their perfect little dinners, to force out of her slim hardness a poignant comfort for all his wrongs, to remain with her—it might be—an hour in fierce and secret rapture, and then to break away and take the wholeness of himself back into the familiar gloom, leaving her broken. . . .

"My God, Susan, I can't change things! I wish you'd keep still."

She was not too loyal to wonder sometimes, now, if the hold of the two old women was still so inevitable. She had made him a different person from the solitary man she had passed upon the street. The compensation and sustainment had done their work. That terrible hold did not sap all his strength or turn his energy into hopeless brooding. He had a secret pride. And although he still shunned dances and social meetings—and made Susan shun them—in his old misanthropic way, he was no longer afraid to meet other men. His training and study, after all these years, were at last beginning to show; and people in physical extremity did not care about the equivocal reputation of their surgeon. He was making money now. Susan knew how much that meant; and fear had slowly grown into her that he could make a place for her if he would. But she dared not quiet the fear by an assurance that would force the last of her pride to break away from him.

And was there joy in her love for him any more? Yes, she had actually come to question that. Joy, which had made her look out at the familiar world through Mrs. Calverton's window one March morning upon thawing patches of snow which shone with a blinding brilliance, and feel that the song of the first spring robin had bubbled in sheer happiness out of her own body and heart? Tenderness which had melted the clear hard edges of her well-known little world and watered the dry exactness of her vision with a living freshness and wondering depth of comprehension? . . . Or had she yielded so much to him that she simply had nothing left for herself?

Then, perhaps, she would get a new dress or discover in a magazine a new kind of cushion she could make for her room. She would shampoo her hair and put in with her skillful fingers just the perfect suggestion of a finger wave. She would be feeling well. The whole affair would change its aspect for her. She would pity those two old women, who clung to the presence of their son, while Susan herself had all the best of him. She could look forward to the time when he would be hers altogether—when she could go to sleep beside him in a warm sweet luxury of ease, and wake up still beside him in the morning.

And she thought that she was glad—yes, ultimately glad. His need, his domination, and his terrible dependence upon her, had forced out of her the sweetness of a compassion she had never known that she possessed. It held her to him with a tightness nothing more equal could have done. Mrs. Calverton was right—Mrs. Calverton knew after all. His dominance, more imperious because more needful than her own, had crushed out of pain a strangled fragrance that without him she would never have known.

His mother died. Susan heard it at noon in the drugstore. Fred Jefferson told her.

"I hear the Doctor's mother died last night."

Things irrelevant to that statement were the first that came into Susan's mind: Fred Jefferson's eyes, curious and cold, betraying the tone he had taken, and the calculated shock of his statement (Fred was an old beau of hers, he had always taken a sneering tone about her affair with the Doctor); and then a painful thrust of anger because she must hear from other people this news affecting the man who was hers. The news seemed to have no other significance, although a kind of sickness made her food tasteless to her.

It was not until she went out of the drugstore, into the open light of the street, that she stopped still—for the barest second—while the meaning of the event opened up dizziness before her.

"The Doctor's mother died last night."

A wildness of impatience thrilled through her. It was agony to go on with her work at the bank. She walked home through a changed, incredible world—it was June, lawns were fresh, roses were out. Susan hadn't noticed that until now. The low sunlight of half-past-five lay across Mrs. Calverton's lawn. The green thick stalks of the peony bush bent over and laid flushed thick blossoms against the cool earth. For the first time in years, Susan thought of the woods . . . in the deep green filter of sunlight, the flush of wild geraniums. . . . Cars sped down the wide bright street. She heard voices of children playing. All the town, all the world, was coming out of the tightness and uncertainty of spring into the open and sunlit freedom of summer.

There was a summery light in Susan's room. A pleasant light lay over the mirror. She stood and looked. Eagerness made the brown eyes sparkle out from the fine lines that were beginning to surround them. It flushed the cheeks and ripened the lips. Her whole white body in its pink summer dress was flushed and open and warm, like the roses, and the peonies, and the wild geraniums. She had not yet lost the youth of her girlhood, but womanhood curved the slight lines of her form. She was at her best this warm sweet hour of late afternoon . . . let him come, let him take her now, claim her, keep her. . . .

He telephoned the bare news to her—a guarded voice, withdrawn and strange. He could not see her just now. He would manage it tomorrow. But after all these years, on this perfect night, it was terrible to be thrown back again into the old tense suspension of living. She ate a solitary dinner, stood at the window awhile, and went to bed.

The news made its small uproar in the town. Not because of the Doctor's mother herself—she had been, in her own person, almost forgotten—but because of the way her death would affect the Doctor and Susan.

"What's been the matter with her?"

There were very few who could actually say. "She used to be quite a beautiful woman. The old Doctor did everything for her." It was rumored, but never quite substantiated, that the old Doctor had taken his own life. But they only knew that for years she had absorbed the care and money of her son; and all reminiscence of her ended:

"I suppose now the Doctor will marry Susan."

And Susan, accepted for some time in a role seemingly static, became a heroine of a sort in the eyes of the town again. Her old challenging interest came back to her. She seemed no longer set apart from the town's life. Again she was appreciated in her shining and immaculate slimness; although now the memory of the affair, the never-ending curiosity and speculation as to exactly how far it had gone—its culmination indignantly denied by the innocent and insisted upon with secret delight and outward cynical derision by the knowing ones—

shed a deeper and more significant aura of romance about her.

But the summer went on and the thing still hung fire. The Doctor stayed on in the brick house. Susan went daily to her work at the bank and back to her rooms at Mrs. Calverton's. The roses were gone, the peonies shed their petals on the grass; there were only bitter-smelling yarrow and boneset in the woods. People wondered, laughed cynically, or were indifferent; women who had loved Susan's mother talked angrily about the selfishness of men; and the rest of the force in the bank, getting their heads together, declared:

"Susan ought to give him a jacking up!"

There were so many things to think of, the Doctor said. There was the old home. There was Aunt Agnes. She trusted him. After all these years, he could not put her in an institution. And when Susan, hard and resentful in her balked desire, would not agree, he called her cruel and cold. Susan, with the heat and confidence of her fresh bloom upon her, fought with him, almost in the old arrogant way.

"It can't stay as it is. Don't you see? That's all I'm saying."

Almost—but without the old straight and clear direction of her free imperiousness—because beyond that statement she dared not go. She was sobbing and angry; her hands still clutching with weakened passion at the edges of the couch, but a feeling of brokenness lay within her. The Doctor sat in the big chair that he claimed as his. His voice was husky. He was almost too tired to speak.

"Susan, I'm tired. I've got to have some time to myself. I've had this strain for years. I can't think of anything. I can't do anything now."

Then go, then go, Susan wanted to say. But it was only telling herself to go. She was bound up in him. The old habit of passionate consolation remained; and she could not keep her strength or her anger at the tired appeal of his hands loosely clasping the arms of the chair, and the bright remoteness of pain in his eyes. She went over and put nerveless arms about him and laid her wet cheek against his hair.

After he had left she lay on the couch; and then tired, more tired than he could be, more tired than anything in the world, she struggled up through a daze of weakness to take off her clothes, fold them neatly, wash her face, brush her hair—as her stern sense of orderliness still commanded—and lie down, on her single cot—lie down to the old dissatisfaction turned now into apathy.

The next morning the lawn outside the windows was not so bright. The green, still thick and deep along the edges, beside the sunken coolness of the old cement walk, was fading into dry brown at the center. The leaves had a look of dustiness.

The Doctor came to see Susan as always. But a sense of estrangement, an actual thing, not the old resentment that had made her turn more passionately to him, had crept between them. Or was he a little more cautious and infrequent, now that the eyes of the town were curiously upon him, and that something else might be expected of him?

Susan was no longer a glittering figure to the town. How had it happened? . . . She was good-looking still. The clear features, the slim, straight figure, the smart perfection still were left. Her red-gold hair was smooth. But the fresh attraction of her bloom had faded out of her. How and when had it gone? A little while ago, and Susan was "looking better than ever." But now when she stared into her mirror it was with a sense of dry and hopeless helplessness. The brown eyes stared back, with the sparkle worn out of them, from a face not altered from its familiar contour but from which the living texture had faded. Her swift white hands had settled into a mechanical rhythm at their work in the bank. The warmth of sympathetic interest that people had felt for a few weeks was gone. They were thinking, while they looked at her curiously, "I wonder if he will marry her!"

For imperceptibly the light which shone upon that image of two had shifted and brought out the figure of the Doctor into relief. The lifting of the strain was beginning to tell. He looked fresher, freer, more vigorous. The gloom had lifted so that his handsomeness was no longer mysteriously perceptible through his aloofness. Any one could see it now. He met people with an awakened interest. Nothing held him back from them— nothing but the still secret, unacknowledged pull of his affair with Susan. And they felt a new respect for him, for it was plain that he was his own man at last.

"Well, the poor fellow," men often said, when women accused him of dealing selfishly with Susan, "he's been tied down ever since he was a kid. Let him stretch himself awhile before he gets tied down again."

Women, on the other hand, to men who still admired and stood up for Susan, often said with a hard, small clarity of perception:

"I think he could do better than Susan now."

So that no one was really surprised when he started going with another girl.

Susan knew it long before she consciously knew it as a definite actuality, long before her tortured imagination began to settle and dig its talons into the actual image of now this girl and now that. She could only turn at night in a restless fever of conjecture and rejection of the fact itself. She wanted to know, and at the same time skirted all possibility of discovery, until finally her torture of uncertainty grew more unbearable than knowledge itself, and forced her to say to him—a laughing hint that couldn't possibly be true, "I believe you must be going with some other girl!"

He answered her impatiently and without sympathy, "Well, good heavens, Susan, you played around long enough! We can't shut out the whole world forever."

He to say that! But when he had been bound and moody, it was just what she must do!—until now, forced into the way he had made for her, she wanted no one but him. Another of her accusations against him. They were piling up into a weight of pain that lay upon her and ruined her happiness with him. Still, they did not suffice to permit her to be the one who broke the tie. Susan had been as calculable as quicksilver with the other men whom she had known. But her rectitude and loyalty, once demanded, once actually forced and given, held her with a grip beyond resentment.

That answer, little as it told and incredible as it seemed, was an admission. And now the torture of her imagination was worse than anything she had gone through before. She did not know who it was. People were thoughtful enough to avoid all mention of the name, and even of the Doctor's name; but she could see their knowledge in the curious, conjecturing glances of their eyes. Her natural swift directness made her crave to go straight to the point and learn the fact. But that long suspension of action seemed to have bound her into itself so that she was unable to move hand or foot out of the new agony of suspense.

Susan was too clear-sighted to deceive herself with false reasons for the longer and ever more irregular intervals between his visits. In these intervals she wondered bitterly why she wanted him to come at all. She had allowed—they had allowed—that brief brightness of recovered June to die out of the summer, and since then it had never been the same. She felt as if their love were going as irresistibly and irrevocably as the summer itself. She tried fiercely to wrench what sweetness she could out of every meeting, giving up in the end to her failure with the same dry hopelessness that came upon her when she looked at her fading image in the glass. She was out of step—could not catch the new rhythm—had responded for so long to his need that she had no response for his new desire for lightheartedness.

But she could have responded! Why, she used to be known as the gayest girl in town! All the boys had said of her, "You can have the most fun with Susan." And after all the years of passionate submission to his unhappiness, that old brightness had been alive in her only a little while ago. It was perhaps her worst accusation against him that he had, at that time—her time—forced out of her tenderness and consolation again instead of fulfilment.

Now, what had she left? But she could not let him go.

Fear had crept into the place of dissatisfaction in the tense center of her mind. It gnawed at her all the time, no matter what she was doing. Sometimes she would stop work for a moment in the bank, caught in an inexplicable breathlessness of fear. She dreaded having him come and dreaded just as much that he might not come. Every meeting might be their last. Then why not make it the last? . . . She understood Mrs. Calverton now.

Still, outwardly, the affair seemed to go on pretty much as it always did. They had their little dinners together. The warm weather lasted on into the fall; and on Sunday they were to drive as usual to the Four Corners.

Susan dragged herself out of her tired inertia and got up in good time on Sunday morning so that she could bathe, wash and wave her hair, and press her white-silk sleeveless dress. Now, in the bright daylight, she wondered why she should dread this meeting. She thought of their long time together. One meeting like this could not really end it—not with the leaves still on the trees, dahlias still scarlet out in the garden, only one red branch on the big soft-maple tree. She tried to wrest confidence out of the immaculate slimness of the figure in the glass—when she turned just that certain way, the long lines of the form seemed perfect, and the brown eyes were dark and bright in the white skin under the faint shadow of the white hat. But she knew that she dared not risk turning and letting the light fall this way and that. The same inexplicable fear kept gnawing under her expectation.

She looked out of the window and saw the Doctor coming up the walk. His roadster stood out in front. He looked handsome, large, well-dressed. Susan felt even more than the old thrilling leap of pride. She wanted to tell every one that this man was hers. The time had long passed when it was enough to know this sweetly in secret. The familiarity of going down the walk together and getting into the car made her fear look small and foolish, like a night terror dragged into daylight.

"Have a good time!" Mrs. Calverton called. She stood and looked after the couple.

All the same, Susan had the feeling that the large, well-kept surgeon's hands upon the wheel were not hers to touch. The profile was strange. She chattered recklessly to keep him from speaking.

The Doctor seemed, after a little while—and that might have been only because the motor wasn't acting well—to be responding to her. It was just like all of their drives, so that, when they came to the top of the One-Mile Hill, turned aside from the main road, and stopped in the midst of the tangle of fall flowers, the silence brought back fear to her with a shock of surprise which blinded her. She sat in incredulous stillness; but her heart was pounding. She tried to say that she would get out and pick some goldenrod.

"Susan, look here."

Even her breathing was suspended. The world was stopping.

"We've had the best out of this. Don't you think so, too?"

Silence.

He turned toward her, and something like the old pleading

broke through the strained huskiness of his voice. It was almost like an accusation.

"You must have known this was coming as well as I did."

Silence. . . . "My God, I wish you'd say something!"

Through her dry throat, Susan forced a muttered, "What?"

"Well, just a response. You make me do it all."

"What is there to say?"

That was all there was to it. Susan felt it, in a terrible tiredness, as she sat with her slim hands loose in her silken lap. The great autumn landscape of brown fields and tufted trees spread out beyond the hill. She saw it. But she could not even feel pain for the difference between this chance final view and all the other happy ones.

The Doctor felt it. He did not even try to explain. There was so much to be said that there was nothing to be said. And yet there was little after all. The thing had come to an end. He sat hunched loosely over the steering wheel and stared at the autumn landscape, too.

There was a sort of ease between them as they drove back to town, the ease of mutual understanding again, and of apathy. But for the Doctor, the apathy was only for the moment. It was the temporary conclusion of one thing. There lay beyond it the fresh and eager beginning of another. Brightness lay just beneath the tired glaze of his eyes.

Susan could not go beyond her sense of final completeness—to her, it was relief, if it was anything at all. When they reached town, she saw the Sunday streets, empty and stony, of the familiar business section, and thought that now she was entering them for the first time in years with love and pain gone from her. There was no emotion in the thought.

It was the Doctor whose face, Susan noticed with wonder, when they stopped in front of Mrs. Calverton's again, was broken up with pain; and he begged her before he could let her out of the car to tell him that she felt as he did about it and understood. They had both had the best out of this, hadn't they? What was the use in dragging it on? And he had never, in his whole life, felt a moment of freedom to be himself. . . .

"I want you to tell me that, Susan."

"Tell you what?"

"Well . . . that you feel this as much as I do."

"Yes . . . I guess I do."

She smiled at him quickly. But she got out of the car bitter with her final resentment. He could not even leave her without her reassurance; and she could not help giving it.

She took off her white hat at the mirror and stared at herself in bleak bitterness. He was right. Why should he care for her now? She hated him because he had forced out of her a tenderness that was beyond her nature. And then, still staring with dry, dark eyes at her faded face, she hated herself as much. It was what she had wanted—what she had asked for—the change, the something beyond herself—the something that would break into her and make her over again. It seemed to her that she had not really understood what Mrs. Calverton had meant until now.

The affair was broken. The small anticlimax of the ending had proved final.

Susan kept on with her work at the bank. She still dressed smartly and immaculately, kept scent of the new styles in hats and scarves and beads and, after a little while, had an occasional date with a traveling man or even with one of her old beaux. But they asked her without much ardent interest— because she was a good dancer and because Susan had always been a man's woman and because she was at hand.

The hard truth was that Susan was passée. Young girls no longer adored the sheer perfection of her clothes. Men coming into the bank no longer had the pleasantly disturbing sense of an exceedingly attractive girl. They did not try to linger at the window when they took the money from her white fingers. Letha Grove spoke to Susan now as an equal, perhaps even an inferior—because Letha herself was full of new interests, planning for a trip abroad that was going to change her whole life. . . . Why? Susan was not old, still good-looking, not much changed. It was only, perhaps, that a suggestion of spareness had hardened the slimness of her form, a set dryness the clear features of her face, and about her clothes and her hair there was some finality of precision from which the interest was gone.

"Yes," Mrs. Calverton thought, "that's the way it goes."

She looked for a moment at her own face in the darkened mirror of the old-fashioned parlor. She saw it faded, sad, old, wise with a wisdom she could not be without, and yet that she might wish she had never had to learn.

The whole town, of course, knew that the affair—whatever it had been—was over. They blamed the Doctor and felt sorry for Susan, but without much conviction, at that. Not nearly as much as one might have expected. "She ought to have brought him to time sooner," the men at the bank agreed. They had always, for the sake of Susan's usefulness and the bank's respectability, taken the line that it was merely a case of "going together," and "not yet able to get married." The Doctor was beginning to show an interest in Marjorie Pratt. She was only three or four years younger than Susan, but gay, wealthy, fresh. The Doctor was having a good time for the first moment in his life. Who could blame him? His affair with Susan was bound up with the old days. She wouldn't make the best wife for him now. She had worked too long at that one job in the bank. There were plenty of men who were indignant; but there were others who said, "Well, we don't know the inside of these things."

The older women who had known Susan's mother, and always taken a particular interest in her because of that, were unhappy to see that the long affair, which they had regarded so fearfully and about which they had tried to give their warnings, had come to nothing. They wondered about Susan. They should think it would break her heart, they said. For reluctant as the innocent and kindhearted among these ladies were to credit "anything bad" about Susan—a girl whose family they had known intimately—they all agreed that "men were selfish" and that there was little hope of happiness in these long engagements.

Nevertheless, Susan did not die when the affair was over. In fact, she was aware of other powers in her that had never been brought to fullness. In spite of the bleak dreariness in which she moved, she resented the finality of her aspect in the eyes of the town.

She was alive. She had to think of what to do with her life. At times she considered marrying. There was even a touch of grateful warmth in the thought of a home. Pride—the obviousness of the reason for the change—was all that kept her from moving away from Mrs. Calverton's. She had domestic and managing instincts that had never been given free play. And if the freshness and ease of her attraction were gone, there was enough of her old sure confidence left to tell her that she could marry if she would. A home . . . she would put everything into that, not into the man; forget the Doctor.

For a while, she looked at the men who came into the bank with a faintly reawakened interest. She would have to work now to get one of them; but that would be all the more reason for doing it. There was old Tommy Rumsey. His wife was dead. He had always liked Susan, if he was not quite so apt, now, to pat her cheek and squeeze her hand. To him, however, she was young. He was a rich old codger. The town would have to yield her, involuntarily, a place among the matrons if she married him; and sometimes it amused one side of her mind—an earlier side, belonging to the old Susan, having nothing to do with the Doctor—to conjecture what she could make him do. Could she force him out of that big old house in the country and into a new one in town? Susan thought she might. Now, when she was walking home at night, she made long, interminable plans about what she would do if she married Tommy Rumsey—only to lose them abstractedly, if her eye caught sight of a new car or a strange person or just anything.

And her intention of attracting him—sometimes seriously decided upon—always failed when he came into the bank in his bluff, sentimental, aged person. What was the matter with her? Had she found that love left her with much? But she could not make marrying Tommy Rumsey for a home seem worth while.

And the other men—the bank examiner, whom she knew to be a bachelor; a certain pleasant traveling man; Sid Bartley who had started out as a mechanic, but now, with a garage of his own, was a new possibility—they were not worth while, either.

In fact, Susan felt with an amazement about which she could do nothing that she didn't want to marry any one. She resented the patronage in the tone of her old beaux—she wasn't done yet!—and the pitying tone of the older women, the way in which the town took it for granted that she was still thinking of the Doctor. In the bleak clarity of her vision, she had admitted the truth when he had said that it was ended. Sometimes she wondered . . . if she had told him this or that at such and such a time . . . but she had waited too long until expectation had frayed out into nothing. His need and demand had crushed out of her more tenderness and passion than perhaps she had possessed. Why should just she, Susan, the most unlikely one, have been sacrificed to that need? But she understood Mrs. Calverton in that, too. She could not really wish it had never been. She might be happier, but she would not be what she was now, not this Susan.

Her love for him had gone too long balked, half fed, unsatisfied. It had sucked her dry. All that it had really left was her practical capability. She took refuge in the shelter of that, away from feeling. It grew restlessly. She was no longer contented in her work in the bank. She began to talk about going West and finding something else to do. Nothing seemed interesting now, but she could foresee—at the end of a long dim vista of change—how an interest might open up. She was not finished.

But it was finished—her affair with the Doctor . . . her heart; yes, her life after all. . . . The Doctor was marrying Marjorie Pratt. He was building a new house and sending off the old aunt to an institution. His practice was enlarging. People took him as he was. But as long as she lived in this town, they would never look at Susan without thinking of the Doctor.

HOME-COMING

. . . . .

"Well, I see you're treating us to some real old corn weather," people who had come back to the Home-coming said.

And the others answered, "Yes, we've saved you a little of the genu-ine brand."

Heat glared back from the asphalt that was all new since the day of the old-timers; but the burned and dusty weeds in the vacant lots, the hot and ragged leaves of the box elders along the sidewalks—those were familiar, at any rate.

How sweltering it was going to be for the Old Settlers this noon! They were to have their dinner in the new United Church. Still, where could you find it any cooler?

"My, what a nice building! We didn't have anything like this in our day," the visitors were saying.

The colored windows were down from the top, and the pews fortunately were stained, not varnished. But people were packed in pretty tightly; more had driven in at the last moment than had sent word they were coming; and there was a desperate rattle of fans made of folded Sunday-school papers in the midst of old and elderly people, fat women perspiring through their silk dresses, fat men who couldn't stand their coats if this *was* the church, and lame old men shuffling down the aisle to greet other old-timers. Here, carefully placed at the end of a pew, sat a frail old lady, withered and small in her thin summer dress, thin, darkened hands trembling slightly on her lap, but her eyes—bright under the film of age—peering up with wistful eagerness through gold-framed glasses, hoping that the visitors were going to recognize and greet Grandma Calkins . . .

"Yes," her quavering voice told them, "I'm still here!"

Most of the visitors were from near by. But there were a few surprises. Some stranger had come in with Mrs. Kirkup. Or *was* she a stranger? A very nice-looking woman in a white summer silk—who could she be? When you looked at her face, prettily pink with bright eyes under the white felt hat, surely there was something familiar about it? Mrs. Kirkup, looking so nice, still so dignified, with her violet-colored hat and her waved white hair, had her hand on the visitor's arm.

She stopped Mrs. Seeley.

"Do you know who this is?"

"Well, seems like I ought to know her. It isn't—!"

"Yes, it is!"

"Bessie Gould? Well, for the land's sake! How did *you* get here?"

The visitor was laughing at Mrs. Seeley's astonishment, Mrs. Kirkup was proudly laughing, and then the two women kissed. Mrs. Kirkup was telling how Bess had come.

"I was just on the point of locking up, when up drives a car, and two people get out. Well, thinks I, I've never seen these people before! And then I heard 'Auntie Kirkup'—and here it was Bess!"

By this time Bess was surrounded. Old people who remembered her only as a girl wanted to hear about her father and mother.

"Well, we didn't know as any of you folks could be with us. This is fine to have the Goulds represented!"

Old Ben Moffatt, who used to drive the sprinkler, came hobbling up. "We was a-hopin' your pa could git here. Say, do you know, I miss him ever' time I go by the old place."

And that was what other people told her, "We've never got used to Fairhope without the Goulds."

Bess listened, happy and moved, with smiling poise.

As she talked with these old people, the more she seemed to miss her own parents from among them. Why, after all—as Auntie Kirkup asked her—had they needed to move away? Oh, of course, people were going West at that time, and "the folks" were comfortably off and could afford to take things easily. Yet they had always been homesick—mother, at least—for their old friends; nor had they ever lost the feeling that it was to Fairhope that they belonged.

Old ladies spoke sadly to Bess of her mother; and she had to say again and again of her father: "Yes, he's grown to like it there. No, I'm afraid he couldn't get away,"—while his recent marriage seemed more utterly incongruous to her than ever before—her own father, A. V. Gould of Fairhope.

Mrs. Kirkup was proudly determined to have every one see Bess. And they were interested in seeing her, too—Bess Gould, Mrs. Roscoe McIntyre, who had been away for so long, had lived in Mexico and South America and all over, and whom they remembered as such a pretty girl.

A woman with stout arms and brown, bobbed hair came running in from the kitchen. "Well, Bess, you old darling, I didn't expect to see *you!*"

It was Verna Kliegle—married now, of course—who had been in her own crowd.

Old Mr. Valentine came up to her, not much older than he had seemed to her when she was a little girl—her nice Mr. Valentine who had said, "We'll have to find you another" when her kitten died, and who had given her rides on his pony.

"Well, well, here's my girl back! Just as pretty as always."

Oh, no—she shook her head—she wasn't that! But pretty enough still, and so very well-groomed and well-dressed that she wasn't at all afraid to meet her old friends. She showed that she had traveled. What an interesting, unusual life she had led—one of their own girls!

Mrs. Kirkup was taking her down the aisle toward the old lady, who tried to hold up a trembling hand.

"You remember Grandma Calkins, don't you?"

Oh, certainly Bess did! She had been Grandma even in those days, a spry old lady nourished on dandelion greens and tea.

"My, my, is this Bessie? I wouldn't o' known ye. But we've all of us changed, I guess. Ye wouldn't have thought to find me here, would ye?"

And when Bess tried to reassure her, the voice quavered on, the frail head shaking:

"To think I should be here today and your dear mother gone! Who'd ever o' thought it would be like that? Well, things turns out queer sometimes, that's all."

Bess felt the eager pressure of a hand on her shoulder and turned to hear Verna say,

"Bess, here's some one you ought to know."

Through a slight confusion, as she turned, Bess saw a man holding out his hand, and looked into pleasant, brown eyes. She had a feeling of a stillness all around her—interested faces . . . But a certain bright restlessness in her gaze had been suddenly stilled—even before she actually realized who he was, stocky, not very tall, a little bald—

"Well, Bess, don't you know me?"

"Why, Charlie!"

She felt an old, quieted sense of the strangest familiarity when she had shaken hands with him. The whole place was suddenly familiar now. But she parted from him a little breathless in spite of her poise.

"You didn't expect to see *her*," Verna was challenging.

But there was a shout: "Form in line! Get in line, folks. Reverend Siddons leads."

Bess turned back to Mrs. Kirkup. They were all going in procession down to the tables in the basement to the music of

"Auld Lang Syne." The eager restlessness had come back into Bess's eyes, only brighter, different. Laughing with an excited animation, she put her hand on Mrs. Kirkup's arm and cried, "Don't lose me, Auntie!"

M rs. Kirkup thought proudly that they were treating Bess almost as the guest of honor. And that was just as it should be. Bess had been the most promising of the girls, and she had grown into the loveliest woman. She was the most interesting visitor at the Home-coming. She was seated at the head table, next to the master of ceremonies, the new superintendent of schools. He hadn't been here, of course, at the time of the Goulds. But he was interested and pleased at having such a pretty woman beside him. He understood that she had lived in South America, he said. Bess answered all his questions and talked to him with her bright animation. She told him funny old incidents of local history.

"Do you know whom I really miss, Auntie?" she cried. "I miss old Gid Caraway. I think we children thought more of Gid Caraway than of any man in Fairhope. It was that uniform. Where did he get it, Mr. Valentine?"

"Well, I guess nobody but Gid knew where he got it! In the wars, no doubt."

The other people at the table laughed to hear old Gid Caraway mentioned again. That certainly brought back old times.

"Well, he's been buried a good while," Mr. Valentine said. "Him and his uniform, too. Yes, Gid was quite a character."

"You mustn't think you really know Fairhope, Mr. Barnes, unless you can remember Gid Caraway."

The old people at the table began to tell about other local characters and local happenings, pleased—Mrs. Kirkup was beaming with pleasure—that Bess Gould should have remembered such things when she had been gone so long and had seen so much of the world. They talked about fires, and blizzards, and tornadoes, and the ancient fight with Petersburg to get the courthouse. All these were drama and humor and nostalgia, now that they were in the past.

Bess listened with delight. The little town, long so remote that it had become a dream to her, was real again. There could be return. She felt as if she were acting for her father and mother as well as for herself, that once again the family was whole.

But all the time there was a bright absence in her eyes. She had noticed where Charlie was sitting. He was almost hidden from her by one of the basement pillars, but now and then she saw his pleasant face. All the time, the consciousness of that face was her background. She was talking to it, acting for it, playing out her part—the part of a mature and happy woman, traveled, experienced, and assured, as she had dreamed of doing so many times.

Now it was happening. Charlie was seeing the woman that she had become. That was all she had wanted, she thought. She was years away from Charlie. And yet, far apart as they had grown, she could never have been satisfied if he had not once seen her as she was, in the very prime of her living . . .

When she had first driven into Fairhope with Mac last night, she couldn't believe in this little town—the weedy lots at the edge, the old frame houses and newer bungalows, even Auntie Kirkup's house, so incredibly unchanged, with its bay-window and wooden lacework. But now she had the sense of entering into Fairhope again. She clung to it—she even wanted to shut her eyes to keep it, as children try to keep a dream when they know that they are waking.

Mr. Valentine said to her:

"Well, Bess, you look more like yourself all the time. I remember when you and Charlie Laird were just little tykes and used to fish for 'minnies' in that 'crick' in the ravine. You each one had a little line fastened to a switch, and you came and got me to put on your worms for you, because you were both too tender-hearted. You remember that?"

Bess laughed—she said she did. And while old Mr. Valentine went on to recall other tales about her, she could see the shine of water in the "crick," the dapple of light and leaf shadows in the deep ravine, and feel Charlie's reassuring hand when they came to a slippery place in their wading. Hours and hours they must have spent down there. They had looked for pearls and precious stones, and had always secretly hoped to catch two little goldfish for pets.

She felt grateful that her family should be so well remembered and that dear old Mr. Valentine should cherish the remembrance of her childhood. It had never been quite the same for the Goulds anywhere else, although presumably they had bettered themselves in moving. Her whole heart seemed to open again, tender and flower-like—every little word touched her. She felt with poignancy the sweetness of returning to old relationships, and saw with tenderness the signs of age on all these dearly remembered faces.

Once, when she looked up and smiled at Verna going past, she almost thought she would ask if either of the women sitting beside Charlie was his wife. Oh, no, that great fat woman couldn't be! Why, that was Lottie Peevy—actually!—who used to drive in to high school with that funny old buggy and blind white horse. Bess could have laughed. And it certainly couldn't be that little, thin old lady on the other side. Perhaps she was waiting on the tables. And Bess found herself looking with intense curiosity and aversion at an animated young woman with bobbed, reddish hair—she grew to detest the creature's animation as she flew about the dining-room.

It was on the tip of her tongue to say lightly, with the woman-of-the-world ease that was second nature to her now in place of the old girlish eagerness. "Which one is Charlie Laird's wife?" But to her amazement she couldn't get it said. She only smiled at Verna, who had stopped in answer to her look, and murmured,

"No, nothing."

She didn't want Charlie's wife pointed out to her. When any one mentioned him, when any one seemed even to glance at Charlie, she veered off with a quick brightness. She was afraid to have them add,

"That's his wife over there."

Now she knew and admitted to herself that she had been afraid of coming back to Fairhope, although she had always intended to come, too. It was because she couldn't quite bear to see the woman whom Charlie had married. She could admit her existence in a vague way—for hadn't she Mac, and hadn't she always said it had turned out the best way? But not to *see* her. All these years—and was it possible that she had never lost the feeling that Charlie belonged to her? That must be at the bottom of it.

The idiocy! She *would* ask. With a wrench of pride and a lift of her head, she got back the sense of herself as Bess McIntyre, a visitor in Fairhope. Yet moments went by—and she found herself resting in the half-false peace and sweetness of return.

An old, lost sense of home and peace. She sank down into it, into the surrounding affection, the intimacy of knowledge that encompassed her life from the beginning and the life of all her household. She didn't look often at Charlie, but she was dwelling in the consciousness that he was there.

They wanted to hear all about her.

"Well, Bess, what have you been doing all these years?"

She had to tell them about Mac and his work: said she was sorry, too, that they weren't going to get to see this husband of hers, smiling at Mrs. Kirkup's praise of him. But he was meeting Gould in Chicago—Gould had been at a summer camp in the East. Jean was a sophomore in college this year. They wanted to hear about her life in foreign countries.

"To think all this had happened to Bess!" the old people said.

Old Mr. Valentine spoke what must always be spoken by some one, "It doesn't seem but a little while since you and Charlie Laird were little bits of things begging for a ride on my old pony—and here you are with children of your own!"

He added: "I don't suppose there's so many here today that were here in those days, either. Charlie Laird's here, though—I guess you haven't forgotten Charlie. D'you know his wife? No, I guess she came after your time."

"Oh, yes," Mrs. Kirkup said, "Bess was gone a long time before Marie came here."

"Who?" Verna paused with the coffee-pot. "Mrs. Charlie Laird? No, she isn't here today. She's visiting her folks. She's in Wisconsin."

Bess felt a sudden, gay brightness. She recognized it as absurd and irrelevant, but she wouldn't have actually to *see* that woman, anyway. Fairhope could still be Fairhope to her. Relief poured sweetly into her, and once more she could let herself go in the half-sad happiness of the return. She felt a sudden liking for the innocent red-haired woman and thanked her with a radiant look when she came to the table with fresh rolls.

She was back for a little while. She listened, smiling, to the letters of old-timers who couldn't get back for the home-coming—while the consciousness of Charlie's presence seemed to mingle with the atmosphere, with the summer heat and the voices, making everything both vivid and dreamy.

"Dear friends and neighbors—"

That was written in a slanting, wavering, old-lady's hand on a piece of ruled paper.

"Regrets from both that we can not accept your kind invitation to return to Fairhope home-coming, Mr. Dilley's health being still very bad, but wish to thank the good Lord that among His many blessings He has seen fit to spare my husband to me."

Why, that was Mrs. Dilley, who used to bring ground-cherry pies to all the church suppers—and written from some funny little town in Idaho!

"Dear fellow ruffians and ruffianesses of the good old days—"

A shout went up. Who could that be but Ira Hawkins—a Coloradoan now, and not seen in Fairhope for twenty years!

There was a brief note from Bess's father in Pasadena—people clapped at the name of A. V. Gould. Several of the old-timers in their after-dinner speeches referred to the Goulds.

The master of ceremonies said gallantly, "We have a member of one of the old Fairhope families with us today, one that I came too late to know, but that I've heard a lot about"—and Bess had to half-rise and nod in answer to all the greetings. The Gould family, in spite of all its changes, seemed really to *be* the Gould family in Fairhope.

All the people at the dinner, awkward old country people and all, felt now a heightened sense of human unity. Old Ben Moffatt was as much a part of the place as D. C. Burnside, its wealthy man. All got their recognition. It was affection, not importance, that counted today. There was applause for Grandma Calkins, the oldest of the old-timers, and her small and darkened face wore a look of curious content, as if now at last her long tenacity was satisfied and, in her own frequent words, she was "ready to go."

After dinner was the time for old cronies and neighbors to get together. Bess turned to follow Mrs. Kirkup, but old Mr. Valentine detained her and took her hand. His memory had been gathering things.

"This has been the best part of the day," he told her, "to see you here again, Bessie. I tell you, you folks ought never to have left. You ought to have stayed here, the way we all expected, and married Charlie Laird. Yes, sir, that's the way it should have been."

Bess answered Mr. Valentine with a smiling shake of her head. Then Mrs. Kirkup, Mrs. Seeley—all the old neighbors—gathered in the group that stood talking near an open window. Charlie joined them. Mr. Valentine was the only one who thought anything of that. Even Auntie Kirkup was reconciled to Bess's marriage, since it had turned out so brilliantly. They had all been interested to see Bess and Charlie meet, but now they took them as they were. That hour of the speeches and the letters had seemed to Bess the high point of the gathering, but now, among the few old intimate friends, there was a natural sense of companionship that was better still.

"What shall we do?" they were all asking. "I expect Bessie would like to rest after that long trip yesterday."

No, Bess said she wasn't tired. But Auntie Kirkup was, she feared.

Charlie said, "Well, Auntie Kirkup, suppose you let me drive you and Bess home."

He had the car here, and he was alone. Mrs. Kirkup accepted—Charlie always looked after her.

Parting then for the moment—Mrs. Kirkup and Bess were invited to the Seeleys' for supper later—they went out with Charlie to the small enclosed car.

"No, you sit in front with Charlie," Mrs. Kirkup said. "You won't have so long to see each other."

Charlie backed out from among the crowded cars. Bess was remembering how overjoyed—and how terrified, too—they used to be when Mr. Valentine had let them drive his pony. She had been used to seeing Charlie's hands on reins—she looked at them now, thicker, not boyish, and yet still with the same quiet control she remembered, on the shiny steering wheel.

"Remember the pony, Bess?"

So he was thinking of that, too!

But it seemed to Bess that they were going out of their way to Auntie Kirkup's—and then all at once she saw why. Charlie was taking them past her old house.

"Know that place, Bess?"

Mrs. Kirkup cried, "Well, I guess we do!"

She had roused herself from a little nap and was looking out at the brown frame house—they were all three looking together, as Charlie slowed down the car. It was not so changed. It had the same narrow porches, and it was painted the same color of withered leaves. Bess had always remembered it in the fall, dry leaves in drifts on the sloping lawn, and herself coming home from school with Charlie through cool and sunny air to get apples before they went out to play. But it had a look of deterioration. The paint was dingy, the wide lawn— once so impressive a part of Fairhope—was unkempt.

"Yes," Mrs. Kirkup mused, "there it still is, Bess."

"We used to have some good times in that house," Charlie said.

"I guess you did. All you young people. I don't believe any young people ever had better times than that crowd you two were in, in spite of all these goings-on today."

Bess said nothing. She looked back at the house as Charlie drove away. It was still itself, yet no longer hers. Yet, although it hurt her, she was glad to have seen it again.

It was Charlie's own way to have taken them quietly past there. It hurt her to recognize that, too—there was so much that it brought back—but she settled back beside him with a pleasant knowledge that the strangeness she had feared was gone.

He was saying: "Well, Auntie, are you tired? Want to sleep a little while I take Bess for a drive? I thought she might like to see some of her old haunts."

When Mrs. Kirkup had gone, with her slow dignity, into the small white house with the bay window, it seemed perfectly natural to be sitting beside Charlie, idle and at ease, while he drove. Bess was pleased, too, that he had taken things in his hands and suggested this—that he had broken through the estrangement. Now she had the happy sense of renewal with the estrangement all melting away.

Charlie slowed down the car now and then to point out other old houses to her.

"The Horton house. Remember that? Both the old folks are dead."

He told her of how the place had changed. "It has a lot of improvements. It's a pretty good little town for its size. But it's not the same place at all. It doesn't seem to me we have the good times we used to have. Maybe I'm just getting to be an old duffer."

"No, I suppose it has changed," Bess said slowly. She was thinking of all the strange interests and activities of her life since she had left Fairhope. "I've done lots of things since then, but I don't know that I've ever enjoyed any part of my life as much. I wonder."

She looked up into the familiar, reassuring kindness and understanding of his brown eyes. And all at once they were conscious.

It lasted only a moment, breathless and undermining. And it seemed to have been needed—that moment of consciousness. It was like a silent and necessary admission. Charlie was still Charlie, and Bess was Bess. They could talk together again.

Now, as they drove along, Bess could admit to herself that it was not the dinner, not the meeting with old neighbors, that was the heart of the occasion, but this hour alone with Charlie. All had been leading up to this.

Charlie asked about her parents. Mac had never really known her mother well, and he was inclined to regard her father's second marriage as a good joke. Charlie's parents both were dead. He said just a little about his father's difficulties—just enough to make Bess realize (although Charlie hadn't thought of it that way)—what a tangle the thing had been, and how hard for Charlie.

"So I'm still at the old stand," he told her.

No matter how she might feel, though, there was little she could say to him about those old days. So much must be passed over.

They had reached the mill pond now. That was where Charlie was taking her. It was the old picnic spot of Fairhope and scarcely changed from the days when they used to go there.

"Do you know it, Bess?"

"I should think I do!"

"Would you like to get out a moment?"

She did, but without taking her eyes from a wondering contemplation of the woods, and the quiet spread of the mill-pond, the stones of the foundation roughly overgrown with weeds, even the very ground. All were here, just the same. But over the stir of awakened feeling Bess kept the cool protection of her poise. She made little comments and asked adult questions, as she walked over to the pond with Charlie.

"Have some of these woods been cut down—or do they only look smaller to me now?"

They might have been thinned out a little, Charlie said, but he was afraid the woods were about the same—it was Bess who had seen too many other places since then.

"There's some pretty fine scenery in Mexico, from all accounts."

"Yes, the mountains are beautiful."

"Well, I may get there some day."

It was all smaller, so real but so incredible. Over all this ground they had been dozens and dozens of times together. As children they had walked out after school to pick bluebells in these woods, and once, when she was ill, Charlie had tramped out by himself and brought back the hugest bunch of bluebells—they had to put them in the lemonade pitcher, she remembered. Sunday-school picnics used to be held out here, and then Bess and Charlie would slip away from the others and go wandering off on their own devices. In the wintertime this pond was the place where they used to skate. Charlie had always put on Bess's skates for her—he had been jealous if any other boy tried to do it. Afterward, when they were older and getting into high school, they would ride out here on their bicycles; and still later this had been the place where the crowd had come for picnics. They hadn't exactly been engaged at that time or ever. They had simply taken it for granted that they would always be together—"Bess and Charlie" . . . and now here they were, long separated, each married for years to some one else, Bess with her home in another part of the country, but walking together over this very same ground . . .

How had it come about? Bess felt as if she were seeing the place from a distance—as if something withheld her from it, all the things that had happened in between. Was she one self or the other self?

When they reached the mill-pond, they stood on the bank for a few minutes. Bess looked down into the water, partly clear and partly stagnant. They stood close together in almost their old, easy companionship, with the sense of sharing all they saw. It was as if the world, suddenly and yet easily, had swung back into its own right orbit—and there was the old singing sense of miraculous peace and rightness together. It was as if all at once the woods and the water came close again, and the right earth was under her feet, the right sky over her head—while the summer landscape, her own summer landscape, intimate and alive, stretched away from that central moment of reunion to its far horizons of green tree-tops.

Bess scarcely tried to listen to what Charlie was saying. She was lost in the ecstatic breathlessness of the swing of the world back to where it belonged. All the rest of her life was alien. She had never felt this singing peace since she and Charlie had been apart . . . Although certainly she loved Mac—had loved him more impetuously, rapturously, with a wilder surprise, than ever she would have been able to love Charlie.

All these years she had said at intervals, "How much better it is this way!"

And yet she had had to say it, to think to say it—to stand sometimes with her hand on the railing, as she was going downstairs, and to repeat that like an answer to the turning of an old thrust of wonderment; or at times when she was happiest of all, when they went up into the mountains, or when she caught a sudden endearing sight of her children, she would have to repeat it again in a kind of glad amazement. Her happiness had always been surprising, had never quite come real. All these happy, active years, through all the interest and variety and astonishments of her life, and in spite of the children—or even more because of the children?—there had been under everything an unassuaged aching. It had put into her eyes that bright absence for which Mac teased her ("Where are you, old lady?"), and which the children recognized as one of the personal, unfathomed expressions of their mother's face.

How could she have asked for a better life? She couldn't. It was only that she had never been walking just in her own path. She had stepped aside and taken a strange turning. It was never quite right that it should not have been "Bess and Charlie." There were moments when she seemed to have to stop and think of that; and Mac, her lover, and so long her husband whom she loved, was still to her that "stranger" whose name it had been so exciting to draw when she used to sleep on seven slips of paper and a crumb of wedding cake.

"Well, Bess, have you had a good life?"

They had been keeping a little clear of personal subjects. But Charlie asked her that now. She had, she told him—for she had married the nicest kind of man, and she had her two children.

"And you've been everywhere."

That worried Charlie, she could see, while she herself feared to regret that she had lost touch with her old home.

"Yes, we've been around more or less."

Well, things had come out pretty well for him, too, he said, although it had taken a good while. He had a fine wife. Sometimes he'd wanted to get away from Fairhope, but it was as good a town as any other, he guessed. Not like it used to be, but it was a good town. Of course—and he looked around at the old picnic grounds with a frown of wondering pain—

"Well, things go queer ways sometimes."

They turned now and walked over toward the woods.

How had they got so far apart? It seemed so slight, now, the reason. The estrangement itself had long ago swallowed up the poor little cause. Charlie's father had failed in business, and Charlie couldn't start into college, and she had got with a different crowd. Charlie had the burden of his family, and his old conscientiousness wouldn't let him ask her to marry him then—but to Bess, bright, spoiled, eager and impetuous, it had seemed that he was willing to let her go. Well, there were other men who liked her! Did he expect her to sit and wait his good pleasure? She had chafed perversely at the bond of their intimacy. And then, when she was visiting at the Lakes, she had met Mac—and in a mood of eagerness, of angry impatience, she had let him sweep her off her feet and wildly into love. She had left school, and married, and gone off into the West; and it wasn't until after her first rapturous hours with Mac that she had found herself crying, in a lonesome, dismal sort of way—not wanting to leave Mac, certainly, but unable to comprehend that she had actually separated herself from Charlie; hurt and aching under her happiness, and feeling that she had entered a foreign country . . . But then her parents had left Fairhope, too, and everything had changed.

Yet she had never quite given up the idea of seeing Charlie again. In her imagination he was always present in a shadowy way at all the important occasions of her life. Even when she bought new ear-rings, when she turned her head and saw them swing against the pink of her cheek, it was with a remote wonder as to how she would look to Charlie if he should see her in them some day. She had never been able to picture her life without some sort of reunion with Charlie.

And now she was having it. Not at all as she had dreamed of it in any of her romantic imaginings; but even more astonishingly right in its actuality. It had turned out to be this moment of hot summer, and here at the mill-pond, the air dense and still, and the sky its bluest blue. They were at the center of the queer, familiar world in its turning.

"So that's the way it goes," Charlie murmured.

He turned to Bess and smiled. They understood each other.

But, after all, there was little that they could say, and this was as close as they could come. The irrelevancies between them were actual and could not be thought away. That was all there was to it. There was no retracing of steps beyond this. Only, as they left the picnic grounds—"Well, would you like to be getting back?"—Bess felt again her old impatience that human beings should move with the irresistible movement of life. Now they had had their moment.

They were really different, she and Charlie. She could see it now, after the first glad shock of finding him still himself. His clothes, his features, his slow, careful movements, had a provincial air. He had settled into a slower rhythm and she into a swifter, and they had lost their peace together. There was, after all, no real renewal of a thing once gone.

No, she had moved away from these little streets—from the graciousness of the lawns, the settled comfort of the aging houses. She ached for the old feeling again, but she had grown too far away. And yet it was here, and with Charlie, that she had belonged. The green of this grass was her green, and the blue of this sky was hers. She felt it when they parted—almost formally after the closeness of their meeting—as she went into the familiar, darkened hall of Mrs. Kirkup's little house.

All the rest of the day, Bess felt restless and strange. With a pained impatience, she wanted Mac to come, and yet she was aware of a queer fear of seeing him. Through the darkened rooms of Mrs. Kirkup's house, the air hushed and cooled, she could move as her own most intimate self. But to work among those sweetly familiar things was like trying to prolong her girlhood when her girlhood was gone.

Mrs. Kirkup was saying comfortably, "So then, Bessie, if you'd like to go out and pick us some flowers to take along—"

They were to have supper with the Seeleys tonight.

Bess went out into the garden, where phlox and dahlias grew in rows, and the background was filled with a straggling mass of pink cosmos. Perceptions came to her with the rough touch of the stems of the summer flowers. The meeting with Charlie—so brief, so momentous—was past. They would never be close again. Yet she had a shadowy feeling of him with her in this garden—together they would have enjoyed its precision and the neat tools in the vine-covered shed. Charlie would have helped her to choose her bouquet, hunted out and brought to her the best of the flowers, and all without the need of a word. That Charlie—the old Charlie. They were both different now. She went into the house with the flowers to wrap the stems in damp newspapers, but she could not get rid of her feeling of aching absence.

"Are you getting ready, Bessie?"

"Yes, I am. I will."

The supper with the Seeleys, so pleasant in prospect, was an anti-climax after all. The whole company felt tired and hot. Oh, it was good—sweet corn, fresh tomatoes were good even in this heat—and Mr. and Mrs. Seeley were glad to have her there; but the highest point of neighborly reunion had been reached at the dinner at the church.

"I invited Charlie Laird, too," Mrs. Seeley was saying. "I thought as long as his wife was away— But seems he couldn't come."

Well, that would have been an anti-climax, too.

The dinner was tasteless, though, without Charlie there. The chief interest of the old neighbors, even, was gone. The white house, as Bess and Mrs. Kirkup came up to it in their slow walk home through the hot twilight, seemed to be withdrawn into the past again under the shade of the maple trees. Bess helped Mrs. Kirkup to lock the doors and put in order the few minutely disordered things. But she moved in a dream, tired and yet restless. She seemed to be in a fever of hurry to end Mrs. Kirkup's leisurely recital of town happenings and to get into the shelter of her own room.

"Well, my dear, I can see you're tired."

She was ashamed when the old lady fondly kissed her good-night.

The Seeleys had been asking her about Jean and Gould. She would see Gould tomorrow, she was thinking with a thrill of eagerness, as she polished her nails with her rose-tinted buffer at the old-fashioned dresser. She could picture him—handsome, sunburned, impatient and eager under the cool politeness of his youthful manner; bursting with things to tell her about his month at the camp; impatient when even his father claimed her attention, and seeing no reason at all why they should stop in a little place like this. But she was queerly alien to him at this moment. She seemed remote from the youthful, cold beauty of his blue-gray eyes. He was hers, but there was nothing of her girlhood in him, nothing of Charlie, nothing of this place.

She sat down on the bed in a daze of pain and loneliness. It seemed as if she could not wait through the night until Mac and Gould should come and take her away. Yet she dreaded them—their impatience—Gould's cool-eyed strangeness here in this little house, and Mac's jesting beneath which lay a dim uneasiness of fear.

"Well, mother, see your old flame?" he would be sure to ask her.

He would make fun, lightly, of the settled slowness of the town. "Well," he had said, when they drove into Fairhope, "I think your dad did well to pull out of here" . . .

But unsatisfied until he had got her at least to seem to agree. And then he would be suddenly gay and at ease. The two of them would demand her at once in her old relationship as mother and wife. Her childhood, her girlhood, were unknown to them. It was only in this place—this little room with the maple trees outside—that she was still Bess Gould.

But after this one summer night what would be left for her

here? The place would be gone even from the expectation of her dreams. She knew what the parting would be—how, as mother and wife again, she would have to yield herself to the impatience of her men to be gone, with only a hasty last glimpse of the small white house, the maple tree, the tall old woman at the door. So hasty and yet so final. In a few more years—who knew how soon?—Auntie Kirkup would be gone. The last of the old neighbors would be scattered. The lawn of the old Gould place would grow more and more desolate, until "Lodgings for Tourists" appeared in the big front window, and it was worse than unrecognizable. Her mother's grave was not among the others in the cemetery among evergreens and bridal-wreath bushes, nor would her father be buried there. The Goulds had gone away. And she and Charlie were apart. There was nothing to which she could return.

Now she wanted to go away. She wanted the night to be over—the last sweet and painful night, home-like and strange, in this place. She thought of morning, hot blue sky over the maples—and with fear, elation, she saw Mac, the stranger, tall and impetuous, enter the little house. She had never, even in her first rapture of impatience when she had let him sweep her off her feet—never wanted his arms with the abandon of desire, the finality of surrender, with which she wanted them now. He had come as a stranger and carried her off from this place before. But there had been something never wholly real about it. She wanted him to take her again, and with no remembrance left. She got up to push back the thin, white curtain from the window, and looked out at the maple tree in the thick heat of the night. The open country lay beyond, and already the little town, so intimate and close about her, seemed to draw remotely into its trees.

She felt lost and all alone, and her heart was wildly begging Mac to come . . . "Take me away with you. Be everything. Make it up to me. Don't let me die away from home."

A PART OF THE

. . . . . .

INSTITUTION

. . . . . .

CHAPTER I

Adams College—"The Pioneer College of the Prairies"—had been founded some forty years ago by a little band of home missionaries from New England, dedicated to "the interests of Christianity and of the higher learning in the West." Then the campus had been prairie land—a few lonesome acres in the great expanse of rolling country. There had been one building, the old Recitation Hall of red brick, dingy and ugly, plain as a barracks, that stood in the east campus. The town had been a few houses, a church and two wooden stores.

Now—in the early nineteen hundreds—the town and the campus already had an established, mellowed look. The frame houses had wide lawns and lilac bushes; and some of them—square, painted white or brown, with shutters and a cupola—began to seem elderly. The elms were tall along the wide, pleasant streets, which were still unpaved. The campus had lost most of its old raw prairie look. The five buildings—Moorish and classic and conglomerate—were softened with ivy. Flowering bushes lined the cinder paths. The big oak that had stood alone in prairie days was ringed about with maples, catalpas and tulip trees. There was a great clump of evergreens which gave age, and shadow, to the campus on the south.

The college already had its traditions, fixed and sacred. The class scrap between the Freshmen and Sophomores, no dates on Sunday night, a man for class president in the fall and spring and a girl in the unimportant between months, chapel attendance, enmity with Billings (the Methodist school), that Ionian girls should "go in for society" and E. B. B. girls for "activities," the social value of Freshman class prayer-meetings. College bards had written hymns to "the Adams spirit." The spirit of "service," of "democracy," of "the good loser," of "ideals." There was an "Adams type." A man not too good-looking, a fair student but not in any alarmingly original way, athletic, a "clean Christian fellow," a good speaker, a good mixer and organizer, a member of the Glee Club and the Y. M. C. A., "the all-around man." A girl pretty, but in a girlish ingenuous way, not too well-dressed, popular with men but felt to be a conscientious student and an earnest Christian, full of enthusiasm, of "the Adams spirit," a worker in the Y. W. C. A., clever but not too intellectual, executive, "in everything," "the all-around girl." If this man and this girl became engaged to each other in their Senior year, then they had fulfilled the best Adams traditions and would be prominent alumni.

The town and college had grown up together. Adamsville— "The State Headquarters of Congregationalism," "Saints' Rest," "The Home of Adams College"—was a residence town. It had a population of about five thousand people, with prosperous banks, but in a business way it was rather slow. The only important industry was the implement factory owned by Josiah H. Porterfield, the leading citizen and chief trustee of the college. People moved there because the town was clean and pleasant, with the wide streets and big trees, "a nice place to live and bring up children." It was a place for retirement. Retired farmers and ministers, church officials, retired business men who wanted the advantages of the college for their children.

To the old ministers and old-timers, the church was the center of the town. A big squat gray stone building on a corner, with a dark cavernous interior in which voices were lost. It, too, had fondly cherished titles. "The Convention Church of Iowa." Conventions of the Christian Endeavor, of the W. B. M. F. and the W. B. M. I., the State Ministerial Association, the Purity League. Houses were always ready for the entertainment of delegates. "A minister killer," it was sometimes less fondly called. The Adamsville church was still looking for "a man to satisfy everybody"—the right wing of ancient "saints" who held firmly by the Atonement, the left wing of "advanced" college professors, and the center of comfortable, prosperous, fairly educated people who went home to good Sunday dinners.

The town was really built around the college. The stores catered to the college trade, with desks for rent in the furniture store, a large stock of "wienies" on hand in the meat markets, a kodak department in the photograph and art gallery, a supply of blue and white felt in the dry goods stores. Houses were built large so that rooms could be rented. Furnaces were stoked by college boys. The restaurants and "Jack the Cleaner's" had college help. Washwomen flourished in the south part of town across the tracks.

College functions made the life of the town. In the fall the football games. Adams was too small to "do much in football." Big husky country boys went to the state agricultural college and the university. But the boys had speed and the Adams spirit. They prided themselves on being good losers. The town "grads" contributed to the football fund, and "Doc" Boardway bound up wounds free of charge. When the college beat Billings, the townspeople gathered in a dusky circle around the athletic field to watch the bonfire celebration. It was not good form for the merchants to say too much when their dry goods boxes were stolen for fuel, although it was permissible to complain to the marshal when signs were taken down and tacked above the entrance of the Congregational church or the old pest-house. Then came basket ball, and later "track." A good track team was an Adams tradition. The merchants knew the names and nicknames, year after year, of the track athletes, could compare records since the founding of the college. Little boys held track meets all spring, and staggered theatrically into outstretched arms after a run across a fifteen foot lawn. The town had rain-stained bunting that was put up every year at the time of the State Meet.

Women followed social events with painstaking interest, as men did with athletics. They knew the names of the most popular girls, and who was going with whom. On the night of the Glee Club concert—the great social night of the year—they walked slowly back and forth in front of the chapel to see the dresses as the girls went in. They had their favorites—"the cutest girls." They were anxious to learn who was to be the heroine of the Dramatic Club play. Everett DeLong, '94, the editor of the Adamsville *Messenger*, "wrote up" the college plays, and compared the heroine of the current play to those of years back, as well as to Maude Adams and Julia Marlowe. His greatest praise was to say:

After last night's performance we must admit that Miss Hutchison takes her place among the brightest stars of the Adams dramatic galaxy, well in line with Helene Royce as Hermione in "A Winter's Tale" of '97, and with James Peacock as Shylock in the 1889 "Merchant of Venice" production, and second only to the superb performance of Daisy Lyons in the title part of the "Antigone" of Sophocles as performed in 1891.

Everett DeLong still kept alive the breathless tradition of Daisy Lyons as Antigone.

Everybody went to the Commencement events. The women of the town left their noon dishes and went over early to the campus on Class Day to get good seats in the rows of folding chairs in front of the outdoor platform, taking newspapers with them so that the varnish on the chair backs would not stick to their clothes in the heat. They made their husbands carry over cushions and camp stools to the campus on the last evening when the Glee Club sang. They knew all the old songs in the Club's repertoire—"Oh, I hope they sing 'Carry me back to old Virginny' next!" They marked their programs at the oratorical contests and agreed or disagreed hotly with the verdict of the judges.

There were snake dances, night shirt parades and hay rick rides through the main streets of the town. Caps and gowns in the spring. The two girls' literary societies—the Ionian and the Elizabeth Barrett Browning—mildly took the place of sororities in the school, fulfilling the Adams tradition of democracy. Housewives were accustomed to coming to their doors and calmly answering questions when initiates took the cat census of the town or the number of women who believed in Carrie Nation.

When school was over the town was "dead." There was nothing in the summer except an occasional baseball game between professors and business men. The town settled into a thick summer languor, under the great trees, in the moist heat of central Iowa. When fall came, and Harvey Higgins, the one lank drayman, carted trunks through the town, and there were hysterical greetings and embracings on the brick platform of the little station, people said, "Well, it seems pretty good to have them back after all."

CHAPTER II

There was only one girls' dormitory at Adams—"the Dorm"—a large brick building on a wide, sloping lawn, with fire escapes where town boys stole pans of candy set out to cool, and a gloomy reception hall where calling youths waited upon the "anxious bench." Freshman girls lived in the Dorm, as recommended by the Dean of Women, but the upper classmen lived in rooming houses on the three long streets that ran parallel to the campus. Some of these had traditions of greatness—the Wilson House, the Harris House, the Trombley House—either because great ones lived there, or because the landladies were good-natured. Everything depended upon "the bunch of girls." The importance of the men's rooming houses was more shifting.

The Harris House was one of the most famous. It was a tradition that some of the most prominent E. B. B. girls should room there, with one or two Ionians to keep away the dread name of sorority. It was an old barny two-story brown house with a narrow porch and big drafty rooms with battered furniture. Since the death of Mr. Harris, a few years ago, the house was in fearful repair. The furnace would not heat the big rooms, the bedrooms smelled like steam laundries in the mornings and the mirrors were dim with vapor; steam would suddenly come bursting through a wall, there were floods in the cellar when tubs and pails had to be collected and girls had to run over to the campus for masculine aid in stemming the torrents. The bathroom was unheated. But still, "nice girls had always stayed there." There were many male callers at the Harris House. It kept its popularity in spite of steam, floods and freezing. It stood on a corner of College Street across from the campus and from the new Carnegie library that was just being built. One large birch tree on the lawn threw a shadow over the porch where couples lingered on pleasant evenings.

The Harrises were one of the semi-important families of Adamsville. Mr. Harris had been a neat, insignificant little man. But Mrs. Harris was in some way related to the Adams family, so that she sometimes appeared in the less imposing reception lines, and as a helping hostess at teas. A little slender gentle, nervous woman, with bright, sweet eyes set in bony, darkened sockets, wearing always a black silk dress trimmed with black lace and a band of velvet around her little throat, making an appearance of appealing gentility. She was a cousin of the Mrs. Adrian Adams who had married her cousin, Adrian Adams, Jr., sole son of the Adrian Adams who had given the land for the campus of Adams College. Mrs. Adrian Adams lived in one of those square, white houses and had the only victoria and coachman in town. Adrian Adams wore the only Adamsville silk hat. A faint traditional glory glimmered about Mrs. Harris.

The older children, Alma and Russell, had both been graduated from Adams and had married classmates. They had been of "the Adams type." Perhaps a little more exclusively devoted to religion than the students of this day. Alma had been the president of the Y. W. C. A. in her Senior year, and an E. B. B. Russell had been in the Y. M. C. A. cabinet and on one of the gospel teams that were sent out to the surrounding small towns to preach Adams ideals and recruit new students for the college. "All-around fine students" and "in everything." Alma was now living in Montana, where her husband was a superintendent of schools, and Russell was in social service work in the East.

Hester, the youngest, had grown up in the shadow of the college. She adored the girls who stayed in the Harris House. Her mother, a shy little woman with delicate notions of gentility, would not permit her to "bother the girls." But sometimes she sat perched on a cot listening with shining-eyed, breathless awe to their talk of dates and classes and "Society."

Some of the girls were always active. Always about the campus, doing all their studying in the library. Others sprawled about their rooms, in kimonos or comfortable, sloppy undress, their hair down or hanging by two pins. They lay on their cots and talked, one girl's head in another's lap. About five o'clock there was a rush for the bathroom. These girls were the ones who "dolled up" for their evening dates, standing in front of the mirror and staring intently, then leaning forward to rub the powder out of their eyebrows with a moistened finger, putting on their corsets again and taking a deep breath as they clasped them.

At times they would suddenly pet and fondle Hester, praising her with school girl extravagance. "Hasn't this child the darlingest smile! I think she has the sweetest expression! Honestly, I think she's got the dearest disposition of any girl I ever saw."

Hester came up to see them when they were dressed for a function and stood adoring. Flowers were sent for the great event, the Glee Club Concert. She was given a bud or two when she helped to hook dresses and powder backs and offered eagerly to press petticoats at the last minute. She opened the door for swains and said shyly, "Won't you sit down? I'll call her"—then sped softly up the stairs to whisper in high excitement. "Somebody's come for Mildred!"

The girls' rooms—the cots piled with cushions, the fly-nets on the wall stuck full of photographs, the Indian heads of tinted plaster, the burnt-wood boxes, the pennants, the toilet things on the dressers, the chafing dishes and tea cosies. "A college girl's room." The girls at Adams took care of their own rooms—the boys, paying less rent, did not—but Hester was sometimes sent up with new castors or tacks. She slept with her mother in the old back parlor downstairs. She tried to make one corner of it look like "a college girl's room" with some of Alma's old pennants, all the kodak pictures that she could gather—known and unknown—pasted on an oblong of shiny black cambric, a covered waist box and some cushions. Babe Dunkel—a girl with flying black fuzzy hair, "a caution"—had a cushion covered with the little colored silk bows from the inner rims of men's hats. Hester would have given anything in the world, she thought, for a cushion like that. But the boys that she knew still wore caps, and she was much too shy and awestruck by the college "men" to beg such trophies from them.

She admired all the girls—all the Harris House girls were "nice"—but she had special ones whom she worshiped. Daisy Lyons, the wonderful girl who had played the part of Antigone, whom Everett DeLong declared to be better than Julia Marlowe, had stayed there for a year. Then she had suddenly married an elderly widower in her home town and never reappeared at Adams. Hester had an old glove box of her mother's, of dark red plush lined with faded, tattered red satin, which she called "my most precious trophy box." In it she kept a little square photograph of Daisy Lyons—a girl with a severely classical face, with black hair combed up into a "psyche" and a square-necked white gown with enormous sleeves—a handkerchief that Mary Purcell had given her for Christmas, a faded sprig of lilac that had dropped from the coat of the 1897 football captain and that Hester had rescued from under the sofa when her mother was sweeping, a letter from Helen Garvis, an ancient bud from Helen's Glee Club flowers. Helen Garvis was her great adoration. She had been called "an ideal Adams girl." She had fluffy fly-away light hair, a sunny fresh-colored face, little soft hands. . . . Hester had worshiped her. She had "gone in for everything"—had been Y. W. president, in the Dramatic Club play, Senior president of E. B. B., had given the mantle oration. She had married John Fellows, the great man of her class—"an ideal Adams couple"—and they had gone to Asia Minor to found a new Adams among the

Turks. Professor Hildebrand called Helen Garvis "the incarnation of the Adams spirit." Helen Garvis . . . oh, she was the most wonderful, most perfect girl who had ever gone to Adams!

Hester was softly, wistfully, eagerly devout. She prayed:

"Oh, please dear Father, please make me grow up like my darlingest belovedest Helen. Oh, dear Father, I pray Thee, *please* make me like Helen, just as much as it is in Thy power for me to be like her—dear Father, and be taken into E. B. B.—if it pleases Thee that I should—but, oh, *please* dear heavenly Father, because I can't bear to live if I'm not. Oh, but *like Helen* . . . for Jesus' sake I ask it."

Then she sprang into bed, glowing with happy, secret shame, and snuggled down under the covers beside her mother who murmured, "Darling, mamma likes to see you good, but you make such long prayers when it's so cold. Your little feet are like ice. Can't you do part of your praying in bed?" "Oh, *no*, mamma!" "That furnace—I'm beginning to despair. I'll have to order coal again . . . eats up coal. . . ." Hester lay shivering and glowing, only half hearing. She was ashamed, far too shy and maidenly, to confess to God that she wanted to marry someone just like John Fellows. But that was in her prayers—and to go and start a new Adams in the most savage part of Africa, an even more glorious John and Helen . . . she wandered into sleep from a savage village filled with cocoanut palms where two noble people in white clothes were going about laying healing hands on the heads of little suffering savage children, braving terrible perils together. . . .

She knew Alma's and Russell's old Annuals—the "Pioneer"—by heart. The names of all the prominent students who had ever gone to Adams. She was sick if some popular Freshman girl turned down E. B. B. for Ionian. She went to every one of the Commencement events, and tried not to weep when one of her favorites crossed the platform of the

Congregational church to receive her diploma with a dipping bow. "Helen Geneva Garvis"—"John Warburton Fellows"— her emotion when those names were called. She lived through the summer until Harvey brought over the trunks in the fall.

She was in High School now. She "went in for" High School activities, because that was the Adams way. She yelled desperately at football games, helped edit "Pebbles," organized class parties, tried to make bright helpful little talks, like those of the college girls, at the Christian Endeavor. She "went with" various High School boys. All this was what the college girls did.

She wanted so fervently to be a real Adams girl. It was her religion, and Helen was her goddess. She believed with absolute trust in every aspect of the Adams ideals. She would die, she thought, if she weren't taken into E. B. B., if she didn't have a man for the Glee Club Concert. But she thought that these were mere selfish ambitions, that they shouldn't matter so violently as her young eager heart knew that they did, that what did matter was "service."

CHAPTER III

Hester was going to make a dear little Freshman, upper-class girls who lived in Adamsville said. She was slight and girlish, with a pretty early bloom—with light straight soft hair, a round delicately tinted face and slender throat, eager, innocent, responsive eyes. She had a lovely, wistful, tremulous, believing smile. The older girls were kind to her, and she repaid them with an utterly trustful, fervent and yet shy devotion.

College opened, and she was a part of it. She went actually to register with the two Freshman girls from the Harris House. She was one of the girls now—an Adams girl.

She was starting well—not through calculation, but through

the fervency of her belief and enthusiasm. She flung herself heart and soul, without reserve, into the activities of the Freshman class. Everything was going like a wonderful radiant dream come true. She had got "Pa" Taylor for Latin and "Bunny" Phelps for English, just as she had hoped. One of the Junior girls in the house was on the social committee for the Opening Reception, and she had "got a good man" for Hester—Randall Doty, a Junior who was a leading debater. There were fewer men than girls at Adams. Hester was one of the triumphant Freshmen who had a man all to herself. She wore her sheer white lace-trimmed graduating dress and the new long white gloves that Alma had sent her. Afterward, Randall Doty asked her for several dates, flattered by her little soft eager responsive laugh and her lovely smile. She was being rushed for E.B.B. Delight Peterson beckoned her into a corner of the library and murmured significantly: "Hester—if you get an Ionian bid don't take it until you hear from me." She was even being rushed tentatively for Ionian, although they knew that Alma had been an E.B.B. and that she went with the girls in the Harris House. That showed her eminence—that, and having dates with a prominent Junior.

She was one of the most popular Freshmen immediately. She and the other two Freshmen girls, Bess and Jinny, scarcely slept the night before the class scrap. They bound veils around their hair so that they need not comb it in the morning, but could dash straight over to the campus when the scrap began. Hester carried water for the fighters—a sign of social supremacy—and tore up three handkerchiefs to bind wounds. Afterward she eagerly handed out coffee and wiener sandwiches from the kitchen of the Harris House. At the first class meeting she was elected secretary by acclamation.

She was chosen to lead the first class prayer meeting, which sinners and all attended, youths eyeing the girls to whom they would say with facetious nonchalance—"You seem to be going my way." She made an appealing, enthusiastic little talk on "Freshman Ideals." Afterward the girls crowded around her, exclaiming fervently, "Hester, you were wonderful! That was the *best* thing!"

"Oh, girls, was it?" she asked tearfully. "I was simply scared to death!"

They fell away respectfully as they saw that Jay Oehrle, a Freshman boy who was "showing up prominently," was lingering to walk home with Hester.

Jay carried Hester's testament and notes for her. He murmured,

"That was a great little speech, Miss Harris. I certainly wish I could do half as well when my time comes."

"Oh, you will!" Hester declared. "You'll do lots, lots better!"

He declared that it wasn't the kind of a night to go straight home. It was chilly, windy, raw. But they walked up and down the cinder paths in the blowing dusk, talking and pretending that they didn't feel the cold. Hester forced her teeth not to chatter and declared, "No, really I'm not cold."

"I don't want to make you catch cold or anything," Jay said, "but I certainly am enjoying this."

They talked about serious "real" things—about what college ought to mean to people, and what class prayer meetings "stood for," what the Adams spirit was, what girl would make the best class president for the winter term. When Jay finally left her on the worn porch of the Harris House, he declared earnestly,

"This certainly is the best talk I've ever had with a girl, Hester. I hope we can have lots more of 'em. I tell you, I think the people that have got the best interests of the class at heart ought to get together. It does a fellow good to talk with a girl that's got some ideals."

A Part of the Institution · 63

When she went into the house with eyes and nose red with cold, Jinny and Bess, who had been waiting for her, exclaimed disgustedly, "Well, he might at least have taken you to the Vienna and got you a sandwich to warm you up after keeping you out in the cold for three hours!" Jinny said she had picked Jay Oehrle "for that kind."

Jay usually took Hester home after class prayer meetings. She declared to Jinny and Bess,

"You know, girls, I like Jay *better* because he just talks about serious things to me, and doesn't take me to the Vienna afterward and everything, just like a regular date. Jay has the most wonderful ideas."

Jay Oehrle was a short slight boy with a thin dusky face and gray eyes, heavy black hair that fell in a thick lock over his forehead. He was going to be a minister. He led the Freshman yells with savage earnestness, screwing his face up into a tortured frenzy of bitter enthusiasm. There were already deep lines in his thin swarthy cheeks. He scolded the class bitterly for its lack of spirit.

There were more boys—"men," she learned to call them now. Some of the older girls told her that it was better not to stick to one in her Freshman year, but to "try them out." Such advice was too worldly for Hester. But she enjoyed with a bubbling recklessness under her earnestness the new delights of going with now this one, now that one, the exhilaration of her Freshman popularity. Of course, the older girls said she might lose out on the Glee Club concert and some other things this way—that was when it was an advantage to have "a steady man." Hester said, "Oh, I like all the boys so well, I think the Freshman class has the most wonderful bunch of boys ever got together!"

She loved the "serious talks" with Jay. And the first class president, Rob Alden, a rosy stocky boy with eyeglasses, was "the grandest boy." Bunty Peterson was "loads of fun." She even went out once or twice with Big Bill Warren, because she was too tenderhearted to "turn him down forever" and he kept patiently asking her. Big Bill came from Winner, a tiny village a few miles from Adamsville. Big Bill from Winner was a joke in Freshman year. A huge awkward bony Freshman whose two long front locks of hair hung down to his heavy eyebrows and whose wrists and raw red hands dangled far out of the sleeves of his shiny coat, with deep-set mournful eyes and an enormous grinning mouth. He was tremendously solemn when he was with Hester, saying respectfully, "Yes, ma'am," but there were already rumors among the boys that that big gawk from Winner was "a regular clown." Of course he could not be taken seriously, like Jay Oehrle and Rob Allen, who seemed like real Adams boys.

Hester was naturally, instinctively among the "good bunch"—except for Jinny. Not necessarily the social belles, but the girls who were "active in Freshman affairs." Ellen, Bess, Margaret, Della, "Crazy Gertie" Bumstead. They asked her to the Dorm for meals and included her in spreads.

Bess Lake was in the Harris House because her Senior sister, Carrie, stayed there. Jinny Woodward had been recommended by a graduate from her home town. Jinny was tremendously popular for the first three weeks, was rushed by both societies—then she was felt to be "a mistake." She was pretty, she could sing and play, men liked her—but she was not the Adams type. She scoffed and would not go in for things unless she pleased. She was felt to be "a little too swift." She went to one of the town dances, with a "town fellow." Dancing was against the Adams traditions, although it was not damning to "be called up for dancing." But town dances were beyond the pale. Jinny always wanted to "do something reckless." She would not listen to the older girls.

She said rebelliously, "I don't know who appointed Carrie Lake my Dutch uncle. I don't care. Dad made me go here and if I'm sent home it's his own fault."

But Hester loved Jinny, although she "couldn't approve of all the things she did." She was fascinated by Jinny—her round, soft-featured, dark, rebellious face, her curling dusky hair and dark starry eyes and piquant uneven brows, strongly marked, one higher than the other. She mourned over Jinny and pleaded with her. Jinny had "another self." Why didn't she show it? Why did she do all these wild things that counted against her? She tried to "get Jinny into things." Jinny could do anything if she would.

As the year went on, and the older girls showed their disapproval more markedly, Jinny grew more reckless. Hester did things for her that tortured her sensitive conscience. She would not tell the other girls when Jinny went out with Dave Greenaway, a "fast" Junior against whom she had been warned. She stayed awake to let Jinny into the house after hours. She opened the upstairs window when she heard Jinny softly call, and, with smothered giggles, climb up the porch post to the balcony. When her own mother was responsible for the girls! She, Hester, who believed so earnestly the little speeches that she made in the Y. W., lying and helping another girl to lie! Yes, and about the things that Adams girls didn't do!

After the episode of the town dance, both societies dropped Jinny, although she did room at the Harris House. Hester got her bid to E. B. B. The upper class girls called her and Bess into Carrie's room and told them, with many ecstatic embraces, before the bids were out. They had a spread for them—cheese dreams and fudge. They said that they were sorry about Jinny but she'd killed her own chances. If she cut out Dave Greenaway and the town fellows, she might have a chance in the spring. Hester could not conceive of refusing an E. B. B. bid, but it was dreadful to go in without Jinny.

They had a queer friendship, disapproving and pleading on Hester's part, scoffing and then suddenly remorseful and affectionate on Jinny's.

"Jinny, if you'd only give yourself a chance, you'd *love* Adams."

Jinny said the whole thing was "too tame." She wrote verses about "purple adventure," furious when Hester found them in her English notebook and declared that they were "good enough to hand in to the *Adams Magazine*." What did she mean by adventure? She didn't know, but "something wild, something crazy."

Hester's friendship for Jinny was the only stain upon the clear shining purity of her Freshman record. She did all the things that Freshman girls should do. She started out on the committee for the first Freshman party, ladling out lemonade on the lawn of the house of the Dean of Women. She was on social committees, prayer meeting committees, committees to get up class yells and services for the Day of Prayer, the first Freshman girl to lead a meeting of the Y. W. C. A. She went with her Opening Reception man, Randall Doty, to the Glee Club concert. She seemed all the more a real Adams girl because she wore her little simple graduation dress. Randall added a touch of imposing elegance by having sent to Farwell City for her roses. Big Bill had asked her, too. She had turned him down, of course—gently, because Hester couldn't help being kind—but it was all the more glorious and exciting to have had two invitations.

Big Bill, in his old blue suit with a choker collar, officiated as an usher—a consolation prize given to single but respected youths. He started the evening in gloom, but his natural clownishness broke forth, his huge grin widened and widened, and he took great glee in seating a frivolous Freshman couple among the faculty and in leading Stub Parker to a seat beside his last year's girl. In the intermission he distributed, with great applause, tiny bunches of artificial forget-me-nots to all the ushers. It was seen at once that Big Bill was coming to the front.

Hester was generously glad that on one occasion, at least, Jinny shone. She looked "glorious"—all the girls admitted it. She wore a pale green evening gown that showed her soft dusky-white shoulders and her black hair was piled and twisted into a psyche knot. Dave Greenaway had sent her two dozen American Beauty roses. Her cheeks and her lips had a dark glowing color. For once that night the girls exclaimed over her, approved her. Dave escorted her to the chapel in the one Adamsville hack. He wore the only dress suit outside of the Glee Club and the faculty circle. It was a night of imposing triumph for Jinny.

But she did not get into E. B. B. in the spring. She had no solid position in the Freshman class. Hester wept and pleaded with her to come back to Adams the next year. It hurt her desperately when Jinny broke into bitter, laughing, biting mockery of all that Hester felt that Adams "stood for," getting more and more reckless as Hester wept, finally calling the leading spirits of the Freshman class "a bunch of rubes varnished with religion."

"You know very well that Dottie Burroughs does as many wicked things as I've ever done. But she makes little sweetie talks in Y. W. and so it's all right. I don't pretend to, that's all. I don't sugar over what I do. People have such fits about Dave. 'Wild'—well, what if he is? Just the same, Dave's one of the most decent fellows I was ever with. I'd trust him any time before I would Jay Oehrle."

"Jinny! You've always been unjust to Jay. But I'm *not* going to listen to you when you say anything against Adams."

Jinny said too much for even Hester. Even when Jinny caught her in the hall the next day and pushed her into her room, throwing beseeching, remorseful, soft arms tightly about her, and calling herself ridiculous extravagant names, Hester—although she smiled tremulously and let herself be embraced—found her tender, trusting, orthodox little heart wounded beyond speedy healing. She couldn't respond wholeheartedly to Jinny's coaxing and embraces and funny remorseful antics.

Not even when Jinny said,

"Hester, beloved. I don't doubt it's largely that I'm peeved because I haven't made good here and I know it."

Jinny cried, when she left.

"Oh, Hester, you're so *innocent*, anyone can make you swallow anything whole! I feel wicked going away and leaving you here."

Except for this one thing the Freshman year ended in radiant glory.

Jay Oehrle was staying on for a week at Adamsville to finish his work at Jack the Cleaner's. He and Hester went to all the trains to see "the last of the bunch" off. Then they sat out on the deserted steps of Blaine Hall in the moonlight until two o'clock, having the best and most serious of all their talks. Jay told her his ideals of a minister's career. He confided to her the details of a love affair with a girl in his home town who was teaching and sending him money to help him through college. Hester gave him earnest shy advice, with a delicious confidential feeling. They talked about what they meant to do next year.

Jay said,

"One thing I'm not going to do, I'm not going to kill time like I've let myself do sometimes this year, and I'm not going to stand for the other fellows in the house doing it. I tell you, we're here at Adams to *work*, and not to just work for ourselves but for the college—"

"Oh, I think that's *true*!" Hester cried eagerly, looking at him with shining trustful eyes in the ivy-shadowed moonlight.

Jay cleared his throat and looked out frowningly over the

slope of dewy campus to where the black cinder paths lay edged with laburnum and bridal wreath. Hester sat beside him with her hands tightly clasped, worshiping the beauty.

She said,

"I think you're *right*. I feel that way, too. I feel as if this year I've done too much, and thought too much—well, just for myself. I know I haven't thought enough about Adams."

Jay declared,

"Well, if *you* haven't Hester, I certainly don't know anyone who has. I think you've got more of the real Adams spirit than any girl in the Freshman class."

His thin, dark, tense hand closed over hers as he spoke. She could not say just why the clasp began to make her uncomfortable. She twisted her hand slightly, and felt his fingers reach higher on her wrist. She sprang up a little breathlessly, cried with forced gaiety,

"If we don't go home Prexie'll be getting the marshal after us!" and ran down the cinder path.

"Silly! What made me act like such a silly?" she berated herself afterward.

Her mother murmured, half awake, "Hester, where *were* you?"—moaned and turned back to sleep. Hester lay with open, radiant eyes, thrilling again over the talk with Jay, the partings, tears welling up when she thought of Jinny, and all the wonderful Seniors, gone . . . smelling again the odor of night and dew and bridal wreath on the campus . . . one beautiful year gone. . . .

CHAPTER IV

That summer seemed endlessly long and dull. Hot—every day worse than the one before. The nights were terrible. Hester and her mother did not pretend to do regular cooking.

After a little lunch, they each took a bath, put on their nightgowns, and tried to read and sleep in the darkened back parlor
until the worst heat of the day was over. At night, Hester
hooked the screen door and lay down on one of the old cot
mattresses before it. The Harris House attic was full of cot
relics.

The town was nothing without the college people. How
could she ever stand it until fall? She went again to the Christian Endeavor. Humphrey Dilley walked solemnly home with
her. She and Humphrey had been in school together since the
day when they had both started into kindergarten in the basement of the old Universalist church. Humphrey was one of
the banker Dilleys, an old, loyal, solid Adamsville family.
Hester knew that Humphrey was "a dandy good fellow," but
it wasn't easy to talk to him, as it was to Jay and Bunty.
They discoursed about their classmates and the prospects for
next year.

"I had a letter from Rob."

"Oh, *did* you? What did he say?"

"Well—I don't know as anything specially interesting."

She tried to talk over candidates for class officers and for
next spring's *Pioneer* Board election with him; but although
Humphrey was a good, solid member of the class, the kind
who is elected treasurer, he could not exchange thrilling confidences over these things as Jay could. Humphrey was not a
leader. Their talks always ended with:

"Well, it'll seem mighty good to see them all come back in
the fall."

He tried with the most conscientious determination to keep
in step with her as they went down the long tree-shadowed
walk, frequently stopping to start over again. He was a big
heavy-shouldered youth with a large, good, dull face and a
massive wave of dark hair. A little too slow to make a football
player. At the door he lingered and lingered, until he could

finally utter the parting word—"Well, I expect it must be getting late."

"But then," Hester thought as she went in yawning, "Humphrey is such a *good* fellow, and I know I ought to be ashamed."

Fall came at last. That hottest week of all in September, when she helped her mother to clean the house, wash all the bedding, put up the cots and get the girls' rooms ready.

Jay came three days early to get his old job with Jack the Cleaner. Hester spent those three evenings with him, wandering about the campus while he outlined to her his plans for the class during the year, and she broke in with,

"Oh, won't it be glorious to see everybody! Jay, I don't see how I've lived through this summer."

They both felt the glory of being important members of their class.

Hester was already in all the activities that she could manage. She was on the committee for the Opening Reception. She promised to give Jay his choice of the Freshman girls. She wore a badge saying "Old Girl," and ran down to all the trains to meet new people and old. She did want to make the Freshman girls feel at home, feel that they had a place in Adams. She took Freshman girls to their rooming houses. They looked at her with adoring eyes. They said, "If all Adams girls are like Hester Harris!"

She was so kind, so enthusiastic about everything, so full of the Adams spirit, telling them to think of her as a big sister and to ask her anything. She meant every word of this, meant it ardently. But she was wondering which ones would do for E. B. B., which was only second to Adams itself in her faith and love.

They were all pouring in now, more on every train. There was such a feeling now of old and tested intimacy with her classmates. Della, Ellen, Bess—Gertie more crazy than ever. Bob Alden cried,

"Hester, I've been watching for that smile all the way from Des Moines! How you was? I sure am tea-kettled stiff to see you."

They were all hilarious because the train had gone sailing past Big Bill on the platform at Winner, where only one local and one freight stopped. They told how he had tried to signal it frantically with a bandana. The boys said, grinning,

"Let's get up a reception gang, badges and horns and stuff, to meet old Bill when he comes into town in the caboose."

The station platform was stacked high with trunks, and everyone was trying to get a promise for quick delivery from Harvey Higgins. Embracings, shrieks—Hester had seen all this since she was a little girl, and now she was "in it."

All back but Jinny. She had thought that she would miss Jinny, and the Seniors, so terribly. But these first weeks were too full. Jinny had gone West suddenly and was teaching a country school, to which she had to ride six miles on horseback.

"Just to be doing something wild," she had written Hester. What a shame that Jinny hadn't come back and given herself a chance to make good.

Activities were so much more serious this year. It was the Adams ideal to go in for as many as possible, to sink the individual in the public good and so advance the school spirit. Hester plunged into them all. She scampered about the campus trying to get items for her "try-out" for the "Blue and White" staff. She tried for the Dramatic Club, very ambitiously with "The quality of mercy is not strained."

Her voice was light, of course. She said, "Oh, I don't expect to make it, but I think as many ought to try out as can for the sake of the club."

She was hurt because Wade Brunner, a Senior, said that she read Portia's speech as if she were giving a talk to the Y. W. But then, Wade Brunner was a "crab." No one liked him because he was "so sarcastic." He thought that no one knew anything about dramatics but himself. Hester knew that she could not make the Girls' Glee Club (at this time an inferior organization, overshadowed by the Glee Club, as the men's organization was called). But she could sing well enough for the Oratorio Society, where all that was needed was to carry a tune, and she joined that. Even the German Club, made up largely of maidens who "had no other activities." She and Ellen had decided that some of the "girls who did things" ought to go into these organizations and raise the general tone. She was on every committee in the Sophomore class. It was "service," "doing something for Adams."

She worried a long time about joining the Volunteer Band. The German Club was merely obscure. But the Volunteer Band was "roasted in the Annual." She still kept her worship of Helen and John Fellows, still talked of going to China when school was over. She believed in carrying the Adams spirit to downtrodden lands. Then wasn't it her duty to join the Volunteer Band? She had long talks with Jay about it. He opposed it fiercely, with strong arguments.

"That's all very well, Hester. I honor you for feeling that way. I may decide to go to Asia or somewhere like that myself, although I think there's a big field right in this country. I tell you it would be about the grandest work a man could do to carry the spirit of Adams over the world. But I'm opposed to seeing you join the Volunteer Band. Its purpose is good—I honor that—but it hasn't much of a standing, as an organization, in Adams. It hasn't the right kind of people."

"Oh, but Jay," Hester cried anxiously, "don't you think then some of us that believe in what it's doing ought to join it?"

"No, because we're putting our service into other organizations. You're doing a whole lot right now for the school through the Y. W. and all, and you can do more there."

Rob said,

"Gosh! I think the heat must have turned your brain this

summer, girl. That bunch of pills. Leonard Stoner and Susie Dykes and Jesse Babcock. Wouldn't you look sweet among 'em? Well, maybe you could make a hit with Jesse. Is that your object?"

She felt guilty, but she was glad to have two fine earnest fellows like Jay and Rob, who had the best interests of the school at heart, advise her against joining the Band. There were Leonard Stoner and Susie Dykes, one of the school jokes as a couple—Leonard a little light wisp of a dried-up youth, Susie a big homely girl with flat feet and stiff black hair and prominent teeth. Jesse Babcock was the biggest "pill" in school, the one who was roasted in the *Pioneer*. Then there was that poor girl with the harelip—Hester always took special pains to "be nice to" her—and the little cripple, and other harmless but insignificant ones. She didn't belong with them, that was true. And of course she hadn't absolutely made up her mind to go to Asia—perhaps she oughtn't to bind herself.

After that eventless summer she wanted to go to everything. She accompanied the Harris House Freshman girls to the Dorm reception, which was chiefly useful for youths who wished to have a good view of the new girls.

Dorm receptions were always supposed to be dull. Hester went about "making people have a good time." She was really shy about approaching strangers, but for an old girl to sit and talk to a few people whom she already knew would be too selfish. Mrs. Potter, the matron, "counted upon her to keep things going." Her shyness kept her from being officious, and colored her soft cheeks delicately. One gloomy Freshman youth sat in a corner, and his dark eyes followed her half sulkily. He listened to her little high, sweet, eager voice that was just the least bit breathless.

Hester said to the other girls:

"That poor fellow's been sitting there all evening and I don't believe anyone's said a word to him."

"Why don't you, then?"

"Well, I do think that someone ought to."

She promised to help Mrs. Potter to get some games going. They were all to play Wink 'Em. "Now I want every boy in this room to get behind a chair, and every girl to sit in a chair. Only Dick Johns. He can't have any girl in his chair."

"Why do you pick on me?" Dick wailed.

The girls seated themselves in the chairs with the aid of Mrs. Potter. A dozen boys wanted Hester. She called on her courage and spirit and slipped softly into the chair behind which the lonesome youth was gloomily standing. She felt a kind of reluctant thrill from the dark strong hands that hovered over her shoulders, closing down with a fearful grip when bashful Freshman boys winked gratefully in response to her shining, helpful eyes.

Then later she found herself near him at the frappé table. He silently brought her a carefully held cup of the reddish frappé. She talked brightly to him, trying to penetrate his gloom. They sat down in one of the long red-cushioned window seats in the big reception hall. She clasped her hands lightly and smiled helpfully at him, ready to respond.

"Do you like your classes? Whom did you get in Freshman English? Oh, it's too bad you didn't get Bunny, he's so perfectly dear, I had him last year. But then, Professor Thurber's very good too. It's hard to start, isn't it? But then, I think Adams does more for its new students than any other school."

His silence intrigued her. She felt that she must enthuse, and rouse him from it. The beauties of the campus, the faculty, Prexie, the new crowd of girls in the Dorm, the fine spirit of the Freshman class. She was horrified when he said gloomily:

"Yes, it's all right if you just fall in with whatever anybody else does. It's all right if you get their 'attitude' but they don't want any fellow to have an attitude of his own."

"Oh, no! Oh, you don't understand Adams at all. They *want*

people to think for themselves. That's what they *teach* people to do."

"Yes, sure, if it's just what they think they ought to think."

She exclaimed: "Oh, but you mustn't start right in criticizing! How can you expect to like things, or to have people like you, if you do that? That isn't the Adams spirit—it's to help and not hinder."

"Yes, but I want to have a pretty darn good idea of what I'm helping first."

"I don't see how you could have listened to Prexie's chapel talk and not know what you're helping!"

"Oh sure, Adams ideals that they all talk about—but a fellow's got to think about and decide these things for himself."

Hester explained and defended Adams with loving enthusiasm. She was flattered in some obscure way by his silent gloomy regard which she could not quite fathom. And besides, she must not let a Freshman get the wrong idea of the school. He was a dark boy, with thick swart black hair and a wide mouth that seemed at the same time sensitive, hurt and bitterly satirical. He wore a cheap, black, ready-made suit and careless scuffed shoes. He told her that he had been working on a farm all summer. She could see that his dark sunburned hands were scarred. But he had none of the uncouthness that offended her in Big Bill. She did not learn his name. When she left the Dorm, she found him silently beside her in the dusk. The other girls went hurrying on ahead of them, and she heard giggles and whispers.

The girls were all waiting for her, in their kimonos, massed on the stairs.

They chorused: "Hester! Are you trying to do missionary work? Where did you pick him up?"

Hester said, a little nettled, "Why? isn't he all right? *I* don't know who he is—from Adam."

"That's that Joe Forrest. That's that nut that wouldn't join the Y. M. and invited Summer Grant to leave his room. Is *that* what you pick up when we aren't there to take care of you! I never thought it of Hester."

"Girls, she was sitting on the window seat talking away to him—I thought she must be trying to convert him."

"Look out—you're getting her fussed."

"Well, I don't care," Hester said, "he wasn't a bit bad to talk to."

It made her feel foolish, though, that she had been so interested in him, and wondered so who he was. That Joe Forrest. She had heard the boys talking about him, saying that a little session with the Damme Club some dark night wouldn't hurt that guy. He might change his tune if they kept him up a tree for a while in his night shirt. He needn't think he could come here and criticize. Who was he anyway? His father was a preacher in a little burg named Pitt. Fred Loomis knew him. Said he'd always been like that—always been "ornery."

Hester felt strangely conscious when she heard the boys talking about him. Rob said he had only made that fuss about not joining the Y. M. to get some notoriety. All the fellows joined the Y. M.—it didn't necessarily mean they had to attend every meeting, or believe every word that was said, either. Lots of good fellows didn't take part. "But this guy had to show off."

Hester said nervously, "Oh, I'm not defending him. But I do think you boys ought to give him more of a chance before you do anything to him. If you'd go and talk to him—I don't think he really means all those things."

"Well, he's starting in with the wrong notions of what he's going to do, I'll tell you, and it wouldn't hurt him any to get a little of it licked out of him."

For a time the advent of Joe Forrest made quite a commotion. He was the only youth who had ever refused point-blank to affiliate with the Y. M. C. A. when he entered Adams—almost an automatic act. Even if a fellow "didn't take much active part" it "gave him a good standing." If Joe Forrest remained until his Junior year, he would be the sole youth who did not have the letters Y. M. C. A. printed after his name in the *Pioneer*, saving letters for those who could claim no other activity. Of course it wasn't that alone. He didn't have the right spirit. He was a knocker. Adams had no use for a fellow like that. For a time, whenever members of the Damme Club— the college punitive society—were seen in conclave, people said, "I bet they'll do something to that Joe Forrest tonight."

But Joe Forrest, after his spectacular entrance, slipped back into obscurity. People let him alone and he let them alone. He seemed to have retired into a state of gloomy silence and inaccessibility. The boys in his rooming house—an unimportant little house on the wrong side of the campus—declared that he was "a mighty good guy" and that "they liked old Joe." He was a good student, a "shark," and only occasionally asked disconcerting questions that made people remember that the Damme Club had never dealt with him. "Oh, he makes me tired," was what was said of him now. But he no longer seemed important enough to concern the Damme Club. He was simply a dark, shabby, taciturn boy, something of a grind, who didn't go out for athletics.

Hester sometimes saw him around the library or crossing the campus. He gave her a feeling of uneasiness, almost of guilt. She had never followed up that "earnest" talk she had had with him. She was ashamed. She would not admit, even to herself, the thrill that she felt when those dark hands had suddenly clamped down upon her shoulder and forced her back into her chair. How dreadful. . . .

Hester and Jay Oehrle took fewer walks and talks together this year. Jay was still prominent, but he had lost a little of his Freshman eminence. People "got tired of his trying to run everything." Hester was with Bunty Peterson oftener.

Big Bill had come into sudden and immense popularity among the other boys. The boys at his rooming house had "got him tamed down a little." His coat sleeves now reached his hands and his front locks were disciplined. Of course he was "always up to something" and couldn't be taken seriously. Hester—remembering John Fellows, slight, fair-haired, fine-featured—could not help feeling an uncouthness and disconcerting levity in Big Bill. She laughed at his practical jokes—as when he attended the Sophomore fancy dress party in the gym as the Bride of the Mistletoe—but still he was not quite what she thought of as the Adams type. There was still a good deal of "taming down" to be done. Oh, she liked Bill, no one could help liking him. But she was glad to accept Bunty's invitation for the Glee Club concert early in the year and fend off Bill's bid.

During the second semester she found that Joe Forrest was in her Poly. Sci. class. It was a sleepy class, conducted by an aged, learned and kindly man, and elected as a "snap" by a large medley of assorted students. No one was expected to do anything in it. But Joe Forrest, although he sat silent and bored most of the time, slumped far down in a chair and digging with his pencil at the initials and fancy designs carved in the desk arm, would sometimes come out startlingly with those sharp, disconcerting questions.

Hester made good grades in Poly. Sci. and kept up her notebook. She was always a conscientious student. It was a joke among the boys to flunk Poly. Sci.—almost an honor— but it would not have done for a girl. Of course she didn't take it seriously, like Major History and Applied Christianity. She was horrified at some of the statements that Joe Forrest made. He "liked to argue," as the boys said. But at the same time she was always conscious of him sitting in the back of the room among two rows of boys who handed about sacks of "red hots" and looked on each others' notebooks. His face was dark against the light from the long windows.

She always had that uneasy feeling of guilt that had troubled her since the Dorm reception. She would try to speak to him. She did one day, a little breathlessly, as they were leaving class.

"Did you hear what Professor Duke assigned for Tuesday?"

He stared at her, and told her. She felt herself blush hotly, until she saw with what care he was opening his notebook and finding the assignment. A few days later he was near her when they left class. He lingered with an air of indifferent carelessness and walked down the long hall with her. Then he began walking back to the library with her.

The girls said lightly, "You must have made a hit with our friend the crab."

At the Glee Club concert, she looked brightly about, telling Bunty, "I wanted to see where Ellen and Tad were sitting" . . . Joe Forrest wasn't there, even as an usher.

He always sat across from her in the library now. When she left the building, he got up after a moment, still with that indifferent air, and followed her, coming up with her suddenly just as she paused on the stone steps outside. They discovered that they were in different divisions of the same Latin class. Hester was pleased to have Joe ask her questions about constructions, which she always worked out faithfully. Joe was "a shark," but only in things that "he could see some sense in taking." He could see no sense in taking Latin. Since he was required to take it, at least he wouldn't study the stuff, wouldn't pretend that he did. He and Hester began "getting their Latin together," she with the constructions all conscientiously learned, he with no preparation but frequently able to throw light upon something that had puzzled her. There was a grassy place beyond the library where Hester liked to sit to study in the spring.

Now Joe always sat there with her. She argued with him the value of ancient languages. There was a kind of fearful pleasure in hearing the statements that he made.

She knew that people were saying, "Honestly, is Hester Harris going with that Joe Forrest?"

Joe was no longer conspicuously obstreperous. He had the respect of several of his professors, the liking of a few boys who knew him intimately. But his reputation was settled as that of "a grouch," "a crab." He seemed to be absolutely the wrong person for Hester Harris.

Hester's arguments with him all settled now about the definition of the Adams spirit and of "Adams ideals."

"The Adams spirit is the spirit of 'pure democracy.' You know very well that you girls wouldn't take that poor kid with the harelip into E. B. B. You know that if any fellow got her name for a party he'd slide out of taking her."

He said, "It's all this simply falling in with things and talking about 'em as settled facts, when you don't know what they are or whether you believe 'em or not, that I'm talking about. . . . You girls at the Y. W., you just repeat the same stuff over and over and never stop to find out whether you understand a word of it. Winnie Parker, down on the poster to lead your Y. W. on the subject of 'Honesty in Little Things,' and then goes and sits by poor old Susie Dykes every day in German so that she can copy her written work."

Hester made an almost tearful defense. She knew what the others would say. "Why do you take the trouble to argue with a grouch like that? What do you care what he says?"

But she was most ardently anxious to convert Joe. She cried, "Well, I know some of the girls do things like that—we all do things we shouldn't—but then, most of them *are* sincere. Winnie's just one instance."

"Sure. But it's this taking things for granted that gets me."

She tried to defend her own sincerity.

He looked at her. "Gosh! I know you believe the whole business, Hester. You believe everything, don't you? Poor kid."

"Why, Joe! I do believe it—of course I do. I just wish I could make you see what I mean by these things."

She knew that the right was on her side—that he was just using little unimportant instances to put her off—but she hated this constant pinning her down to exact definitions. "Well, what do you mean by 'democracy'—if it isn't that? Just what do you mean? What are 'Adams ideals'? 'Service'—serve what? And how and why, and where's it going to get you?" Hester cried in despair, "You have to *feel* these things, Joe. You can't define them in so many words."

"Well, how you going to make me feel them?"

Once he burst out: "Gosh! People can act the way they please for all I care. It's this damn sugaring things over that gets me, all around here. It was just the same in my dad's church. Have to hit every nail just a little on the slant."

But she liked Joe so well, "in spite of the way he talked." She wanted to "change his viewpoint about these things," to "make him see things in a better light." A kind of intimacy had unconsciously grown between them. Joe told her things that made her feel that she could understand him better. He was the alien among four stepbrothers and sisters. He "wasn't happy at home." His father wanted him to do one thing and he wanted to do another. He hated Pitt, but he loved the woods and the river.

She was more than flattered—touched and stirred—by these confidences. They sat out in their own little grassy spot near the cool stone foundation of the "lib," Joe looking down at the ground and poking at it with a little stick as he talked. He said that she was "the only one he'd tell about these things." She felt his sensitiveness and loneliness under his armor of hurt callow cynicism and "orneriness." And yet there was something mature about Joe, something that the minds of

the other boys didn't have. His cynicism, his occasional rude-
ness, his angry bluntness, wounded her. He told her, when she
was elected to the *Pioneer* Board, "You know you don't even
pretend to write. Susie Dykes can write a darn sight better
than you can, Hester, and you know it. You got on on the
platform of general compliance." Yet there was something almost childlike, oddly grateful and shy, in the way that he
turned to her softness and gentleness and responsiveness.
That little eager, trustful way of hers. It seemed to soften the
harsh, bleak outlines of things, and he wanted it even while he
mocked at it. There was all the special pleasure, too, of being
the chosen one of someone who cared for few people.

"Hester Harris and Joe Forrest! What's Hester thinking of!
What on earth does she see in him!"

But with the spring, it was seen to be "a case." They were
constantly together. The girls in the Harris House declared
that it was no use trying to talk Hester out of it, they believed
Joe had a kind of power over her. She did the things that he
loved to do—went with him on long tramps into the woods
near Adamsville, instead of driving out in picnic parties of
four. She read the books that he picked out for her in the library, although some of them seemed "terrible." He would
not stay in the parlor of the Harris House, declaring that he
could not stand Dolly Rowen and Fred Davis, who had "a
terrible case" and sat in the corner in melting-eyed silence. He
and Hester walked until they were tired, and then stayed out
under the birch tree talking.

He was going to come back next year because of Hester.

CHAPTER V

Joe went out through Iowa and South Dakota during the summer selling paring knives. He made enough to start him at

Adams the next year. He wrote Hester letters with little odd, appealing strains of boyishness cropping out. She agonized over whether she "ought to keep on going with him next year." When he came back, his dark, thin, strong face with the black hair fascinated her as it had done before. Joe got a job working in the Vienna Café, one long room with a counter and stools and a row of "drug store tables," the ceiling festooned with ancient red and green tissue paper.

Their career as "a couple" was stormy and fitful this year. Hester was always breaking it off, to the satisfaction of the girls. Then after a period of lonely agonized weeping, it would be on again.

Hester had looked forward to the *Pioneer* Board as the pinnacle of her college course. She could never forget the glorious times that Alma's Board had had, that had seemed so wonderful to a small sister. That was when Alma had got to know Herschel, whom she had later married. That little sacred room on the third floor of Recitation Hall where the Annual Board met had been her goal. '03 had a wonderful Board. Gertie, Ellen, Bess, Bunty. Rob Alden was editor-in-chief. Bunty Peterson was business manager. Big Bill was on the Board. He was editor of the joke department. If it had not been for Joe, Hester might have "gone with" Bunty. He was a slim alert boy with "lots of the right spirit," a leader of mass meetings. More personally attractive than Jay, not such a clown as Bill. Everyone said that he and Hester would "make a grand couple." Why did she have to stick around with Joe?

The boys talked to her, when she and Joe were temporarily "off." They told her that they had nothing against Joe Forrest, that he had brains, but he was a knocker, a crab, not her kind. A fellow like that did nothing to help the school. It "made them tired" that she had always turned down Big Bill, and then would go with a fellow like Joe who wasn't anything in school.

She knew that everything was different this year because of Joe. She had got him to "go in for debate," but she sometimes felt that he had had more influence with her than she with him. She could not go in for things as fervently and innocently as she had always done. Echoes of Joe's sarcasms stayed with her. She did not enjoy the *Pioneer* Board as she had expected to do. Joe was jealous of Bunty, even while he scorned him, declaring that Bunty was the worst bluffer in school, that he'd talk just the same about any "set of ideals" that happened to be on tap where he happened to be, that he was out for Bunty Peterson and nothing else. "Bluff" was Joe's great word that year. He was seeing bluff everywhere. He worried Hester by declaring that debates were mostly bluffing, too.

"You want to be smart, not wise, to win a debate," he said. "Sure it's bluff—isn't your whole object to pretend there's no truth on the other side, when you know there is?"

Junior year, with all its importance and prestige, was not at all what she had thought it would be. Their tempestuous career was followed with disapproval, but intense interest by the girls in the Harris House. The few of these whom Joe liked stood up for him violently, the others detested the sight of him. But they all agreed that he and Hester were "a queer couple." Hester and Joe had desperate disputes. When they were at enmity, Hester could not study, could not work, burst into strange fits of weeping. He was always wounding her most cherished beliefs—bitterly and consciously, she thought in agony—and then being sorry when it was too late.

"Joe, it seems to me that you deliberately try to hurt one of the deepest beliefs in my life."

"Belief—but why do you believe it?"

"Why, because—why, because I *do*."

"That's just what I'm saying. You've never thought about it at all. You just take all they cram down your throat. Gosh,

Hester, you'd believe anybody. What I'm objecting to is acting as if Prexie was the Pope, sitting on the chapel platform sending out bulls. Prexie's a darn good chapel speaker, and he's a darn good money-getter, too. Has to be. His right hand and his left aren't always on speaking terms. Well, that's all right, it's his job—but don't try to make him infallible."

"Joe Forrest! You don't understand Prexie. No wonder you've got the reputation of being a knocker."

"Sure! That's just what I'm talking about. Slide over everything and never take a straight look at anything—might see something. That's my point exactly. Fellow doesn't swallow everything in one big lump, and then he's a knocker."

"Well, you are a knocker. I try to say you aren't when people call you that—"

"Well, why should you say I'm not if you think I am?"

"Joe! Oh, this is hopeless. Why do we ever try to agree?"

He answered gloomily, "Why do we?" But after that he would show his contrition for hurting her. He would say, "You believe things so darn hard, Hester. I'm afraid you're going to get an awful jolt some day. It scares me."

The Adams way was to trust fervently, without reserves. Joe had to question into everything. He "couldn't let anything alone." Criticism was "crabbing," and he was always criticizing. He said that he wasn't going to be fed with pre-digested ideals, like Mellins Food, whether they were good for him or not. That it wasn't the business of a college to "teach ideals," anyway—just to lay the facts before you and let you make your own deductions. That you weren't here to "do things for the school"—that stood to reason—but to make use of the school.

He criticized the Adams heroes and great men. Jay Oehrle was his pet aversion—and Joe took pleasure in his aversions. Jay—slender, dark, intense—rubbed Joe all the wrong way.

Jay's ferocious earnestness about class politics and "spirit," his political maneuvering, his speeches, his officiousness—Joe hadn't a good word for him.

"Look at his mouth," he said once to Hester, "if you want to find out what the Reverend Jay is like."

The worst of it was that she couldn't help noticing Jay's mouth. She knew that it had that vague something that had always repelled her. A kind of tortured sensuality—poor Jay, it told all too much about him. Although Hester didn't recognize it as that, only as "something she didn't like." It made her remember that night on the steps of Blaine Hall. Hester tried to defend Jay against Joe—but after that she shrank from having Jay near her. Joe's comments were always affecting her that way, and she thought that it was wrong, that she wasn't "seeing the best in people" as she should.

But Joe was not one of those who rejoiced when Jay Oehrle failed by three votes to make the *Pioneer* Board, a thing for which he had been maneuvering since his Freshman year. He said that it was mean to beat a fellow out of something he'd set his heart on. Sure, he was "a politician." Only not so slick as some of the others.

Joe and Hester had some wonderfully happy hours in the fall, when Joe rented one of the old livery teams and they went out to Sandy Creek for an all-day picnic. They sat in the long coarse grass on the shaggy bank of the creek, in an open place ringed about with oak trees. Joe brought out of his pocket a small, thumbed copy of "The Rubaiyat," which was then his Bible. Hester would not admit that she liked the sentiment— she didn't think it was "a sorry scheme of things" and she didn't want to smash it—but the rhythm was lovely. "A book of verses underneath a bough"—that she liked. Joe told her about the times when he had camped out in the woods "when he was a kid." They had a bonfire and roasted wieners and marshmallows, and then Joe blew up the sacks.

Joe was "a kid still" in some ways, in spite of his maturity in others. When Hester quarreled with him, he had to do something to prove how bad he was. It was one of those silly, childish things that caused the final trouble. Joe had scoffed at the idea of activities being "service." He told Hester that she went into activities because it was the thing to do, and she couldn't bear not to be approved and popular. And that was all right, if she felt that way—only why call it "service"? Poor Hester denied, and then agonized over whether there wasn't truth in it. They went on to quarrel. She charged Joe with callousness and showy defiance. The next day, to prove her case, he appeared upon the campus smoking a big cigar.

Men were permitted to smoke in their rooms—unless their landladies banished them to the cellar—but not on the streets or campus. Joe was summoned to the President's office. It was not just the offense—his "attitude was wrong." There was no rule about chapel attendance—merely a tradition—but Joe was never there. He had openly scorned the Y. M. C. A. It was the "attitude" which all these things revealed. "Prexie Jim" was a warmhearted, impulsive, autocratic man whose attitude was wholly personal. Joe knew that he could have "worked Prexie's sympathies," he saw clearly and coolly the exact way to do it—but some perversity, perhaps a little disdain, held him back. He felt uncomfortably that he liked Prexie, liked even his hastiness, if he hated to admit it. He had "knocked" Prexie because Hester thought she must worship him as a god.

Joe went back across the campus to his little room and began packing immediately. When the other boys came in he told them coolly that he was "canned." Oh, of course Prexie called it "suspension," but he was not coming back, so why not simply say "canned"?

But he was not cool. His hands—red from the dishwater at the Vienna Café—shook a little. His old feeling of being a "lone wolf" had forced him into defiance. He had said that he hated Adams—but it was not easy to leave it. He had a queer underlying, unspoken love for the campus, the cinder paths, the big, dark clump of evergreens on the south, the little pale-green birches on the north, the tree-lined road to Sandy Creek, the big birch in front of the Harris House, even the noisy, smelly Vienna Café, where the boys shouted—"Hey, Joe! Hurry up with those sandwiches!" He could not believe that he was going. He would not believe anything until he had talked with Hester. He had a feeling that she would force him out of his perversity, that that would give him an excuse for going back to Prexie. He wanted to tell her that he had been a crazy fool.

The first that Hester heard of it was in the library—"Joe Forrest is canned for smoking on the campus!" She was in an agony of humiliation. If Joe could deliberately get into trouble for such a silly thing as that, he could not care for her. Everyone was eyeing her, wondering how she was taking it, whether she sympathized with Joe. People were "called up"—for dancing, for Sunday dates. Even Rob. There was no disgrace, even a little swaggering glory, in that. She, too, felt that it was Joe's "general attitude." He didn't care for Adams or for its ideals, he was bitter and a pessimist and a crab, as the boys had told her. He had hurt her too terribly.

When she came hurrying off the campus from her 3:15 class, she saw Joe, with pretended carelessness, hanging about near the big oak. She knew that he was waiting to speak to her. She was instantly aware, as always, of his dark eyes and carelessly tossed black hair. But she was still too terribly hurt to look at him. She went straight on past, talking vivaciously with the other girls, pretending that she hadn't seen him, although her cheeks were flushed. She knew when he turned sharply away and went off across the campus.

He left town that night without a word to her. He preferred to consider his suspension "canning," and did not come back.

The other girls, and the boys on the *Pioneer* Board, were kind to Hester. She was grateful for their trying to show her that they were glad to have her back as one of them. They speculated as to whether Hester and Joe had been engaged—whether she heard from him. But to her they never mentioned Joe. She did not speak of him.

She flung herself again into "activities" that spring, with a kind of revulsion against Joe and all that he had said. She had a feeling of having returned to the fold. She went passionately back to her old beliefs. She entered into things feverishly, trying not to give herself time to remember last spring. There was the day when the *Pioneers* came out. She helped Bunty and Big Bill "get up the stunt." They got an old covered wagon, and the boys scoured the country for oxen, renting them finally from an old farmer near Sandy Creek; and they made a gratifying commotion driving upon the campus, the girls dressed in calico and old sunbonnets, the boys in broad-brimmed hats. They handed out the *Pioneers* from the back of the wagon. Big Bill wore a false beard and overalls, with an enormous plug of tobacco sticking out of his pocket, and he led the oxen. "The cleverest *Pioneer* stunt ever pulled off." Afterward, the Board, still in wide-brimmed hats and sunbonnets, went to the Vienna Café for refreshment. Hester talked and laughed animatedly to smother that feeling that Joe must come in a moment from the swinging kitchen door. She let Big Bill take her home—he was now the only unattached male member of the *Pioneer* Board—and they sat on the steps of the Harris House all evening, refusing to move to let anyone pass them.

There was such a comfort in going back into orthodoxy, in being "one of the bunch" again.

Commencement was so beautiful—the lilacs, the bridal wreath, the girls in white, the June evenings. Hester returned to it all in passionate devotion. How could anyone criticize

Adams? She felt the Adams spirit all about her. She served frappé at the President's reception, on the lawn of his old yellow stone house, she ushered at the Commencement exercises in the Congregational church. She won second prize in the Girls' Extemporaneous Speaking Contest, with "What Adams Ideals Mean to Its Women." She did not have a good voice for speaking, but her devotion, and her ardent, shining eyes, her almost tearful earnestness, made one of the judges mark her first.

She "went to things alone" this Commencement. Bunty was now devoted to Ellen, who was the most prominent girl in the Junior class. Big Bill was going to sell "The Century Book of Facts" that summer and did not stay for Commencement. Hester went with her mother to hear the Glee Club sing on the campus. The Glee Club sat on the steps of Blaine Hall, and on the grassy slope before them was a scattered mass of people. The great trees stood duskily motionless. There was a scent of flowers and dew. Hester sat on the cushion that her mother had urged her to bring, pulling at the cool grass blades and listening silently to the cadences of the songs in the evening air. Tears kept welling up in her eyes. This was the first night when she had admitted that she was lonely for Joe. She had been with him last year. He had spread down his coat for her. She remembered the line of his shoulders as he sat beside her, and his dark lifted profile.

There was the long, hot, dull summer. She felt that she must struggle, that she must put Joe out of her heart. She could not bear to see the grassy place beyond the library, across the street, where she and Joe had sat to "get their Latin together." She felt a dry agony of waiting, every morning, until the postman came. But when he finally did bring a letter from Joe she half hated to open it.

For a while they wrote constantly. Joe had gone to Des

Moines and got a newspaper job. The newspaper business was "all bluff," but then so was about everything else. He wanted to come to Adamsville and see Hester. He knew that he had acted like a fool in going off that way. Hester decided and re-decided, lay awake at night and agonized. She was torn between Joe and her beliefs. She wrote him finally that "it had been a mistake." She cried through half the night, but after that she felt a kind of peace. She had returned to her old loyalties. Next year would be her Senior year. She had conquered herself. She would give the college, this year, all that she had.

CHAPTER VI

Senior year.

Hester took her old place in the class. Everyone knew now that "it was all off between her and Joe." She did not have the presidency of the Y. W. C. A. Ellen had that. But she was given an important position on the cabinet. It was service that counted, not what she had for herself. She had lost prestige a little because of Joe. But she got it back now as one of the prominent Senior girls. She tried to make devotion to her class and college take the place of Joe. She had more than she could do, which was one of the Adams ideals. She was overworked, as a prominent Senior should be. A little thin now, her early bloom already fading, girlish but without the appealing, innocent, joyous trustfulness of her Freshman days. Her enthusiasm was a little less spontaneous now, her smile—"Hester's smile"—just the least bit conscious, and there were two fine curved lines beside her lips. Most of the Freshman girls admired her. With her spirit, enthusiasm, loyalty, sweetness, she was "an ideal Adams girl." There were a few, however, who spoke slightly of "the Y. W. smile."

Hester was the only girl chosen to speak at the mass-meeting before the Billings game. In spite of the lightness of her voice, and her slight presence, every one told her that the speech was "wonderful." It was her spirit, her belief in what she said. A slim figure in a blue sweater and a dark skirt, so girlish up there on the platform in the big, echoing gym— leaning slightly toward her audience, her eyes shining with eager enthusiasm, her fine light hair fastened with amber combs, her lips parted, speaking with such ardor that her slender throat tightened, "giving herself out." . . .

"People, it isn't just the team that's going to win this game— it's every one of us. The team will do their best—we know that—but they must feel, we must *make* them feel—that every man and every girl in Adams is right there back of them— every minute. And I know they will be, because they're Adams men and women. And people, if we want our team to win for us, it isn't enough to *feel* enthusiasm—we must *show* it. Girls, *don't* be afraid to yell tomorrow. What if you do make your throats a little sore? A sore throat will be a badge of honor after that game! We girls can't go into the game—we can't risk broken collarbones and broken arms—well, then, we oughtn't to be afraid to risk our voices!

"People, we know our team is light. They haven't the weight that some other teams have; they haven't the brute strength. But they do have one thing that no other team can boast. They have the Adams spirit. And *that's* what will win tomorrow's game!

"People"—her voice quivered—"when I look at our boys, I don't feel that I'm simply looking at eleven men—I feel that I'm looking at the Adams spirit made visible."

She turned quickly and stretched out her arms to the foot-ball team, sitting rigid and shamefaced on the platform. Her eager voice broke as she quoted, in the breathless silence of the building:

"Our hearts, our hopes are all with thee—
Our hearts, our hopes, our prayers, our tears,
Our faith triumphant over fears—
Are all with thee, are all with thee!"

Jay Oehrle leaped upon the platform. His voice was already strained and husky from four years of yell-leading, but he forced it fiercely into service. Small, thin, dusky-sallow, a lock of black hair tumbling over his wildly screwed forehead, waving his arms frantically, he led the cheering with even more than his old savage ardor. His strained, hoarse voice, that was at times only a harsh breath, added to the effect.

"Now, people, all together—oh, *yell*, YELL—you aren't YELLING!

Adams we cry!
Adams we cry!
Adams! Adams!
Do or die!

". . . And now for Hester, people, YELL!"

It was a serious, responsible year. The Y. W., E. B. B., the college spirit, were all felt to rest upon the shoulders of the chosen few—Ellen, Hester, Bess, Margaret, Gertie.

Jay was still a leader, but he was not liked. Rob had steadily kept his popularity, and so had Bunty. Everyone liked Big Bill. Now that he was sure that "there was nothing between her and Joe," his old devotion to Hester began to crop up again. But—besides his being so immense and awkward—it seemed to her that he was not earnest enough over things, that he turned the most serious things into a joke. Of course, Adams had improved Bill immensely, as everyone said. But he did not seem quite the type of Adams man. There were still crudities about him, and there was that love for "acting the fool."

Bunty and Ellen were engaged. Rob was rushing a Freshman girl. Hester had scattering dates, but no longer her reckless Freshman popularity. She felt that she had climbed into a region of grave responsibilities. She knew that Jay wanted to confide in her again, tell her about the mysterious girl at home—but somehow, since what Joe had said, she evaded Jay.

It was time to "begin thinking about next year." Hester wanted, as they all did, to use her Adams ideals for the service of humanity. She thought of a dozen things—of "going into Y. W. work," of social settlements. Just teaching wasn't enough. Prexie meant more than that when he spoke of "going out to larger service." Her brother Russell was out of social service work now and in the insurance business. He wrote her "for the Lord's sake not to get into anything like that." She and her mother felt that Russell was not the same. Something had embittered him. Perhaps he was not happy in his second marriage. Frances, his first wife, his Adams classmate, had died. Her old ideal of taking the Adams spirit to Asia had been founded upon the vision of herself as helpmate for a John Fellows, as Helen had done. To go alone was so lonely and perilous, and it was not what girls like herself did. But she did want to "really do something."

It was so hard to find just the thing—to find it and do it. There seemed to be nothing but teaching, after all. She put in her teaching application with the other girls, had her picture taken looking very severe to impress superintendents of schools with her dignity. She and the other girls mourned: "Oh, girls! Just three months and it'll be all over! What shall we do?"

It seemed to her that she had never really contemplated anything beyond college. How could she leave Adams? She had grown up, really, in the school.

She went with Bill to the Glee Club concert that year. He said that he'd realized one ambition, at least, before he left school. He was proud of her little girlish, simple semi-evening dress. She still fulfilled his honest notions of what he called "the *i*-deal Adams girl." With her eagerness, her earnestness, her sweet smile, her innocence, her girlish slightness. After the maidens of Winner, she was a vision of refinement and "culture" to him. Some of the Freshman girls thought that "he wasn't the one for her," but still they made "a grand Senior couple."

The Glee Club "stunt" that year included a song of the Senior girls, among other local hits. All the favorites—Ellen, Margaret, Bess, Jessie, Hester. Pride shone all over Big Bill's face when they sang:

> *"Oh, Hester Harris,*
> *Sweetest of all we know,*
> *Your smile shines brighter*
> *Far than the sunshine's glow."*

It was not possible that she was going away from it all. Her last Glee Club concert—it could not be.

But she must do something. She was just debating whether or not to accept a position at Hobart, Minnesota, when Prexie called her into his office. She came out with shining, ecstatic eyes, dove into the crowd of Senior girls who were standing near the library steps, threw her arms around Bess and Della and swayed them rapturously back and forth.

"Oh, girls! I'm not going away, I'm not going away!" she chanted.

Prexie had asked her to stay and teach Latin in the Academy. Her salary would be small—smaller than at Hobart—but she would be serving the college. She would be *here*, she could stay at Adams! Wasn't it wonderful! The girls exclaimed, envied her. Next year they would all be gone, and lucky Hester would be here still.

A Part of the Institution · 97

She had had the most wonderful talk with Prexie. He had shown her all his charm, all his sympathy, when she had told him of her vague but ardent aspirations, of how she wanted to do something "real." He had made her see how much she would be helping by taking this work in the Academy. The old Academy was running down, and he wanted her young enthusiasm to put new life into it. Of course she would want "enough money for hair ribbons," he told her playfully. The college could not afford to pay much for the Academy work. But she would have the honor of serving it. He wanted someone who lived in Adamsville, who understood the school. He did not mention the fact that the position did not pay enough for anyone who had board to pay. He assured her that even if she did feel young and inexperienced it would be the spirit of her work that counted.

Commencement came—her own Commencement. Hester had no part in the class play. Ellen was to give the Mantle Oration. But Hester must have something. She was chosen to give the Ivy Oration when the class ivy was planted with vain hopes of growth beside the chapel wall. Her name figured prominently in the class history and the prophecy.

"And Hester, having married our other loyal citizen of Adamsville, Humphrey Dilley, remained to welcome back the class of '03 with her own sunny smile to old Adams."

Her smile was a little set and strained when she was called forward to receive her class gift from Gertie on the campus, in the less serious part of the Class Day exercises, when local hits were given. A photograph of trees—"a souvenir of the Forest," Gertie said. She thought that that was a little cruel of Gertie.

Her own Commencement Day exercises, in the hot, gloomy cavern of the church. It seemed only half real when she went through the long, familiar ceremony. "The candidates for the degree of Bachelor of Arts may rise." Then the roll of the well-known names—"Robert Burns Alden" . . . until Prexie came to "Hester Grace Harris." She crossed the platform, made her dipping bow.

When the exercises were over, the graduating class lingered outside the church. The boys took off their black gowns and the stiff mortarboards from their perspiring foreheads. Big Bill was there with his mother and father, who had come from Winner "to see him graduate." The father a huge, gaunt, bent, old countryman, the mother a tiny scared, prim, bright-eyed woman in neat, old-fashioned clothes. Big Bill had asked Hester and her mother to go with him and his parents to the Glee Club singing on the campus. There was something very conscious and solemn about Bill that night, so that Hester tried nervously to stay near the older people. Yet she could not help admiring Bill's simple, genuine manner with his old-fashioned parents, his big-boy affection for his mother.

She was with Bill at the Senior Picnic the next day, out at Adams Grove. They were on the social committee together. They buttered dozens of buns and roasted beefsteak over a blazing fire. She had never liked Bill so well as that day. In his shirt sleeves, his great arms glistening with heat, his hair rumpled, his huge mouth grinning. He set her up on the bough of a tree and helped her to climb fences and to ford the creek. It was hot in the woods under the oak trees, where bushes of wild gooseberries and the leaves of May apples grew among the long grass. Hester was exhausted when the committee was through with its work. She and Bill went off to the bank of the creek and sat there to rest.

They talked about what they meant to do in the future. Bill said it was all right for Hester to stay, but she wasn't to wear herself out teaching Preps. He was going to teach and save money to study law some day. He'd been offered a job teaching and coaching athletics, but he hadn't made up his mind yet whether to take it. It depended on something else. He might decide to go out West and try his luck out there.

He rolled over, found a pebble, took aim elaborately and made it "skip" the creek. She knew that something was coming, from the rigid, conscious line of his big shoulders, the husky note in his voice when he spoke.

"Hester, I'd be mighty glad if you'd tell me just how much there is between you and Joe."

She said, a little tremulously, "What makes you think there's anything?"

"Meaning there isn't? Well, I'd kinda figured that out, I'm glad. I always liked Joe myself, and I could kinda understand his orneriness. He had a lot more to him than folks gave him credit for, if he ever does anything with it. Joe kinda started in wrong—I don't know. But he's a good guy. I don't think he'd ever make you happy, though, Hester. He looks at things too different."

Hester was silent.

Bill said: "I guess you know what I've always thought of you, Hester. I don't see how you could help it the way I've more or less camped on your trail. I guess you've always thought I was pretty much of a roughneck."

"I don't think you're a roughneck, Bill. I think you're an old peach. Everyone thinks so."

"Sure, I'm a Winner!" he laughed huskily. "But then I don't blame you if you did think I was a gawk. I guess I was about the crudest thing that ever struck Adams. Bad enough now—but I feel a lot different about things, even if I don't show it. This school has sure meant a lot to me. You have too, Hester, a lot more than you know. You were the only girl that was decent to me when I blew in at that first Freshman party on Mrs. Lewis' lawn. You were so darn nice to everybody. You've always seemed like—well, the *i*-deal Adams girl to me."

She tried to murmur something deprecatingly. She wished nervously that he wouldn't go on. There was something pitiful to her about his great, awkward body, his big hands and feet, his big mouth and his deep-set, mournful eyes.

He tried to grin at her. "Well—if you could stand it to take me in hand, Hester, I might turn out the pride of the college yet."

Hester slowly shook her head. Her eyes filled with tears. She wanted anxiously to soften her refusal, to tell Bill how much she did like him, almost to give in, after all. But the others broke in on them. "Hey, you two! Come out of that. You're wanted." They had to pretend as much as they could that nothing had happened, and go back to the rest. Just before they left, Bill managed to whisper to her:

"Sure you won't change your mind? . . . Well, that's all right, I don't pretend I'm good enough for you, Hester."

Tears filled her eyes again.

They all rode back in a bumping hay rick. Bill was solemn and gloomy, would not be roused to retort by any jest. Glances were exchanged among the others. Hester did not sit beside him when they drove out of the woods, but in the back of the hay rick with the other girls. They dangled their feet over the soft, cloudy dust of the road as they bumped back to town between the trees and the fields in the late afternoon.

Hester went to the two evening trains to see them all leave. At the familiar station, with the long, covered brick platform and the row of box elder trees bordering the vacant lot, they talked about their next Commencement.

"Oh, people, you *must* all of you come back!" Hester cried.

Big Bill had not appeared at the station. He had jumped off the hay rick before they got into town and disappeared. Hester was remorseful at the memory of the tragic look on his big, gloomy face, with the heavy eyebrows and the deep-set eyes and the two long front locks of parted hair. He would go back to Winner later on the freight. She tried nervously not to let anyone speak of his disappearance, not to hear when the boys said, "What'd you do to Bill, Hester?"

There were all the good-byes, hurried at the last. "Take care of the school, Hester. Don't let it run away. Be good to the Preps. We expect you to be waiting here for us next spring."

The last train went. The plume of pale gray smoke melted into the paler sky. The station had that too familiar summer emptiness—more than that. They could hear the humming rails and the evening sound of insects from the vacant lot. There was only Humphrey Dilley left. He and Hester walked solemnly down College Street together. They made plans for the return of the kitchenware they had rented from the china store for the Senior picnic. Hester did not care if Humphrey did see the tears that kept coming weakly into her eyes.

He stood awkwardly on the porch of the Harris house, not knowing how to leave, as always.

"Well," he said finally, "guess we'll be here, anyway, next year."

CHAPTER VII

Hester was tired out during the summer, so that at times her mother declared anxiously that she was "not fit to teach" next year. Hester would not listen to that. But she was apathetic for a while. Something vital was gone. She let her mother take her to old Dr. Burns, who said gruffly that she'd been doing a hundred or so too many things, like all these college girls, and that she must "keep outside all she could, forget about these other things." He tried to get her interested in the study of botany afield, but after spending one morning in the pasture north of town with Russell's old botany handbook, she gave that up. She drank a tablespoonful of olive oil after every meal and lounged through the hot weather.

For a time it seemed to her that everything was over. But there was "next year" still to look forward to. She would still be a part of things, she would not lose interest just because she had her diploma. Humphrey escorted her from some of the Christian Endeavor meetings again, and they talked over plans for the first '03 reunion. She talked over prospective members with E. B. B. girls who lived in town, and did a little discreet rushing of flattered high school girls who would soon enter college.

When fall came she was fully alive again, and, although her mother still complained over her thinness, she impatiently refused to keep on with the olive oil or to "take things easily this year." She was not going to lose all her spirit just because she was out of school now, as so many people did. It seemed strange and lonely at first not to have her own classmates back. It seemed that she must come upon them in the old familiar haunts—the library reading room, the cinder paths. But there were so many things to do. And the Harris House was full of girls again.

Much of her old Senior glory still hung about her. She was given a Freshman man for the Opening Reception. She was welcomed at E. B. B. meetings and helped with rushing. She was asked to lead an early meeting of the Y. W. C. A. She had a few dates with Senior boys. She was "not going to lose interest in a single thing." She still felt herself as more or less a member of the student body. "Prep" teachers were not really considered among the faculty. She felt that she loved Adams more deeply than ever this year.

She went with the consecration of an acolyte to her work among the "Preps." She tried to put her old enthusiasm into her class work in the Academy. She was not going to belie Prexie's trust in her. She would "build up the Academy," she would "give it all that she had." It might be hard at first, but she would not let herself be discouraged.

"Prep" classes met on the third floor of Recitation Hall—"the roof garden" it was facetiously called. There were three flights of steep battered stairs, with little square landings, to climb. The dingy, high-ceilinged rooms were cut up into strange shapes and sizes. They were so cold that Hester wore her coat in her classroom all winter. The old radiators banged and pounded. Little hailstorms of plaster fell suddenly from the ceilings.

In former days, when high schools were few, the Academy had flourished. It had been lively and overflowing, with its own literary and debating societies, its own singing society and baseball team, which had occasionally beat the college team. Now only a dwindling number of raw-boned boys and dowdy girls came from the little nearby "burgs," such as Winner, where full high school courses were not offered. The Preps were like the Volunteer Band, in general a sorry lot, except for a few faculty children whose parents felt that the college expected them to patronize the Academy. "Prep" was a joke now to the college. Its few little activities were swallowed up by the glory of college affairs. About the most that could be mustered were a Prep picnic in the spring, and an annual German play which none but the members of the class attended.

The Latin classes were the largest, but also the least hopeful. They were filled with bored, superior and disgruntled college youths who were "making up credits" in Cæsar or Cicero. They meant simply to get their credits, no more. Hester's enthusiasm flung itself day after day against this stony row of youths sitting slumped down upon the ends of their spines in the ancient chairs that had been relegated to the roof garden. She would not believe that they could not be aroused, that she "might as well give them their credits and let them get out." She worked and worried over her teaching that year. She meant to "put spirit into Prep." She wanted to "make Latin interesting." She was conscientious about grammar and constructions, however, as she had been when she had "got her Latin" with Joe.

She meant to do all kinds of things for her Preps, although, of course, she couldn't start everything this first year.

She still felt that she was a part of things. Of course she no longer held offices or made speeches at mass meetings. But there was a new pleasure in being turned to for advice by the E. B. B. and the Y. W. girls. She promised the Junior girls to "help think up things for the *Pioneer*." She helped them to steal snapshots from the other girl's rooms. Humphrey Dilley took her to the Glee Club concert. Of course it wasn't very exciting going with Humphrey; but she would not have liked to stay at home when all the girls were going.

All year she could look forward to the first class reunion. Hester had been chosen secretary at their last class meeting, as at their very first. That meant she heard from every one. She sent out the class letter. She wrote the '03 items for the Alumni Bulletin. She was the one to start the circle letter which her old "bunch of girls" had agreed to keep going as long as they should live—Bess, Ellen, Della, Margaret, Crazie Gertie. To think of seeing them all back at Commencement, of hearing about their teaching experiences, of their plans for the next year!

She wanted '03 to "get up a grand stunt" for their first Alumni Day to show that their spirit was still alive. There was no one but Humphrey with whom to talk it over. Humphrey could always be depended upon to help, but he wasn't the one to be looked to for ideas.

Under her anxiety for the reunion was a secret, unadmitted thought of Big Bill. Sometimes when she was crossing the campus from the roof garden in the chilly late afternoon she would suddenly realize that Big Bill was gone, that he wouldn't come,

huge and grinning, from around the corner of Recitation Hall
to walk home with her. She wondered how Bill would seem to
her at Commencement time this year. Where was he?—he
hadn't sent in his class letter.

So that she felt a strange twinge of disappointment when
she met them all at the station and heard that Big Bill would
not be back. He was teaching, the boys said, in a Colorado
mining town—having a pretty hard time of it, too. They looked
at Hester.

Of course it was glorious. The girls were full of teaching
tales. Della was engaged to her superintendent. Ellen wore a
diamond, and she and Bunty were constantly together. Ellen
was to stay at home the next year. She had "broken down"
and had to leave her teaching. Her pretty, vivacious face had a
languid, spiritless look. She didn't seem to take her old interest
in things. Bess was going with her family to California and
was going to take her master's degree at Berkeley. They all
united in begging Hester to tell them everything that had happened at Adams this year. She was their link with the old
school. They told her that she must never leave, so that they
would always feel that '03 had a place there.

They had the "grand talks" for which she had been hungering. Some of the girls said that the Adams ideals meant more
to them now than ever before, now that they saw how the
world was. But they despaired of ever putting them to practice
in their teaching. All but Hester. But Hester, they declared,
had always understood them better than anyone else. Hester
would keep her enthusiasm.

Hester murmured, contrite:

"Oh, girls! And I feel that I haven't accomplished a thing
with my Prep people this year."

She felt that she hadn't tried hard enough. She was ashamed
that she had ever had that feeling of looking down on Prep—
instead of trying to lift Prep *up*.

Well, she would see them all again next year—oh, they *must* come, they must have '03 better represented again than any class on Alumni Day.

She was not given a name for the Opening Reception the next fall. But at the last moment one of the Junior girls in the house could not go, and Hester took her place. She felt very motherly toward the Freshman boy whom she took under her protection—a very engaging, eager little fellow with blue eyes and a funny grin. He called on her several times and she "advised him about his college course." Then he suddenly sprang to eminence in the Freshman class and became the possessor of a popular Freshman girl. Goodness, she hadn't been expecting to go with a Freshman at this late day! But she missed the boys whom she had known.

She couldn't help feeling just a little more out of college things this year. They didn't ask her to lead a Y. W. until the year was half over and they ran out of leaders. There was no one but Humphrey again to take her to the Glee Club concert.

She turned to her Preps. She tried to make them realize that they, too, were a part of Adams. She wanted them to have more of a place in the college life. She urged them to go to mass meetings and to the Billings game.

There were fewer at the reunion this year. The second reunion was not so important. Their five-year reunion was what they must be planning for now. Think of having been five years out of college! Two seemed bad enough. Still she heard nothing from Big Bill.

Her third year she felt that she was no longer a real part of the college undergraduate life. The Seniors had been Freshmen in her day. The others had known her only as a teacher in the Academy. She felt that she hardly knew the girls at E. B. B. now. She was asked to lead the Y. W. only as a last resort when someone failed. No one thought of assigning her a Freshman man for the Opening Reception.

This was the first year that she had not had a man for the Glee Club concert. Humphrey, who was in his father's bank now, had gone out of town. But would he have kept on asking her, anyway? To stay at home on the night of the Glee Club concert! She said gayly to the girls in the house: "Oh, no, I'm not going this year. I think it's time for me to quit."

She was very helpful in pressing clothes, opening the door, telling whether petticoats showed, as she had done before she entered college. She kept smiling when the girls went off, bright-eyed, carrying their flowers. She exclaimed over the flowers, helped the girls to clip the stems and put them in water the next day. She went into their rooms after the concert to have them tell her all about it. As she sat smiling and eagerly listening, her mind was repeating and clinging to those maxims: "It is more important to learn how to take a defeat than a victory"; "It isn't whether you win or lose, it's the spirit with which you do it." There was a consolation in the effort to take this with the Adams spirit.

There was another consolation, that showed that perhaps all these little defeats had a purpose. They made her turn to her Preps with renewed enthusiasm. She tried to reorganize the old literary society, to make it as important as the college societies. She entertained the Prep teachers at a little tea—the English, History and Commercial teacher, of the Susie Dykes type, the Principal and his wife, a little elderly woman who taught everything that was left over. She tried to discover latent genius among the Preps. She declared to the girls in the circle letter that the Preps were wonderful when you came to know them. She was young, alive, "sweet-looking." Awkward Prep girls declared that they adored Miss Harris, that she had the most wonderful smile. Her old smile, that was a little defensive now when she went to E. B. B., could beam out warm, encouraging for her Preps. Even if she couldn't do much with her Latin classes, she might rouse the Preps to take part in activities. And that was where spirit was developed. She urged them to get up parties, and she acted as chaperon. She said to the other teachers: "We mustn't *let* Prep run down." The bashful adoration of the girls who waited to walk home with her from the roof garden consoled her for the growing tendency of the girls in the Harris House to look on her as simply the landlady's daughter, almost a member of the faculty. They did not invite her to spreads very often.

The next year she still kept her ambition for Prep. She tried heroically to keep the literary society running. She could not hope quite so much from her Latin classes. She hinted that she might not stay, but no one would hear of that. Prexie praised her, convinced her that she was doing something after all. Of course her salary was small. But she wasn't working for money. She was working to "serve the college." She was the only one who was really trying to do something for Prep.

Every spring brought the five-year reunion just that much nearer.

She had at last given up thinking of herself as still one of the student body. She suddenly found a new interest among the "Scrub Faculty." They were inclined to look down on the Prep teachers, who had only A. B. degrees. Hester was not with them at the Faculty Boarding Club, where the college students who acted as waiters reported gay times. But a little new instructor in the English Department showed a sudden interest in Hester, whom he met at a faculty tea. He insisted that she be included in the Scrub picnics and parties. She was starved for pleasures, and wrote the girls that "the Scrubs were a wonderful crowd, more fun than she had ever dreamed."

You couldn't help having a good time with Mr. Willius, although no one could really take him seriously. Hunter Hollingsford Willius. He had come from the East somewhere. He was a strange, vivacious, irrepressible little man, very light, very pale, with an exaggerated Harvard accent. He flew about, the women of the faculty said, as if he were being pulled by wires. Nothing could "faze" him. He proudly exhibited the new *Pioneer* in which he had received more "roasts" than any member of the faculty—even than old reliable "Strongpipe" Jones who cut the grass on the campus and smoked the only pipe seen in those precincts. "Little Willie" was the campus joke.

Hester said that sometimes she felt rather "funny" going with Willie to things. But it meant nothing. He was all kinds of fun on a picnic. There wasn't a thing the man couldn't cook. He rented two rooms in the old Beasley house, where he sometimes gave dinners cooked and served entirely by himself. He had a flattering, caressing, restless, irrepressible manner. Faculty men professed to despise him. He was attentive to nearly every woman on the faculty, married or single, for at least one day. But Hester, surprisingly—for the new French instructor, Miss Wylie, with be-curled hair and much jewelry, ogled him shamelessly—was his favorite. He called her "Merry Sunshine" in public, and in private—under his breath sometimes when they went to the spring for water at picnics—"Little Buttercup." Of course he was foolish, but you could have fun with Willie.

The astonishing thing was that he should be a good teacher under his flippancy. He did far more modern reading than any member of the faculty. He gave good advice on themes. But he "didn't fit in at Adams." The students did not have the right respect for him. He smoked cigarettes incessantly. All Eastern men did that, though, Miss Wylie said. He was a "lightweight." Imagine his leading the chapel exercises! No one was surprised that he was not asked to come back the next year. After he had gone it was learned that he had been engaged to some girl in the East all the time—and think how he had run around with the women on the faculty!

It was silly to really miss Willie. But now the Scrub Faculty good times languished.

The fifth reunion. Over half the class was back—a wonderful showing. There were changes now. Some were married, many were engaged. They were getting into different work than the first inevitable teaching.

Jay Oehrle made the great sensation of the class. He was only one year out of the theological seminary to which he had gone, presumably with the help of the girl in his home town—for the boys asserted that Jay "didn't have a red." He had taken an assistant pastorship in a large church. And after three months there he had married, not the girl from his home town, but a wealthy spinster nineteen years older than Jay himself, who was a member of his congregation. She was working strenuously for his clerical advancement. Jay had brought her to the Commencement exercises, at all of which she stared with an elaborate graciousness through the first lorgnette seen in Adamsville, except in a Dramatic Club play. She had a strange, admonishing and yet ingratiating manner toward Jay, whom she considered as a youthful genius of humble origin whom she had discovered and whose career she would "make." Jay was more dark and savagely earnest than ever, but he had developed an impressive mysterious silence and an entirely new manner. Adeline—"Gosh! Sweet Adeline!" Rob Alden said, rolling his eyes and leaning faintly against a tree—was much concerned for the "delicacy" of Jay's throat. It had never recovered from his efforts as yell-leader, although its huskiness still had a queer impressiveness of its own. She was always appearing at his side with a silken scarf whenever he strayed from her. Well, they had always known that Jay would "do something," would "get ahead somehow"—but who in his wildest dreams could have pictured this!

Rob Alden was much more himself, although just the least

bit bald. Bunty had not come. Ellen was still at home, still trying to gather enough strength to marry him. The girls said that they were afraid she never would.

No one had heard from Big Bill. He seemed to have dropped out of sight. Only his old roommate said that Bill was still in the West and that he had gone through some pretty hard times. He believed that Bill had to support his old parents. But they needn't worry, old Bill would come through, he "had the stuff in him."

Some of the girls were better dressed than they had been in school. They were earning their own money now. Hester still dressed in the old girlish Adams way, still fastened her light, straight hair with amber combs, wore shirtwaists such as she had worn in her college days. She "looked just the same," they all said.

CHAPTER VIII

Hester admitted that she got discouraged sometimes. In spite of all that she could do, the Academy was dwindling year by year. There was less and less interest in it. The brief enthusiasm that she had managed to instil for activities, and for parties, was gone. She thought of leaving, of getting away. But she hated to add one more burden to those that "Prexie Jim" already had. There was a faction now among the trustees and the faculty who wanted to get Prexie Jim out. He was not doing enough for the advancement and broadening out of the college. There was a party working for President Heller of little Southern Iowa College, a man of determination and vision, of less personal charm than Prexie Jim, but with more of a business head. Prexie Jim could get money, but he could not use it to advantage. His were all the small personal methods that did not suit the present growth of the institution. It would be hard for Prexie Jim to find someone to take her place. She would stay as long as he needed her. He had never wanted to give up the old Academy in which he had once taught years ago.

Yet it seemed as if she were doing so little. She thought about social service work again, about applying for a place in the college in Asia Minor. John and Helen Fellows came back to Adams that year, partly to make a plea for more funds for the college. John made "a wonderful talk" in chapel, everyone said. But he was smaller than Hester had remembered him as being, and with something thin, hard and strained about him. He could no longer think, talk or dream of anything but his work. The life of that little precarious missionary college over-shadowed the life of everything else in the world. Helen was spoken of as "his devoted wife and most valued helper." At first Helen seemed curiously unchanged. She still had a look of belated girlishness, her hair was combed as it had always been, her way of talking was as eager as ever. It was just that the old charm had mysteriously evaporated from her person and her manner. The old soft, sunny look was gone. That fly-away fluffy hair was somehow dead-looking now. As Hester talked to Helen her desire to "take part in the work," that she had been feeling, ended in a kind of ache of obscure disap-pointment. Yet she wanted to "do something."

Leonard Stoner and Susie Dykes had married and gone as assistants to the college in Asia Minor. John Fellows spoke of them impressively in chapel as the stand-bys of the school.

Yet, when she really thought of it, how could she leave Adams? Not to be a part of it any more, not to enter into its life and help to keep even a small and seemingly unimportant part of it going? Not to see her classmates when they came back, not to be here to hold her class together. . . . How could she ever live apart from these things? Where could any place be found as wonderful, and as nearly perfect?

When Prexie Jim finally was forced to resign, when President Heller was appointed in his place, when there was nothing to keep her from going if she really wished—she knew that she did not want to go. She clung to her place in the Academy with increasing loyalty and fear. To have to leave Adams would be like being sent into a cold and unknown waste. She could never love anything again as she had loved the college.

There was her mother. Poor little Mrs. Harris was very frail. They had had to give up the Harris House and take the two rooms that "Little Willie" had once had—small, low, gloomy rooms, with the addition of a kind of overgrown closet for a kitchen. These were some of the only light-housekeeping rooms for rent in Adamsville. They took what was not too battered of the old Harris House furniture, with the pieces and the treasures that had grown to have special meanings to them. The house and the girls had "got to be too much for mamma." The old Harris House was more of a wreck than ever now. For a year or two they managed to rent it to a club of boys. After the girls' and boys' quadrangles were built, they sold the lot to the Dean of Men and the house was torn down.

Their friends said, with tactful intent:

"I'm so glad you and your mother are so cosy up there in your little rooms, and haven't that big house to look after. It must have been quite a burden. I always wondered how your mother could do it, she looked so frail."

Hester said, "Oh, yes, indeed, it's so much better for mamma."

But she missed the house and the girls—the house as it used to be—the old shabby rooms where so many eventful things had happened in the lives of herself and of other Adams girls. To think of boys living in the Harris House! She hated to go past that corner, past the big birch tree. Its glory had finally passed from it, and the Harris House was no longer a factor in college affairs.

People wondered: "Do Hester and her mother both live on that little salary? Perhaps Russell sends them something."

"Russell! Not if that wife of his is what everyone says she is. It will take more than Russell Harris can ever make to support her."

Mrs. Harris had a tiny bit of independent income. Hester paid most of their living expenses out of her little salary. It was hard for them to dress as they were expected to do, to contribute to this and that. But people worked for the college for its own sake, and not for the sake of money. They felt the shame of mentioning the money side. The college paid in other things than in money.

Now that the Academy was in actual danger, Hester felt how dear it had become to her, how much she had hoped from her work there. And perhaps she hadn't failed. Her students, few as they were, still liked her. They said, "Oh, Miss Harris, don't you leave or Prep won't be anything!"

She still went to college functions. Now she went to the Opening Reception with Miss Howell, the other Academy teacher besides the little elderly one, and with Miss Keats, who worked in the registrar's office. She went to basket-ball games with them, and with some of "the older town girls." The teas, the games, the receptions, meant much to her, as her other pleasures and activities dwindled. There was what Miss Keats called "a snippy crowd" among the Scrub Faculty now. They scorned to have anything to do with the supernumeraries around the college, from the Academy and the President's office.

Humphrey Dilley, of course, was still in Adamsville. Hester saw him only when they were planning something for '03. He still kept his old loyalty. He was now vice-president of the Adamsville State Bank—his father had died—and one of the important bachelors in the town, a stand-by in the college and the Congregational church. He would be a trustee in both organizations when he was a little older.

The ten-year reunion made a happy break. Hester had been writing letters all year urging people to come back. With her old spirit, she worked to have a splendid, big reunion. She boosted for '03. "Boosting" was almost as important a word now as "serving." She rejoiced ecstatically over every letter announcing that another member of the class planned to come. She would see people that she hadn't seen since her own Commencement!

Fewer and fewer of her classmates wrote to her now—none of the men. Sometimes it would be months before the circle letter reached her. She wondered if this time she would see Bill—what he would be like. She thought of him with a little excitement. She thought back, with a kind of gratitude, to his old devotion.

She declared that she was absolutely praying for good weather. She would weep if it dared to rain Alumni Day. They were planning the grandest stunt!

She felt a grateful return of the old sense of importance and value in the class in writing all the letters and knowing just who planned to come.

Not Jay this time. His Adeline had won for him a parish in the East. Rob had seen Jay on a recent trip. He reported that Jay wore a clerical coat and his collar "wrong side before, kind of like one of these Catholic priests," although he still seemed to be a Congregational minister. There were rumors of trouble between him and his Adeline, although she was as ambitious for him as ever.

Bunty would not come. Nor Ellen. Poor Ellen had never regained her health, had never married Bunty, and only a little while after the fifth reunion she had died in California.

But Rob was there, of course, stocky, rosy, really bald this time. Rob seemed to keep track of everyone. He had seen Bill, too. The old fellow had begun to make really good now, out there in the West. Bill was going to be a big man out there some day. And you ought to have seen him, Rob said. Actually, old Bill was a fine-looking man now. He had grown up to those hands and feet of his. He still had his old jokes, but Bill had changed, he had got a lot more dignity, too. There was a rumor—Rob didn't know how true it was, couldn't get much out of the old fellow—that Bill was going to be married to some girl out there. Rob himself had married an '07 Adams girl.

Hester wanted eagerly to show them all the new buildings, the improvements on the campus. The new chapel, the science hall. They declared that she was the most familiar thing at Adams, that she was just as she had always been, that she had the same old Hester smile.

She was still slender, girlish. She dressed as she had always done, in the simple, fresh, not too fashionable way that Adams girls had affected in her day. She wore the amber combs still. But the old soft look had left her face. Her small features were a little sharpened. She had no color. Her smile had in it a bright, strained sweetness, not exactly forced, but over-eager. Thin, fine, curved lines were etched sharply about the corners of her mouth.

They said that Hester was as enthusiastic as ever. She kept the old spirit. She had held close to her ideals—more than the rest of them had been able to do. But then she had stayed right at Adams.

She cried, "Oh, people, do you think so? I've—honestly, I have—got so discouraged sometimes."

"Oh, Hester, I've never seen you discouraged."

Some of them said afterward: "What makes Hester stick there in the Academy? I should think she'd want to get out."

The next year did see the end of the old Academy. It could

no longer compete with the High Schools. The time for it was gone.

Hester had long been expecting this. The Academy had been doomed when Prexie Jim had asked her to stay. And yet it was like tearing something out of her life, she felt, to have it go.

And what would happen now? Would she have to leave Adams?

She felt that she could not go into public school work. It lacked the prestige, the atmosphere, of anything connected with a college. But if she did go she would have to take her mother with her, and then what else was there for her to do?

Carrie Lake, '00, had been asked to come back to the college this year as Dean of Women. Miss Keats said angrily to Hester, "Why couldn't they have given you a decent job like that? It's just that you've been here so long that they don't really know how to appreciate you. It's always the folks around here that do the most that get the least credit for it." Hester would not have said such things. But sometimes she did enjoy having Miss Keats say them for her. Martha Keats was red-haired, with a kind of roughness and a tendency to sputtering that had at first offended Hester. But she had found that Martha was "really more loyal than those that said less." She had developed a kind of angry protecting affection for Hester, whom she believed that the college had used and not rewarded. Martha Keats herself was not a graduate, except for a short course in commercial work at the Academy. But she always admitted, too, after a spasm of sputtering, that she supposed she had got too much attached to the place to leave it, like all the rest of them. She supposed that she would go right on putting up with everything.

There were only a few things about which Hester did wish to complain. She still accepted with fervor. And these were such little personal things, she said, compared to the institution itself. Think of all it gave them! Think of the wonderful chapel talks, and the beautiful Vesper services in the new chapel. The institution was so much greater than themselves. All that they could do for it would be little enough.

She did not leave. President Heller—"Prexie" now—had a new place for her. The big million-dollar endowment campaign was beginning now. Many extra helpers would be needed at Adams and it was desirable to have those who need be paid as little as possible. Hester was to work in the President's office. In the feeling that she was really doing something for Adams, she did not feel so keenly the closing of the Academy, the turning of the old roof garden into office rooms. For those three years she lived for the endowment campaign. She hunted up statistics, kept records. Think what success would mean to the school! The new dormitories could be built, there would be a new organ in the chapel, a new men's gymnasium. This was something to which she could "give everything" again.

She became now one of the staunchest devotees of Prexie Heller. Oh, of course she worshiped him from afar. He was not like Prexie Jim, who called her "Hester" and held her hand warmly while he spoke to her. Prexie Heller was grand, sublime, distant, Miltonic. She transferred to him the devotion that had once been given to Daisy Lyons and Helen Garvis. She felt that she was in the presence of a great man.

"Well, I wish I could believe in things the way you do," Miss Keats told her. "But I'm such an old grouch I can't help seeing the other side of things. You're the least selfish person I ever saw."

There was the glorious night when the college bell was rung and all the whistles were blown, when men threw silver dollars upon the platform of the chapel to make up the last five hundred dollars of the endowment fund. The speeches and the yells, the singing of the new Adams song that a Junior boy had written:

"Spirit of Adams,
We give to thee
Our hearts, our faith,
Our loyalty."

She went home exalted, uplifted. What did any personal life matter beside the immortal spirit of Adams? What did it matter if she was cramped next year, if she had promised every cent that she could wring from her little salary for the next five years, in answer to very definite solicitations? It was all for Adams. It was so little—if she could only have done more!

CHAPTER IX

Immediately after the endowment campaign was concluded, another was begun. Only half the things could now be done that were included in Prexie's great vision of Adams. Adams could not stand still. A few "pessimists," "croakers," declared that the change was all on the outside, that new buildings couldn't make up for the loss of the old free life. But that wasn't the spirit which got things done. The campus, certain aspects of the college life, were transformed. Everything in Adams had gone forward except the salaries of its professors. Hester was still contributing to succeeding endowments from her princely wage.

She stayed on. She would probably have a permanent place in the President's office. She was getting to be one of the fixtures in the college. Of course she would stay, Miss Keats said grimly. People couldn't be picked from bushes that would do all that Hester was doing for sixty-five dollars a month. That was her salary, a chastely guarded secret which only Miss Keats certainly knew. Miss Keats knew all the salaries. She "could have told some things," she sometimes remarked. When she saw old Strongpipe driving leisurely over the campus with his grass-cutting machine, she would remark with grim pleasure, "You'll never get the salary that he's getting, my girl! Oh, well, what's a simple A.B. compared with a degree in Smokeology!"

Martha Keats still did all the grumbling for both of them. Hester could never bring herself to more than a wistful "Well, I do think that I ought to be getting more than I am getting. But then I know how in need of money the college is." Her affections, her whole life, were too closely entwined with the thought of the college for her to really complain. She kept up the idea that it was better to work for little or nothing at Adams than for millions elsewhere. The college could give something that mere money could not give.

Hester would never criticize Prexie Heller, whom she associated with the college in her devotion. She defended him hotly when she heard people say that "it was personal ambition on Prexie's part." If they had seen Prexie as she had seen him! He lived for the college. He hadn't a thought, he hadn't a desire outside of it. He had more than taken the place of Prexie Jim in her worship. But it wasn't a personal feeling, she always told Miss Keats. Prexie was too aloof and awe-inspiring and grand. When she saw him in his doctor's gown slashed with orange and his mortarboard with the silken tassel, a splendid figure, the embodiment of all for which Adams stood, she felt that she was worshiping an ideal, not a person. But these people—Martha Keats was one—who said that Prexie was too grand to be human, were wrong. She had seen Prexie almost discouraged, almost heartbroken at moments over the terrible disappointments and difficulties of the campaigns. She cherished these instances of his precious humanity in her secret heart, and they made him infinitely more beloved.

Because of her loyalty to Prexie she would not admit that the spirit of the campus life was changing. Oh, in accidentals, of course, but Adams could never change in fundamentals. Of course there were things that seemed strange. The dormitory life couldn't help spoiling some of the old free companionship between men and girls, such as there had been when they ate together at hilarious boarding clubs. There was all this new formality and "red tape" at Adams. It was a shock at first to have dances upon the Adams campus.

But then the privilege of belonging to such a splendid institution! The pride of feeling that it was unique. A little, beautiful world of its own, sheltered, keeping to its own standards, not heterogeneous and miscellaneous like the great universities.

If she had ever felt that some of the old "spirit of service" was dying out, during war times it flamed gloriously to life again. She thought of what Prexie said: "The spirit of Adams is the spirit of democracy, of service for humanity, and the spirit of democracy and service is the spirit of America."

At first, Adams could not believe in the war. It had seemed like the defeat of the Adams ideals. The whole spirit of Adams was "against conflict." Great things were hoped from the peace ship. The professors sent a petition to the President.

But when the United States became involved, it was seen that Adams had stood for peace when peace was possible, but not for the dread name of pacifism. Now the professors who had signed the petition scrambled for positions with relief commissions, with the Y. M. C. A. It had been whispered for a time that Prexie had made "pacifistic utterances." Strange rumors filled the campus. But these were stopped when Prexie was given a post of importance in the Government service. Adams rose valiantly and proved its spirit when the day of testing came.

Not Carlson, "the most brilliant man on the campus," to whose chair Josiah Porterfield had given an extra endowment to keep him at Adams, was chosen as Acting President during

Prexie's absence. Instead, Dr. Seeley, from the science department, a good, safe, solid, not too brainy man. Dr. Seeley had always seemed a pleasant, quiet, serious man. Now strange things came to light. The submerged jealousies and resentments of years ran rampant. Now had come the happy day, long despaired of by Dr. Seeley and his colleagues, when Carlson could no longer have things all his own way, when it was proved that brains were not all that made a man, when this talk of "originality" was shown for what it was, when evidences of disturbing intelligence were revealed in all their danger. Now was the day when the old guard came into its own, and heresy received its just punishment.

They were "after Carlson," in faculty meeting, where he was questioned by a band made strong by unity. It was a serious matter, of course—he had a wife and family—but his strongly cut lips twitched a little as he saw the childish joy which these men took in their new ferocity, like little boys playing Indian. This was better even than dressing up in plumes and swords and parading with the Knights Templar if it wasn't at the same time a display so infinitely sad. Documents were circulated to be signed, there were investigations by trustees. To be able to strike at Carlson, almost in the open, and with motives of glorious and exalted patriotism!

But they did not "get Carlson." "Carlson can run circles around those old boys, he's a wise guy," the students said. But their thirst was slightly appeased by running down a few other instances of "dangerous opinions."

The little old lady who had taught in the Academy and was now teaching a few extra classes and assisting the Dean of Women. She would not sign one of the documents, declaring with tears that "Christ had said to turn the other cheek, to love one's enemies, to do unto others as ye would have others do unto ye." She wavered a little when the now favorite text of chapel and pulpit was brought forward—"I come not to bring peace but to bring a sword." But that was only one instance, and Christ was called "the Prince of Peace." People regretted it—but an example like that, however harmless it might seem, could not be passed by. There was a young German instructor with a tubercular wife. He must go. Fraülein Hoeffner, who taught violin, a large and buxom person suspected to be fond of beer in the privacy of her room but forgiven for the past six years because of her efforts with the Girls' Glee Club, left in a storm. People shuddered when it was discovered what a viper they had been cherishing unsuspected in their midst.

Hester saw none of this. There were regrettable things—but life was great and exalted. Adams was glorious. There was a new, fascinating severity and suggestion of danger in the sight of boys in uniform on the Adams campus. The terrible sorrow, that both thrilled and hurt her, was that these beautiful boys might go away to be killed. Hester, as always, believed fervently.

And there was an exciting stirring-up and change in the Adams life. So many professors were gone. She was set to teaching Freshman Latin classes. She helped with the Red Cross. No one knew what might happen.

Yet how quickly things settled down into sameness again. The old interests came back. The breath from the great world which returning professors were to bring back with them was only a breath. Dr. Seeley stepped back into the chemistry department. Carlson, after showing that he could remain if he wished, accepted a position with a large university. Hester was put back into the President's office, where she now had the noble work of keeping war records.

Her youth was now definitely gone. She was a fixture on the campus—"Hetty G." the students called her. They laughed at her little enthusiasms, at her ardent middle-aged manner, at her sidecombs and the coat that she wore year after year. In the Annual, she had taken an insignificant place among the other worthies who were subjects for "roasts"—that band of whom Strongpipe Jones was head. They wondered if she took off her smile at night.

She still religiously attended college functions with Miss Keats and Miss Crowley and Miss Summerson. She went to the Opening Reception in the evening dress that she had worn for eight years. Cream-colored, trimmed with wide lace, semi-low-necked, with a skirt that was lengthened or shortened according to mode, but never quite enough of either. She belonged to a decorous town club. She assisted at teas held by connections of the Adams family, her mother now being too frail. To Miss Keats and Miss Crowley she had a faint traditional family glory. One thing that hurt her dreadfully was the discovery that she and some of the other Adamsville "girls" were no longer welcome at E. B. B. But they still loved their little old plain gold pins better than these expensive pearl-encrusted ones that the girls were now wearing. At least she had never lost her loyalty. She would still do anything for E. B. B. She still rejoiced, unselfishly and without personal resentment, when popular new girls joined E. B. B. But her smile was defensive when she met the girls at teas.

She was still excited over the results of the Billings game. Those in the President's office had early intelligence of the Phi Beta Kappa appointments. They were sometimes asked to be judges at oratorical contests. They held hot discussions as to who best deserved the medal that was now being given for "The most distinguished service to Adams during the four years." They knew minutely the achievements of all the prominent undergraduates, they had favorites over whom they "simply raved"—"Oh, I think she's the loveliest girl! She has the most wonderful voice that was ever heard at Adams."

She must take her pride in the growth and advancement of the college.

The town, too, was so changed, although she did feel that

in spite of her pride in it she could mourn over its lost aspects a little. It had long been paved. It had more asphalt than any other town of its size in Iowa. The character of the houses was changing. Those that had been built in the early nineteen hundreds—large frame houses with big, plain porches rounded at the corners—now looked elderly. There were new bungalows and stucco houses with hot, red splashes of geraniums at the windows. The character of the stores was different, with the little new ready-to-wear shops. The old Vienna Café had long passed away; giving place first to "Wick's," with its one long, dusky room with oaken compartments and yellow-shaded lights, where chocolate pie à la modes were consumed; and now to tea rooms and an "inn."

Hester's personal life, beyond the religion of the college, was fed by her worship of Prexie and her loyalty to her class. She was still the Alumni Secretary of '03. She wrote letters indefatigably, gathered the class news for the *Alumni Bulletin*. She felt that the old, precious class spirit was in her keeping. It was, in a way, a principle with her to wear her hair as she had done in the old days, to be in every way "the same Hester." Miss Keats, who had had "no chance for such things," liked to have Hester tell of the girls and boys of her own class, the "stunts they had pulled off," the flowers she had had for the Glee Club concerts. Miss Keats knew all about Big Bill. She was going to look for him at that twentieth reunion, to "see what he looked like."

Humphrey, of course, was still in Adamsville. He was as loyal and dependable as ever. These qualities now quite overshadowed his slowness. Her meetings and talks with Humphrey made her think of the old happy importance of committee meetings. Humphrey had married, a few years before, a woman whom he had met at Lake Okoboji. She was a social leader, "not just the Adams type." But his old class was still nearer to Humphrey's heart than any later acquisition. He was a trustee and a solid citizen now, still chosen as treasurer of organizations. Heavy, with creases in his chin, a grayish skin, and hair that he still tried to keep in its own massive wave. He too was a fixture.

Hester and her mother lived in their three small rooms. Hester did practically all of the housework and the cooking now. Little Mrs. Harris was nearly blind. The brightest time of the year for her, as well as for Hester, was Commencement, when some of "her dear girls" who had stayed in the Harris House came to see her and talk to her, holding her frail, wrinkled little hands tenderly in theirs. She could remember the girls, but she could no longer remember their classes: '95 and 1915—they were all the same to her.

Hester was living now for her twenty-year reunion.

CHAPTER X

That Commencement feeling in the town. The long cement walks burning through light shoe soles, but over the walks and over the asphalt a dappling of grayish elm shadows. Girls and boys going endlessly up and down. Cars purring over the asphalt, parked at the south of the campus, hot light flashing off the smooth black hoods and steel radiator caps. Downtown eating-houses crowded and warm—the dining-room of the old Adams House, the Wild Rose Tea Room and Pickwick Inn. Warm, moist green June grass on the wide lawns of the big frame houses; and along the cinder drives lilac bushes that gave the scent and feeling to the days.

Little touches: Professor Hendries' dog, Collie Prince, strolling in through the open, sunlit doorway of the chapel. A doctor's gown thrown over the big lilac bush on the lawn of the little old-fashioned house, with sharp white gables, where old "Pa" Taylor—long retired—lived. Humphrey Dilley meeting speakers and prominent graduates with his Cadillac.

Now Commencement was half over. Baccalaureate and Class Days—sunny, perfect days. Showers, but brief, sparkling, summery showers that sent people scurrying over the campus with hastily folded chairs, and left the green June grass and the lilacs fresher and richer scented.

Then Alumni Day. Old grads thick on the campus. '96 wore little purple and gold hats. Girls and boys wandering down the cinder paths watched these antics with tolerant, superior, amused and careless eyes.

A little group of idle girls came down College Street, their arms about each other. Hester passed them.

"Good-morning, girls."

"Good-morning," they chorused.

Their eyes followed the figure hurrying past them.

"Where's Hetty G. going in such a hurry?"

"I suppose she has to arrange everything for Commencement. Didn't you know Commencement couldn't be pulled off in this institution without Hetty G.?"

"She's going to her reunion, girls."

"What reunion—for heaven's sake!"

"Didn't you know Hetty was graduated in naughty-three?"

"Didn't know Hetty had ever been graduated! Thought she'd always been here, like Recitation Hall—"

"Like Bunny's straw hat."

One of them called softly,

"Hurry, Hetty old dear! She's running to 'get things started,' girls. There's Humphrey—girls! Don't they make a darling, frisky little couple?"

They giggled with light, unconscious cruelty, and loitered in the sunlight through the elm trees dappling their shining heads and smooth, entwined arms and pretty frocks with shadows.

Hester hurried on, with an eager, wistful look on her face. Now that she had passed the girls she was not smiling, but the imprint of the smile remained in the fine set lines about her mouth.

She thought she had never seen the campus so beautiful. The green grass and the dusky evergreens; the flowering bushes along the black cinder paths; the little, delicate, silver-stemmed birches. Oh, lovely, lovely. . . .

She was almost late for her class meeting on the lawn of the Quad. She had had to help with the diplomas, post notices, order the little parasols for the class stunt. She hadn't seen half of those dear people. Bill Warren was coming from Seattle, Leonard and Susie Stoner. She had just heard this morning that Jinny Woodward—*Jinny*—would be here! They were all to carry little scarlet and white parasols. And the horns, what about the horns?

Humphrey Dilley caught up with her.

"Oh, Humphrey, you *do* have the horns!"

Good old Humphrey. He performed a stately little foot dance on the cinder path trying to get in step with her hurrying feet.

"Oh, isn't it all beautiful!"

Her glance took in the ivied buildings, the leafy trees, the grassy, open spaces, as they went on together down the paths that were so much more than familiar to both of them. They saw the shade-dappled lawn of the Quad, sloping to the path, a little group of people. . . .

She began to smile and to hurry. She left Humphrey several steps behind as she climbed the grassy slope, waving excitedly and calling, "Hello, you aught-threes!"

"Why, it's Hester!" . . . "Hester Harris!" . . . "Well, well,

well—welcome to our circle!" "Hester and Humphrey—isn't that exactly like old times!"

She was in the midst of the happiness for which she lived—being greeted, and kissed, welcomed and welcoming . . . with misty eyes . . . catching sight of one face after another, with little gasps of remembrance. . . .

"Bill! Of course I know you." Bill—think of it! She felt a little consciousness. "Rob! Margaret, my dear, I'm so *glad* to see you!" Poor darling Margaret, she was so changed, so terribly changed. "Gertie Bumstead! Yes, I do." But there was nothing except the familiar brown glint of eyes in that large, massaged face to identify the old Crazy Gert.

"Do you know who this is?"

A low, beautiful voice, a fleeting touch on her arm, a dark face with soft contours and dark, starry eyes—one strange dash of silver in dusky hair—

"Jinny Woodward!"

They embraced. The contact with Jinny was thrilling—with her soft, fragrant arms and breast, the touch of her exquisite garments. But Hester drew back from it somehow shaken with a disquieted sense that changed into excited admiration as she took in the loveliness of this half-strange, half-familiar Jinny—her manner of laughing ease, her indefinable splendor. There was time only for a breathless glimpse—

"People, here are your parasols. *Please* like them, because Humphrey and I have scoured the country for them."

She laughed excitedly while Humphrey, with his solemn air, unwrapped the absurd toy parasols with their scarlet ruffles and rosettes—

"Oh, boy!" Big Bill shouted. "Will my mamma let me out?"

He seized one in his enormous hand and went mincing down the lawn, simpering and bowing to the laughing Quadrangle girls who passed. Bill *was* still the same—although he had seemed at first so different, with his long locks shorn and the new, easy, well-fitting clothes, the new manner. "Same old Bill," the laughing, pleased glances said. But Bill was the leader at once.

"Hester, are we actually to carry these things? Goodness, I feel so foolish!" Della was half shocked. "If my Sophomore son should see me—"

"Oh, but let him see you! Show him you're a good aught-three!" Hester cried. "They've never balked at anything."

"Right! And never will. Every man shoulder his parasol—forward, march!"

Big Bill led them off, stalking at the head, carrying the little absurdity in martial style, they all following after, some embarrassed and laughing, Della protesting, all of them conscious and hilarious, carrying it off gayly before the laughing eyes of undergraduates. Hester went along happily, not seeing the glances and the nudges of the students who passed her—"Look at Hetty G.! Isn't she having the time of her young life?" Hester moved up and down the line, distributing the little knots of scarlet and white ribbon that she had sat up to make the night before.

"Still on the job, Hester!"

"Still on the job."

She saw in a kind of dazzle of light the sunlit campus, the big group of people under the birches, the colors, streamers, badges, the old gymnasium standing red and solid in the sunshine.

'03 had a lovely level spot in the shade of the tallest birch. "How splendid—Hester, I know we owe this to you." People clapped them as they sat down. The smiling faces were all irradiated. The class of 1903—Hester's heart swelled with proud appreciation. She looked about—she saw the classes each in its own place. The two dear old white-haired members of '79; '96 with their absurd hats; last year's graduating class back in full force, radiantly excited; her own class, the dear old bunch, '03.

She thought of those who weren't here. Of Ellen. Bunty had married—"My dear, a regular flapper type, I nearly fell over when he introduced us!" Had they heard about Jay? He had run off with another woman in his congregation—or something—anyway, he had got into a terrible mess and Adeline was suing him for divorce, he had lost his church—it was all in the papers.

Horns were being tooted and trumpets blown, class yells were being fervently given, boys and girls were darting about with paper plates soggy with yellow potato salad. Big Bill led their own yell—

Osky-wow-wow!
Skinny-wow-wow!
'03!
Wow! Wow!

Hester yelled so enthusiastically that the tears stood in her eyes.

Hester must help with the picnic luncheon. She was in and out of the gymnasium, urging the girls to make more sandwiches, sending the boys on hurried errands, running about. "Hetty G.'s all excited—what would the Pioneer College of the Prairies do without her?"

She did not hear that.

"People, what can I get you?"

Her thin, delicate face was flushed and glistening with heat, her light hair escaped from the amber combs in fine damp strands.

"Aren't you dead, Hester?"

"Oh, no," she gasped happily.

She looked up with shining gratitude when Big Bill took her gently but firmly by the shoulders and forced her down upon the thick green grass. He fanned her with a paper plate with exaggerated fervor. She had thought that there might be some discomfort in meeting him, that he might hold resentment. She glanced up—saw in his face only a kind of special gentleness, something a little pitiful, as she had seen in Jinny's face. She smiled her brave determined smile.

The luncheon was over. The grass was littered over with bits of paper, ribbons, scraps—work for Strongpipe. Martha Keats would be delighted with that. It was hot. People stirred and whispered through the last of the speeches. But there was the class meeting to look forward to. In that, again, she had a place.

"Well, people," Humphrey began ponderously, "I suppose it's time we were adjourning for a little business meeting."

Della moaned that it was too hot for business.

"Humphrey!" Hester cried eagerly. "That little clump of evergreens behind the gym! It's always cooler there."

"I remember no such place in my day of campus perambulations," Bill asserted.

"Oh, well, there's lots you don't remember!" . . . Heavens! She hoped he didn't think she was referring to *that*!

When they all sat down, with groans of pleasure, on the brown needle-matted ground under the evergreens close to the cool stone wall, they were suddenly silent. Humphrey sat down facing them, clearing his throat in his old deliberate way. Hester could see from the eyes, some looking intently, brightly at him, some turned consciously, with pretended carelessness, away, that they were realizing Humphrey—his dependability through twenty years. Twenty years . . . the sunlight, cooled and darkened by the evergreens, fell upon them, voices sounded remotely from the campus, the June air touched their faces poignantly.

Humphrey was beginning, with that look of dumb agony that always came into his eyes when he tried to make a speech:

"Fellow classmates . . . of the class of nineteen-aught-three

. . . I feel as if on this occasion . . . something ought to be said. As I believe you know, I am not a speaker. But our friend Bill Warren always did like to talk—" A gust of appreciative laughter, "so I've asked him to say a few words to you. Bill . . ."

The eyes turned toward Bill, sitting hunched over tailor-fashion, poking at the pine needles with a little stick—they took in his big, pleasant, ungainly figure, that was impressive in some strange new way, the smile curving his wide mouth, the air of exuberance that made them say he was still the same Bill. He looked up slowly, they felt the gray glow of his deep-set, mournful eyes. Then he began to speak in an easy, deep-toned, direct way:

"Well, fellow classmates, naughty-three's more naughty than ever—after the base insinuations cast upon me by our talkative friend Humphrey, that I—I—a grave man, a silent man—"

The same Bill—no, not the same, more changed than any of them. She had heard them say, "how wonderfully Bill had developed," that "Bill had come into his own." She felt with a strange pain that it was true. Hester sat listening to the deep tones. In a kind of fear she realized how long and how intensely she had been looking forward to this—now it was happening. She forced herself, smiling, to follow Bill's words:

"Well, classmates, I hate to stop talking, but I see you're all sitting on edge to get in a word—especially our friend Humphrey, here. Well, that's a little of what I wanted to say."

"The secretary will read the minutes of the last evening."

Everything seemed breathlessly still. Her fingers trembled a little as she opened the familiar red-and-black book, holding down the leaves that flapped in the soft June wind. Her voice went thinly through the words that were like food to her— "The class of 1903 met June nine, nineteen twenty-two, and was called to order by the president—"

"If there is no correction to these minutes they stand approved."

"Mr. President!"

"Mr. Warren."

Big Bill leaped to his feet. "Not a correction exactly, but I would like to make a motion—resolution—whisper to me, Gertie, what do you call it?—resolution, *she* says, to be incorporated, by force if necessary, in the record of today's meeting. Fellow classmates, there's one member of this band of the faithful who's more faithful than all the rest, who's been largely instrumental in making this day a tumultuous success. Boys and girls, I move we give three rousing cheers for Hester."

They gave them. "Speech! Speech!"

Hester's heart seemed to pound and stop. Her smile quavered tremulously on her lips. This was her tribute. Her work, her loyalty had been worth while. For the first time in years her heart had again its own food.

There were other speeches.

"I move we hear from Leonard and Susie Stoner, brethren and sistern."

Leonard Stoner, just as he had always been, little, with a wave of lightish hair and an Adam's apple, not much more dried up than he had always been, talked somewhat pompously of the work of himself and his wife in Asia Minor, speaking patronizingly of "the corner in their hearts that they would always keep for dear Almas Mater." He would have been glad to have spoken more. Susie Dykes Stoner—big, plain, homely, with the same black hair and protruding teeth—had now an air of mature authority before which Hester felt uncertain. She had brought up, besides the Asia Minorites, a family of young Stoners, all of whom would receive their training at Adams. The Stoners were full of their great work "establishing the ideals of Adams College among the downtrodden peoples of Asia Minor." John Fellows had had a nervous breakdown, and the Stoners were now in power. They were listened to with respect. They had gone far afield; they had seen "conditions."

Jinny laughingly refused to speak. She declared that she was too black a sheep. Hester learned that she was here because her husband, James Broderick, the geologist, had been asked to speak before the Scientific Society. Jinny had "got out," as she used to darkly threaten. The music of her voice thrilled and disquieted Hester with its suggestion of experience, of some unknown richness and plenitude of life. Her dusky, cloudy hair with that one sharp dazzle of silver, her brows piquantly uneven, the shadowy, deeply dented corners of her mouth, her light, exquisite gown . . . Jinny had defied everything that Hester counted best. But she was more wonderful than ever.

It was so soon over. They seemed to have held the meeting and then dismissed it—an event in their lives, but only one event among others. They were sitting about talking of other things. The Stoners of Asia Minor to whoever would listen. Humphrey seemed a little out of it. Embarrassment came over Hester. They knew each other and the place so well. It meant so much to them. They were both at the disadvantage of caring more than the others. It was like a guilty secret between them.

Her warm sense of gratitude toward Bill left her. He was taking it all so easily. He had given her her tribute—and now it was over. She had met all the slow closing-in, the insidious disappointment of her life, with the same smile. Now it seemed carved upon her mouth, as if she could not move her lips out of their set painful, valiant line.

She felt a faint deep resentment. It was she who had kept the faith. But those most listened to—Big Bill, Jinny, even the Stoners—were those who had not been the "real Adams people." Her heart began to feel chill and wonderingly depressed.

Prexie's reception was a welter of light dresses, black coats, frappé and afternoon shadows. She was useful again—running off on her aching feet to find chairs for tired ladies, going in search of people for other people. There was even a martyred exaltation in having no time to see her own "dear people." A crowd surrounded Jinny. They had no chance to talk together, although Jinny pulled Hester gently to her side and held her there, conspicuously. She had one sharp, amazed vision of Big Bill's wife. She was young, a radiant and assured person, gowned and made up with delicate exquisiteness. Not like his "*i*-deal Adams girl."

Hester got away just in time to go down to the seventeen train. The little, dingy brick station with the arcade, the trunks, the boys and girls in laughing groups, the late-afternoon sunshine. Her own group she found near the door of the baggage room laughing at a tale told jointly by Bill and his wife. They waved—"Here's Hester! Bless her heart; I knew she'd get here." She hurried up to them on tired, aching feet, valiantly eager, helpful and smiling.

Humphrey came out of the depot room. "Ten minutes late."

"Then you'll be here that much longer!"

"Isn't Hester wonderful! She never loses her enthusiasm."

Big Bill was looking at her thoughtfully. She strove to say, with wistful appeal, "*Has* the day gone off well, people?"

"Perfect!"

They were leaving again—and she was watching them go. There were so many things unsaid. Jinny left her husband and stood near Hester, taking Hester's hand in her own, warm and vital through the light silk glove. Jinny seemed trying to convey a kind of comfort.

"How is dear Mrs. Harris? I wish I might have seen her."

"Well," Hester answered brightly. "Frail, of course, and she doesn't see well."

"And you're not in the old Harris House!"

"Oh, no, that's gone. But we're very cozy in our little rooms, just mamma and I."

The talk included them again.

Rob was saying, "Coming back next year, folkses?"

"Of course they are," Hester cried.

They shook their heads doubtfully. "No, I imagine it will be a little harder to get back every year from now on."

The little group of people, the station, the well-known row of box elder trees seemed to recede and waver. She could not hold them.

With the sound of the whistle they were eager to be off. The women gave Hester hasty, preoccupied embraces. She made no effort this time to press forward, but let the surging crowd of careless young people have their way. She stood back until the train was gone.

The rails still shook. A thin plume of smoke drifted across the pale clear June sky. The dray man—a new one—said, "Well, I'll be glad to be rid of the last of them darn trunks." Hester looked back and saw Humphrey close behind her; and with inner reluctance, with that sense of a guilty secret, they walked sedately down College Street together.

"Well—it's over again."

"Yes," she said bravely, "but we'll see them again. Now there's our thirty-year reunion to look forward to."

CHAPTER XI

Humphrey had left her. Her steps sounded loud on the wide cement walk. The tall elms stood up thick-leaved, motionless, as they would stand all through the long hot summer, throwing gray dappled shadows on the asphalt. There was that after-Commencement feeling—a growing languor, a sadness and a uselessness in the fragrance that floated out over the thick, moist, solid mid-June heat.

She hated to go back up to those three small rooms. But suddenly she wanted to see Martha Keats. She had never really admitted Martha. But all at once she wanted to talk to her, to feel her blunt, affectionate, admiring interest, to explain to her, for instance, how she had felt about Joe Forrest and Bill Warren and to feel the consolation of her loyalty.

VISITING

· · · · · · ·

Dale had told Bea that she was foolish to get so worked up over this visit. It would be no trouble to entertain "the folks." They would be satisfied with whatever she gave them, and mother, he knew, would pitch right in and help. Bea knew from kodak-pictures, however, and from things that Dale had said, how well the Masons lived at home. They had a big house—and here she had to try to pack them into this coop of a bungalow! They were used to all the conveniences. Bea was sure that Mother Mason was one of those perfect housekeepers. Well, she couldn't help it—with a baby, and all the washing that made, and two extra men to feed—

"Sure! Mother'll understand all that. She worked hard enough herself when we were all kids. She'll be doing more than anybody else before she's been here a day."

It was his father whom Dale was dreading. He wouldn't admit it, but Bea could see how nervous he was. The quarrel between them had been made up, supposedly, when Dale had written home that he had taken over the garage and was getting married. But the writing had all been done by his mother, the messages of reconciliation had all come through her—and it was never against her that Dale had rebelled, anyway.

He had seen neither of his parents since he had left home and struck out for the West. Now he did so want to impress his father, who had admitted no faith in him, with his success as a business man and responsible householder.

Bea had got Junior all dressed and cleaned up first. That wasn't very safe, he was such a little villain, but she would rather risk having herself, than him, not ready if Dale should bring the guests back a little too soon. Her strong brown hands shook a little with anxiety and haste as she put on her blue dress and pulled down the hem. Oh, Heavens, but how sun-burned she was! It was this terrible sun. She supposed that the girls Dale's mother knew at home all had nice complexions.

That girl whom they had wanted Dale to marry was in her mind. Bea had felt quite superior and contemptuous toward this Margaret, knowing that Margaret had no chance against her with Dale. But now she had to prove herself to Dale's parents. It would seem to reflect on Dale if she failed. She stared into the glass, seeing everything that was wrong instead of what was right.

The picture of Margaret among Dale's old snap-shots, of which she hadn't thought much at the time, grew prettier and prettier until it seemed to her that they must think that Dale had made a mistake—and that the hard life here, the plain little house, all were her fault for marrying him.

She turned and seized wildly upon the baby, crushing up his pink freshness, his warm smell of ironed clothes, of washed and talcum-scented flesh against her.

"They can't say that *you* aren't nice, anyway! They can't say that if Dale had married their old Margaret he'd have *you*!"

She took Junior and went out to the porch. Cars and cars and cars spun down the road. Bea tried to look, squinting her eyes, into the blinding brightness of lights and radiator-caps through the whitish swirl of alkali dust. She held Junior so that he wouldn't creep and get dirty. That was the car! She could tell by the way that Dale drove.

She took Junior into the house and put him down in his little pen in the living-room. "Now, *stay*, honey!" Then she went out to the porch again. She was trying to smile. Her heart was pounding. Oh, how she hated to meet them! She felt sick inside. The car was stopping. They had come!

And then they got out of the car. Dale's father first. So that was the way he looked!—a thin man, not very tall, with gray hair and glasses. Bea scarcely knew why she was so surprised. Dale had told her about his parents. His mother was coming toward her, and Bea had an impression of a large lady with a comfortable bosom, a smiling face, younger than she had thought, grayish hair, bobbed and curled.

"Mother, this is Bea!"

"Well!"

The softness of large arms embraced her. Bea was squeezed a moment against the silken comfort of that bosom, saw misty eyes, felt her eyelids curiously smarting.

"And this is my dad."

Dale's voice was embarrassed but proud. Bea felt the grasp of Mr. Mason's firm, dry hand. She tried to hold onto her old resentment against Dale's father, but it was fleeting when she actually saw them face to face. She had met them. It was over. She was asking them into the house. Her knees were weak and shaking, but she had a funny desire to laugh.

"And this is Junior!"

The two young parents stood back smiling but proud. Mrs. Mason tried to take the baby, laughed, patted him. "Grandpa, see here! See your grandson!"

Mr. Mason said, "How do you do, sir?" He tried awkwardly to shake the baby's little curled hand that drew quickly away from him.

Mrs. Mason said, "Tell grandpa you'll know him after a while."

Bea told them, "Well I expect maybe you folks would like to go to your room."

Supper was going much better than Bea had dared to hope. After her first relief at finding them so much more—well, natural—than she had feared, all sorts of anxieties had come up. Their nice luggage, and Mrs. Mason's well-dressed opulence, had seemed to absolutely overflow their little bedroom. If they wanted anything, Bea had anxiously told them—but no, no, they were all right, Mrs. Mason had assured her.

Bea had run down into the kitchen, after a glance at Junior. "Dale, you keep him. Don't let him get himself dirty." Still feeling weak and queer, she had flown about trying to do everything at once.

"Can't I put things on or something, Bea?"

No, she'd rather have him entertain his father and mother. They were sitting in the living-room, rocking, trying to make friends with Junior. When she went into the dining-room Bea could see her mother-in-law's plump, crossed, silken ankles and strapped slippers.

"Well, I guess we can have our supper now."

Bea had been so conscious—nervously, defiantly conscious—of all that wasn't just as it should be. But there had been only praise.

"Such nice, thick steak!"

"I'm afraid perhaps it's a little too done. I never thought—maybe you people don't care for it that way—"

"Oh, no, it's lovely!" Mrs. Mason said.

Mr. Mason, who always ordered rare steaks, echoed dutifully, "Fine!"

Then there were the two boys from the garage. "Boys," Bea called them—only one of them was a boy. She had to board them because they had nowhere else in Brownfield to eat.

Harry was just a nice young kid. He had come out from Pennsylvania hitch-hiking and had stopped here because he was broke and had to get a job. Bea didn't know what the Masons might think of Blackie. He looked like a desperado. His coarse black hair grew straight up from a wrinkled, rocky forehead, and he had terrible black mustachios, and a scar across his cheek. Not even Dale knew what his history had been.

But the Masons, shocked or not, seemed affable. And the boys took the visitors better than Bea had feared. Both looked scrubbed and subdued. They didn't say much—Blackie nothing; he was in an agony of dour embarrassment—but they kept their implements busy and made the most of the special meal. In spite of its early stiffness, the supper had quite a festive air.

Mrs. Mason talked about their trip. No, they hadn't driven. "I wanted dad to get a real rest. If we'd had the car he would have had it on his mind." The Masons, it was evident, were going to let nothing disturb them. Even when Junior upset his cup of milk, and began to roar, Mrs. Mason said, "Well, grandma's used to things like that, isn't she?" She did most of the talking. But Mr. Mason echoed her at the right times. He was under strict orders in regard to behavior during this visit, it appeared.

"Well, Mother and Dad, maybe we'd better go out where it's cooler."

Bea wouldn't hear of letting Mrs. Mason help her with the dishes. Her company mustn't do anything on the first night. All she had to do, anyway, was to put things together. Mrs. Strobel, the mother of Charlie, the lame man at the garage, would come in to do the washing.

"Why don't you take them over to the garage?" she said to Dale.

For one thing, she felt better with them out of the house while all this work was going on. And she felt a kind of diffidence—she wanted to give them some time with Dale. It gave her the strangest feeling, lonely, and yet self-reliant, to think how close his relationship was with them, while she had none at all.

"Well, then, let's walk over to the garage," Mr. Mason said.

That was really a great concession on his part. It made Dale feel both eager and relieved. He hadn't known how much he could say about the business to his father. He was proud of the place, altho it didn't look like much now, and he wanted to show it to them. They all went along the half walk, half path, where the weeds were white and stiff with the alkali dust, to the big, sketchy, barnlike building.

"Of course we haven't got much of a building yet. But we've got the business. The building will come."

"Well, if you've got the business that's the main thing," his mother said consolingly.

Mr. Mason was silent at first. But Dale was aware of him all the time. He knew that his mother would be sympathetic. All the time that Dale was showing them the new gasoline-tanks, the little, oily-smelling office, the big room littered with cars in all stages of wreckage, the contrast between this place and the bank was in his mind; and he knew it was in his father's.

Those last embattled weeks at home and Dale's stormy leave-taking were pretty hard to get over. Mr. Mason felt that his son should have been following him in the place that he had made—and here he was, away off in this little, God-forsaken burg in Colorado, that was only a repair-station for the stream of cars endlessly whizzing through. Well, he had chosen it!

But Mr. Mason had made promises. He felt the silent pressure of his wife's anxiety. At least he had to admit that the boy was making a go of it; and he couldn't help being impressed. He was secretly sick of being estranged from Dale.

"So you do a good business?" he said.

"We sure do. Location's fine."

"What tires do you sell the most of?"

Mrs. Mason smiled in happy relief. But she scarcely bothered to listen any more. All that concerned her was whether Dale could make a living and didn't have to work too hard; and she was anxious, too, to learn what they gave this poor lame man, Charlie, to do. Tires meant nothing to her.

"Employ three fellows all the time, do you?"

"Yes, and it keeps us all busy. Charlie's just in the office."

"Well, certainly looks as if these wrecks would keep you tinkering for a while!"

It was a tacit acknowledgment of the success of the garage. Dale felt exultant and amazed. His father had been forced to see that Dale really could do something with machinery. Away from home now, and away from the bank, his father was curiously unformidable. Dale had a feeling of something like compassion for him. Why, mother and dad were getting older! They had always seemed to Dale to stay at just the same age. He had got away from them; this place was his own; and now he felt strangely remorseful.

Dale had longed for and dreaded this visit. It had taken the visit, tho, to make him realize that he had actually broken away from them. They looked lost and incongruous, in their nice, somewhat expensive, Middle-Western clothes, as they walked back to the bungalow along the weedy path—out of their old familiar setting, with these great bare plains stretching all around them and rising dimly to mountains in the distance. Still, dad was dad. He wouldn't always be so mild as this. To-morrow, probably, he would be criticizing and trying to take the running of the business into his own hands. Dale wouldn't have it!

Mrs. Mason was making some sort of signal to Mr. Mason.

"Got a drug-store around here, Dale?"

"Drug-store? Sure. Anything I can get you, Dad?"

"No, no." Mr. Mason was rather mysterious. "Just thought I'd go over and make a little purchase if you'll show me where it is."

"Well, we'll be on the porch, Dad," Mrs. Mason said.

It was ice-cream that he was after. Dale knew it the instant that he saw his father coming back across the road, carefully holding out a package.

"Got any dishes around here, Dale?"

"Sure."

"Dad thought we might all like a little ice-cream," Mrs. Mason explained.

Dale went to the kitchen for dishes. Bea was still there.

"Aren't you about through, Bea? Come on out on the porch. Dad brought us some ice-cream."

Dale reached up into the cupboard for dishes. This made him think of Summer nights at home. "Dad, I think we'd all like some ice-cream," his mother would say. Then they would eat it, sitting on the big, comfortable screened porch, with the June-bugs knocking against the mesh and circling the light, the air warm and close under the big dark trees. His chest ached with homesickness. He seemed to realize actually for the first time that he had left there, he was living here. But all the same, he was going to fiercely keep this place for his own, not let his father get hold of it.

"Very nice!" All were praising the ice-cream, Bea because Mr. Mason had bought it; the Masons because it had come from the Brownfield drug-store.

The cars still went whirring past on their way to Denver. Bands of light whitened a piece of flat plain out of the limitless darkness. Alkali was heavy and stiff on the sparse weeds. Across the road stood a line of houses, the post-office, the combined grocery and meat-market, the drug-store. One tall cottonwood rattled its leaves. But Mrs. Mason was determined to praise.

How nice and cool the air was! How clearly they could see the stars!

Mr. Mason tried to follow her lead.

Bea was still constrained and very respectful. But Dale felt that queer pity breaking through his uneasiness and anxiety as he saw his father—his mother, too—try to stifle yawns. It had been a long journey. He wouldn't come home, wouldn't give up, and they had been driven to coming here. His father had left the bank for him! Bea was afraid to suggest bed for fear they might be offended, and Dale had to do it himself.

"Wouldn't you like to turn in, folks? You've had a long trip."

Mrs. Mason would have stayed gallantly talking, but Mr. Mason couldn't force himself to that. Dale had a moment of worry again as he wished that he could make them more comfortable. They did look pathetically out of place. His defiant anxiety melted into pity. He hoped they weren't going to miss the things they had at home. He thought guiltily of their big, comfortable room with the twin mahogany beds. But it was only the night, the strange place, their weariness that gave them this strangely pathetic look. Nothing pathetic about dad at home!

"Hope you sleep well, folks!"

"Oh, we will," his mother assured him. "Good night."

They walked carefully about the tiny room. Mrs. Mason took pains to make Mr. Mason lower his voice. She let herself down on the bed with a big sigh, hoping that she could get some sleep.

"Mama! Where on earth do you wash here?"

She showed him. Bea had set out wash-basin and towels on a stand. This might be all right for the young people; but, at their age, to come back to not having a bathroom! Mrs. Mason was really appalled. But she tried to warn Mr. Mason.

"Now, Dad, be careful. They can hear everything in this little house."

The great, silent, treeless view from the window struck fear into her heart in spite of the nice air and the lovely stars.

She crawled into bed with cautious sighs and moans, longed for her own good bed, but wanted her husband with her for comfort.

"Aren't you coming to bed, Alvah?"

She lay close to him. But she was worried and must instruct him before she could go to sleep.

"Now, don't let them think you aren't having a good time."

"Why do you keep thinking about me?"

"Because I know how you are away from home."

If she could only keep him satisfied somehow for the three weeks—the three weeks they must stay unless people at home were to think the visit a failure—keeping him satisfied, keeping him from interfering with Dale. This visit had to give back her boy to her. Nothing must happen. It had been all right tonight, but without the bank, without the radio, for three whole weeks—

The next morning Mrs. Mason insisted on helping Bea with the dishes. Bea would rather have had her out of the kitchen—not seeing things. But Mrs. Mason in a voile housedress was not so impressive. Her face was older, too, in the morning light, full of soft wrinkles. It was impossible not to become friendly over dish-washing. The two women could almost forget the wariness and embarrassment of their relationship. Bea did not say much about Dale yet, but Mrs. Mason began to talk about Mr. Mason.

"I wonder what dad's doing with himself."

Bea thought she had seen him go out to the porch with the paper.

"You know, I was amazed that I could actually pry him away from that bank!" Mrs. Mason confided. "But we'd stood it without seeing our boy as long as we could—and our little grandson." Mrs. Mason sighed. Dale's quarrel with his father was still too tender a subject for her to speak of it directly.

"Where do these plates go, Bea?"

"Right up there in the cupboard. I guess it isn't a very good place."

Mrs. Mason looked affable, but made no comment.

"I must go and see where he is."

She was so afraid that he might have gone over to the garage. There would be trouble between him and Dale yet. She must get them together, and still keep them apart. Business simply filled dad's mind. But she found him sitting on the hot little porch, looking at yesterday's Denver paper. She thought he looked lost and dreary, and she asked:

"Well, Dad, can't you find anything else to do?"

He muttered, "What is there?"

Well, there didn't really seem to be much!

"Look around the place. You haven't done that yet. I'm going to take that paper away!"

"Here! Give me that!"

He made a futile snatch for it. But then he seemed to resign himself quickly to obedience. The last that Mrs. Mason saw of him he was standing out beside the one cottonwood-tree testing the thick, gray bark with his finger. She had a moment of dreadful remorse. Poor man!—and it was she who had made him come; her passion for her children warring again with her tender loyalty toward her husband. He looked so pathetic and queer away from his own place. Maybe she oughtn't to have made him come with her.

How could she still expect to change him, transform him (as she did) at his time of life? If there was a quarrel now with Dale it would be her fault. She ought to have come alone. But he was here—and oh, if only the visit would turn out right! But she must get him started doing something, or he would be thinking about that bank all the time or else interfering at the garage.

Mrs. Mason went back into the house. Perhaps she could make the beds. She felt guilty about their visit; didn't want it to be a trouble for Bea. She was so strange and out of place. She was almost afraid to turn around. There were so many things about which she might have advised Bea; but she wasn't going to add to any trouble; wasn't going to let Bea think of her as "one of those mothers-in-law"! Mother-in-law! This was the first time Mrs. Mason had really thought of herself as that. Because the two "boys" whom her daughters had married, and whom she had known from the time they were infants, were just like her own. She could run into the girls' houses at any time.

Her own bed she could make, but when she saw the confusion in the other bedroom—much as she yearned to straighten it out—she tactfully closed the door. She was a visitor here. She had eaten more than was good for her last night, because she knew dad didn't like brown steak and had been afraid he wouldn't eat his; and now she must manage to get a little hot water without letting anybody know she was sick. She couldn't bear just to sit, tho, and to see all the things that needed doing.

"Oh, I don't want you to work," Bea said shyly.

Mrs. Mason sat down in the living-room. She tried to look at one or two household magazines that she had already seen at home and to hide the signs of her bodily distress. That rough, empty plain shimmering with heat was barren to her after the green lawn at home with all the flower-beds still wet with heavy dew at this hour in the morning. She had to be so very affable with Bea to cover up the resentment she couldn't help feeling. If Dale had married Margaret he might have been living next door to her now in that white house with the nice little garden. Mrs. Mason turned to Junior in relief.

"Look at this little mannie! How dirty he's got his rompers! Granny ought to make him some—yes, she ought."

Mrs. Mason went to her room and took out the nice folded

piece of fadeless gingham that she had brought in the big bag. Well, that was something that couldn't offend Bea. She took the gingham into the living-room, with her scissors and work-bag and glasses for close sight; and when Bea came into the room she was already at work.

"I can just as well get some things done for the baby while I'm here. Let me show you this pattern, Bea. I've made little Dorothy Jane several of these."

After that, Mrs. Mason was in charge. She had Bea bring out all her sewing for Junior and showed her new devices. And then it was so late that she must help Bea get dinner. She would make some hot biscuits.

"The men'll all enjoy those."

The work took her mind off her stomach troubles. She was so deep in cutting and basting and advising that she forgot all about Mr. Mason until she actually realized that it was noon.

"Where's dad?"

He hadn't been at the garage, Dale told her, looking a little foolish as he thought of his defiance. He wasn't in the bed-room asleep. What on earth had the man done with himself? Mrs. Mason was actually worried. Dale felt as if he were some-how to blame.

"I'll go and hunt him up, Mother," he reassured her. He stopped to hug his mother. "Hard at it, aren't you?" he whispered.

"I'm getting a few things done for the baby." She smiled, and then took off her glasses to wipe her eyes.

Dale was looking all around the place. Had he showed too plainly that he didn't want his father at the garage? "Dad!" he called. He thought he heard a "What?" from somewhere—and then all at once he thought of that old barn that had be-longed to the place when the old shack stood here. He didn't know what on earth his father could be doing there, but that was where he was!

"Dinner, Dad!"

How idiotic that they should have been worried! There were some old carpenter's tools in the barn and Mr. Mason seemed to have been working with those. But even when Mrs. Mason anxiously questioned him at dinner, the two "boys" listening and grinning, he wouldn't say just what he was up to. "Were you making something?" He wouldn't say. But as soon as dinner was over he was right out there again.

Mr. Mason now was busy all the time. But no one could get a word out of him. Mrs. Mason was consumed with curiosity, and all of them began to feel the same.

The children—what children there were in Brownfield!—had found out that something was going on. They clustered about the door of the old barn, and they were the only ones whom Mr. Mason would let into the secret.

That was another amazing thing—the children! "They were helping him," Mr. Mason said imperturbably.

They spent most of the day with him in the barn and they were tagging him whenever he went down-town—"down-town," Mr. Mason persisted in calling the three stores and garage of Brownfield. They visited the drug-store, and the helpers were seen to return sucking lustily at lollypops. To be sure, he did remember his family enough to bring them ice-cream as a peace-offering at night! Mrs. Mason, in the intervals of loud whirrings of the sewing-machine, exclaimed and marveled. He was never "much of a one" for children at home. But here he quite outshone her.

Even the baby took the greatest liking to him. Junior laughed and began to bounce whenever his grandfather came near. "Look at that!" they all cried, amazed. Junior was not half so fond of his grandmother. He didn't like to have little rompers put over his head and sleeves measured to his arms.

Bea was tremendously pleased. But Dale was astounded, a

little resentful. "I can't remember dad ever playing that way with *us* kids," he said.

Mr. Mason worked all morning in his shop; but in the afternoon he took time off to put Junior to sleep. He was spoiling the baby. Bea would have a time with him after they were gone. Mr. Mason paid no attention to that. He said to Junior, "You and grandpa have to have a little confab together— h'm?" Mrs. Mason, tiptoeing near the living-room, heard him singing old songs she hadn't even known he remembered.

> *I went to the animal fair.*
> *The birds and beasts were there.*
> *The big baboon.*
> *In the light of the moon,*
> *Was combing his auburn hair.*

Junior giggled happily at the tune and at the contortions of his grandfather's eyebrows. He was warm, safely held, and he began to drift into sleep. Mr. Mason was chanting softly his lullaby, a look of anxious quietude on his face.

> *It ran into a drifted bank*
> *And we, we got upsot—*

Why hadn't he done that with his own children? But perhaps it was true, he actually could be transformed!

Bea was reproachful when she talked with Dale that night. "You never told me your father was like this!"

"He never was at home."

Bea couldn't believe that. She wondered how much the quarrel had been Dale's fault; and Dale resented any withdrawal, however silent, of her fierce loyalty. He resented, too, that she seemed to like his father better than his mother. Mother, just as he had fondly prophesied, was getting everything to rights. She was cutting, mending, sewing, cooking, hemming curtains. He tried to tell Bea that it was always mother, at home, who had had time for the children.

"Why, dad was always at the bank. We hardly knew him, compared to mother. And gosh, if we'd tagged him around the way these kids do here!" Bea didn't believe it.

Every one in Brownfield was interested in Mr. Mason and the mysteries of the barn. "The old gentleman," the boys at the garage called him—rather to Mrs. Mason's horror. "Old!"— well, that made her old, too. The man in the post-office asked about him. "How's that machine or whatever it is of your father's getting on?" He was in some kind of league with the man in the drug-store. "Your dad get his paint?" the man asked. Paint! Then that was the mysterious package Blackie had brought back from Denver! Blackie was delighted to be a messenger for the old gentleman.

Mrs. Mason grew more and more curious. He had taken his visit out of her hands—and he wouldn't tell her a word! Dale was even a little disappointed, in a queer way, that he hadn't tried to come near the garage. He was cutting up something— they knew that much. They could hear the saw.

"I didn't even know you could use carpenter's tools!"

"Didn't you?" he said imperturbably. He helped himself to potatoes. He was eating largely now of everything, and Bea encouraged him.

"Vern—" Mrs. Mason began warningly. Vern was their doctor son-in-law.

"Oh, don't talk Vern to me! We left him back in New London." Then, when he had finished a large bite, he admitted. "Sure, I can use carpenter's tools. When I was a kid I wanted to be a carpenter. Always had kind of a hankering for it if I had the time."

"Why, Dad, you never—!"

Well, she was too amazed to finish it. Dale couldn't help thinking of all the fuss his father had made—the stern commands, the hot quarrels—because he had insisted on "fooling around with machinery" instead of going dutifully into the bank. What had got into his father? Dale had never actually seen him on a holiday. His feeling wavered all the time between resentment and that queer compassion.

His mother kept wondering how Ava and Marian and the children were getting on, kept looking for letters, and poring fondly over kodak-pictures slipped inside; but the bank never seemed to enter Mr. Mason's thoughts. When he stepped into the garage it was strictly as a visitor.

Mrs. Mason was bewildered. To think how she had worried about this visit!—to keep dad contented was all she had asked, until it was decently time for them to go home. And here he was enjoying himself, more contented than she was herself—and she was shut out of it!

"Well, I can't stand it any more," she declared. "I'm going to see what's happening in that barn."

She made Bea go out there with her. Mrs. Mason's face was determined. "Well, he certainly has fastened this latch!" There was an old, cracked box. Mrs. Mason drew that over and stood perilously upon it, trying to look in through the one glassless square of the little old window. The panes were too dusty for her to see through them. "There's something red—" The box gave a dreadful crack, she shrieked, and Mr. Mason came to the door.

"You girls stay out until I'm ready for you."

They tried to plead, but he was inexorable. Mrs. Mason marveled and conjectured as they went back to the house. "I thought he'd spend every minute in the garage if he did anywhere! I never dreamed I could keep him away from home this long! I don't know what's come over that man!"

But there was still work for her to do. Dale was going into

Denver. He could just as well visit the fruit-stores and bring them back a crate of peaches, she said. She'd noticed in the Denver papers how cheap peaches were this week. Then she could get a whole lot of them put up for "you children" before she went home.

"I hate to have you work so, Mother. Seems as if we ought to be doing more to entertain you. But the time—"

"Oh, I know you can't take the time! Not with three big men to feed!"

Mrs. Mason was so busy that when Mr. Mason came for them she actually hated to stop. He walked in on the two women in the kitchen, fragrant and hot with the steam from the peaches.

"Now, ladies," he announced, "you may come with me."

They were astonished and excited. It didn't seem possible the mystery was going to be solved at last. But they must finish with the peaches. After all, it was only some foolishness, and here was all this fruit—

"Thought you were so anxious to see it!" Well, they were. They decided that the peaches could stand. Oh, but they must get Dale, too! They mustn't go without him.

Mr. Mason grumbled, "Women always have so many things to do first."

He sent one of his little followers to the garage for Dale. The follower came back panting. "He's coming just as soon as that fellow with the car leaves. He says for you not to wait." The women hurriedly washed their hands. Mr. Mason let them get Junior. Then they started.

He was taking them, not into the barn, but to that old chicken-yard outside. That was the first surprise. Mrs. Mason actually felt breathless. She felt like—goodness, Christmas! The old board and wire fence around the unused chickenyard was grown up to weeds; the wire was bulged and matted.

What on earth could he have concocted here? One little silver maple-tree stood inside.

"Dad, hurry!"

"All in good time."

He was maddening.

"Well, here we are!"

"Dad!"

And this was actually it! The very last thing in the world of which they would have thought. "Why, it's pretty!" The children were showing it off proudly as if they had done it themselves. And that was how he had used the paint!

Bea cried, "It's the prettiest thing I ever saw!" He had actually made the chicken-yard into a garden. He had raked all the ground—how that man must have worked! And this was why they had heard the saw. He had made the nicest little bird-house, with windows, and gables, and a porch, just like the old Captain Perry house at home—Mrs. Mason recognized the model; and then below it, on the stump of an old post that he had painted green and festooned with vines, he had set a bird-bath.

"Where did you ever get hold of that bowl?"

He told them, "Part of an old crockery set I dug out there in the barn." He had found two kitchen chairs, painted them green too, and set up a little bench.

"Why, he's really made a garden!"

They were loud in astonished praise. Dale came to look at it, and when he had left the two boys came over from the garage. Blackie was highly gratified to think he had bought the paint. Children stood all around, saying proudly, "The bath's for the birds!" And before night the post-office man, the drug-store man, Charlie, and Charlie's mother had all come to look at "the garden." Mr. Mason was a famous man in Brownfield.

But still Mrs. Mason couldn't drop her wonder. She looked at him with eyes puzzled, remorseful, fond. She talked about it that night in bed. Where did he learn? How had he thought of it? She hadn't known he cared for anything like that. Until he said to her:

"Well, Mama, perhaps you can find out a thing or two about me even yet!"

Bea and Dale came back in the car after taking "the folks" to their train in Denver. It was a relief to be alone together and to say just what they pleased. Company always made work. But the visit had been very different from what they both had dreaded. And the house, when they went into it, seemed terribly lonely. Their family was so small. Dale was standing in the living-room, looking at the curtains.

"Gee, mother did a lot while she was here!"

He would always love his mother best. But Bea was going to miss his father. He was so original, she said. And so would Junior miss him. Dale said jealously it was always his mother whom the kids tagged after at home. Mother was the same wherever she was.

The crowd in the little house had made Bea feel at times that she couldn't breathe, couldn't wait for them to go home. She hadn't expected it to be so empty now. The room where they had slept still showed signs of their occupancy. "Your mother left her glasses! We must send them." The whole atmosphere of the house had changed during the visit.

The boys came in to supper, to the shrunken table. "We sure will miss your folks." Dale was gratified to have Harry speak longingly of Mrs. Mason's biscuits. But they both talked still about "the old gentleman." They said, "It certainly was an entertainment to have him around."

People in town seemed to miss them, too. Dale was proud that his parents had made such an impression. But it was "your father" again for whom they asked. Charlie's mother added, "Your mother was an awful nice lady, too."

The children kept asking after Mr. Mason, all his little con-
federates. "Has Mr. Mason gone home?" And what were they
doing to do with the garden?

"Oh, leave it!" Dale and Bea both said.

There the little garden stood, gay and incongruous, hidden
by the fence and the chicken-wire, in the great burning landscape. Bea carefully filled the bird-bath again. Dale repeated,
"I didn't know dad could ever think of anything like that!" He
looked soberly at the bird-house. Now they were gone home
again—had he and his father always misunderstood each
other? It made Bea and Dale both homesick to stay here. But
they hated to go back to the porch. There would be no ice-
cream to-night.

"Shall I get some?"

"Oh, no, we can't have it all the time, so we'd better begin
without it now." To-morrow everything would be just the
same again. Except for this funny little garden. Dale was going
back to the house, but Bea stayed and looked at it again. It was
the only gay, different, pretty spot in this whole, harsh, hard-
working place—and if they hadn't come it wouldn't be here.
She followed Dale, and said lonesomely:

"Your father and mother are on the train now."

They were just getting into their berths.
Mrs. Mason was satisfied. She had had her visit with
Dale. The family was complete again; and nothing wrong had
happened the whole time. Her years of hunger had given way
to a blissful sense of rest. But it was queer how anxious she
was now to get home. She seemed satisfied to leave Dale.
After all he was settled, he had another home; she and dad
could only be visitors there.

"You *did* enjoy yourself even if I had such a time getting
you there!"

Mr. Mason even admitted it. Mrs. Mason sighed as she bent to slip off her silk dress before going to the dressing-room. It was hard work to visit, in some ways, she said. He told her:

"That's because you don't know how."

But she couldn't help seeing how many things those children needed. She couldn't simply put them out of her mind. When she came back from the dressing-room washed and refreshed, in her nightgown and kimono, she began to take a happy pride in remembering the success and surprises of the visit. Mr. Mason was sitting in her berth before climbing to his roost above.

She thought of the garden, thought of him with Junior. It made her ashamed to remember how she had doubted him. Years and years ago she had almost brought herself to decide that in certain ways she would always be lonely, that there was something she would always miss, but she had never quite made up her mind to it, after all. Now she was eager to get home with him.

"Well, Daddy, I didn't know you had so many talents!" He looked half gratified, half foolish. She kissed him. She told him happily, "Now you must make *us* a garden when we get home!"

He had pulled away from her, wary and ashamed of too much sentiment; and was just ready to mount to the upper berth. But he turned, looked at her as if greatly incensed, and told her:

"No!"

She cried, "But why not? I thought you enjoyed it! We could hardly get you in to eat! And every one thought it was so pretty!"

He seemed ashamed and indignant that she had suggested such a thing. He'd be busy when he got home. He wouldn't have time to fool with things like that. Mrs. Mason stared up at him in amazed disappointment, slowly giving up the transformation of the visit, slowly yielding the picture of herself and of him wandering through a lovely garden in the twilight, perfect companions at last.

She told him, "You can do such things while you're visiting!"

"Well, that's different," he said.

THE CRICK

. . . . . .

Always about their skirts was an irregular stained watermark, yellowish, with a crusting of sand about the hem. "You've been down to that crick again!" the mothers accused them.

All summer they lived in the "crick."

"If you children could ever keep out of the water!"

When they took off their shoes and stockings at night, dribbles of sand shook out. Their legs, even above the knees, were coated with fine, grayish dirt, and between all their toes, and crusting the embroidered edges of their little white panties, was sand.

"How can any mother keep you clean as long as that crick is there? It's a nuisance!"

In the winter, while the boys were skating down beyond the bend, all Susan and Delight could do was to stand on the bridge and trace the gray scalloped edges of the crick and watch the cold black streak of wicked current. In February spreads of rough, thick, gray-white ice were cracked and tilted up, one side in the water and the other broken-edged above it, like the crusty film that hardens over sugar syrup left standing. The broken-down stalks of the thin brown weeds stuck through a glazed crust of dirty snow that lay down the gullies in the banks. The black iron railing of the bridge, with its crisscross pattern, made their hands ache with cold.

They longed for summer, for the hot dreamy hours when they explored beyond the bend where the weeds grew rank and high. Fearfully they would extend their orbit a little farther and farther, knowing they might be cut off from the safety of the house by Cricket Larson and those other girls from down the crick; but they had to experiment.

All through August the stream was dry, or sometimes only a slow trickle over at one side. The crick bed, deep between the split banks, was dry, burning dirt firm under a thin surface of dusty, glittering sand. Crossing the bridge, how the iron railing—brown now over the black—burned and shone against the blaze of blue sky! The splintery boards were so heated that they had to hold their bare feet stiff and walk gingerly on balls and heels . . .

Summer—if only summer would come! Now there was a hope of it. The little girls were outdoors now; the games around the house couldn't hold them any longer. The sun began to have some warmth in it; and the crick—the crick down beyond the lot, between its rough banks—its water was shining, almost as if it were ready for wading again.

Anyway, Susan and Delight could look for the big girls— their own big girls, Susan's sister Irene, and Elsie and Gertie Cartey, who lived across the crick. They always played together on Gertie's side.

They bet they were down at the crick.

"Shall we look?"

"Yes, let's. I'm not afraid—not if we get switches and take them along."

They hunted all about the yard. Out under the plum tree they found a big dead branch with a lot of little twigs. It had broken off during the ice storm in the winter. The bark was black and flaky, and some of the twigs caught in their skirts as they tried to lift it. There! Let any Cricket Larson dare to run after them when she saw them with a stick like that! It was so big that both of them had to carry it. Their eyes were bright with danger as they stole around the corner of the church next door to the parsonage where Delight lived, and out to the vacant lot.

"Oh, Bluebell's following us!"

The Maltese cat had been sunning itself on the back porch, but now he wanted to see what they were doing.

"Oh, no, Bluebell, you mustn't come. Go back, go back," both little girls warned him earnestly.

"You hold the stick, Susan." Delight made a dive for him, caught him by the hind quarters, hugged him in her arms, and whispered anxiously: "Don't you know we can't take you, Bluebell, and have Cricket Larson and those girls get you? Now you go in the house—there!" She scampered back breathlessly to Susan.

There was no one at all in the vacant lot. Cricket Larson wasn't hiding behind the little tree or in the elderberry bushes. The last year's grass shone pale in the sun, and stiff brown weeds were standing. They could see the little pink house where Cricket Larson lived down the crick near the bend, with the yard empty and some one's washing blowing desolate on the line.

"Listen, I hear somebodies' voices!"

Awed and frightened, they stood clutching their plum branch, but inclined to drop it and run if Cricket Larson and those other girls should appear in the vacant lot. Yes, there were voices, very faint, a long way off, the voices of Elsie and Irene and Gertie.

"They're down at the crick!"

They dropped the plum branch, forgetting all about the dangers of this side of the crick, and scampered as fast as they could to the bank. The bright shallow water dazzled before their eyes. There they were! Elsie and Irene were clinging together at the edge of the stream—and then, with a run and a slide, a splash, a shriek, Gertie was in!

"Hurray! I'm going to be the first in the water!"

"What's it like?" the other girls called fearfully. "Is it cold?"

"Why don't you come in? It's grand!"

Elsie held on to Irene, and Irene stiffened her little ankles to bear the first chill shock of the water, bent perilously to reach out her hand to Gertie.

"We're in, we're in! We're in the crick!" they sang out joyously.

The little girls stood away up on the edge of the steep bank. Their small figures were outlined forlornly against the blue of the big spring sky. Their skirts stood out uneven and stiff above the wrinkly knees of their stockings. At the very moment that the bigger girls saw them, the two little pairs of thin legs went scrambling down the bank.

"Don't you come down here!" Irene shrieked. "Susan Green! You go back."

"If you're in, we're coming in."

"Don't you dare! Nobody knows we're here. You stay where you are. Why, Mamma'd—Mamma'd—"

"It's too cold for you little kids in the water."

Now they were sitting squat on the bank, pulling off shoes and stockings.

Susan was wailing: "Irene! I can't get my garter unfastened."

Irene cried severely: "I don't care if you can't. I'm not going to help you. I haven't said you can come in the water."

"*I* can though! Mine are off!" Delight cried gleefully.

How wonderful it was to feel the bare earth warm under her feet again! She stepped down gingerly, squealing with glee as she felt the prickle of the old weeds. It was so dark and cool and strange down near the shadow of the bridge. "Nobody can see me down here," she thought happily.

Her mother might come out of the house, but she wouldn't know that Delight was down at the crick, or that she had her shoes and stockings off. She stopped and, standing on one foot, picked a tiny stone from the tender, dusty sole of the other.

"Don't you come in. Don't you dare!" the older girls were shouting.

"I do dare!" she shouted back at them; and tantalizingly, "Here I come!"

But she stood for what seemed a long while at the very edge of the crick. The bright water kept flowing, flowing past her. She thought, "When that little ripple gets past, I'll step in." And still the ripples went on and on, and there was never a moment when the water would stop for her.

"Go back, go back," they were calling.

She stepped straight into the water. It closed, chill and circling, around her little ankles. She started to wade across. Her feet left little hollows which filled with dirty water that spread slowly. The bright flow past her made her dizzy. There was nothing, nothing but water. She stood teetering above it, while the cold ripples lapped her ankles and her feet sank deeper and deeper into the cold slimy mud that went down, down in soft sucking pockets and slithered over her toes. It was so far—she would never get across. She stood weeping, small and lonely, out in the middle of the bright moving stream.

Then she heard Gertie's warm, protecting voice.

"I'll get you, 'Light. Gertie'll get you."

Gertie came splashing toward her, seized her scared little hand, and together they ran panting out of the water on to the warm sand.

Susan stood alone on the other side, still tugging at her garter. "Wah—wah! I'm all alone! I—RENE, get me. Help me open my garter."

Irene said hard-heartedly: "Let her stay there. No, I don't care if you can't open your garter. You little kids have no business down here today."

"Look!"

Elsie seized her hand, and they stood transfixed with horror. There, in the lot, were Cricket Larson and those other girls.

"Susan! Look out!" they cried together.

"The bridge—run to the bridge!" Gertie shouted.

It was too late. They had seen her.

"Yah, yah, yah!" they began to yell while they danced along the bank in horrid triumph. They were picking up—sticks, stones, *rocks?* Susan gave a dreadful "Moo—OO!" of terror. A pebble hit her foot and she danced, shrieking. Forgetting all about her stocking, she scrambled up the tiny weedy path to the bridge and started wildly across, panting, sobbing, stubbing her toe and going on. Halfway across, Irene met her and dragged her into safety. Those other girls had stopped at the end of the bridge. They dared not come across. It was so high, so different, up here. The pale brown wood of the foot-walk was warm to their chilled feet, and the soft dusty splinters did not hurt. Sunshine glared on the black iron. They were safe on their own side, where the road led, steep and brown, over the hill.

"You didn't get her!" Gertie shouted victoriously.

And then they all began to chant—"Didn't get her, didn't get her—ha, ha, ha!—ho, ho, ho!"

The water was really cold. It was early to go in wading—the first day in the year they had been in the "crick." They sat down on the rough warm earth holding out the chill pink soles of their feet to the sunshine, that glinted bright on the scattering of little stones all down the bank. Cricket Larson and those other girls couldn't touch them when they were on this side. But it was time to put on their shoes and stockings—

"Oh!" Irene exclaimed in horror. "Their shoes and stockings!"

The other girls were ahead of them. With howls of triumph, Cricket and her tribe slid and scrambled down the bank. Cricket Larson snatched up Susan's stocking and waved it gleefully. She was going to throw it into the "crick"!

"You put that down!"

"I've got it!"

Only when a man in a delivery wagon came driving over the rumbling bridge, looked down and out, and exclaimed goodnaturedly, "Hey! What's the trouble down there?"— Cricket flung it on the ground and made off up the bank with her thumb at her nose.

The girls, standing all together, were taking counsel together while Susan and Delight sobbed and whimpered on the edge of the circle.

"We've got to get those shoes and stockings. I don't dare take her home without. Mamma'll know we've been in the 'crick.'"

"Maybe that deliveryman would get them. Let's run after him!"

"He's gone 'way up the hill."

"Some one will have to cross the 'crick.'"

Oh, but the water was so cold and cruel now, so shining— the "crick" was so wide! Cricket Larson and those other girls taunted and shouted from the vacant lot. The shoes and stockings lay in a forlorn huddle, and the toe of Susan's draggled little stocking moved this way and that with the water.

With a last resolution, they formed a concealing circle around Gertie, who, pale, her green eyes shining, was once more pulling off her shoes.

"You don't dare. Gertie, you don't dare."

"I've *got* to dare."

All at once the circle broke and Gertie went plunging down the bank and into the water that splashed up muddy and bright as she ran blindly across. . . .

"Delight! Wake up—you must!"
The little girl tore herself out of sleep and sat up blinking wildly. There was a strange, rushing roar outside the windows; voices in the house, too, and a sense of hurry and flight.

"We must hurry. Mr. Granger's here to take us up on the hill."

Still crying and resisting, terrified at all the tumult and at the disordered, agitated air of the grown-ups, she was dragged from her warm bed and wrapped hastily in a quilt.

"What is it, Mamma? Why do we have to go up on the hill?"

"The crick," they told her; and Mr. Granger shouted, "This is the time when the dry run ain't so dry!"

What did they mean? The crick, where only last Saturday she and Susan had been wading, trying to find gold in the stream bed like people in Alaska? She stared into the wild darkness outside the windows. The roar of wind and water was closing around the very house.

"Better hurry," Mr. Granger was saying. "We want to make it over the bridge in time. Let me take the little girl."

He picked her up with her quilt trailing.

She wailed: "Mamma, dress me! Mamma, I don't want to go like this!"

"Be still, Delight. Do you want the bridge to be swept away? We must get across."

Her mother gave a hasty, strained look about the little room with its beloved furniture and books and keepsakes. It was no use trying to save anything. They would not know where to begin. All that they could do was to shut their eyes and leave it.

"Bluebell, Mamma!" Delight began to struggle frantically in Mr. Granger's arms. "Papa, we haven't got Bluebell!"

"Come! We have no time to look for cats now."

"But he's my kitty! Papa—*Bluebell*! We can't go off and leave him."

As they carried her struggling to Mr. Granger's buggy, she kept straining to see through the pitch darkness, shrieking piteously,

"Come, Bluebell, come kitty, come kitty."

It almost seemed to her that she could hear his little miaow above that dreadful noise of water. But the buggy would not stop.

They drove through the dense black night. The bridge was still there. But as Mr. Granger's horses went pounding across, shaking their heads and rearing, it felt as if the roaring water were just beneath the buggy wheels. Her mother was sitting very still, clutching her with tense, quivering arms. The bridge was shaking, almost whirling with the water, with the wind that came suddenly driving across. Then all at once the horses' hoofs made a different sound that told they were across and going up the hill.

"She's still holding!" Mr. Granger shouted back at them.

Windows on the hill were lighted. Another team came thudding past them. People shouted, "Hi!"—and something else that they could not catch, something about the flats being under water. Then they went from the damp blackness of the tumultuous night into the lighted hall of the Grangers' house that stood square and safe on its high lawn. Mrs. Granger was waiting for them in the doorway. She took Delight in her arms.

"The poor little thing! She's scared, ain't she? Come in, folkses. You're right at home here. You do just the same as you would in your own house. Don't cry, sweetie. We won't let that old crick get you."

While she spoke, she was hurrying out to the kitchen, where the red fire in the cracks of the cookstove, the warmth, and the smell of coffee put a sudden familiar cheerfulness into the strange commotion.

"While Mister was gone, thinks I, I'll just put on a little coffee for the folks. I knew you'd be chilled, tore out of bed like this. Well! And the water ain't reached the church yet! Ain't that a mercy? Who'd ever thought that old crick would take to rarin' up like this?"

"It ain't the first time," Mr. Granger said. "I remember back in—"

"Well, Mister, it ain't any time to stand around telling old stories about it when maybe other poor folks are getting their homes carried right out from under them. Them poor folks across the crick!"

He roared: "Well, I'm a-going! Let me git down a cup of coffee first."

The warm smell of the coffee filled the big clean kitchen.

"Mister, you go in and get some rockers," Mrs. Granger said.

Delight and her quilt were deposited close to the stove. Mrs. Granger stopped her bustlings to feel anxiously of the little, cold, bare feet and to tuck them up. The men put down their coffee cups and started out again.

"Don't cry, dearie. Your papa'll get across," Mrs. Granger said soothingly. "Men know how to take care of themselves."

The two women, left alone, talked it over as they drank more coffee out of cups patterned over with faded brownish leaves. How each had first heard the flood; how Mrs. Avery had wakened her husband and cried, "Richard, I believe the crick's overflowing!" how Mr. Granger had said, "The church is right next to the bridge, and it'll be the first thing to go," and Mrs. Granger had told him, "You hitch up this minute and go bring the minister's folks up here"; of how safe the crick had seemed, with the children beginning to wade only a few days ago!

Delight sat cuddled in her quilt, only her scared round eyes and ruffled hair showing. The tears had slowly dried on her cheeks, although she felt little thrusts of pain when she thought of Bluebell. Here beside the warm stove, in this familiar kitchen where so often she had watched fresh cookies baking, here with Mrs. Granger in her white apron, and the light making a yellow glow in the big lamp, the water could not touch her.

The school bell had begun to ring, sending a hard, frightening, iron clangor through the night. There were vague shouts, sounds of teams thundering past. Again and again they went to the window, straining to see something but blackness, thinking that any noise meant that the bridge was gone.

At last there were hurried steps, a commotion on the porch. Mrs. Granger rushed to the door. Delight hopped down from the big rocker, trying to hold up her quilt. It was her father and Mr. Granger. They had got across the bridge! And they had brought some one with them—Cricket Larson and Cricket's mother! Mrs. Larson had on an ancient coat over her rumpled nightdress. She was sobbing, and Cricket clung to her coat and sobbed, too. Delight looked at them in awe.

"Why, 'Lecta, these poor folks are all out of house and home. I found 'em over by the bridge."

"Land! Ain't it a shame?" Mrs. Granger cried. "Now, never you mind, Mrs. Larson. You come right into the kitchen and get warm. You're welcome to stay here as long as you please. House carried away! Why, ain't that awful!"

Mrs. Larson's torn nightdress was bedraggled with mud, her shoes were soaked. They had had to run right through the water in places. Just as they had got to the bridge, they had heard the crash and known that the house was gone! Mrs. Larson began to sob again, and to mourn in queer, disjointed phrases.

"All we've got in the world . . . I had Mrs. Dennison's washing in the house . . . I s'pose all those nice dresses of Maudie's . . ."

"Don't worry about Maudie Dennison's clothes!" Mrs. Granger cried indignantly. "Do her good to lose a few of them." She added angrily: "I always knew that crick was a dangerous thing. Right there in the center of the town—dividing the town in two. One side's always bound to suffer. And now for it to go on a rampage like this!"

Delight was staring gravely. Cricket Larson was here in

this room. She was not so big after all. When she stood on the bank of the crick, shrieking and brandishing a whip that she had picked up on the bridge, she had seemed a giantess. Her hair was all ruffled above the skinny little pigtails, and her freckled face was swollen with tears. Cricket Larson! When Delight and Susan had found their palace down near the crick spoiled, all the little shells broken and the "precious stones" scattered, they "bet Cricket Larson had done it." Always, whenever they waded, they had kept an anxious watch on Cricket's house down the crick. And now the little pink house, with the washing blowing in the wind, was gone.

Cricket buried her face in her mother's draggled coat and sobbed. "My little chickies!"

"What's that?" Mrs. Granger asked anxiously.

"Oh, them little chicks she thought so much of," Mrs. Larson said, a little shamed. "Yes, if they was all we'd lost—"

Her rough, veined hand crept over Cricket's head. She began to cry again, weakly and helplessly, with a faint sense of apology because of the other ladies, making unobtrusive dabs at her overflowing eyes with the handkerchief that Mrs. Granger brought her.

"Poor thing!" Mrs. Granger whispered. "I expect that house was all she had."

Cricket leaned against her mother's arm. She had stopped crying, and now her bright small eyes were full of a shrewd childish curiosity. She and Delight stared solemnly at each other.

"Why, look what that child's got on!" Mrs. Granger cried. "She's wet as sop, and so are you, Mrs. Larson. We needn't all wait for them men to come back. I'll get some of my nightgowns."

And when Mrs. Larson protested, saying that they "would be all right here," she urged:

"Why, those children can hardly keep their eyes open! Why don't we put 'em in together in the little room upstairs?"

At that, Delight began to cry wildly, clinging to her mother and sobbing: "No! I don't want to go to bed! No! I won't leave Mamma. I want to stay here."

Her mother and Mrs. Granger urged anxiously; but she would not go upstairs with Cricket, she didn't want to go to sleep, she didn't care about the little room. Although she could not say it, she would never, never stay in a room with Cricket Larson.

There was an interval of sleep, as she sat cuddled on her mother's lap. Then she woke again to noise and voices. The men had got home, this time to stay. They were telling about the flood. It was a story now, exciting, wonderful.

Was the bridge gone? No, the bridge was still there. But they were bailing water out of the stores in town.

"Papa, is our house gone?"

No, it was standing—the house and the church. Delight settled back with a little sigh. Everything was safe: the piano, the little doll cradle—perhaps even Bluebell had got up in the barn, as Mrs. Granger said, and was crouched away up on the dusty rafters. But Cricket's house was gone. Maybe it would land somewhere away off, with the furniture still in it—and the little chickens—and Cricket and her mother would live there.

The epic of the flood was thrilling as they listened to it in this safe, warm kitchen. Sheds had come floating down the crick; trees, fences, barns were carried away. The flood had come from above Langley. It had started with a cloudburst. The whole town of Langley was washed out, people were saying. "Wiped off the face of the map."

"Katie Rausch and her mother slept through the whole

thing. Didn't know there was a flood until Wesley Hobart went with a rowboat to the upstairs window after them."

"Land, Mister! Have they got rowboats out?"

"Duck boats and everything they can find. There's fugitives all over this town tonight."

They were talked out at last. There would be another day, Mrs. Granger reminded them. Little enough of the night was left, but they might get such sleep as they could.

"Now will you go to the little room?"

Delight trembled. But Cricket Larson did not look so dreadful, leaning against her mother's shoulder and crying again as she thought of the flood. Her little chickens were gone. Her house had gone down the crick. And Delight's own house was safe, just as she had left it; Papa had said that it was. Her little bed, the dolls that she had left in their red chairs with the one boy doll tucked into the doll cradle . . .

No, she wouldn't "put Mrs. Granger to so much trouble." She wouldn't "be a nuisance." She would go upstairs with Cricket Larson.

"Now!" Mrs. Granger cried. "You two can have this little room all to yourselves. I can make up your ma's bed on the lounge—then we're fixed." And she went away.

The two children eyed each other. Cricket looked small and frightened in Mrs. Granger's big nightgown with the sleeves dangling and the long skirt festooning the floor. Slowly they crept into bed, where they lay self-conscious and stiff, the two little bodies side by side.

In the kitchen their eyes had been dazzled and closing. But now they were wide-awake again. Cricket began to wiggle. She sat up in bed and stared around her, bounced down. After a while she whispered:

"I ain't sleepy. Are you?"

"No. I'm never going to be sleepy."

"I bet you're afraid up here!"

"Honest, I'm not."

It was strange, but now she wasn't afraid. Mrs. Granger's feather bed was warm and soft. She couldn't see Cricket in the darkness. Cricket didn't seem like that mean Cricket Larson. It was fun to be here in the little room. They began to giggle and hop about on the bed.

"We won't go to sleep tonight, will we, Cricket?" Delight whispered confidingly.

"No, we won't *ever* go to sleep."

Two little hot hands fumbled for each other and clutched. Face to face, they clung to each other, laughing, gleeful, and naughty.

"I know what I'm going to do when the water goes down," Cricket whispered. "Gonna explore. Because, gee, you don't know what might have got carried down the crick!"

"Cricket, are you going to look for your house?"

"I'm going right down the bank looking until I find it," Cricket murmured dreamily.

"What if it's gone clear to Sioux City! What if it's gone clear to *Chicago*! What if it's gone all around the world! Cricket—" she gave a little jump—"what if you should find it upside down?"

"Then I'd live in it upside down."

"Eat upside down?"

"Yes, and sleep upside down."

"And *dress* upside down?"

"Yes!"

They giggled wildly.

"Cricket. Listen. Wouldn't it be fun if you and me'd go exploring, and instead of your house we'd find a lovely little playhouse come down the crick—just big enough for us to get into—and we'd have it for a palace! We'd take all my doll furniture—my little doll cradle that Uncle Charlie sent me. You never saw my little doll cradle, Cricket. And my little piano. Oh, my little piano's so *cute*, Cricket!"

Cricket said jealously, "No, there'd be furniture already in it."

"Oh, yes, what if it would be all full of furniture! Cricket, if it was little gold furniture! Little gold dishes, and gold knives and forks—"

"And gold things to eat!"

"Yes! Gold bananas—and gold candy—"

"And gold ice cream!"

Again they laughed hilariously. Delight popped up and looked at the door; and then they giggled harder. She snuggled close to Cricket and whispered:

"We'd keep it for a secret, wouldn't we, Cricket? It'd be all hidden in some bushes, and nobody but us would know where to find our little door. Only we'd let Bluebell in! We'd let *animals* in! Rabbits could come in, and birds could. I guess maybe we'd let Susan in, too. Maybe once I'd let in Harvey Taylor. When he goes past our house, he says, 'There's *my* girl.' But don't you ever tell, Cricket."

She flopped over, thinking ecstatically of the palace, planning the little gold meals . . . The lights, the shouts, the roar of the water, the pounding of the hoofs on the bridge, Cricket and the palace and Harvey Taylor going past the house in his red jockey cap—all blended into sleep.

Morning—was this morning? Sunshine flickered on the tree leaves outside. Bright, motionless, a faint muddy scent in the air . . .

It was Mrs. Granger's little room! There was the dresser, and Mrs. Granger's winter dresses hanging in a corner. Cricket was gone!

A murmur of voices went on downstairs. Delight sat up in bed and called plaintively,

"Mamma!"

No answer but that interminable feminine murmur.

"Mamma!" She pattered out to the hall. "*Ma*-muh!" The nap of the stair carpet was harsh to her bare feet. The kitchen door was open, and she stood there, sleepy and forlorn.

"Well!" Mrs. Granger cried. "If here ain't our little girl! Did she think she'd wake up this morning?"

"Mamma, come and dress me."

"Why, sweetheart, you haven't any clothes. You'll have to wait until Papa comes back with some."

That was dreadful. She felt sleepy and queer, and began to whimper. The kitchen clock said nearly eleven. She sat at the kitchen table in her bare feet and her nightgown while Mrs. Granger brought her a biscuit and a banana.

"Your papa went a long time ago to see how your house was."

"Why don't he come back with my clothes?"

"He'll come; don't you worry. Do you want to get home?"

"I want to find Bluebell."

Cricket's uncle had come for her and Mrs. Larson hours ago. The two women talked about it as Mrs. Granger whacked down the rolling pin and busily opened the oven door, and as Mrs. Avery sat picking over cherries that were bright and red in the morning sunshine.

"I hope Bert Fitch does something for poor Mrs. Larson now. There he's got those three children and no wife. Why don't he keep her to look after things?"

"Well, I suppose he doesn't make much."

"He makes good wages when he's a mind to work. It ain't that—he could provide. He's after that Miller girl that lives down by the tracks. Lot of a mother she'd be to those young ones! No, he won't do anything for his sister. I was surprised he even come for her this morning. Oh, some men is so selfish!" Mrs. Granger slapped down the rolling pin. "Think of that poor thing losing her home—just the one that couldn't afford it. Well, that's the way. Yes, sir. In spite of the Lord's care, it does seem like when a flood or anything comes, it takes away from those that need things most. Well, there's lots of things we don't understand."

Had there really been a flood last night? The yellow roses were sweet and warm outside the window. Bright drops glittered on the leaves and on the rich grass. The cherries were red and clear in the thick white bowl. Morning peace lay over the hill.

The little girl listened dreamily as the two women talked about the flood. How much the banks had caved in, how deep the water was in the stores; all the epic of the night, exciting and stirring even now, but with a faint foreshadowing of aftermath that was like that dank scent of mud lingering in the fresh air.

"It's a treacherous thing!" Mrs. Granger said. "These they call dry runs is always the worst. You can't count on 'em. This old crick has ruined more property than a river twice its size. And yet I guess it's what makes the land valuable. If it wasn't for that, I suppose we'd have it as dry as it is over in Dakoty.

"Them poor families down by the bank!" she cried. "I never did like the idee of the crick cutting the town in two, like. Why couldn't they all build over on this side? But that's it—the town's gone and made all these lots so high. No, sir, I ain't got any use for that crick. It's the meanest thing around here."

Delight listened solemnly. Was this her crick, where all the girls went wading, where they sat and watched the boys turn tiny fleets of black water bugs this way and that with a dry stick? She remembered how it was down under the shadow of the bridge, squatting on the cool smooth strip of bank and leaning away over to dig "cornelians" from the crick bed; calling up to the feet sounding hollowly above them and casting momentary moving shadows over the bright cracks—"Hi! Look down here! You don't know who we are!" They were hidden and secure, no more than faintly echoing childish voices to the people passing. Even the hot summer water cooled and flowed more silently, as it went through that deep shadow with the fiery cracks of light. A horse and wagon crossed, going over their heads with hollow mysterious rumble and thunder. It would seem that the bridge was coming down, and they would stand trembling, ready to flee out to the hot open brightness . . .

"But it's a mercy how it left the church property alone!" Mrs. Granger went on. "I always said it was a mistake to put the church on that side."

"Well, of course it's on high ground."

"But it ain't all that. No, I tell ye, Mrs. Avery, I think after all, and with all we can't make out, God kind of looks after these things."

Delight's eyes were wide with awe. It was true, then. God, with a big curly beard and His arms spread out, sat on a cloud watching. He had kept the water from their house. She could not help feeling the fine importance of being specially looked out for by God. But it was mean of God to have let Cricket's house—and the chickens!—be carried away. She wanted God to have sent a little board down the crick for the chickens to float on.

Her father came back. Mr. Granger had the horse and buggy waiting, and they went off down the hill.

The bridge stood. But where were the old weedy banks with their familiar cracks and gullies? Brown water covered everything, wide as a river, with wicked foamy swirls and branches and debris floating. Gone were the tiny bays, the ripply wading places. Great chunks of yellow clay had caved in on the banks. The little tree at the bend was gone, stood no more glistening and green against the summer sky, would drop no golden leaves to make "kings' and queens' crowns" in the autumn. Delight cried in hurt, bewildered protest at this betrayal:

"I think the crick's mean! I *hate* the old crick!"

The church was safe on its rise of ground, the house dry and snug beside it. But Cricket Larson's little pink house—the back yard, the line, the washing—all had disappeared. The other little houses stood, but water-stained to the windows, their yards a muddy waste. The vacant lot was under water, the weeds crushed level with the ground and crusted with mud. Part of a buggy lay in the middle of the lot.

There were the dolls in their chairs, the boy doll still asleep in the cradle . . . Bluebell! Delight's heart began to thump. She ran out into the back yard. "Bluebell! Come, Bluebell!" she called.

She went into the barn. "Bluebell!" It was all silent.

"Miaow!"

She was sure she had heard it—a faint little miaow somewhere.

Away up there among the packing boxes in the dark corner just under the rafters, there was a moving, a little cracking sound. Bluebell stood up, stretched his hind paws and then his front, looked at her, gave two or three reluctant squeaks, and leaped down. She caught him up and snuggled his furry head against her cheek.

"Precious Bluebell! You knew where to go. You knew it was safest in the barn. The water couldn't get you, Bluebell. God saved our house and our church and our barn."

She felt the thrill of his purr in his soft furry sides. She loved his little whiskers and his round golden eyes, his dainty paws with the silvery toes that made her think of pussy-willow buds. His little claws were as pretty as shells. They would never scratch *her.*

"Bluebell, I didn't want to go off and leave you. They made me, Bluebell."

Her eyes filled slowly with tears. In spite of all her warnings to Bluebell when he started off for the vacant lot, mousing, now she murmured, with her tears dripping into his fur: "Oh, Bluebell. All Cricket's little chickies got drownded! We're sorry, aren't we? We *hate* the old crick, don't we?"

Oh, yes, the crick was a mean old thing, just as Mrs. Granger had said. It had drowned horses and pigs and cattle, and even some people in Langley. It had rooted out the trees and covered the ground with mud and branches and leaves and fence wire all tangled up together.

And yet, for a few days, there was strange excitement all about. The crick, after dividing the town for so long, had brought it together through disaster. All the men were bailing water from the cellars of the stores. And all the children gathered in the vacant lot to dig and explore. Patiently day after day they went over the evil-smelling ground, poking about through the mud with long sticks and broom handles, and digging up here a broken buggy shaft, there a draggled chicken. They found no little house with gold furniture. But other things consoled them: a twisted shoe, the rocker from a chair, the buggy shaft that Harvey Taylor said could be made into a teeter-totter. They all toiled together: Delight and Susan and Irene and Gertie, and Cricket Larson and those other girls. Cricket, whose house had gone down in the flood, was the heroine among them. Feuds were forgotten while the high water held.

Then it was only a memory. The summer was dry. The water stayed muddy, and receded and receded. The new banks grew familiar, weeds sprang up, paths were trodden by bare feet down the sides. The children played again in the crick. Cricket Larson began to say that they couldn't take any pebbles from her side; and Gertie Cartey, that *they* couldn't pick any flowers on *her* side. Soon it was:

"This is our side of the crick! You can't have anything on this side."

"If you come over to *this* side, you know what you'll get!"

"Wear white pants and think you're smart! We found more things on our side than you did on your side."

"We wouldn't have your old drowned side!"

"You throw back that buggy wheel."

"Come and get it if you want it!"

Cricket Larson was the worst.

Now when Cricket came to the back door of the parsonage, with the washing in a clothes basket covered with a blue apron on her little wagon, she stared at Delight with bright hostile eyes. Delight picked up Bluebell from his snug place on the chair and stood clutching him. When Cricket was gone, Delight whispered in solemn warning:

"No, Bluebell, I can't let you out. I can't let you go where that Cricket Larson might get you. Because she's mean. She throws rocks. She lives 'way down the crick, and she plays with those other girls."

W H A T   H A V E   I ?

.   .   .   .   .   .

To-day the Club met. It was called just that, The Club, needed no other name. Of all the women's organizations in Battle Bluff—and they were innumerable—this was the most desirable. Membership was a passport to the center of the center of social life in this old Midwestern river town. Except in a few special instances, it was passed on down from mother to daughter, or from grandmother, or grandmother-in-law; people were just coming to realize that The Club was an old institution. And by tradition The Club had a literary and artistic flavor along with its charming social intimacy.

Even The Club had not been immune from the troubles of the times. The Frank Hood affair, that had upset the whole city, had struck right into The Club and shaken its long-established security. Some of Lenora Hood's old friends had felt they could never bear to meet again without her. The affair had left bitterness behind it. People—even people like the Richmonds, the Kitchens, the Butterfields, the Beardsleys—hadn't known for a while where they stood or what they had. During the worst period of all The Club had suspended meetings, a thing that had never happened since its founding just after the Civil War. But of course for The Club to disband was unthinkable. The meeting this afternoon would be a gala occasion, held at the old Bliss home on the river bluffs, a mile or so from town: one of the most delightful old places in the whole region.

Winifred Serles—Mrs. Alton Serles—came rightly by her place in The Club. Her mother, Mrs. Dr. Wallingford, had been one of its most dearly loved members; and her grandmother was one of the founders. It seemed a very long time though since Winifred had gone to a meeting; not since before the break. She had been ill and forced to drop out of things. This past winter she had spent in Florida. Now as she dressed for The Club she felt excited and happy, much as she used to feel, eager to show the girls her new outfit and the improvement in her looks generally. She had stopped in Chicago with her married daughter Nancy, and the two of them had shopped wide and handsomely. This gown was a sheer, of dusty pink, with hat and accessories of iris purple. Pink had been Winifred's color in her girlhood, and it was as becoming now as then, together with the purple shade that went so marvelously with her dark eyes and wavy silver-streaked hair. In the oval-shaped glass above the dressing-table she and her costume were mirrored at their best. The new draperies, in white and deep red, made a rosy light all through the large room.

Winifred called, "I'm going to The Club now, Mrs. Bjorn-son." The housekeeper came to the door. "I needn't leave you any instructions though." Mrs. Bjornson gave a slight, kindly, professional smile. "Has Mrs. Bolton come?"

"Yes, she's in the den, Mrs. Serles."

The den was an odd little room just off the lower landing. Winifred looked in on her way downstairs. Edna Bolton sat there mending. Winifred nodded at her brightly.

"How are you?"

"All right, I guess." Edna stared with a slowly gathering, subtle contempt, as if daring her to follow up that question. Winifred caught the satiric undertone in Edna's voice.

Saying hastily, "I'm on my way to a meeting. But Mrs. Bjornson knows about everything—more than I do now!" Winifred went on downstairs. In that last admission she had been asking for a little acknowledgment of her own troubles, her illness and all; but she had felt rather than seen how Edna's slight grimace in response turned into a contemptuous twist of the lip.

Her heart was beating very fast, and she had to stand a moment in the cool paneled hall, waiting for it to calm down.

She felt how lightly and quickly she had spoken, with what a false smile. She could hear herself go tripping downstairs, the high heels of her new slippers shining and unmarred.

She couldn't meet Edna's challenge. She *hadn't* dared go farther and ask about Don. She had to skirt round mention of Don's name as if blandly unaware that he still existed—and after she'd been so sympathetic. She had been glad to try to find work for Don Bolton when he had come over, saying somewhat defiantly that he was out of a job and the whole family almost down to rock bottom. It was the natural thing. Don's father used to do all the fixing and tinkering for their old neighborhood, and Winifred had known Don since he was a little bit of a fellow. Her mother had got all the Bolton kids to go to Sunday School—"gathered them in" was Mrs. Wallingford's phrase.

Winifred hadn't dreamed she was running into anything! Now it turned out that Don Bolton had been fired from the Richmond Plow Works and was bringing some kind of suit against Hal Richmond. The government was mixed up in it somehow, but seemingly on *Don's* side. Alton was Hal Richmond's lawyer, as he had been Grover Hurd's.

There were no explanations this time. Both of them remembered too well. But Alton wouldn't let Winifred employ Don even to mow the lawn. He would give no encouragement to that element. Winifred just couldn't think of Don Bolton as a part of a horrifying "element."

But she could when it came to Edna. It was awful having Edna in the house.

Winifred felt she would like to go straight back up to the den and have a real set-to with that woman! Because Edna was *mean*, Winifred felt she really was, and she found herself almost crying with resentment. She had kept her promise the best she could, had given her household odd jobs to Don's wife, since she couldn't help Don directly—paying Edna out of her own money too. She had done everything for the Boltons that *she* could. The little bit she paid wouldn't keep them, but that wasn't her fault. Winifred had learned her ways from her father and mother, "some of the very best people who ever lived"—those who remembered Dr. and Mrs. Wallingford still spoke of them in just such terms: the kindest people, the most conscientious. She had always been on good terms with her help. There hadn't been any barrier except what she thought of as just the natural one. Winifred Serles had never in her life—no, not even under the scrutiny of a surgeon—been forced to meet anything like this hostile, cold, implacable stare. It judged and classified her according to some rule she had never learned. It opened an unknown dimension.

What was she afraid of? What could Edna Bolton do, poor thing? She ought to be pitied, Winifred thought, trying to find her way back to what should be her natural attitude.

The clock sounded a mellow chime. Yellow iris glowed in the old stone jar. These were her own surroundings, what she thought of as simple and real and down-to-earth after the rackety gaieties of a winter playground. She was going to The Club, into the midst of her own old friends, to have a delightful afternoon, to be welcomed back to the pleasant, natural ways of existence.

Marlin was waiting out in front with the car.

"Hello, Marlin. How are you?"

"Fine. Hello, Mrs. Serles. Swell day, isn't it?"

Alton took the small car downtown nowadays and left Winifred the Packard. Dr. Barnes said she oughtn't to have the strain of driving, and so Alton was hiring this boy to be on call for her every afternoon. He was a nice youngster, amusing company as well as a good driver—played seven musical instruments and said he was "studying" to be an orchestra leader. Having Marlin was an extravagance, but oh, what a pleasure! Winifred sank back into the soft retirement of the back seat with luxurious relief.

But even now, as they swung round the curves under the scattered shade of oak trees out in the semi-rural wooded addition where the Serleses lived, Winifred had not come out from under the cold spell of Edna's stare. Suppose, she couldn't help thinking, *I* had to go out, if something happened to Alton, and grab what little I could from someone I hated, should I have the bitter resolution just to put it through? She felt chilled, pampered, feeble, and distraught. There was no reason for thinking about anything of that kind. It was morbid and she must stop.

"What's that, Marlin?"

"I said, they've sure got swell gardens out this way."

They were driving along the southwest road. It was a highway now and the old farms had been cut up into semi-suburban places, with small trim houses, and landscaped gardens—white gates guarded by wooden bulldogs, stony pools watched over by wooden birds.

"Don't miss the turn, Marlin!"

Marlin leaned forward and peered, putting out his hand with a sweeping gesture as he turned into the narrow side-road.

"Gol-*lee*. This is sure some road."

"Oh, I've driven out here, Marlin, when it was lots worse."

"Sure enough?"

She had driven out in all sorts of conveyances and in all seasons—in the family surrey, in long-ago autumns, come to pick wild grapes; in hayricks, through the deep green summer; in bobsleds, on winter nights; in carriages, by moonlight, going to dances. The old Bliss place used to be the gathering spot.

The road didn't look much different now—lonelier, if anything; for people kept to the highway. There were deep mud holes that Marlin approached with elaborate care. Sometimes the car had to scrape through branches that whipped back and hit the glass. An old frame house some distance from the road seemed to be deserted. It stood dark and forlorn among its flowering lilacs.

Winifred began almost to dread seeing the old Bliss place. Flora Belle and Kerwin had been so hard up for a while that their friends hadn't wanted to come out and impose any extra burden. The two of them, brother and sister, had been living here together ever since the old General had died.

But the place when she came to it looked almost the same—except that Winifred hadn't remembered how beautiful it was. She used to take it for granted. The four-storey brick house, one of the few surviving pioneer mansions, was built on a lofty spot overlooking the river. The weathered white cupola rose embowered in great trees. On the sloping grounds, each under his own tree, stood the statues of the Civil War leaders—Grant, Sherman, Sheridan, McPherson under whom General Bliss himself had fought. "The greatest loss the Union cause ever suffered was in the death of McPherson. Do you realize that, young lady?" The girls used to think they would perish if they ever had to hear about McPherson again! The lilacs were blooming, a lofty hedge. Out at the back stood the windmill, which Kerwin had kept, since this was too far out for city water. The gasoline engine was pumping. At this distance, in this rural stillness, it had a romantic sound.

"Thanks, Marlin." She let him help her out with great éclat. "You did awfully well over that road."

"Oh, I like to drive something like that once in a while. Gosh." He stared about him frankly. "I didn't know there was any place like this."

"Why, Marlin!" Winifred was shocked. "This is one of the oldest places near Battle Bluff. The most historic."

"Is that right? It sure looks historical. Boy, look at the statues. Are they of anybody? Civil War! Gee, 'way back then?"

The great front door of carved walnut stood open. Mr. Hawley was holding open the screen.

"Why, Mr. Hawley, how are you? I'm so glad—" you're still here, she was going to say; but thought she'd better not. "You know me, don't you? Mrs. Serles?"

"Mrs. Serles. Oh, yes! Miss Wallingford."

Before Winifred had time to ask after Mrs. Hawley—and maybe it wouldn't have been safe anyway; who knew whether she was still alive?—Flora Belle came hurrying. "Winifred!" They kissed. "I'm *so* glad. We've missed you terribly. You know where to leave your wrap, don't you? *Dar*ling outfit. You look so nice, you sweet thing."

Winifred went on upstairs to the guest-room. The great rosewood bed was strewn with brightly colored spring coats and scarves; and in the cool, leafy, springtime light, in the large north room, women were moving about, crowding round the dressers, examining themselves in the wardrobe mirror, picking up and putting down some of the odd old knickknacks.

"Winifred!" "How wonderful to have *you* back!"

Others kept coming in, all with the same enthusiastic greetings. Just as in old times, when they had driven out for a dance, a group went out laughing and chattering together, down the broad walnut stairway toward the green-gold light from the open door.

Winifred went into the front parlor with Dorothy Kitchen. The new spring hats were all she could see at first! Then the girls crowded round, saying how joyful they were to have her back, how perfectly grand and absolutely stunning she looked. Mrs. Burnham smilingly rescued her and led her over to the old Victorian chair with the footstool.

"Girls, do let her get her breath. There, my dear. You have the place of honor."

Winifred could sit back and enjoy it. She could enjoy being in this house. During the worst period Flora Belle and Kerwin had closed off most of the rooms. But now all the great doors stood open. The hand-carved cornices, the mantels, the beautiful faded furnishings—all were visible in the afternoon light; and with flowers massed everywhere. People had urged Flora Belle at various times to have the two parlors thrown into one. But in holding devoutly to things as they had been in her father's time she had really preserved the character of the place. This arrangement was more interesting, more in keeping.

The girls began coming up to Winifred, telling her she looked marvelous, they didn't believe she'd ever been sick. She'd just wanted a winter in Florida.

"Yes," Stella Beardsley croaked, "and get out of serving on our renowned Civic Board."

"*Is* that so awful, Stel?"

"Is it *awful?*"

Stella launched into the tale, using gestures freely. The dramatic play of her features and the hoarse animation of her voice did more than justice to her mild story. The cerise of her hat was really too brilliant for her sallow skin. Her thin face was withering. The others laughed with the old indulgence, and Winifred smiled. But her glance wandered uneasily seeking relief among the other groups.

The whole scene gave her at first a sense of joyous reassurance. The break had been only temporary. The Club seemed just the same—except for the new clothes, and they were part of the pleasure. The organization took in all ages of course. There were still a few of the old ladies, her mother's friends, although these were becoming almost as rare as Civil War veterans. Winifred smiled across to Carol Mann, a chum of Nancy's, who had come in lately. Winifred's own crowd, those she called "the girls," were the matrons now and predominated. But all were of the inmost group where the associations were oldest and the ties strongest in the end; although one might actually *like* someone better who didn't fit or belong. Now she was back in her own atmosphere. Here she was accepted at the natural value and needed to make no assertion.

But the program was about to begin. The women round Winifred's chair finally stopped talking, Stella giving the last of her recital in hoarse whispers . . . then Stella too scurried for a seat.

Mrs. Burnham was presiding. She took the chair that Flora Belle had placed beside the mahogany table near the long front windows. A sweet-faced, broad-faced, silver-haired, ample-bosomed woman of a generation older than Winifred's, she smiled with maternal complacency upon all. She called the meeting together by playfully tapping on the shining table top with the silver thimble she had reached over to borrow from the *petit-point* in Lucille Countryman's lap. The Club had none of the official atmosphere of the Federation meetings in the Civic Center. Members sewed or not as they pleased.

"Girls—most of you *are* girls to me," Mrs. Burnham began. "We hoped Marianne would give us the account of her visit to the Scandinavian countries. We're all so interested in the Scandinavian countries these days as offering really a *middle* way. Not that I don't believe the American way is best. As all of us do. But as I suppose you know, Marianne left this morning for the East. So I'm going to suggest—if our hostess agrees— that we take advantage of the day and spend most of our time in these beautiful grounds we all love so well and don't see half often enough."

"Then I'm let out!" a dark-haired girl cried, springing up.

"Oh, no, you aren't!" Mrs. Burnham waved her back. "Fellow-members, I was about to add that first of all Gail Salisbury has promised to play for us. And we all know what a musical treat *that* means."

The dark-haired woman, shaking her fist lightly at Mrs.

Burnham, made her way between chairs to the grand piano in the back parlor, where she was invisible to at least half of her audience. "Little girls should be heard and not seen," a voice cried mockingly. Winifred had thought at first, why, are there people in The Club I don't know? But now she could place them both. That rather distinguished-looking girl was Gail Salisbury, young Glenn Salisbury's wife, and the unfamiliar voice belonged to Mrs. Billy Butterfield: two young matrons, fully eligible for The Club, although both had entered by the mother-in-law route.

The members seemed to wait in their usual complacent, half-attentive hush. There was a slight tension of expectancy however. Gail Salisbury had studied in the East and abroad. If she hadn't married Glenn she might have gone on the concert stage. So people said.

Winifred sat softly and brightly smiling, thinking of all the times she had listened to music in these rooms. Then this music suddenly sounded, hard and expertly careless, in sharp dissonance. Winifred gave a slight gasp. It wasn't at all what she'd been waiting for or wanted to hear. It was like a rude assault. The discords struck against her tender flesh.

All at once without warning she was brought back to the edge of that hour when the ground had opened—the solid midland ground her own parents had cultivated for her benefit—and she had looked down in and seen the foundations of her established life. She could smell the secret earthy rot, here in the springtime air of the cool old parlors.

Winifred took hold of the smooth walnut arms of her chair. She closed her eyes—not for long; but in that tiny space of darkness she relived at a distance the hour that had been covered up and forgotten, because it was unnatural and couldn't have been.

Now it was clear how she had come up to it step by step but blindly, and every one of the steps incredible in itself. First there was the shocking news about Frank Hood. She couldn't believe it of *Frank*. But he didn't deny it. Rumors spread that others were implicated. Frank Hood was by no means the worst. Grover Hurd was the big boy who was actually behind the whole thing. It was partly because Frank didn't know so well what he was doing that he had got out in front. The others were better covered. It looked as if Frank would have to take the blow. But then, Winifred had very earnestly asked Alton and Phil Gibbons, who happened to be at the house, oughtn't people to *tell* what they knew—those who did know—and do what they could to help Frank? Both the men had looked very strange. Finally Phil (who had always admired her, always said Winnie Serles was his ideal of a lovely woman) had told her gently:

"Well, Winnie, I'm afraid it's more complicated than that."

Winifred couldn't be satisfied though—not this time. She couldn't bear to see what Lenora was suffering. Frank, it seemed, couldn't speak—couldn't, wouldn't, she didn't know what. There was something peculiar about it. Winifred had never dreamed of meddling in Alton's affairs. She was proud of the position he had reached. She confided in him absolutely. But she was driven to go to Alton at last and put it to him outright: if the other men knew anything to Frank's advantage why didn't they *tell* what they knew? Frank was their friend. Why should they all back up a dreadful person like Grover Hurd? It seemed to her they were being almost cowardly.

Winifred kept her eyes closed but she was conscious again of the flower-filled rooms. Could the girls ever have dreamed there had been such a scene between her and Alton?

She wasn't good at discussing business matters, and the details of this awful affair were still vague to her. All that had clear import was the point they finally came to, the point between Alton and herself. She ought to have been warned by what led up to it, by the glint in Alton's eyes, by his too carefully explaining tone; but she wasn't.

"Win dear," he had finally said, "you *must* understand what an attorney's relation with his client is! We've gone over that so often, and you've always seemed to understand."

She thought she *did* understand! She had said, "I know that, Alton! And of course that's all you have to do with that terrible man. You had to defend him of course." And then she had gone on, never dreaming she was driving him into a corner. "But you've always been Frank's attorney too! Why couldn't you have defended him at the same time if they were both on the same spot? Why, I should think it would have been good *business* as well as common decency to defend Frank Hood while you were defending Grover Hurd!"

She had felt righteous saying this, and hadn't noticed how Alton's look had changed. Only afterward she realized that he had got up, taken one or two nervous steps, and then had faced her with a harassed yet grimly determined look, like someone unwillingly turning after being forced against a wall.

"Frank Hood," he said in a biting, deliberate way, "is a fairly decent fellow, if not too bright. I haven't anything against him. But that's beside the point. The point is, and you've asked for it, all this"—his arm had taken in the room in a sweeping gesture and he had actually glared at her as if she were only part of the surroundings—"this didn't come from playing ball with Frank Hood! Not in a town like this, with a man like Grover Hurd where he is in this town."

That was all, but it was the moment that had stood like something unreal and at the same time too acutely real. The look in Alton's eyes for that moment had seemed to open the very ground under her.

Alton's whole attitude had quickly changed then, and he was sitting beside her, his voice sounding husky, but still with an undertone of warning. "When I married you, and promised to love and cherish you, and told your dad that was going to be the main object of my life, I meant just what I said. I meant to do the most I could for my family and myself. For you first. All right. I have. And I will. You can depend on that. But you can take it that way or not at all."

No more was said. It had all been covered over, never referred to by either of them. Alton did everything he could to obliterate those words except to speak others. Winifred had somehow recovered herself without showing much hurt. The times were unnatural. Alton wasn't his normal self, or perhaps she hadn't been; she hardly knew which. But things would right themselves. All would be as before.

That was how it seemed and must be. No catastrophe had struck. She had been ill but she was recovering. Alton was better to her than ever. Their two children were happily married. Their marriage was the most successful in their crowd. They hadn't lost their money. All had turned out as in her happy girlhood dreams, when she was waiting in the warm confidence of the old home nest to be married to the grandest man she knew. No one had a suspicion of that one lurid hour . . . which perhaps after all couldn't have been real.

Winifred became conscious again of hearing the music which had passed into a quieter interval. She realized that she was sitting with her eyes closed, and that people might notice and think she was ill. She opened her eyes and glanced round very brightly.

But she had a curious feeling of being a looker-on returned from some strange planetary distance. She was seeing everything from a changed refraction of light, in this uncertain flowery springtime. The air was warm and then suddenly chilled in the lofty rooms. The faces under the new hats had become remote.

Gail Salisbury's first selection had ended, and an encore was of course demanded and given. Winifred changed her position slightly. She couldn't see the performer, away off in the back parlor, but Mrs. Billy Butterfield was seated not far from her. The two girls didn't look alike—Jean Butterfield freckled and fair, while the other was the dark kind always described as "sophisticated." But Winifred put them together. Both were of a type that seemed to have grown up while she wasn't keeping count; and something about them daunted her. They took things for granted, but not the same things she did.

They brought an alien element into The Club. But The Club itself had changed. At first it had seemed to her the same, but now she could see the difference. New members had entered, old ones had dropped out. Old Mrs. Kearns, "Aunt Katie," The Club's veteran member, had died just after New Year's. How was it possible not to have missed Aunt Katie sooner? Ida Lauermann, Carol's mother, had moved to California. Lenora Hood had dropped her membership. She was gone.

Winifred felt her heart beating rapidly and disturbingly again. For a long while she had tried not to think about Lenora. She tried to think of her now as she would of anyone else. Things happened to people. Women in The Club had not been immune. Think of Mary Wilkerson, the terrible thing that had happened to *her*, husband, son, and son's wife and baby, all blotted out in an instant when another car had struck theirs. Mary's friends seldom heard from her now. Not that they didn't care! It was her own desire. Unhappy things must be dismissed as far as possible. It had been reassuring to know that Lenora wouldn't be at The Club. But Lenora's absence only made her more vivid. Lenora's friends couldn't get round her predicament just by not looking at her. It touched them anyway. They were all mixed up in it. Was that what Edna's contemptuous look had meant?

The program ended and now they could go outside. Ava Gibbons came up to Winifred and said confidentially, "Do you want to go, Winnie? I noticed you while Gail was playing and I was afraid you were tired. I do think she plays difficult stuff—it's over *my* poor head. Well, you and I can go slowly."

"I don't want to make you go slowly, Ava dear."

"Oh, Winnie, I'm not so young and spry. I don't want to admit it, but I'm getting rheumatics. We'll both lag back and pretend we're studying the birds and flowers."

Flora Belle of course was leading, with Mrs. Burnham beside her, panting a trifle but smiling and resolute. Groups wandered off and lingered here and there, running to catch up again. Jean Butterfield cried that she must see the Generals. She'd heard about them ever since she'd been living in Battle Bluff. She dragged the younger women after her, Gail Salisbury and Carol Mann, running from General to General and staring in rapture; while the older women, following more slowly, laughed indulgently. They had gone through a period of thinking these statues were perfectly frightful, of saying Flora Belle ought to cart them out of sight. Some thought so still. And now hear these girls raving about them!

"Iron things are all back," Alma Kite was earnestly insisting. "People in the East have been collecting for a *long* time. They're getting terribly valuable."

"Oh," Stella groaned, "I can't keep up with old things getting valuable! *I'm* not getting more valuable, I know that."

"Now my dear, don't be so sure," Mrs. Burnham chided.

Dorothy Kitchen was crying that she wanted to see the grove. She hadn't been out there since they all used to go nutting.

"There isn't much to see," Flora Belle said sighing. "But then one can't keep up *every*-thing."

Ava and Winifred followed the others slowly. The larger group was moving on again when they came to stand at the edge of the grove. It looked denuded and scanty. Ava whispered, asking if she knew they'd burned this wood during the depression?—Kerwin and Flora Belle? It was actually their only source of fuel.

But after all, even this remnant of the grove was lovely, situated so beautifully here at the head of the slope. The sun made aisles of light between lofty trees. Winifred began to wish she could look at what she pleased without this running murmur of explanation. When they went over to the iris Ava said, "You know for a while Flora Belle sold these flowers on the highway. She tried to have a stand." And as they went down the slope of the great front lawn again, round which the Generals stood in a silent, broken ring, their bronze faces darkly inscrutable under their campaign hats—Ava murmured: "She would have taken tourists. But this place is too far from the road. They simply wouldn't come out here. They'd rather stay in some little dump. Well, if she and Kerwin can just keep going . . . The place ought to be bought for a museum." Now and then Winifred caught Flora Belle's voice. "Oh, we don't try to do anything new. It's all Mr. Hawley can keep up, and, girls, you don't know all *I* do. I suppose there are possibilities, but—" Mrs. Burnham interrupted warmly:

"This is just what we want. To have the old Bliss place remain as it is. Girls, isn't that true?"

Now the women in their fresh spring costumes began trailing, by twos and threes, up the slope to the house. Winifred and Ava were about the last. Candles were lighted and there was a fire of pine in the beautiful old fireplace in the front parlor. Carol ran to get Winifred's oval-backed chair. She said quickly, "I'm going to sit near you," and took the footstool for herself.

They always had such marvelous teas at Flora Belle's. "Does Mrs. Hawley still make all these grand cakes and things herself?" "Oh, yes. She has to. My dear, we don't have anyone but the Hawleys." "But to think you still have both of them. And to think of being honored with sherry from the General's old stock!"

"Why shouldn't The Club be honored?" Mrs. Burnham smilingly asked. "Such a band of queenly ladies."

"This is in Winifred's honor!"

They lifted the glittering small glasses. Stella shouted for a speech, but Dorothy quickly said Winnie needn't do a thing. All they asked was that she should once more grace their meetings with her charming presence. Winifred, sitting smiling, with a worshipping younger woman at her feet—adoring her because she was adored by her husband—was back in her own world. For a little while she had what she had come to find. The fire crackled with delightful incongruity in this flower-filled room with the deep-green May foliage outside.

But Winifred, even while she was having her close little chat with Mrs. Burnham, so soothing and bright—"How are you, dear? You do remind me so of your darling mother, more and more"—had begun to realize that Katherine Burchard was talking about something she wanted to hear. She wanted terribly to know just what it was, but she hadn't the courage to ask directly. There was a private, secretive air about the group. Helen Redding kept glancing over her shoulder. Katherine spoke with sober earnestness, in lowered tones. Winifred dropped Carol's soft little hand, murmured something about the fire, and moved her chair.

". . . Well of course I didn't see much of her. But I was de-*ter*-mined . . ." The narrative was lost while Ava told one of her stories about Dick, her young son. Then Winifred, sitting very still in the oval-backed chair, caught it up again.

What Have I? · 201

"She has that terrible creature to look after. Oh, I can't describe her—I don't want to. Lenora has to be with her night and day. . . . I know my dear, but jobs aren't so easy these days, and Lenora hasn't had any training, people have to have *training*. . . . Oh, *I* admire her too. I admire her ter-*ri*-fically. . . . We didn't talk about things here. I don't know whether Lenora wanted to hear or not—or was even glad to see me. But girls I just *had* to . . ."

Mrs. Burnham had turned back. "Excuse me, Winifred." Winifred felt the comfortable plump pressure of her elderly hand. "You do have good help, don't you? It's so hard these days. But I needn't ask whether Alton has everything arranged!"

"I have marvelous help," Winifred said hastily. "She's had *training*." Her face flushed, but she went on with tales of Mrs. Bjornson's efficiency. She heard with wonder the self-satisfied sound of her own voice. The girls were impressed. All repeated how lovely she was looking. Those colors were grand for her.

"You never got that outfit here!" Ava said enviously.

"Well, Nancy simply forced me to shop."

"Oh, Winnie, tell us about Nancy!"

This she did joyously—but still with a nervous attention on Katherine's group. Stella broke in, and Winifred let her. ". . . Oh, yes she shows it. Girls, I was shocked. She looks really old. Oh, and you know, it was a shame because it did more than anything else to spoil her looks—but that front tooth of Lenora's, you remember it was knocked out when she was just a kid—well, the peg tooth is gone and there's that awful gap. . . ."

Winifred turned away.

She heard Mabel Richmond going on now. "It's the government. Our own government! That's the real enemy."

Ava shrieked, "For heaven's sake! *Don't* let's talk politics, economics, labor troubles, or war, or *mention* the President or the W.P.A. Let's not bring such things into The Club. I make it a motion!"

"Second! Second!"

Mabel looked both hard and hurt. "We know how we feel about these things," Mrs. Burnham told her soothingly. "It's just that we don't want to arouse any differences, dear—if there *are* any." Jean Butterfield stared with big solemn blue eyes. Mrs. Burnham felt annoyed however. She too had caught some of Katherine's words—and she didn't feel it was quite right to bring such matters up just now; it was out of place.

She hastened to say to Gail Salisbury, "How do you keep it up, you wonderful child, with your beautiful house, and everything else? And you and Glenn never miss out on any good times. I think that's *so* wonderful."

Gail answered drily, "I don't keep it up."

"My dear, why say that?" Ava Gibbons demanded. "Now don't set your standards impossibly high! We don't ask you to be absolutely pro-*fes*-sional."

"I know you don't," Gail answered even more drily.

Winifred felt she couldn't listen to anything more. She was back in the midst. Her friends were her friends again, close, and not remote. But, whether they knew and admitted it or not, all were in a sense survivors. All must have experienced, in some degree, the same shaking of their own solid ground.

But were things really much different? Some had gone through bankruptcy but apparently weren't much the worse; where formerly they had kept two maids they now kept one. Stella's animation had worn thin, but even Stel couldn't keep it up forever. Flora Belle looked exactly as she had for years, wearing the same type of printed chiffon dress for afternoon, with her gray hair marcelled, and the marcel flattened down by a net. Mabel Richmond, the girls complained, howled constantly about how frightful conditions were, as if she were standing in her custom-made sandals on the edge of doom, bitterly resentful, and trying to point to the personal enemy who had pushed her there. Here Mabel was sitting though on the Victorian sofa beside a bouquet of white lilacs, ostentatiously youthful, her hair blacker than black, in her red-and-white costume and lacquered red hat. It seemed to Winifred she must have dreamed that awful time.

But she kept having a strange feeling among her group here, her own rightful desirable circle, in the beautiful old house in its romantic seclusion, as if a gulf had widened between these bluffs and the smoky town, and they were set off here by themselves with the candlelight, firelight, and flowers.

"Winnie, haven't you your car?"
"Yes, it's here, Marlin's driving up now."

"Oh, I forgot you're bumming round with a chauffeur these days! You're as grand as Mabel, aren't you?"

Winifred laughed. Mabel, in her brilliant red-and-white, was standing at a little distance. She was taking this chance to tell her troubles. Winifred heard the hard, aggrieved voice, caught the glance of the wandering, resentful eyes. But she didn't go over although she realized that she had scarcely spoken to Mabel to-day. Guilt was heavy on her, because she was employing Don Bolton's wife. Mabel would regard that as a traitor's act. And it was perhaps according to some strict division of loyalty. The knowledge hurt Winifred, and she felt sickeningly that she didn't like Mabel Richmond, never had— no better than she liked Edna Bolton. She really did like Don. She felt as if she were a tiny, soft, tame animal that had got helplessly into some gigantic trap.

"You have room, haven't you, Winnie?"

Flora Belle had come up with Gail and Jean Butterfield. These two reckless girls had driven out without a spare and here was their car with a flat. Winnie quickly and generously offered to drive them home. *Please.* She was ashamed to have this big car all to herself.

"Where do you both live? Of course I know where Gail lives, but—"

"I should think you wouldn't know where we live," Jean said, laughing, and gave the address. Winifred was really taken back. She hadn't been through that district for ages, but she had always supposed it was the jumping-off place. Billy Butterfield—Sherman Butterfield's son? Would he live in such a part of town, bring his bride there?

The bride seemed to feel no shame. She was still talking about the Generals. "Yes, he was stunning. But I want the little man. He would be sweet under our big oak tree." Now she turned to explain to Winifred how she and Billy had bought an old house out in the slums. "I want to prepare you for entering our depressed area. Gail's never recovered from the first shock. She thinks it's slumming to come to see *me*."

"It is," Gail said coldly. "You're W.P.A. people and I'm an old royalist. So is Mrs. Serles."

"Oh, I'm not anything," Winifred protested. "I don't know enough."

The girls both laughed, and Winifred felt all at once that they approved of her. On close view Gail Salisbury didn't look so formidable. Her color was bad—as so often with these pared-down girls who smoked too much and nourished themselves on green salads and black coffee. The dissatisfaction in her face was familiar. Jean's healthy good looks were reassuring in a different way, making it plain to Winifred's practiced maternal eye that—no matter how unorthodox her views— she had had the right things to eat during childhood. But it did give Winifred Serles a shock to learn that Sherman Butterfield's son was working for the government.

The shock was worse when they drove over ancient railroad tracks, sunk in deep grass, and on into the outlying river section. Then Winifred could scarcely hide her astonished distaste. Jean spoke with enthusiasm. This was the oldest part of town, older than the bluffs—as if that made it the best. A few of the original buildings were left. Of course there were the railroad tracks and some factories, but the district had kept a rural wildness.

"We can walk right down to the river, to the old landings."

"And smell the nice little muddy-water fishes!" Gail said.

The houses, the shacks, the muddy yards, and weedy lots— they made Winifred shudder. And she was afraid to look at them for she wondered if Edna and Don might not be living somewhere out here, maybe in some place like that awful trailer. . . . Don had said they were going to lose their house. Jean told now, her eyes big and excited, how interesting it was in this neighborhood. They lived with people on the real bottom level, right among these people, so they got the chance to know them.

"What a chance," Gail drawled. "No wonder I can't compete."

Winifred was too courteous to make any comment. And to her relief, she was able to admire the Butterfields' house, to agree with the girls that it had good lines. She could say, with her own responsive charm, how interesting it must be to make an old house over—reserving her suspicions of what it must cost, sure that the plumbing could never be right. The large white house, still needing its second coat of paint, stood in forlorn seedy dignity in a big flat yard that had kept one magnificent tree. Winifred *could* admire the tree.

As Jean stepped from the car she cried, "Look over there in the lot! That old woman. She's getting dandelion greens. *I'm* going to dig some. There isn't any reason why Bill and I should buy our vitamins. Gail, I invite you to the mess. Greens are a mess, aren't they?"

"Thanks. Yours will be."

Winifred laughed. She felt with tender relief that Jean was a romantic child—as much a child as Carol Mann, more than Nancy. Yet there was something daunting and disturbing in her eager freshness. Gail looked jaded by comparison.

The old woman stood up just then and turned to stare. Winifred looked straight at the sunken old face. The mouth was open showing a few hideous tusks. Winifred shuddered again.

She felt homesick for the comforts of her own lovely room. She was glad to get rid of both the girls, and to reach there.

"Gosh that sure smells, down there by the river," Marlin observed with gusto as he helped her out of the car.

Winifred said good-night gaily—she'd call about to-morrow—and walked slowly up the flagstone path between the purple and yellow iris in the cool sweet air of early evening. The front door was open, but no one seemed to be about. Alton was probably in the garden surveying his peonies. Thank heaven Edna Bolton was gone.

Winifred stood a few moments in the panelled hall looking into the mirror as she took off her purple hat. She saw the lovely faded image of herself that had changed little throughout the years. She recalled the approbation of her friends; she had always lived and moved in its warmth, and she hadn't lost it. A cold memory touched her. What was herself in this image, with its charming colors, against the dim background? Would that self still have sustenance if she were like the old woman out picking greens—if her streaked gray hair was cut raggedly with the scissors and a gap in her front teeth gave everyone a shock who saw it? How much of the "sweetness" and the "dignity" that had always belonged to her, as Winifred Wallingford, and Mrs. Alton Serles, was fed by her pleasure in her own physical loveliness? Could she live without that—if, instead of being pleasing, so that Marlin felt set up to be driving her . . . She didn't finish it. But her delight in her new clothes was dimmed. She couldn't bear the faint, expensive scent of Nancy's perfume, that Nancy had given her because it went with the costume.

The question rose clear that for all this long while had been aching in her mind beneath the shifting confusions: suppose Alton *had* come out and told all he knew, paid whatever it would have cost to get clear of Grover Hurd—suppose we'd lost everything—could I have stood it?

Lenora had. What gave her the power? If she had any particular religion, nobody knew about it. Lenora was like the rest of them in that respect; went sometimes to the church where her parents used to go. Love of Frank? But Frank Hood was—oh a nice fellow, they all liked him; but if his wife felt any great devotion nobody knew about that either. The Hoods' one child had died years ago.

Once Winifred would have said—as Alton had said—that their happiness together was the main object of her life. It had included even her devotion to her children. But her love had been her trust in Alton—in his splendid competence and his worshipping care. It had been her security. The smitten ground had closed again but that one vision of old roots and rotted foundations had stayed with her.

It might be just that Frank and Lenora had been the ones hit while the others had all escaped. If they hadn't escaped—or if it should happen to them still—something might stand clear, if only for an instant. She might learn what she really had. Whether—though having dwelt, with becoming grace, in the pleasant places ordained for her—she really had anything.

A GREAT MOLLIE

. . . . . .

Mollie Schumacher drove into the yard of the Bell farm. At first she thought there was no one about, it was so quiet. The garage doors were closed, however, and Frank always left them standing open when he took out the car.

She shut off the engine. But she kept on sitting in the car with her hands on the worn steering wheel, so comfortable that she hated to get out. She noticed how dry the September sunshine made everything look. The heavy pale grain of the grindstone was warm in the sun. Milk had been spilled at the corner of the corn crib where the cats were fed. It made a whitish stain on the bare ground and flies were thick above it. There was a look of country peace about the old red barn. The loft window was open, and shaggy, dusty hay stuck out. In the open wooded pasture behind the barn, the oaks had that dry look, too, in the sunshine.

Summer was almost over again! Mollie felt a thrust of fear. Summer, no matter how hard any one worked, was an interlude. It didn't really matter. But just as soon as that first crispness came into the air, it was different. The handle of the pump burned with cold when she went out to the vine-covered stoop to get the water before breakfast . . . again she was impatient because they kept on living in that old-fashioned house at the edge of town where they couldn't even have city water or a furnace—things everybody had nowadays! In the summer, it was pleasant enough, with the flowers, and the birds for which Charlie had made a dozen queer little houses of bark and boards. But the cold spurred her ambition. When frost came, you had to decide things. It might come any time, now. It would get harder and harder to start the Ford. It would be too cold to drive in an open car. Her summer work would be over.

Nearly over . . . These days when she started out early, eager to get away from the puttering routine of home; packed her bag of samples; called back impatiently that they could expect her when they saw her; and then, after long dallying with the starter and heated attempts at cranking, heard joyously the loud steady noise of the engine, sprang in quickly before it had a chance to die down, and at last was out on the open road. . . .

She had been grumbling all summer about the annoyances—having to fool with this old car; getting caught in the rain somewhere out in the country and driving home over slippery roads; her goods not coming on time. But she had an affection for the Ford, which she had bought second hand at a sale in the country—although she got so furious at it sometimes that she called it every name she could think of. "You damned hell-fired old SKATE!" once she had sobbed at it.

But when it was running well, when the road stretched long and smooth, when the fields were fresh and the sky was blue, when the engine hummed noisily and the fenders rattled, she squeezed the steering wheel with both hands and felt that she loved the old rattletrap. She was so happy that she sang. She drove on and on and on, trying new roads, pretending that it was because she was enterprising and was looking for new customers. When she came to a patch of woods where it was shady, she stopped the car, took out from her handbag the sandwich of homemade bread and summer sausage she had stolen into the kitchen to make when Luisa wasn't around, and ate it luxuriously. She liked to sell things and to dicker.

"Hoo hoo!" Mollie called.

Mate came to the door at last in an old bungalow apron.

"Well, look who's here!"

"I thought you folks must be all asleep."

"I was lying down. I don't know, I've felt kind of bum ever since I had those teeth out. I ought to get my ironing done today, there's some pieces I need, but—come on in, Mollie, what you standing outside for?"

"Wait. I want to get some things out of the car."

Mollie ran out and opened the back of the car.

"Land, you do pick up the most things! Where'd you get all that junk?" Mate demanded, in amusement.

"Oh, I don't know," Mollie said, laughing and blushing, half sheepish and half proud, like a child caught in some game of its own. "I see things when I'm driving around, and folks give me things. Gosh, Mate, I don't know where it all does come from! But I always seem to come home with the old bus loaded."

She had some seed corn that Henry Fuchs had given her to try out, and a bag of crab apples, a jackknife she had found in the road, a few hazelnuts she had picked to see whether they were ripe, a pail of honey, a spray of sumach, and half a dozen melons.

"Where'd you get the melons?" Mate demanded.

"Oh, some girls back here on the road had a stand and were selling them. I always like to take something home to Lu and Charlie. Here, I want you and Frank to try one of these."

"Oh, no; we'll have melons of our own before long."

"Oh, take this one—it's supposed to be a new kind. Go ahead, Mate."

"Well, but I hate to."

Mollie followed Mate into the parlor and sat down with a luxurious sigh, in the cool room shaded by pine trees. She took off her hat and wiped her face and neck until they were red. Her hair felt stiff with dust.

"You're sweating like a man," Mate observed.

"I have to work like a man, I can tell you."

"Ain't it awful hard work for you, going around with that Ford?"

"Oh, well, I can do it!" Mollie boasted. She laughed, and her eyes sparkled. "I came across a fellow in the road—couldn't get his car started, so I got out and tinkered around with it a while—and I don't know just what I'd done to it, but the darn thing started up the minute I turned on the gas! You ought to have seen that fellow's face!"

"You ought to have been a man," Mate said, admiring, yet disapproving.

She looked at Mollie.

Mollie was big all over, and Frank always said, when she helped him lift anything, that her arms were as strong as his. Her reddish brown hair grew rough and thick and slightly curling, and below the dusty roots was a tiny gleam of perspiration. There were dark hairs on her upper lip and chin. Her lips were full and vital, and her nose had a bold outline. But her brown eyes were childlike. They had an ingenuous glow in the coarse vigor of her tanned face. There was something defenseless in their warm darkness. When she was pleased, or touched, they misted over.

"I expect I look like thunder by now," Mollie said, uncomfortably. "Well, who could keep fixed up, running around the country, and doing the things I do?"

"You're all right," Mate lied politely. Really, she was disapproving of Mollie's dusty shoes and her blue gingham dress with big hoops of perspiration under the arms and the hem of a dark brown slip showing at the back. "You've got a smudge, though, on your neck."

"Oh, well, when I get home I'll have a good scrubbing. I start out clean, Mate, but gosh, I can't keep that way! Who can, that runs a Ford? Anyway, I caught an old biddie for Lena Toogood, when I was there, that she couldn't catch, and I had to chase that female devil all over the landscape."

Mate did not answer. She had always disapproved of Mollie for not thinking more about her clothes, although—when they were off together after nuts or elderberries—she depended upon Mollie to shake the trees and find a way of getting over fences. Mate herself had never learned to drive their car and had to wait to go to town until Frank could take her. She regarded the car as beyond both her management and her comprehension, just as she did some of the farm implements—and this although she had been brought up on a farm, had known how to milk since she was an infant, and would have no help with either her stove or her washing machine.

Mollie opened her sample bag.

"I brought along that underwear I thought'd be nice for Frank," she said. "And then I got your corselette, in the other bag. I think this is the nicest thing yet I've struck for men. Look here."

She held up a winter weight union suit, eying it with proud satisfaction and discussing all its good points in detail, while its pathetic legs dangled.

"I don't know," Mate said, dubiously. "Frank's never worn that kind."

"Best of reasons for wearing it now!" Mollie said vigorously. It always made her impatient that the people around here were so afraid to try new things, which were the very breath of life to her. "I know what Frank wears—those old clumsy two piece things, still! It's not that I'm so anxious to sell, Mate, but I'd like Frank to try a good handy piece of goods like this and get rid of those old contraptions. I want the people around here to take up new things once in a while! Now, I'll tell you, I'm going to leave this sample here, and as soon as it gets cold, I want Frank to try this, and if he don't like it, all right; I'll take it back—give it to somebody for Christmas, or let Charlie wear it."

"I don't think we ought to take your sample," Mate demurred.

"Oh fudge! Season's ending, anyway."

"Did you say you brought my corselette?"

"You bet!"

Mollie talked while she fitted it. "I had another nice suit of men's summer underwear, but I sold it to a fellow I met on the road. That was a funny sale! I passed him, and I saw he was walking, so I says, 'Want a ride?' He says, 'Sure!' We got to talking. He told me he was a lightning insurance man. His car broke down and he was walking out to see Bert Gulley. He asked what I was selling, and I told him I had the best line of men's underwear he'd ever seen. I says, 'Don't you want to look at some of it?' and he says, 'Sure,' and I stopped the car and got out my samples, and he bought that one—it was just his size. He told me he'd get me a job selling insurance if I wanted it!" Mollie gave an eager, delighted laugh. "I bet I could make a go of it, too!"

"Aren't you afraid to ask strange men like that to ride with you?" Mate asked, in horror.

"Afraid! What of? Think they're going to run off with me?"

"They might rob you."

"Oh fudge! And all they'd get from me—!"

"Well, I think it's awful risky."

"That don't bother me any. I like it! Oh, anyway, I can't pass somebody walking along in the heat while I'm riding and not at least offer the fellow a chance to ride if he wants it. I had a tramp one day—I took him as far as the creamery."

"Weren't you scared to have him in the car?"

"No, he was a real nice fellow! He'd been bumming around

out in California, and he told me a whole lot about raising honey from onion blossoms—I'd like to try that! I learn all kinds of things from these bugs I pick up on the road."

Mollie laughed delightedly again, and rocked strenuously. It was fun to horrify Mate—and then it was so cool in here, and she wasn't anxious to get home where they all disapproved of her "going around selling things."

"You better stay for dinner," Mate urged.

"Oh gee, I can't, Mate! I've got to get on. I spent half the morning chasing that old biddie for Lena. Say, though, if you'll let me do a little of that ironing for you—"

"Oh, I couldn't let you do that! You've got your own work."

"Oh, come on, Mate, I'll be glad to do it for you. It'll give me a change. I can just as well help you out a little while I'm stopping here."

There was no resisting Mollie when she was determined to do something for you, Mate knew. So Mollie was soon hard at work with the electric iron in Mate's back kitchen. Mollie always worked harder at anything that wasn't her own work, and wasn't what she was supposed to be doing.

Frank Bell came into the house shortly before noon.

"I thought I saw a car out here that didn't belong! Hello, Mollie," he said, heartily. "How you was?"

"Fine, boy! How's yourself?"

He stuck out his hand and grinned. "Want to shake with a nigger?"

Mollie said, "Sure, you bet I do, yours aren't much worse'n mine."

"Well, us fellows that handles engines can't keep tony, can we?" Frank asked. He shook Mollie's hand with jocular vigor until Mate squealed:

"Frank, let go, you're hurting her!"

He retorted, "Aw, Mollie's not hurt so easy as all that. I'm working up her strength so she can crank that Ford."

"Well, you aren't going to set down in any of these chairs in those clothes you've got on now."

"Oh, I ain't!" Frank retorted jubilantly. He waved his blackened hands at her until she ducked and squealed again. "Say, what's that melon I see out in the kitchen?"

"That's Mollie's."

"No, it isn't," Mollie said, eagerly. "I brought it for you folks. Come on, let's have a taste of it."

"Now? Before dinner?"

"Sure!" Frank said, heartily. "Mushmelons, any time."

"I'm not going to have Frank Bell sitting down here in this room and eating melons in those awful clothes."

"Aw, say, I can't change my clothes every time I step in and out of the house!" Frank began, indignantly.

"He can eat outdoors," Mollie broke in. "Come on, Frank, you do get treated pretty mean. I got some more in the Ford. You come out mit."

They ran away from Mate's expostulations, and Mollie rummaged through the miscellany in the back of the Ford until she'd found a nice little melon for Frank. "Here, boy! How's this?" He stood, eating it happily, letting the juice drip into the road and caring nothing for his black hands.

"Gosh, look at the plunder!" he said, marveling. "Here, Mollie—want a bite?"

"Sure, I'll take a bite."

He broke off a dripping hunk of melon, orange-tinted and coolly juicy in its pale green rind. Mate stood on the back porch watching them in disapproval. They were spoiling their dinners. Frank and Mollie were like a pair of kids when they got together. Mate was glad to have Mollie stay, though, in spite of the extra work any company made. Mollie livened things up, and took a hand at helping with all kinds of work.

Frank went back to finish his job with the machinery, and Mollie washed luxuriously in the cool soft water at Mate's sink. She was going to stay for dinner after all.

"I oughtn't to. But the morning's gone anyway—gosh, I don't know where to! Well, I got some of that ironing out of the way for you, Mate."

Mate's being so particular was all right when it came to a meal. Frank came in, scrubbed and with his hair wet, in a pair of clean, faded blue overalls. Mollie loved to eat in company. It wasn't the meal, she always said, but the sociability. Still, Mollie could get away with a pretty good meal, too, as Frank Bell had often noticed with amusement.

"Well, Mollie!" he began. "Business pretty good?"

"Took in fifteen dollars' worth last Friday!" Mollie boasted.

"Zat so! How much you taken in to-day?"

"Oh, not so much to-day—so far: I don't know what I may do this afternoon," Mollie said, easily. "I haven't stopped many places. Kind of got stuck. Well, Lena Toogood was chasing around after an old biddie, and I stopped and caught it for her, and I don't know—did some more things."

"She ought to save you a good order for that!"

"She ordered fifty cents' worth, I guess. One pair of cotton stockings."

"Well, that was pretty good for Lena."

Mollie ate with gusto of mashed potatoes, pork, and gravy. She had picked a big stiff bouquet of zinnias for the table, and it made her happy to look at the bright, gaudy colors.

"Well, if you can take in fifteen dollars' worth in one day," Frank told her, "I expect you'll go on selling union suits and stockings."

"No, that's only pick-up work."

"You've got the car, and I should think you could get all

around the country here, and do a lot of business. Work up a good trade. I always thought you were a good salesman, Mollie."

"No, it's almost over. No, sir, what I want," Mollie said vigorously, and scowling, "is real work, something that'll call out the best there is in me. Oh, it's fun to sell stuff for a while . . . but *that's* what I'm after—something big!"

"Yes, something big . . ." Frank began, dubiously.

But she went straight on: "This is nothing! This is something I can do with one hand. What fun is it to make money that way? No, *this* isn't what I'm after."

Her face glowed darkly and her eyes sparkled. Frank was impressed, as he always was when he talked with Mollie face to face. She was a strong woman, all right, and a mighty capable one in lots of ways, about as much so as a man. But he asked facetiously:

"What do you want to do? Some more vi'lets?"

Those "vi'lets" . . . That was the trouble with Mollie: always wanting to get into some fancy kind of business that nobody'd ever heard of; not contented with straight buying and selling. That showed that she was a woman. He got rid of his respect and got back his amusement, which suited him much better . . . but still with a little uneasy feeling that Mollie might make a go of one of those crazy businesses some day: she could do things.

"That all fell through," Mollie answered him, robustly.

"What was the trouble? Couldn't you and Artie get together? Thought you and him was all ready to do down South and make your fortunes!"

"We might have, too," Mollie answered, looking back over the plan with a reminiscent glow—her schemes were always radiant to her in anticipation and alluring in retrospect. "There's something in it for the fellow that takes a-hold. No, the trouble was, Art got cold feet, and the Missus, I guess, got 'em first—heard about the snakes down South and was afraid to go down there."

She wanted to turn it off, but Frank was started on it now and wouldn't let it go. He asked, mulling over his amusement: "What was you and Artie going to do with the vi'lets when you'd raised 'em? Going to take 'em into town and stand and sell 'em to the visitors on the street corners? Say, Art Gilbert would have made a cute flower boy!"

Mate was listening to all of this nonsense without a smile, with her hand on the handle of the coffee pot, ready to fill the cups again, if anybody wanted coffee.

"Pass Mollie the meat, Frank. She's out of everything. You better tend to your knitting here instead of talking about vi'lets," she said, with a dry coldness. Mollie's schemes neither impressed her nor gave her any amusement. If Mollie had any real sense about things, she'd marry some farmer around here—a widower, somebody who needed a good, strong wife and would be glad to have her; her friends would help her look around for somebody—or else she'd make up her mind to settle down where she was, with Luisa and Charlie, and attend to things at home.

"Well, I still think it's a good plan for the fellow that can work it," Mollie affirmed, stoutly. "Why shouldn't people raise violets as well as raise potatoes?"

Frank was now highly amused. "Sure, and so was the goldfish a good plan!" he said. "What become of them? Last I heard you was chasing old man Davies all over town to try and rent his crick from him and set up a goldfish farm!"

"Well, now that was all—"

"And then once you was going to fence off half your place and raise skunks there and go into the fur business along with John Jacob Astor. Wouldn't you have a sweet place? Talk

about the slaughter house! On summer nights—wow, pugh!"
Frank laughed hilarious, and made appropriate gestures.

"Frank Bell, you're at the table! You act nice or leave,"
Mate said with frozen dignity.

Mollie was red, but she stood up under it. "That's all right,
too, there *is* a fortune in that for the right fellow. I looked that
up and I've got bulletins and reports to prove it."

"All I can say is—give me the pigpen!"

"*Frank Bell!*"

Frank saw, then, that he would have to behave for a while.
To show her disapproval of the whole conversation, Mate
began to ask dutifully now about the other Schumachers.

"How are Luisa and Charlie getting along these days?"

The sparkle went out of Mollie's eyes and she looked
scowling.

"Oh, the same as they always do! Lu don't have time from
five o'clock in the morning to eight o'clock at night to pick all
the grass by hand around the trees. Charlie goes back and
forth to the office."

Mate, however, would not talk satirically about the two,
whom she considered more sensible than Mollie because
they stuck to home, although they weren't such good friends
of hers.

"I suppose Luisa's got lots of sewing done this summer,"
she said, primly.

"Oh, yes, she's made over a lot of flour sacks into shirts and
nightgowns that neither Charlie nor I will wear, and thinks
she's accomplished a lot. Oh, yes, they're both the same as always: everything at our house is."

Mollie's face was dark as she stabbed her fork into her goose-
berry pie, that had a sparkling crust of sugar upon the flaky,
bubbled crust of dough. She said, defiantly:

"I may go away this winter!"

"Where to?" Mate demanded, with resentful skepticism.

"To Chicago," Mollie answered, pretending to be nonchalant.

"Chicago! What would you do there?"

Frank, a little remorseful for the way he had teased Mollie, and thinking that she had more ability than Mate would ever give her credit for, said, judiciously:

"Well, Chicago's got room for lots of people."

Mate looked as if Mollie had said the South Pole.

"I'm thinking about going there."

Mollie was too eager to unburden herself, however—too helplessly and expansively communicative—to keep up the barren triumph of mystification and reticence.

"Well, I s'pose you'll have a fit when you hear who—"

Then she told them about the letter from Dorrie Parker. No matter what people in White Oak had predicted, Dorrie had been getting on well, after all. She had been working in a beauty parlor, and now some *person* (Mollie went over that very hastily—she didn't want Frank and Mate to know that the person was a man) was going to help her to set herself up in business. She wanted Mollie to come to Chicago and go in with her.

"I'm not crazy about that business," Mollie said. "It always seems to me as if folks ought to have something better to do than just fool with their looks. But I'd kind of like to help out for Dorrie."

As Mollie had expected, Mate had "lots to say." While there was nothing absolutely definite against Dorrie Parker, her reputation had not been good and she had left White Oak under a cloud. There had been rumors of her carrying on with other men at the time of her divorce. Mollie Schumacher was about the only person who still heard from her. Dorrie had written, sentimentally, that Mollie was the only friend she'd ever had in White Oak. (Well, that wasn't true, but maybe it seemed so now.) She wanted to get Mollie out of there. Between them, they could work up a good business.

Frank Bell, however, was inclined to be on Mollie's side—perhaps it was just to oppose Mate.

"Dorrie Parker's a good worker," he declared. "Folks is patronizing those places now."

"Yes, the big fools!" Mollie put in, with a snort.

Frank said that Dorrie might have made a few mistakes, but she was a smart woman—knew where she was headed better than most women did. Mate listened, in silent indignation that he should defend Dorrie and urge Mollie on—she was scatter-brained enough without any urging—to desert her home and "go in with that woman."

"Well now, *that* sounds like a scheme that might work, Mollie," Frank said, in generous approval. "I'd rather polish up folks' fingernails, if I was to choose, than get up meals for skunks."

"Well, I think I'll do it," Mollie said, vigorously, "If only . . ."

"If only what?"

That warm mist filled her dark eyes.

"Oh, well . . . if it wasn't for Charlie and Lu. They needn't think they can stop me! But, I don't know . . . if they should really feel bad about it—if I thought they couldn't get along without me . . ."

The mist gathered into large tears. Frank was astounded. He saw no sense to that at all. With the quarrels that went on in that household, and Luisa doing all the housework anyway, and Charlie Schumacher such a mild soul he could get all the amusement he needed in life out of making those gimcrack bird-houses—! Mate thought it very proper, however, and something that Mollie ought to have been thinking of before.

"I don't know whether this pie's very good," she apologized. "I believe I got a little too much lard. Let me warm up your coffee, Mollie."

"Well, I oughtn't to—coffee upsets me—but then—"

"Oh, have some more!" Frank said. The ready mist had dried from Mollie's eyes. Frank felt happy and convivial. He said to Mate:

"Shall we treat wine?"

Mollie's coming was a fine excuse. Mate never touched Frank's wine. He went down into the cellar, found a bottle, and came in from the kitchen with the two miniature glasses almost slopping over with a deep red brightness that held all the warmth of the late summer—that was like the sparkle of dew in the morning and the grapes growing ripe on the fences and the dark velvety red of the blossom tufts on the sumach. Mollie liked to be a good fellow with Frank—and she liked the looks of the stuff, she said.

"This is my last year's grape. Time to drink it up and make some more. Well, Mollie—good luck!"

"Good luck, boy!" she responded heartily.

They drank.

Mollie, in spite of all the orders she'd meant to take that afternoon, didn't get away from the Bells' when dinner was over. Frank, when he'd had one glass of wine, had to have another; and then he thought about the cigars his cousin in Chicago had sent him for his birthday, and had to have one of those. The wine made him think about making more wine; and that made him remember his old cider press and how he had been wondering if he couldn't get the thing fixed up.

"You know, I'd forgot we even had it. Father used to run it every fall. But then, I don't know, guess it got out of kilter, and it got stuck into that old shed and I never saw it until I went out to look for something else."

("Yes, and you'd find plenty more things if you'd go through those sheds!" Mate put in.)

Mollie had to see the press. She liked to tinker as well as Frank did.

"Come on, finish up that cigar, Frank; let's go out and have a look," she urged. "I can just take a squint at it before I go. Maybe we can get the thing to working."

She followed Frank out of the back door, calling back to Mate:

"Wait with those dishes, Mate, I'll be in to help you—now, don't you go and do them."

Mollie and Frank went off through the farmyard. The ground was dry and the air was warm and the sun was a glorious gold in the blue September sky. A string of cats, adult and half grown and mere little scampering infants, trailed after Frank. He made pets of the cats, and fed them.

"Oh, stop and give 'em their milk, Frank!" Mollie pleaded. Her eyes grew warm and humid. She had slapped Pete Heim in the face once for beating his old horse. "I can't bear the little beggars mee-owing like that. Here, kitty, come, kitty."

"You won't catch none of them!" Frank told her, with admiration for the adroit elusiveness of the cats. Mollie made a dive for them, and the whole tribe fled at once, with soft vanishing evasion—all but one little tiger with white mittens and round emerald eyes, who stood poised, with eyes glittering, until Mollie's fingers almost touched his whiskers . . . and then was gone, in one flattened furry dive, beneath the woodshed.

"Little villains! Confound 'em!" Mollie said, hotly. She adored cats, but they always ran from her.

Frank laughed uproariously. "You'll never get any o' *them*, Mollie! Not if they don't want you to. They're smart! . . . Well, here's where I dragged the press. I kind of gave it a looking over, but—I don't know, something's out o' whack—I ain't figured out what."

Mollie's eyes darkened into concentration. "Well, now, sir, we're going to find out what's the matter with this thing!"

Both began studying it, Mollie bending over it, and Frank crouching with knees bowed out. He had set the press outside the woodshed, and the pleasant sunshine of early autumn burned down glossily upon their heads as they conjectured and tinkered.

"Think it's this here that needs tightening?"

"I think it is, Frank. Then I think she'll run."

Mate came out when she had finished the dishes and stood watching them. She looked slightly satirical, but she had brought out a hat and a sunbonnet, and she said:

"You better put these on your heads if you're going to stay out here."

The dryness of her tone made them both feel guilty. Mollie exclaimed:

"Say! I wonder what's the time."

"It ain't late," Frank assured her. "Let's finish the job. Course, I hate to take you away from your canvassing—"

"Oh, well," she told him, robustly, "that ain't the only thing on earth. I'd like to see you get this thing to working."

It was late enough, when Mate told them the time. Frank said:

"Well, the afternoon's gone now, anyway, Mollie. Better stay on and have supper with us, and make a day of it."

"I can't!" Mollie cried, in a panic. "I was going to stop at all those places along the road this afternoon. I haven't sold a thing to-day but these cotton stockings and one of my own samples. Well . . . oh, well, why not go the whole hog!"

She threw away her afternoon with splendid recklessness. Her eyes sparkled and she was warm with sunshine and happiness. She and Frank were like two children playing hooky from school. They tinkered with the cider press for another hour, coming at last to the conclusion that they couldn't make it go, anyway.

"But I found out what was wrong with it!" Mollie boasted, with a triumphant laugh. "I'll look for a bolt when I go through town, and then Frank can make his cider."

Frank told her, seriously:

"I sure am grateful to you, Mollie. Hope I haven't taken too much of your time."

She answered generously:

"Oh, shoot, Frank, forget it! It wasn't what I'd planned to do, but I guess it was just as good as selling a few stockings. You and Mate might just as well be enjoying some cider this winter."

She glowed under Frank's praise of her mechanical prowess.

When they had finished with the press, he wanted to take her to see his melons.

"Here's old Rastus! Why, what's the matter with him?"

"Oh, I don't know, he's hurt his paw some way," Frank said.

"Rastus! Did the old boy hurt himself? Well, that won't do!"

As soon as she reached the melon patch, Mollie sat down on the bare, hot ground, and took the dog's paw in her hands. The paw was swollen, and sand and burrs were tangled in the coarse, black fur. Frank told her: "Oh, I guess it'll heal up, Mollie," impatient to have her look at his melons. But that wouldn't do, for Mollie. Here was something that called for help, alive, and more absorbing than the cider press. She made Rastus go back with them to the house, and then called for warm water, a cloth, and a darning needle from Mate. Mate thought that was a dreadful fuss to make over a dog. Rastus yelped and snarled, so that Mate shrieked, "Be careful!" and even Frank was worried; but Mollie held him until she had got out the splinter.

"See there, what it was! No wonder! Now, old boy, just a minute—"

She laughed with triumph again. She forced Rastus to stay while she put salve on the wound and bound it up in her best surgical style. Frank laughed at her.

"How long do you think he'll keep that on?"

Still, he and Mate both, although they derided so much to-do over an animal, were glad to find out what was the matter with the dog and to have the splinter out.

"There now!" Mollie cried.

Mate was beginning to get the supper ready. Mollie remembered about the dishes—she was full of contrition and helpfulness.

"But there's always so much. If I'd done that, I couldn't have done the other things."

She insisted on gathering the eggs for Mate. Mate considered that a task: Mollie adored it. She hunted through old boxes with hay pushed into one corner, through folds of the harsh old dusty robe in the ancient cutter, through the mangers and the loft. She carried the eggs in a basket into the house through the low shafts of sunshine. The excitement of all her accomplishments was upon her still, of the praise and gratitude they had yielded her, and she sang, happily, and off the key.

"Well, I certainly didn't think when I stopped in here I was going to stay for supper! But I guess I've done a pretty good day's work of it, after all."

When Mollie came to leave, the glow and triumph of her visit were still upon her. She was taking more plunder with her: eggs, and a glass of fresh jelly, and an old rooster in a gunny sack mysteriously moving and plunging on the seat beside her.

"Now, you keep that sample, Mate," she was urging. "Frank, you try that suit when cold weather comes—you'll never wear anything else, I'll tell you that!"

"We sure are grateful, Mollie, for all the help you've given us—"

"Oh, shoot! Forget it!" But she glowed happily. "I think that press'll run now, Frank, when you get the bolt. Put some more of that salve on the dog's foot. He'll get some good out of it even if he does lick off most of it."

"Aren't you afraid to drive home alone at night?" Mate asked, fearfully.

"No! I enjoy it. There's nothing I like better in this world than to get off in this old car by myself, and get the wheel under my hands, and go it!" Mollie said, with shining eyes.

"Sure, you bet! That's the truth," Frank told her. "Mollie ain't one of these scared she-males that always think she's going to be run away with."

"You bet I'm not!"

She tried the starter, but it had a streak again, and wouldn't go.

"You crank it for her, Frank," Mate said anxiously.

Mollie cried:

"No, I'll crank the old beast, I'm used to it. Here, boy! Give me hold of that crank."

But Frank would not let her go. The car started, and Frank shouted at Mollie above the loud noise of the engine:

"Well, Mollie, we're glad you stopped. And we're sure grateful—"

"Now you forget it! If we can't do a few things for folks once in a while when we get the chance, why, what's the use? Well, I've had a fine day of it—and I'd like to know why that isn't just as good!"

"Sure!" Frank said heartily.

"You're going to get the engine heated," Mate told her.

"Well, good-by, folks!"

"Good-by, Mollie!"

She started with a suddenness that almost killed the engine—recovered, went on—and stuck her head out of the car, to Mate's horror, just as she was turning out of the driveway, to shout back to the dog:

"Good-by, old boy!"

Mate and Frank listened to the loud rattle of the car as it went on through the country stillness.

"Well, sir," Frank said with relish, and with a laugh, "she's a great Mollie!"

He thought over all Mollie's escapades, and the goldfish, and the violets, and laughed again.

"I bet she didn't do fifty cents' worth of business to-day. She'll have to hump when she gets to Chicago with Dorrie! Well, it's a good thing she's going, although I'll hate not to have her come around. Charlie and Luisa, you couldn't move with a derrick. If the town burned up, Charlie Schumacher wouldn't notice it as long as he could go on puttering with those bird houses."

"Well, I don't know what Mollie does so much more!"

"Fudge, Mate, she's got three times the get-up to her! Yes, sir, I'd like to see her to go to Chicago. Those girls haven't got a thing but that old place and what little salary Charlie gets. Now's Mollie's chance. Mollie may be left alone some day."

Frank felt satisfied. At last Mollie had a scheme that wasn't crazy. She was finally going to get to do something.

"She won't go," Mate said calmly.

"Why won't she?" Frank demanded belligerently.

The idea was a fine one. What was to stop Mollie this time?

"Because I know she won't."

Frank stopped to take this in. All at once he had a memory of the darkness of Mollie's eyes, warm and defenseless, and he seemed to see them mist with ready tears. Yes, sir, Mollie was a woman! After all, she was unaccountable. She could do anything for anybody but herself. Then Frank said, as if in defense of his own statements:

"Well, anyway, Mollie gets a darned good time out of it!"

Mate still had her look of small, calm, satisfied wisdom.

The last far-away rattle and hum of the car was lost, now, in the hugeness of the evening, and the crickets took up the sound in a thin, shrill, minor chorus.

THREE, COUNTING

THE CAT

Mrs. Hubbard was out among her flowers picking a bouquet to take over to Grandma Parkins. The summer garden was at its final loveliest now; and if she had to leave it for these next few days, there was no use in just letting it go to waste. All her flowers! She wondered if she could count on that little Dorothy across the street to remember to water them. She thought up anxious bribes and nice rewards, as her fingers thrust in among the thick leaves to find the hidden stems.

"Ouch!"

Something had nipped at her foot. But she smiled, knowing what it was even while she exclaimed.

"Yes, you!"

The kitten had followed her out into the garden, although she hadn't seen it come.

"You have to be with your mama, don't you?"

She supposed herself to be a silly old fool. She wouldn't have had any one else hearing her call herself "mama" to a cat. She with her four grown children! But after an unsatisfactory compromise with "mistress"—when she knew the kitten did just as it pleased—she had let herself lapse with humorous contentment and shame into the old word.

The kitten played around her as she picked the best of the flowers. It dashed in among the leaves and stems for bugs; leaped and turned over in the air after a small white butterfly;

crept and cautiously smelled the flowers; and then lay trust-fully blinking up from the warm dirt, waiting for petting. All the antics! Mrs. Hubbard wished that Ira could see her.

She had heard Ira wandering around the house a little while ago. She had better go in and hurry him up, set him to doing something, or he would be finding a reason why he couldn't go. They had everything arranged. Harold could take care of that creamery for three days. This was a trip that she had al-ways been wanting to take, and she wasn't going to let Ira slide out of it.

She said to the kitten, "You go and see if papa's getting ready."

Then she started for Grandma Parkins' with her flowers.

"Now, don't follow me."

Plants were set along the edge of the sloping, weathered porch next door. But they were a pretty seedy lot: a few slips of this or that in a dented can half bright and half rusty; a crooked geranium tied to a kindling stick; a flower pot filled with cracked, dried earth and a withered spear of something. Mrs. Hubbard had to smile a little at Grandma's array. Ancient silence lay behind the bulged screen door.

"Oh my, my, my! Such lovely flowers! Are you bringing them to me?"

"Ira and I are going away for a few days, and I thought you might as well be enjoying a few of these."

"Well, that's jist lovely! Now you wait till I bring a pitcher. Don't you go!"

Mrs. Hubbard sat down in the little old dining-room-sitting-room. The clock ticked in its case of smooth light wood, and out in the kitchen the old woman's steps went pattering about. An embroidered cloth hung down in neat points from the pushed-back, unused table. Mrs. Hubbard wondered. Could she ever bear to be alone like this? She had thought that she and Ira were lonely enough after Harold married, but it was nothing like this slowly measured solitude.

She saw a little face and whiskers at the door.

"Oh! You go back."

Grandma came in with the flowers crowded into a big, white, crockery pitcher with a triangle of hole in its lip. "Somebody at the door?"

Mrs. Hubbard laughed. "Oh, it's just our little cat."

"Yours? I thought Iry never liked cats."

"Oh, he always said so, but he's sillier about this one than I am."

"Yes, you can git awful attached. Let it come in if it wants to."

"No, it's run off. She's shy of every one but Ira and me."

"Well, you hain't said where you was going?"

"To the Falls," Mrs. Hubbard answered.

"Oh, ain't that lovely! It's real lovely up there. Haven't you ever been?"

"No, sir, we've lived here all these years and never seen them."

"It ain't so far."

"I know it isn't. But we just never seemed to get the time to go."

"You and Iry didn't go along when the Star had their picnic?"

"No, Harold was sick. One of the children, anyway."

"Well, now's your time," Grandma told her. "We've got that anyway when our children leave us."

"Yes. We have! . . . It's hard to leave a place, though, when you have it," Mrs. Hubbard added.

"Yes, there's always something. That's the truth. I only been to the Falls once, myself, and that was years ago. So I oughtn't to say much. I thought, I was always so kept down when the children were little, when they was grown me and

Mister would go places again. But I don't know—he didn't seem to care about it any more. Well, he didn't have his health. That was it. And now I don't care either. . . . But then you and Iry's young."

"We feel pretty old with five grandchildren!"

"Well, you wait till you get some 'greats'!"

"I sort of hate to go away just now and leave the garden. The flowers are right at their best. I almost wish I didn't have any garden. I wish I didn't have anything around the place."

"Oh, no, Myrtie, you wouldn't be satisfied."

"I don't see why I'm always tying myself down!" Mrs. Hubbard exclaimed discontentedly.

"Well, that's the way. We've all got to have something. We ain't satisfied, otherwise, seems. Ettie wanted me to stay with her last winter, but I don't know, I hated to leave the plants and all. I wouldn't go when it come to it. But you and Iry's not like me. You ought to go some while you're young."

"Oh, we're going! I want to go. I've always wanted to see the Falls. Think of living only forty miles from such a place and never getting there in your lifetime! It's absurd. Anyway I wouldn't disappoint the children. They're coming after us. No, I wouldn't let Ira go to the creamery this afternoon. I've got him staked out right at home where he can't find anything to keep him."

No, she hadn't reached the age of Grandma Parkins yet, at any rate! She guessed she and Ira had a little go left in them. Poor Grandma and her plants! Crossing the lawn, she glanced around for the kitten, but it didn't seem to be anywhere in sight. But she saw their place, the house so comfortable and trim in the midst of grass and trees and flowers—at its final, settled, established comfort now, exactly now, when only she and Ira were left in it. It was hard to believe that they were actually all alone there. But time had moved again—it had moved on from the awful, despairing dreariness after Harold left to a kind of equilibrium once more. This summer she had felt quite contented.

She went into the house. If they were going away, she ought to be getting some things together. She had boiled some eggs at breakfast and some potatoes yesterday. Now she would make her salad. She started to go about it, frowning, with the old slapdash fervor of the days of hot weather when she had four children and company besides in the house and was called upon at the last minute to contribute a cake to the church supper. She glanced around for the little cat. It liked to be given little pieces of cold potato.

"Tiger!"

She and Ira hadn't thought up any better name than that. But it was the funniest kitten! Of all the queer things that cat would and wouldn't eat! Mrs. Hubbard cut bits of potato and olive into the chipped white saucer. She couldn't keep from worrying over how it was going to get fed, and it seemed treacherous to anything so trusting to leave it to Dorothy's haphazard mercies. The little thing went leading her out to its saucer in the morning. The kitten often woke them up.

At first, it was taken for granted that they must have it stay outside at night. But it seemed so little. She didn't care what Ira said. It was raining the night they got it, and Mrs. Hubbard fixed a bed with gunny sacks out on the porch. But it wailed perseveringly. In the middle of the night she felt Ira start up, disheveled and angry, while she lay dutifully crushing down her sympathy.

"Where's that cat? I thought it was to be left outside."

"Ira! Where are you going to put it?"

It didn't do to demand an answer. So she lay and listened and tried to figure out the sounds. After a while, Ira came sneaking into bed again. She couldn't keep from it.

"Ira, what did you do with it?"

He answered, shamefaced: "Well, I thought maybe it was hungry. I can't be kept awake with that yowling!" and then turned over, and she refrained from comment or question.

There were no more sounds that night. She didn't really know until morning, when she found the kitten curled on Ira's old jacket on the kitchen floor. He had used the morning cream. But she was too delighted and stealthily triumphant to say a word. It gave her another example of how well she had learned to distinguish Ira's bark from his bite.

Now the kitten slept where it pleased. If they were too late in the morning, it wakened them by patting their cheeks with its paw. She believed that Ira, that old fool, stayed in bed so that it would come.

"Where are you?"

She looked around for it and thought of that big dog of Utley's. She was disgusted at herself. A lifetime of worrying over children, and now she had to worry over a cat!

Where was Ira, too? It was time he was taking the car to get it filled with gas. She called him—"Ira!"—thinking of all the excursions from which he had absconded, and wondering if he had dared to go back to that creamery.

"Well, for heaven's sake!"

She had found him sitting out in the car in the garage and reading through an old almanac that somebody had thrown on to the back porch.

"Is *this* all you can find to do?"

"Well, the kitten jumped on my lap."

Of all the excuses! She saw that little rascal now. No wonder it hadn't appeared. It blinked up at her with drowsy eyes, and kneaded its claws with smug contentment into Ira's trousers. What a sight for the children to see!

"Good heavens! Do you want the children to find you out here? They'll all be coming soon. I've got my salad all made.

I'm waiting for the rolls. I thought you were going to get gas an hour ago. Give me that kitten!"

She started back on an indignant march to the house, holding the kitten with stern hands in spite of scramblings. But she hesitated, and turned, and almost went back to the garage. They hadn't decided yet what to do with Tiger. Well, it was no use asking Ira. She could leave it well filled up anyway. In the house she set it firmly down to its dish.

"Now, eat!"

But she couldn't help smiling. That old snide of an Ira! To find him sitting there holding the cat! "The kitten jumped on my lap." Well, it was all they had. She didn't know that any one need blame them if they got some satisfaction out of it. And it had made the house a different place this summer— filled its silence with little scamperings and frolics, brought out the old foolish words they had put away or never dared to use with such abandoned freedom, set them up again in their old parental places, and given the home a tiny center that let the old contentment live again. It was eating olives and all! She wished that Ira could see.

Going up to her room, she started to dress in the same old hurry of the days when she used to have four children to look after before she could get dressed for church herself—as if to prove to herself that she was capable of it. The hurry seemed foolish in the settled quiet of the bedroom where Ira's shoes, that never in all these years had he learned to put in the closet, held a place beside the bed as precise as if that were really where they belonged. In the midst of it she heard a car, heard it driving up noisily beside the road, looked and saw Margaret's family getting out. They were all in festal array. She felt with excitement that she was going somewhere. The house filled suddenly with noise.

"Well, Mother! How are you? Ready? Where's Dad?"

"Gone down with the car to get some gas."

"Then you actually got him out of the creamery?"

"Oh, yes!"

Little Herbert gave a shout, and made a gleeful dash for the kitchen. "The little cat! See the little cat!"

Mrs. Hubbard cried hastily, "Oh, Herbert, you'll scare the little cat!"

She hurried out after him into the kitchen. A striped tail was just disappearing down the cellar stairway. She quickly and stealthily shut the door. Heavens! Was she protecting her kitten against her grandson? But Herbert was rough. She thought privately—it had to be privately—that her grandchildren were rougher than ever her own children had been permitted to be. And it was theirs, the kitten, hers and Ira's, not for her grandchildren to chase and torment. The children needn't know what fools their parents were. It was none of their business. She came back into the living room.

"You taking to cats, Mother?"

"Oh, we have this one."

"I thought it was one of Margaret's greatest bones of contention with Dad that he wouldn't let her have any pets."

"Hmp! You ought to see Dad."

She was going to tell them about finding Ira out in the car, but she stopped. She couldn't give Ira away. The children would think it a great joke, and so did she—a little joke—but to be smiled at by no one but herself.

"What kind of a cat do you have, Mother?"

"Oh, it's just a little tiger."

She began hastily to get them to talking about the trip.

"What do you think we ought to take in the line of wraps?"

"They say the Falls are a good bit larger than they were last year."

"I knew Grace's wouldn't be here yet when we got here."

"Well, just so they appear in time with that chicken!"

But she kept an eye on Herbert, and in the midst of the chatter she found herself half missing the quiet that had filled the summer rooms.

Mr. Hubbard appeared silently in the living room.

"Well, Dad! We were beginning to wonder. Thought you might have absconded again."

"Just went for gas. It's clouding up a little, though, outside."

A hoot went up from the children.

Mr. Hubbard sat unmoved.

"Clouds, nothing!" John declared, coming back from the porch.

"Aren't there any clouds?"

"Oh, Dad might call them that, I guess." John sat down again.

"Pretty bad roads out that way," Mr. Hubbard observed.

"Bad roads? You're behind the times, Dad. They got those all graded this spring."

"Don't you let him go back on us, Mother!"

"Oh, he's just talking."

Mr. Hubbard made no comment. After a moment he got up and went out to the kitchen, and Mrs. Hubbard followed him.

"Did you bring me the rolls?"

He silently handed them out to her.

"What else is that you got?"

He was looking around for the kitten. "Where's Tiger? I thought I'd leave him a little hunk of kidney to chew on."

"Goodness! She's had enough already to founder her."

"Well, he won't get much maybe while we're gone."

"I don't know whether you can get hold of her," Mrs. Hubbard said. "She ran down cellar when Herbert came out here."

"Herbert after him?"

"Oh, just wanted her. Tiger got scared. After *her*, Ira. Oh, dear, you'll never say it!"

"Oh, well, what difference does it make?"

"We may find some day it makes quite a difference!" Mrs. Hubbard observed.

She began to pack their basket. Margaret came into the kitchen.

"Where's Dad?"

"I don't know just where he is."

But she had a good idea. If it hadn't been too mean, and if she hadn't known that she was about as bad herself, she would have liked Margaret to overhear some of the consolation that had just been going on in the cellarway.

"Did he get scared, the little rascal? He'll stay down here. That's right. His old pop won't let anybody find him." (His "pop"! That old fool of an Ira! Well, they were a pair of them!)

He came up from the cellar stairs, dry and noncommittal as always.

John asked from the doorway, where he was leaning and smoking, "Go down cellar in case of storm, Dad?"

"Ump." He went on into the other room.

John wandered out into the yard to look things over, and presently was back again. "Well, Dad's cloud is getting bigger!"

But the other car was arriving. It drove up noisily, packed with children and provisions, and the other family—Grace's— came roistering out. These were a country set.

"Bring the chicken?"

"Brought two of them!"

"We brought chickens and eggs and—"

"Sh! You don't need to tell it all."

"Say! We've just been waiting for you. Threshing done, Bert?"

"All done."

"They get it done early these days. A farmer never used to be able to leave at this time of year."

"Oh, Bert and I always leave to have a good time."

The talk and laughter filled the house as loudly as when the children were all at home and getting ready for a high-school picnic. Mrs. Hubbard almost felt the illusion of those old days. The girls seemed to be taking charge of the kitchen, and she let them. She felt a little out of it.

Mother oughtn't to have prepared so much, they said.

"Why not?" she demanded. "I've got more time than the rest of you."

This was the old gay hubbub that she had missed so dreadfully after the children had left. But it seemed noisy to her now. It seemed at a distance. She had the queer feeling that it was she who had finally been weaned from her children. She had grown used to the fact that they had their own concerns— and it might even be that she and Dad had theirs!

She went to the door and looked at Dad's cloud that was distinctly visible to more than Dad now. She didn't like to admit that it worried her, because she had always had to hold out against Ira's concern over weather. But she considered that John and Bert were reckless drivers. Well, perhaps any one would seem a reckless driver after Ira, who coddled his car as if it had been an old horse ready to drop in its tracks. The boys never thought of paying any attention to rain. They would laugh at any anxiety.

She wandered off from the commotion in the kitchen and into the living room. From there she could see her flowers blooming. A breeze rustled the leaves of the magazines on the porch. A queer, regretful homesickness possessed her. It was as if she were leaving more than the house and the cat and the garden—as if she were putting an end to the contentment that she and Ira had found in the old place this summer.

It had been there before at certain static periods, like summer light over everything—when the children were all in school, when for a few weeks, after they had begun to scatter, she had them all together again for the last time; but it was something she could never make or hold—it had simply come. When she had thought it was gone forever—they were too old, their household was broken, their children gone—it had come silently swinging back and enveloped the two in its happiness.

It was altered and shifted now, the long, low light of late afternoon across the grass; but an aspect of the same, and not less happy; happier, if anything, because it was something like a gift—good measure, the hundred and one, the Indian summer. The household had only the vestiges of its old abundance—but a lingering touch, a hint, a memory, was enough now to keep contentment poised, to bear within it and around it the sense of all that had gone before.

Why were they going racing off in the rain to look at a waterfall?

Ira came in from a silent survey of the weather. "Say, Mother, those clouds look pretty bad."

In revulsion she gave him the look of indignation that he expected. Were they going to back out now? He was ashamed to say anything more. But he wandered restlessly from door to window, and, a little later, she heard him go surreptitiously down the cellar stairs and come up again. Like a conspirator, remembering the exile, she met him at the doorway.

"Did you see her?"

"Nope. Under something, I guess."

They were whispering.

"We haven't decided yet what to do about feeding her."

He evaded that. Besides, the whole tribe was trooping in from the back yard where it had just been congregated.

"Well, sir, it really is raining!" Even John had to say that.

"Can we go?" the girls cried anxiously.

"Sure! Who stops for rain? It'll all be over tomorrow."

And with added hilarity, the children racing and shouting, they began to take the things out to the cars.

"Get ready, Mother!" some one was commanding.

Mrs. Hubbard went to the bedroom for her wraps. Mr. Hubbard, after more wandering and a brief excursion to the car, followed and encountered her as she stood putting on her hat before the mirror. She had been waiting for it.

"Look here, Myrtie, I hate to set out like this."

He had expected one withering blast of indignation and stood sheepishly prepared for it, unable, in spite of it, to refrain from uttering his caution.

She had a wild desire to laugh. "*Ira!*"

"Well, it's a fact just the same."

"Oh, you never fail!"

He answered testily: "I haven't said we wouldn't go. I've just said it was a bad time to start out."

He was at the window again and missed the hasty gleam of relief in her eyes. Then she cried, thinking of a hundred past times—of ties and claims and withdrawals and duties and last-minute accidents,

"Oh, that's the way it always must go!"

She took off her hat and flung it on the bed and her hand bag beside it—the hat that she wouldn't have bought this summer if she hadn't expected to be going somewhere. Mr. Hubbard stood abashed and convicted.

"With all this stuff fixed!" she stormed. "With the children out there and waiting!"

"Well, Mama, if you're so set on it . . ."

She said despairingly: "No, we won't go. You'll be fussing. We won't have a moment's peace. I knew it."

"We'll go then."

"No, we won't."

"I said I'd go."

"Oh, keep still, Ira. You know we aren't either of us going."

Three, Counting the Cat · 243

Plunged in guilt, he could only stand and watch her put the hat back in the closet, take her handkerchief out of the bag, and snap the bag together. But his relief was deeper than his guilt—which made him all the more guilty. He turned and went discreetly down the stairs.

Mrs. Hubbard stayed and hung her wrap in the closet. There was no need to hustle around any more. They could take their leisure. The brief storm had relieved her feelings, and up here alone for a moment she did not have to deny her shameful relief to herself. So here they were again, like a pair of old fools, happy to get out of a good time and stick in the same place where they had been sticking for thirty years! She wouldn't have to lose her flowers. Ira wouldn't have to miss a day from that old creamery. She wouldn't have to make plans for the little cat. They could let it up from the cellar. What a couple!

As she went downstairs to face her children, a clap of thunder came to give a reasonableness to her excuses that they did not deserve. She accepted it thankfully. But the chorus of protest was all that she had expected.

"Mother!"

To back out of a trip like this for a few drops of rain—because it happened to thunder! They would have expected it of Dad, but they had thought better of Mother. The roads all graveled, except fifteen miles or so, and if Dad couldn't navigate those, Marvin, the ten-year-old, would drive them for him.

"I said I'd go," Mr. Hubbard affirmed mildly from a rocker. "Mother's the one. She took off her hat."

"Well, Mother, you put it on again. Don't you let Dad beat you out of this."

No, she didn't want to put on her hat. It was off now.

"Dad won't be happy."

"Don't put it on to me!"

"Well, we aren't going, anyway."

She was ashamed to feel that the children were so disgusted—more ashamed because it was Ira whom they were blaming.

Little Herbert started to wail, "Aren't grandma and grandpa going?"

She kissed him and tried to console him, but nothing could move her now.

They needn't drive, Grace pleaded. Dad needn't risk his car. They could squeeze in with her and Bert.

No, they weren't going. That was all there was to it.

The children, in disgust and despair, refused to wait for the shower to let up, and scurried out to the cars through the downpour—Grace running back, to her mother's shame, to leave cake and roast chicken for consolation. The parents stood safely in the doorway watching the start, Mrs. Hubbard guiltily imagining the sputterings of the sons-in-law, until the cars had left.

They sat down on the porch. They did not look at each other. The rain was changing quickly from a beating shower into a mild, steady downpour that might easily let up before evening and might with luck keep up until night.

Mr. Hubbard said, "You needn't blame me."

She had taken up her sewing. She did not reply.

"I don't trust what the boys call good driving. May be worse, too, over in those hills. They may see themselves stuck before evening."

He tried to take up a magazine, but he was too uneasy to read about either business or new inventions. He wandered around again and then stopped near her chair. He couldn't quite make out what she was thinking.

"Well, we can go some other time, Mama."

A skeptical lift of one eyebrow, but still no reply.

"It's no fun to be off somewhere in a storm. No telling

where we'd been staying. Who wants to traipse around to see a waterfall in the rain!"

She turned for her scissors. "Oh, sit down, Ira. You're the one that's doing the fussing, not me."

Her tone was as unexpectedly mild as the rain, that was now only a veil between them and the scented freshness of the summer lawn. This rain was just what things had been needing. He lay down in the porch hammock and after a while reached over and with a grunt of contentment took off his shoes. Her smile was faintly satirical as she heard them thump on the floor. He turned over the pages of the magazine, thought of going down to the creamery and decided he needn't, and finally said:

"Well, let's go in. It's getting damp out here. I'd like some supper."

In the kitchen she unpacked their basket and put the things away. She took out the silver tied with picnic threads of scarlet, and hung up the tin cups on their nails. He stood and watched her uneasily. She emptied the twists of salt and pepper into their own cans and set aside a small dish of potato salad—she had given the rest to the children.

"Disappointed, Mother?"

She wouldn't answer.

But it was still herself at whom she was disgusted—if she was disgusted at all. She wouldn't let herself admit the relief of being in her own kitchen. All this cooking that she had done! But the children would enjoy the salad. They could drive as fast as they pleased over those hills. They would have enough to worry about with their own children. With the salad that she had kept, and all that chicken that Grace had given her, there wouldn't be much cooking for her to do for the rest of the week. She and Ira could take it easy. It would give them a kind of holiday of their own.

"Let the kitten up."

Poor little thing! It needn't stick down there in the cellar. The house was quiet enough now. Ira came bringing it up the stairs.

"He was 'way back under the house. I saw two big eyes staring at me. He was right at the edge of the cistern. We've got to get that thing covered." (When she had been at him to cover that cistern for years!) "Hear the little rascal purring! Look at the cobwebs in his whiskers. Look here, Mother! Here's some one glad we didn't go, anyway."

"Yes, I expect so," she answered dryly.

But when Ira had gone out to close the garage, she bent down and petted and herself consoled the little cat that rubbed off the cobwebs against her shoe. Well, it wouldn't be wailing about an empty house for food, anyway. They would look silly telling people that they hadn't gone, after all! Taking those flowers to Grandma Parkins! Harold would be the worst. But they didn't have to explain things to the cat, anyway. Ira came in just as she was putting down a piece of chicken.

"We might as well," she defended herself. "Grace left us more than we can eat."

She had set out a supper—salad, chicken, those fresh rolls—on the kitchen table that she herself had lately painted in blue and white from a design in the household magazine. She had heated on the gas stove some cocoa that steamed up richly from the cups, and made a centerpiece of the nasturtiums left unwilted from the "bouquet" that Herbert had picked and strewn.

Ira washed his hands and sat down at the table. "Disappointed, Myrtie?" he asked again.

The rain pattered on the low kitchen roof that was part of the old first house standing long before they had built on and remodeled. It was the same room where they had sat down to their first meals together, but now at last they had it fixed just as they wanted it. Then there had been just the two of them—and now there were just the two. Except for the little cat.

Well, that was somebody! She heard it growling over its chicken. Now they couldn't feel quite themselves unless they had something to look after between them. This was the Ira that she had discovered and cherished, unknown to people who saw a dry little man running a creamery—going contrary in indulgent practice to all he might agree with in public as fixed principle. He had his peculiarities, but he would do for her. If they wanted to play a little now with the old, accomplished responsibility, take their old parts again behind the scenes for no one but each other, who was to know or to stop them? Who but themselves!

They listened with satisfaction to the mild continuance of the rain. The chicken tasted better here than it would have heaven knew where.

The little cat tipped the dish in the effort to get the last piece. A last piece after the last slipped down surreptitiously to the floor from Ira's hand. She saw it. She smiled inside to hear him say with satisfaction,

"Well, we won't have to find any one to feed the little rascal, anyway."

MIDWESTERN

. . . .

PRIMITIVE

. . . . . .

Bert went flying over to get May Douglas to come and look at her table. It was all ready now, and she had to show it to some one. There was nobody at home who knew or cared about such things. Everything that she did there was done against indifference or opposition.

"May! Busy? Want to come and see the table now I've got it fixed?"

"Oh, yes!"

May was delighted. She left her ironing where it was and followed Bert with eager excitement. She was one of the people in Shell Spring who stuck up for Bert Statzer. She thought that Bert was a wonder.

"We'll go right through the kitchen. Smells kind of good, don't it? There! Do you like it?"

"Bert!"

May was fairly speechless. She gazed at the table with fervent, faded eyes. It seemed to her the most beautiful thing she had ever seen. She didn't see how Bert managed it!—how she ever thought of such things and how she learned to do them. Bert was just a genius, that was all.

"You really think it looks nice?"

Bert drank in May's admiration thirstily. She knew it didn't amount to much, that May would admire anything she did; but she had to get appreciation from somewhere.

"I think it's just too beautiful for words. You little marvel!"

She hugged Bert's thin, tense little form in fond worship. "I just don't see how you do it!" She sighed.

"Well, I'm glad you think it looks nice." Bert relaxed, with a long gratified sigh; but stiffened again to say to Maynard, who had tagged them into the dining room, "Be careful, Maynard! If you move one of those things—!"

May was looking at everything: the little fringed napkins of pink crepe, the tinted glass goblets that Bert had sent away for, the spray of sweet peas at every place, one pink and then the next one lavender, made of tissue paper—such a pretty idea! She had never seen any napkins like those. Bert went on talking excitedly.

"Well, if it's good enough for these folks, it'll be good enough for any one. I'll think that I've arrived, May!"

"I don't see how it can help—"

"Oh, but they're real big bugs. I've never had any one from Des Moines before. It scares me. This looks nice to us, but those people have all seen things—oh, my! Then, you know, they're going to have that famous writer with them. That's what I'm so excited about. If he likes it, then I thought maybe I could use his name. You know that'll help to get me known— if I can get his recommendation. Like those cold cream ads and everything—they're all doing that. Oh, I'm so excited, May! Feel my hands? Aren't they cold?"

"Why, you poor child!" May took Bert's tense, thin little hands and rubbed and fondled them. "You don't need to feel that way. I don't see how anybody could ask for anything nicer. If *this* isn't good enough for them—"

"Oh, I know, but people like that who have been places and seen things—! Well, I don't care, I've done the best I could. Maynard, look *out!*"

Bert's face was still gratified but screwed with worry. She knew how she really wanted things to look. She wanted flowered curtains instead of these old ones, and little painted tables instead of this big old thing. . . Of course, here was this stuck-in-the-mud little burg always holding her back, and her mother, and Arlie . . . Well, *she* didn't intend to be stuck in the mud, anyway! She had put up her sign where people could see it. "Hillside Inn." It made people in town laugh. They wanted to know where the "hillside" was. But she'd made a go of it so far, all the same.

She burst out: "The only trouble is mother!" And that was true. She couldn't do a thing with mother. Arlie would stay out—he didn't want folks like that to see him in his old working clothes—but mother thought she had to go in and entertain them, just the way she did with any one who came to the house. "I was so ashamed when those people from Cedar Rapids were here. The way mother came in! Now, of course May, I know mother's good as gold and means it the best in the world, but what do folks like that think of her? I can't get her to fix herself up or anything. She doesn't understand. 'Ach, well, if they don't like the way I look, then they can look at something they do like.' That's the way she is. She doesn't *see* things. She doesn't know one person from another—doesn't see why these people are any different from any others." May kept making little distressed murmurs. She did know how Mrs. Hohenschuh was. "Now, May, I went and bought a nice up-to-date dress for her, like people are wearing, when I was in Dubuque last. She'd look awfully nice in it if she'd wear it. But do you think she will? No, sir. Won't so much as put it on. 'Ach, I never wore anything like that. I'll stick to what I been wearing.' You don't know, May—" Bert's voice tightened into bitterness—"nobody does, they all talk about how good-hearted mother is, and everything like that, they don't know how stubborn she is. Honestly, if mother didn't want to move, I don't believe a motor-cycle running into her could budge her one inch! She's just hopeless."

"Oh well, Bert, it'll come out," May said soothingly.

"I suppose. But she gives these people who come here the wrong idea. I don't want them to think we're all like she is."

"Oh, well, I guess they won't think that about you!"

Bert felt encouraged after May's visit. It was nice to have somebody appreciate what she was trying to do, anyway! She was excited, flying around the kitchen, doing the last few things, watching out for Maynard so that he would keep his little suit clean. Where was mother?—she thought in exasperation. Oh, there!—out in the garden—*digging*! Why didn't she come in and get ready? Bert had no time now to run out after her. Bert snatched a look at the clock. Almost time for them to get here! Oh dear, but she did want everything just right. What was mother thinking of? Did she want to get caught looking like that? She was hopeless. "Maynard, if you don't keep away from that table—!" Bert thought she would go crazy.

Then mother came serenely waddling in.

"Want I should help?"

"Not at this late date!"

That was all Bert was going to say. But she couldn't hold in, even if it was more of a triumph to be simply cold and cutting and bitter; she had to let it all out.

"Here I am working, trying to get everything nice, with everything all fixed, and you don't care, you just go on with your old digging out there in the garden, and don't see or care!"

Mrs. Hohenschuh looked abashed. "Ach, well," she began; then she retorted: "Well, I ain't wanted around here. You wouldn't be satisfied anyway with things the way I'd do them. Ach, all this fuss! What are you making all this fuss about? All this business!"

She finished with an angry mutter, and went waddling off to the door. Bert didn't know whether she was going to change her clothes or not. Well, if she wanted them to catch her looking that way, if she didn't care, didn't know any better . . . Bert was left weak and trembling with anger. She flew about the kitchen, put a few more nuts on each plate of salad, with shaking fingers changed her old apron for the bright green smock she was going to wear to do the serving . . . it was what they were wearing; it was like the one she'd seen in the photograph of "Betty Lee's Tearoom" in the cooking magazine. . . .

She went into the dining room. The shining glasses twinkled up at her, the sweet peas were rosy and stiff, the dishes looked so nice, the little napkins were so pretty . . . was everything right? She had got ideas wherever she could, but was she sure? It had to be right! Everything was so lovely. Her anger and fear changed into a shining glory. The whole table dazzled before her eyes. She caught hold of Maynard who was tagging her. "Look, Maynard!" she cried. "Isn't our table pretty?" She snatched a kiss from him in her trembling happiness.

Then she heard a car outside on the road. The people were coming!

A large green car rolled up to the cement block that still stayed in the thick grass beside the road as a relic of horse and buggy days. Bert in her green smock stood waiting, a tense dynamic little person with her thin face and shining black eyes and short black hair threaded with early white. It seemed to her that it took the people a long time to get out of the car. She had time to wonder and to agonize over the place— the old frame house . . . she wished they could have it stuccoed . . . what would these people think? Then the people were out and coming up the walk, and she had just a confused, eager sight of two men and three women. . . .

One man was in advance. A large man with a rosy face and shell-rimmed glasses, smooth blackish-gray hair—he came toward her smiling. That must be the one who had ordered the dinner, the Des Moines man, Mr. Drayton.

"Mrs. Statzer?" Yes, that was who he was. "We heard you gave such good meals here that we thought we'd have to stop and try one of them."

Bert was so pleased and flattered that she scarcely heard his introductions—forgot the names just as soon as he mentioned them. She had been trying from the first to pick out the writer. It was that tall man, then, with the thick gray hair. She hadn't expected him to look like that, somehow. She wanted to show him that she knew who he was, even if most of the people here in town didn't. They hadn't known whom she had meant when she said Harry Whetstone was coming here. She held out her hand, alert and eager.

"Oh, this is the writer, is it? I certainly was honored when I heard we were going to entertain you. I haven't read any of your works yet, but I intend to—I don't get much time for reading . . ."

"No hurry, no hurry," the writer said with affable nonchalance.

She was looking, too, at the women. She hadn't got the relationships between the women and men figured out yet. One looked older, one wore that smart little green dress and hat, and then there was that one who might be any age—where did *she* come in? They were looking around. "Isn't this lovely!" one of them was saying. What did they mean? Bert's brilliant eyes were watching them. She wondered what they thought of her sign. People in town made such fun of that sign. They were pointing to that terrible old brown tile in which mother had some geraniums planted. "Look, Harry! Isn't that lovely?" They couldn't really think it was *lovely*. Lovely had a different, suspicious meaning as these women used it. Bert's eyes were devouring the details of their clothes. She led them into the house. She was burning with anxiety, sensitiveness, eagerness. She knew how many things were wrong.

"I suppose you people would like to wash a little after your drive. We haven't any bathroom, I'm sorry to say, we want to have one, but this town is so slow, they've never piped the water out this far . . . But if you don't mind just washing in the old-fashioned washbowls—"

She hated that so. But they were nice about it. She was relieved.

"You know you're out in the country," she said with a nervous laugh, "and you have to take us the way you find us."

She ushered the women into her best bedroom, the guest room off the parlor. This was the one room in the house in which she could take some pride. She didn't mind showing them this room. She had fixed it up with furniture she had enameled herself, and white curtains with green ruffles, and she had put the stencil on the walls—all after the plan of the Model Bedroom she had seen in the household magazine for which she had taken subscriptions last winter.

"Now, if you'll just take off your hats and put them wherever you find a place—" She was eager and flustered. "I'm afraid I'll have to take you gentlemen upstairs."

"Well, now, can't we go out and give our hands a little shower bath under the pump?" Mr. Drayton asked genially.

Bert was horrified. He meant it for a joke, though. She was ashamed to take them up to her old room, full of horrid old dark furniture . . . was afraid, too, as she sped up the steep stairs ahead of them, although she knew it was all right, she had been up at four o'clock cleaning and getting the house ready. She banged the door of her mother's room shut as she went past. "Now I think you'll find everything—" She ran down.

The women were murmuring in the bedroom. She heard a soft laugh. She lingered in the front room, sensitive and alert, but she couldn't hear. The smartness of their clothes actually hurt her, showed her all sorts of unsuspected deficiencies in herself—although it pleased and gratified her too.

But when she went into the dining room and saw the table, she was exultant again. "If you'll excuse me," she called, "I'm afraid I'll have to be in the kitchen." They answered: "Oh, certainly!" She was in a flush of happiness. They were nice! Oh, dear. She had forgotten to ask the author to write in her visitors' book. Well, she would! And yet she was obscurely hurt and smarting. She wasn't sure they weren't laughing.

In the kitchen, she hustled about. Arlie had come in and was washing his hands at the wooden sink. "Well, are they here?" he asked. He didn't exactly like their coming, or to have Bert always fussing around with things like this—he didn't see why she wanted to do it—but then, he was all right, he kept out of the way. Bert was getting the roast chicken out of the oven. Roasted not fried. She thought that was what these people were used to. "People in the East never think of *frying* chicken." She remembered hearing Mrs. Elliott say that when she came home from the East. Bert wanted these people to be able to say they had eaten as good a meal here in the Hillside Inn as ever they had got in any city restaurant. She had taken recipes out of cooking magazines. She was so excited now that the ordeal was on that she felt herself working in a kind of tense calm. She could manage everything, nothing could upset her. She gave Arlie his dinner in the back kitchen. These people, with this famous author, were even a notch above those wealthy people from Dubuque whom she had served, and who had told Mr. Drayton about the place. If she could make *them* satisfied—!

"You can come in to dinner now."

There was a moment of quiet and formality as she seated them. They didn't exclaim like those Dubuque people. "Well, well, I didn't know we were going to find a first-class hotel here in Shell Spring!" the Dubuque man had cried. But then, these were a different kind of people. She served them, wondering if she oughtn't to have got in Donna Peterson to help her—but then, Donna wouldn't "know," and she wanted things right. She didn't talk as she was serving. She tried to remember what things should go to the right and what to the left. When she went out into the kitchen, she ordered Maynard to keep back. She was going to bring him in after the meal, all dressed up in his new little suit, and just introduce him. "This is my little boy Maynard." She had read somewhere that that was the way people did other places.

Through her preoccupation with the food and the serving—wondering if everything tasted just right—she heard snatches of the conversation. It was low-toned. The people seemed a little tired, maybe from that long drive. "Well, this is familiar." What did they mean by that? Did they like the little napkins or were they laughing at them? But those napkins were exactly the kind that were used in all the tearooms now! They must be right. "Standardization, I tell you. It gets into all corners." That meant nothing to Bert. They certainly must like these salads that May Douglas had said were simply too beautiful to be eaten. Nice salads were things people here in town didn't want to fuss with—"all those do-dads," mother said. The people were all affable and talking among themselves, and yet Bert could sense that the dinner didn't seem to be going just exactly as it should, and she couldn't see why. Her thin cheeks were flushed. In the kitchen, it was as if she were working in a vacuum, not in that shining flush of triumph she knew and craved. How fast everything was going—how soon this great dinner would be over!

Mrs. Hohenschuh had come into the kitchen from the back way. "Mother, you went and put on that old percale dress of yours, and I had that new one all laid out for you ready!" That seemed the crowning catastrophe. Bert suddenly began to tremble with anger. When she came into the kitchen the next time, she whispered furiously. "You aren't going to let those people see you in that! Since you had to go put it on, just to be stubborn, you can stay out of sight." How could she ever get anywhere with all this family to pull up after her? Mother looked like an old farm woman. Bert felt trembly and ready to cry and could scarcely bear to hear the quiet sound of the voices in the dining room.

The coffee cups were all set out on the little old sewing table that she was using for a serving table. She was going to serve her coffee with dessert, the right way. "Ach, let 'em have their coffee!" Mrs. Hohenschuh pleaded. She thought it was terrible to deprive people of coffee all through a meal. She didn't much mind Bert's reproaches, either. "Ach, Bert, she always gets so cross when she's got anything to do, I don't know." The old lady made off into the garden. But Bert knew how mother was. It would be a miracle if she let any people get away without talking to them—and probably telling them the whole family history!

Bert took in the fragrant coffee and the homemade ice cream. They *must* like that. They did, too. They were much more complimentary. The woman in the cute green dress (she didn't seem to be the author's wife, after all; that was the one that didn't look nearly so much like "somebody"—it surprised Bert) said very flatteringly: "What delicious ice cream! Did you make it yourself?" The older woman—that was Mrs. Drayton—smiled up at Bert. They all praised the ice cream. The talk was freer now. The author seemed to be saying the least of any of them, though. That seemed funny to Bert. Mr. Drayton was lots more talkative and full of fun—peppier. She bet he could write awfully good stories, better than the other one, if he just wanted to.

She was almost happy, when she happened to look out of the window and saw mother climbing up from the cellarway outside, lugging something—a bottle! Oh, for . . . Before she got any chance to get out to the kitchen, the old lady came shy but beaming into the room, with a great big bottle of that dandelion wine. Bert was in torment. As if these people cared for anything like that!

But there mother stood and there was nothing to do but introduce her. Bert suffered agony. It was all the worse, somehow, that they were being so polite and nice. "This is my mother." Mother began to beam at that. She loved to entertain people . . . that was all right, of course, but then she had never learned that people didn't do things the way she used to any more.

And mother was starting right in.

"Well, I thought it was mean you folks had to go all that time without your coffee, so I just brought you something else to drink." That awful old dandelion wine—mother was so proud of it! Bert hated it. "If you ain't afraid somebody's going to get after you—ach, it's all so funny these days—maybe you'll take a little drink of this wine. It's dandelion. I made it."

Bert couldn't stand it. She made for the kitchen. She sat down there, clenched her fists, and felt that she would actually fly to pieces.

The voices were louder in the dining room. She heard delighted laughter. Yes, now mother had some folks there, she had an audience, and she was just laying herself out for them—Bert knew how! She burned with humiliation. The whole thing was spoiled. How could anybody in this town try to do things the way they ought to be done?

Her mother came smiling out to the kitchen.

"Where are them little glasses gone?"

"Mother, why did you have to go in there with that stuff?"

"Ach, what are you fussing about? They like it."

After a while, Bert got up and began feverishly to get the messy plates cleaned off and stacked together. She couldn't eat a thing herself, not even good little crisp bits of chicken that were left. A lump in her throat was choking her. Mother had hold of them now. She heard them leave the dining room, and then the whole party trailed past the kitchen windows. Mother was waddling in the lead. She was going to take the whole bunch out and show them her flower beds.

Maynard was whining. "Are you going to take me in and introduce me, mother?"

Bert looked at him, cold and remote.

"No. I'm not going to introduce *any*-body."

They were all out in the garden. Mrs. Hohenschuh always thought it her duty as a hostess to take her guests out and show them everything she had. Here where she felt that she "had things nice," too—this place in town which she and Mr. Hohenschuh had bought when they moved in from the country—she could take real enjoyment with visitors . . . even if Bert did go on about the place and say how behind the times it was now. But it was a long time since she had got hold of any people as appreciative as these. Most folks came to see Bert. They only pretended to like the kind of things she had in her garden. These people were really enjoying it. Mrs. Hohenschuh expanded.

"Well, I don't know as there's anything you folks'll care much about looking at—" (she didn't mean that; she said it in a rich, comfortable tone)—"I only got the same old kind of flowers I've always had, they ain't any of these new-fangled kinds with fancy names here—"

"Oh, we adore seeing them!" the woman in the green dress cried enthusiastically.

Mrs. Hohenschuh beamed. "Well, I think they're pretty nice, they suit me, but there's lots of folks nowadays wants different things, I guess. Ja. Anyway, that don't worry me. I let 'em talk. I go on doing things the way I want to."

The people all laughed and she was gratified.

"Well, here's what I got! I put in all these things myself.

Bert, she don't want to bother. She's got too many irons in the fire all the time."

"This is lovely!"

Mrs. Hohenschuh stood fat and beaming while they looked and wandered about. She thought her garden was pretty nice— ja, you bet she did! And these folks all seemed to think so too. Why, they was awful nice folks! Why had Bert got so fussed up over having them here for dinner? Why, they was real nice and common! That one in the green dress (she was older than she wanted to let on, too, Mrs. Hohenschuh shrewdly judged) did the most running around and palavering! but those other two, that husband and wife, enjoyed things just as much. The man in the glasses was *real* nice. Well, so was his wife, although she didn't have so much to say. But those other two, she kind of liked the best of the bunch. The woman was real sensible, the things she said and the questions she asked! and the man kind of trailed around after the others, and looked at things on his own account, the way Mrs. Hohenschuh liked to have folks do. That showed he wasn't putting it on, he was really enjoying himself.

Along with her answers and her explanations, Mrs. Hohenschuh managed to get in a good part of the family history. Bert had a fit when she told things like that; but Mrs. Hohenschuh never felt right until she'd . . . well, kind of given folks the facts and the right idea about the family. They'd hear it all anyway, so she might as well tell it herself.

"Have you had your garden long, Mrs. Hohenschuh?"

"Ja, ever since we moved into town. That's—how long is it a'ready?—ach, it's twenty years, I guess! Bert, she was only just in high school, then. That was partly why we come. The boys, they didn't get to finish, but Pa he said Bert was to get her diploma, he was going to see to it, she was always the smartest, anyway. Ja, how old was Bert then? She was seventeen, I guess. She's thirty-seven now. Ja, she's such a thin little sliver, I don't know, women seems to want to be that way now, but she's thirty-seven! Her and Arlie's been married twelve years a'ready—and then this here little fellow's all they've got! Ach, I don't know!"

As she talked, all in her deep comfortable voice rich with chuckles and drolleries of German inflection, she waddled about among the flower beds, pointing out this kind and that. "These? Moss roses, I call 'em. I guess that ain't the right name, some folks say not, but they grow just the same—ain't that so? Ja, the old lady Douglas over there, when she was living, she had to have the right names for all her plants, but I told her mine grew better'n hers did if I did call 'em wrong! Ach, these names I know 'em by, them are the ones I like to call 'em!" The moss roses in their flat matted bed on the hot earth were gay spots of scarlet and crimson and yellow and cerise and white. They made one of the women think of the colors in old-fashioned patchwork quilts, she said.

"She's got the real old honest-to-God peppermint! I haven't smelled any of that for years. Come here, Mary!"

"Peppermint? Ja! That I always have. That I like too."

The woman in the green dress came running and clutched the other younger woman. "Come here, Jean! I want to show you. The pump! Isn't that just right? And see here—all these little flower pots set out and slips started in them . . . just see, this foliage stuff, this old red and green funny leaf stuff, my grandmother used to have that. And look back there! One of those great big green wire flower stands that I suppose used to stand in the bay window. Didn't you just *yearn* to take your dolls promenading on that, and they wouldn't let you, because you might spoil the plants? Isn't this *per*-fect?" Mrs. Hohenschuh had told them, "Ja, sure, you look around anywhere you want to, what's the use of hiding what you got?" Charlie Drayton was enjoying the old lady's naïve revelations, but the other man lounged about poking into the woodshed where the light fell dim and dusty through a little square window high up in the wall, and into a tool shed where pans of seeds were set about in the midst of a clutter of ancient furniture. It was like going back thirty years.

There was a little apple orchard at the side, grown up to tall grass now; and there, on one of his silent excursions, he discovered a two-foot china troll plated down in a tiny hollow with grass grown about his base as it binds in ancient tombstones, and a little casual offering of fallen apples about his chipped feet. He stood looking at it. The woman in the green dress saw him and came running over.

"What have you found, Harry? *Oh!* Oh, isn't that *marvelous?* Oh, Mrs. Hohenschuh, we've found something simply wonderful, won't you tell us what that is?"

Mrs. Hohenschuh wandered over. "That? Ach, is that old thing still out there? Ja, it's funny, but then, I don't know . . . Pa, he was the one that got that thing."

"It's German, isn't it?"

"Ja, it's German, all right. Pa, he come from the old country, he come over here when he was only eighteen years old, he had just twenty dollars when he landed in this country. Ja, it's German, is what it is. Pa, he always wanted to fix up the back yard like the places he'd seen in the old country—that was why he got this funny fellow, that was one reason we moved into town when we did, because Pa wanted to fix up a place . . . ja, and then we hadn't lived here but a year or two when Pa got killed. He got run over, he was thinking of things the way he always done, and didn't hear the train coming . . . ja, that's the way of it!" But after a moment, while they all stood about her soberly, she roused herself and went on. "Bert, she always had a fit over that fellow. She was the one to put him out of the front yard and lugged him out here. But I don't know—" Mrs. Hohenschuh chuckled—"I always kind of liked the little fellow. Maybe because Pa thought so much of him. Well, I guess he's where she ain't likely to find him. She's too busy inside there to fool around out here much. I'm the one does that."

Slowly, Mrs. Hohenschuh in the lead, they trailed away from the orchard. The troll, with his colors faded to dim faint tints and curls chipped off his beard, stood smiling a one-sided but jovial smile at the rotting apples about his broken feet that had almost grown into the orchard ground.

Mrs. Hohenschuh picked some of each kind of flowers for every person. "Hold on, now! You ain't got any of the pansies yet." A circle of sticks set upright—little thin sticks with flaking bark—enclosed the massed, butterfly colors of the pansies. The tiger lilies grew in a straggling bunch tied with twine. "Pick yourself some if you like 'em. Go ahead!" What else were the flowers here for? "Here's a color you ain't got if you like them zinnies, Mrs. . . . well, you'll have to excuse me. I can't remember all you folkses' names." The sun shone down brightly on the garden, bringing out the hot colors of the moss roses, throwing clear antique shadows from the grape arbor, glinting and losing itself in coolness in the thick wet grass around the pump through which silent little streams of water soaked slowly. They all had a drink before they went into the house. The sides of the glass were frosted with wet. The family story was twined with their wanderings among the little paths of the garden, tangled with the bright colors of the flowers, and brightened over with sunshine.

The house seemed cool when they went inside.

"Oh, you don't want to go yet! Come in and set awhile and let's finish our visit."

Mrs. Hohenschuh led them into the parlor.

"There's lots of things you ain't seen yet."

Mrs. Drayton was tired, even Mr. Drayton—although still

genial—was ready to stop; but the other three seemed insatiable. Bert had heard her mother's invitation and burned with helpless shame. What else was mother going to show? And it was hopeless to try to lead her off now. Bert followed the others into the front room.

"I'll show you Pa's picture, Mr. . . . ach, that name's gone again! Well, I guess you know I mean you, don't you? Sure! That's right."

She got down that old faded purple plush album that held all the family pictures—Bert and the boys when they were youngsters, Mr. Hohenschuh when he first came to this country, wedding pictures of hired men. The two younger women sat eagerly close to her, the writer looked at all the pictures with a gravity that Bert couldn't fathom, Mr. Drayton laughed and made funny remarks about the clothes that pleased mother, and Mrs. Drayton looked at the pictures last with a pleased but tired smile; she wasn't quite in all the things the others were, Bert thought. "Ja, look at that one now! Ain't he funny-looking though? He was a cousin of mine. Ja, now they all look funny." Bert sat and suffered. Maynard sidled in. He couldn't give up the promise of being introduced. They were all nice to him. The author showed him a funny pin he had, carved by the Indians, and the women all smiled at him. But they went on making that fuss over mother.

When she had showed them the photographs, she had to let them see her other things: the shells and the "curios" that she prized so, and that she kept on a shelf in the bookcase. "Look here! Did you ever see anything like this before?" How could they act so pleased, unless they were just false and putting it on to get mother to make a fool of herself? Bert could have cried. That shell! Of course they'd seen shells. They'd been everywhere. Those old feathers from the tail of the peacock they used to have out on the farm, the cocoanut husk, that big long German pipe, the glass paper-weight with the snowfall inside. What else could she find to show them? They were asking about fancy work. Did she ever make the real old knitted lace? Ja, not so much knit' as crotchet', though—wait she'd show them! It would be just like her to ask them to all go up to her room with her and look through those terrible drawers—and if she did that! Bert was ready to kill herself. That room of mother's (and it wasn't any use talking to her about it, Bert couldn't make her do a *thing*) with dresses hanging on nails, and quilts piled up in the corner, drawers filled with junk—a perfect museum!

Well, they weren't paying any attention to her and Maynard anyway, so Bert went back to the dining room. She might as well finish with the table. . . . At least they were staying a long time and seemed to be enjoying themselves. In that way, she supposed the dinner was a success. But she couldn't understand them. It was she to whom they ought to be paying attention—she who appreciated them, and knew how different they were, and wanted to be like them; they couldn't really mean it when they made such a fuss over mother? Why should they? They must be laughing at her. What on earth could they see in all this old junk? It was so perverse and contrary and cruel that she wanted to cry. All the very awfullest things in the house—things *no*-body had any more! What kind of an idea of the town would they get? She looked into the parlor, and there was mother getting out all her old fancy work—that terrible piece, that huge table spread, with horses and dogs and cows and roosters crocheted into it . . . and they were saying "lovely"! She heard them.

"That dress. Isn't it perfect? The real thing."

"Oh, she's a jewel!"

"Lovely!"

They were going at last. They were very nice to Bert then. The women sought her out in the dining room. "Such a wonderful dinner you gave us!"

"Well, I'm glad you liked it. I didn't know . . ."

She followed them into the parlor, feeling appeased and excited again, even though she seemed to scent a tactful patronage. But they were all complimenting her now, and she drank in the praise, eagerly, but afraid to believe they meant it.

Mr. Drayton had taken her aside. "And what do we owe you for this fine meal you gave us?" he asked her in a low, genial tone.

"Well . . . a dollar apiece." Bert said firmly. She blushed, but held her ground. She had heard that all the city tearooms charged a dollar and a quarter now. Of course, she couldn't ask quite as much as a city tearoom, that had everything just up to snuff; but her dinner was good and she knew it, and she was going to stick to business. He didn't seem to think that she was charging them too much, however. He counted out some bills and handed them right over to her. But when she came to look at them, there were too many—a five and an extra one!

"Oh, I can't—why, you've given me—"

He tapped her shoulder. "That's all right. Don't notice it. Doesn't begin to pay for the entertainment we've had here."

She still protested, flushed and happy, but he wouldn't listen to her; so she guessed there was nothing else for her to do. . . .

She hadn't forgotten about the visitor's book. She got it out now. All the tearooms in the East had those, Mrs. Elliott had said. She had seen several famous names in one place where she had eaten. It advertised the place; and then it was an honor, too, to think such people had eaten there. Bert was a little bashful but determined.

"I hope you don't mind before you go." She laid the new visitors' book, a notebook with black covers that she had bought at the drug-store, before the author. "I'd like to have you put your name in my book so other folks can see you've been here."

He didn't seem very much flattered about it, she thought, but anyway he wasn't going to refuse. How funny! She would have thought it would please folks to be asked to do things like that. The others teased him a little. "You can't escape 'em, Harry!" They seemed to think it was sort of a joke. Bert stood flushed, waiting and determined. She was satisfied when she saw, at the very beginning of her book, the small firm signature: "Harry Whetstone."

"How little you write!" she cried in amazement. It was funny for a man to write so small as that. "Now I want all the rest of you folks' names."

They protested.

"Yes I do. You're all along with him."

"Well, go on, girls. Sign yourselves," Mr. Drayton commanded.

They all signed. Mrs. Drayton blushed when she did it.

Bert wasn't through with the author yet. Before she let him go, she was going to get all she'd meant to get out of him.

"I wondered if you'd let me use your name, Mr. Whetstone."

He still had that funny, kind of bored way. His wife was really nicer.

"Say he ate with a large appetite, even mightier than usual," Mrs. Whetstone said.

But it seemed to Bert they were all amused.

She wanted to talk to the writer about his books. "You know I never met an author before," she said. "I've always been wanting to, because—" she flushed—"well, I've always wanted to write myself. I always thought I could if I just had the time to do it."

"Oh, don't," he assured her solemnly. But he wasn't as impressed as she had thought he would be. "It's much better to cook biscuits like those we devoured this noon. Infinitely better to make dandelion wine like your mother."

He was joking, of course. But Bert didn't quite like it. She had meant what she said, seriously. It was something she'd thought about all her life. He didn't seem to her a bit like an author.

Mrs. Hohenschuh came into the house, waddling and breathless.

"Dandelion wine!" she cried. "Ja, if you liked that, then you come back here and you'll get some of the wild grape I'm going to make this fall. You come and let *me* get you up a dinner. I'll give you some real genuine fried chicken and you won't have to wait all meal for your coffee."

They all laughed. They seemed to think that was *funny*.

She had been out in the garden again. She had dug up some plants, and wrapped them in newspapers and brought some slips for the women to take along and set out.

"You take these along with you. Oh sure, you go ahead!"

She parceled them out right and left and gave directions. The people went out to the car swamped with packages. They were thanking Mrs. Hohenschuh profusely, and promising to do just what she told them, laughing delightedly at everything she said. She went right up to the car with them, as she always did with people who were leaving. Bert stood back with the bills wadded up in her hot hand, and with Maynard beside her. They had complimented her on the dinner, and said nice things to her, done all that she had asked them: but she stood hungering for just the one thing they hadn't said to her.

"Good-by, Mrs. Hohenschuh. We certainly have enjoyed this."

"You come again. All of you. You just drop in any time you feel like it."

"Good-by, Mrs. Statzer! . . . And Maynard!"

But they had to remember to say that.

Mr. Drayton took the wheel, the big engine started humming, the car rolled ahead. They waved—they were going. . . .

"Well!" Mrs. Hohenschuh said gratified, climbing back onto the walk. "They was real nice folks! I don't see why you made such a fuss over having them."

"Look at your hands, mother!" Bert said bitterly.

"Ja, I know. I dug up them plants. Well, it don't matter now, they're gone anyway."

She waddled serenely to the house.

Bert stood looking after the car. She didn't know just what she had expected this dinner to mean to her. Anyway, she hadn't thought that everything would be just as it was before, that mother would be the one they got on with (mother, who hadn't really lifted her hand!), that she would just go back into the house with a lot of dirty dishes to wash. She didn't yet see what their idea was.

THE LITTLE GIRL

. . . .

FROM TOWN

. . . .

"I wonder who that is coming here," Mrs. Sieverson said, looking out of the kitchen window.

"Somebody coming?" Mr. Sieverson asked from the sink. "Oh, I guess that's Dave Lindsay, ain't it? He said he'd be out."

"Yes, but he's got someone with him. Oh! I believe it's that little girl from back East somewhere that's visiting them. Leone! Children!"

Mr. Sieverson went outdoors, and then Mrs. Sieverson, and, by the time the car stopped, rounding the drive, all four children were on hand from somewhere. Even Marvin and Clyde, the two boys.

"Anybody home?" Mr. Lindsay called out jovially.

"You bet!"

They were all looking at the little girl in the car beside him. They had heard about this little girl, and how "cute" she was. Her mother was some relative of Mrs. Lindsay. Leone and Vila looked at her eagerly. The boys hung back but they wanted to see her. Mr. Lindsay was proud. He said:

"Well, sir, I've got somebody along with me!"

"I see you have!" Mr. Sieverson answered with shy heavy jocularity and Mrs. Sieverson asked, "Is this the little girl been visiting you?"

"This is the little girl! But I don't know whether she's visiting or not. I've just about made up my mind I'll keep her!"

They all laughed appreciatively. Leone pulled her mother's

dress. She wanted her mother to ask if the little girl couldn't get out and play with them. "Now, don't. We'll see," Mrs. Sieverson whispered. The little girl was so pretty sitting there with her soft golden-brown hair and her cream-white dress that Mr. and Mrs. Sieverson were both shy of saying anything directly to her. Mr. Sieverson cried, still trying conscientiously to joke:

"Well, ain't you going to get out?"

Mr. Lindsay asked, "Well!—shall we, Patricia?"

The little girl looked gravely at the other little girls, and then nodded.

"All right, sir! Patricia's the boss! I've got to do as she says."

She consented to smile at that, and the two boys giggled. Mr. Lindsay lifted her out of the car. She put her arms around his neck, and her little legs and her feet in their shiny black slippers dangled as he swung her to the ground. The children felt shy when he set her down among them. Mr. and Mrs. Sieverson didn't quite know what to say.

"*There* she is! This is the first time this little girl has ever been out to a farm. What do you think of that, Marvin?"

Marvin grinned, and backed off a few steps.

"Yes, sir! But she and Uncle Dave have great times driving round together, don't they?"

The little girl looked up at him and then smiled and nodded her head with a subtle hint of mischief.

"You bet we do! We have great times."

The Sieversons all stood back in a group shyly grinning and admiring. Leone's eyes were as eager as if she were looking at a big doll in a store window. They had never seen any child as pretty as this one, and Mr. Lindsay knew it and was brimming with pride. Her short dress of creamy linen, tied with a red-silk cord at the neck and embroidered with patches of bright Russian colours, melted its fairness into the pure lovely pallor of her skin. The sleeves were so short that almost the whole of her soft, round, tiny arms was bare. Her hair was of fine gold streaked and overlaid with brown—the colour of a straw stack with the darker, richer brown on top—but every hair lay fine and perfect, the thick bangs waved slightly on her forehead, and the long soft bob curved out like a shining flower bell and shook a little when she moved her head. Her skin wasn't one bit sunburned, and so white and delicately grained that there seemed to Vila, in awe, to be a little frost upon it . . . like the silver bloom on wildflower petals, picked in cool places, that smudged when she rubbed it with her fingers.

Mr. Lindsay became businesslike now that he was out of the car. "Well, Henry," he said, "you got it all figured up and ready to show me? I think we've got Appleton where we can make a deal all right."

"Yeah, I guess it's ready."

While the two men talked, the little girl stood beside Mr. Lindsay, her hand still in his, with a grave, trustful, wondering look. Leone, smiling at her, was getting closer. Mr. Lindsay seemed to remember her then and looked down at her.

"Well, Patricia, what about you while I'm looking after my business?" He smiled then at the other children. "Think you can find something to do with all these kids here?"

Leone looked up at him and her blue eyes pleaded brightly in her eagerness. "I guess they's plenty of them to look after her," Mr. Sieverson said shyly but still grinning. "They can entertain her," Mrs. Sieverson put in. She could do the baking without Leone this morning, she thought rapidly, but feeling hurried and anxious.

"You going to play with them for a while, are you?" Mr. Lindsay felt responsible for Patricia. All the same he wanted her off his mind for a while until he had finished his business. "I don't know whether—"

"Oh, Leone'll look after her," Mrs. Sieverson assured him, and Mr. Sieverson repeated, "Sure! She'll be all right with Leone."

Leone came up now, smiling eagerly and with a sweetness that transformed her thin freckled face. She shook back the wisps of uneven, tow-coloured hair. She took the little girl's hand protectingly and confidingly in her hot palm that had a gleam of dusty perspiration along the life line and the heart line. The tiny hand felt like a soft warm bit of silk—or a flower.

"That's right! Uncle Dave won't be gone long. Don't take her out where it's too hot, kids. You know she isn't used to things the way you are."

"No, you be careful," Mrs. Sieverson warned them.

"Will you go with Leone?" The little girl did not say that she would or wouldn't, but she was courteous and did not draw back. "You'll be all right! *You'll* have a good time! Oh, I guess Uncle Dave didn't tell these kids who you were, did he? This is Patricia."

"Can you say that?" Mrs. Sieverson asked—doubting if *she* could.

Vila drew shyly back, with one shoulder higher than the other; but Leone laughed in delight. "I can say it!" She nodded. She squeezed Patricia's hand.

"You can say it, can you? All right, then. Well, now, you kids can show this little girl what good times you can have on the farm. That so? All right then, Henry."

Mrs. Sieverson went into the house to get back to her baking. She had a lot to do to-day. She wasn't at all worried about leaving their little visitor so long as Leone was with her. But she turned to call back to the children, who were still silently grouped about Patricia in the driveway:

"You better stay in the yard with her. Mr. Lindsay won't like it if she gets her dress dirty. Leone! You hear me?"

"I heard. Do you want to come into the yard, Patricia? You do, don't you?" Leone asked coaxingly.

Patricia went soberly with her. Her eyes, gray with threads of violet in the clear iris, were looking all about silently. Her little hand lay quiet but with confidence in Leone's. The other children followed, the boys lagging behind, but coming all the same.

"There, now! Here's just the nicest shady place, and Patricia can sit here, can't she, and just be so nice?" Leone placed Patricia in the round patterned shade of an apple tree, and spread out her linen dress, making it perfectly even all around, and carefully drew out her little legs straight in front of her with the shiny black slippers close together. "There!" she said proudly. "See?"

She sat down on one side of Patricia, and then Vila shyly and with a sidelong confiding smile sat down on the other. The boys hung back together.

"Leone!" Mrs. Sieverson called from the house. "Ain't you got something to entertain her with? Why don't you get your dolls?"

"Do you want to see our dolls, Patricia?"

So far Patricia had been consenting but silent. "You go in and get them, Vila," Leone ordered, and when Vila whined, "I don't want to!" she said, "Yes, you have to. I can't leave her. I have to take care of her. Don't I, Patricia?" But when Vila came back with the scanty assortment of dolls Patricia looked at them and then reached out her hand for the funny cloth boy doll in the knitted sweater suit. The boys laughed proudly and looked at each other, the way they had done when the swan in the park at Swea City took the piece of sandwich they put on the water for it. "Isn't that doll cute, Patricia?" Leone begged eagerly.

Patricia touched its black-embroidered eyes, and its red-embroidered lips—done in outline stitch—and then looked up at the eager, watching children and smiled with that gleam of mischief.

The boys laughed again. They all came around closer. "That's mine," Vila said softly. She reached over and touched the big stuffed cloth doll, with the hair coloured yellow and the cheeks bright red, that was smooth along the top and bottom sides like a fish but crisp along the edges from the seams. Patricia took it and looked at it. She looked at every one of their dolls—there were five, one of them was a six-inch bisque doll from the ten-cent store—and then smiled again.

"I'll bet you have nice dolls at home, haven't you, Patricia?" Leone said in generous worship. "I'll bet you've got lots nicer dolls than we have."

Patricia spoke for the first time. The children listened, with bright eager eyes wide open, to each soft little word.

"I have fifteen dolls."

Marvin said, "Gee!"

"Have you got them named?" Vila leaned over the grass toward Patricia, and then quickly hitched herself back, frightened at the sound of her own voice asking the question.

"Oh, yes, I always name my dolls," Patricia assured them. "My dolls have beautiful names. They're all the names of the great actresses and singers." And she began gravely to repeat them. "Geraldine Farrar, and Maria Jeritza, and Eva LeGallienne, and Amelita Galli-Curci . . ."

While she was saying them, the boys looked at each other over her head, their eyes glinting, their mouths stretched into grins of smothered amusement, until Clyde broke into giggles.

Leone was indignant. "Those are *lovely* names! I think Patricia was just wonderful to think of them!"

Vila stretched across the grass again. She touched the cloth doll and drew back her fingers as quickly as if it were hot. "Her name's Dor'thy," she whispered.

After Patricia's gracious acceptance of the dolls, the children wanted to show her all the treasures they had—even those they had never told anyone else about. Everything, they felt, would receive a kind of glory from her approval. They liked to repeat her name now. "Patricia." "She wants to see the little pigs. Don't you, Patricia?" "Aw, she does not! Do you, Patricia? She wants to see what I've got to make a radio." Patricia looked from one to the other with her violet-gray eyes and let the others answer for her. But after a while she said with a cool, gentle, royal decision:

"No. I don't want to go anywhere. I want to stay right here in this round shade."

The children were highly delighted. They began to bring their treasures to her. Vila had run off to the edge of the garden and dug up two glass precious stones she had buried there, but when she came back to Patricia she was too shy to show them and kept them hidden in her hot little hand that got sticky and black from the earth clinging to them. The boys were getting quite bold. Marvin said:

"I bet you never saw a mouse nest, Patricia."

"Patricia doesn't care anything about that," Leone said impatiently. "I wish you boys would go off somewhere anyway and let *us* look after Patricia."

"I can show it to you, Patricia."

"*She* doesn't want to see that!"

"Yes, I do," Patricia assured them with an innocent courtesy that made Clyde giggle again.

The boys ran off to the woodshed to get it. It was all made of wound-about string and little bits of paper and a soft kind of woolly down. Patricia examined it with her large grave eyes. She reached out one finger toward it delicately, and drew the finger back. She looked up at the boys.

"What is it?" she breathed.

"A mouse nest," Marvin said nonchalantly.

The Little Girl from Town · *277*

He held it carefully in his brown sturdy hands, partly to keep it together, but more because he liked to have Patricia's soft little fingers come near his. They were as smooth as silk, and rosy at the tips as the pointed petals of the dog-tooth violets he had found near the little creek in the woods, when he was out there one day last April all alone. A happy shiver went over him at the thought of their touching him, silvery and cool.

"Do the mouses—*mices*—live in it?"

"Sure! They did before we took it away."

"Oh, but can't they live in it any more? What will the mices do?"

"Gee! What can they do?" Marvin swaggered. Clyde giggled.

Her pink mouth opened into a distressed O. She looked from one to the other for help, and the violet in her eyes deepened. "But they won't have anywhere to live! You must put it back." She was very serious.

"Shoot! Why, they've run off somewheres else by this time!"

What did it matter about mice anyhow? Gee, they were something to get rid of! Why did she suppose Pop kept all those cats and fed 'em, if it wasn't to get rid of the mice? But she looked so distressed that Leone, with an angry glance at the boys, assured her hastily leaning over and hugging her:

"No, they haven't, Patricia! Boys just like to say things like that."

"Aw, gee—!"

"But what will the mices *do?*"

"The boys'll put the nest back, and then the mice'll come there," Leone warmly promised her. She didn't care if it wasn't true.

The boys had never heard anything so funny in their lives. Gee whiz! They despised her for such ignorance, and could hardly keep from laughing, and yet they felt uneasily ashamed of themselves for they didn't quite know what. They had just wanted to bring her the mouse nest to make her interested and then to show her, too, that they weren't afraid of things most people didn't want to touch. But they seemed to be out of favour. They hung around while the girls talked a lot of silly talk, and laid all the dolls out in the grass in front of them.

"I'll bet you've got awful pretty clothes for your dolls, haven't you, Patricia?"

Patricia didn't like to say, or to talk about her dolls because she didn't really think that these dolls' dresses were one bit pretty. Leone went on questioning her, with naïve admiration, and Vila listened with her eyes glistening.

"I'll bet you've been into lots of big stores, Patricia. Did this dress you've got on come from a big store?"

They both bent and examined the creamy shining linen with its coarse silky weave and the large roughened threads that Vila scarcely dared to touch with her fingers all dirty from the precious stones. Patricia graciously let them touch and see until, gently but with a final dignity, she drew the cloth out of their fingers.

"Now you mustn't touch me any more."

The boys giggled again at this, admiring but feeling abashed.

A striped kitten came suddenly into sight at a little distance—became motionless, saw them—and flattened and slid under the cover of the plants in the garden. Patricia gave a little cry. Her face bloomed into brightness.

"Oh! Do you have a kitty?"

"A cat! Gee!" They all laughed. "*One* cat! I bet we got seventeen."

"Really seventeen kitties? Did your father buy them all for you?"

"Buy them!" The boys shouted with laughter. "Gee, you don't buy cats!"

"Oh, you do," Patricia told them, shocked. "They cost

twenty-five dollars, the kitties that sit in the window in the shop."

"Twenty-five dollars! Pay twenty-five dollars for a *cat!*" *Cats*, when you had to drown half of 'em and couldn't hardly give the others away! The boys were hilarious with laughter over such ignorance.

Leone couldn't help knowing that Patricia was ignorant, too. But she gave the boys a hurt, indignant, silencing look— it was mean of them to laugh at Patricia when she didn't know! Anyway, she was so little. Leone put her arm around Patricia, in warm protection.

"But they do!" Patricia's eyes were large and tearful and her soft little lips were quivering. It was dreadful to have these children not believe her, and she couldn't understand it. "Some of them cost a hundred dollars!"

"Oh, gee!" the boys began.

"Maybe some of them *do*," Leone said quickly. "You don't know everything in the world, Marvin Sieverson." She knew, of course, that cats couldn't—but then, she wasn't going to have the boys make fun of Patricia. "Come on now, Patricia," she pleaded. "We'll go and see our kitties. Shall we?"

The boys watched anxiously. They didn't want Patricia to be mad at them. They wanted to take her out to the barn and have her look at everything.

She considered. Her eyes were still large and mournful and a very dark violet. At last she nodded her head, held out her hands trustingly to Leone to be helped from the grass, smoothed down her skirts—and the whole tribe went running off together.

Patricia had to climb up the steep stairs into the haymow one step at a time. She felt along the rough sides carefully with her little hands. The boys would have liked to help her and were too bashful, but all the time Leone was just behind her, telling her, "Don't you be afraid. Leone's right here, Patricia. Leone won't let you fall." When they got up into the haymow Patricia was almost frightened at first; it was so big, and there were such shadows. A long beam of sunlight fell dimly and dustily golden from the high window in the peak, across the great beams and the piled hay, and widened over the great stretch of wooden floor.

"Haven't you ever been up in a haymow before?" Clyde demanded.

"Of course she hasn't," Leone answered indignantly.

Patricia looked around at them, and her face was pale with awed excitement. "It's like the church!" she breathed.

"Gee, a *hay*-mow!"

Still, it really was. Even their voices and the way they walked sounded different up here. The boys were tickled and a little embarrassed that Patricia had thought of that.

"Is this where the kitties live?"

"The little ones do. Where are the little bitty ones, Marvin?"

"*I* know!" both the boys shouted. They leaped up into the sliding mounds of hay, calling back, "Come on if you want to see, Patricia!"

"I'll help you, Patricia," Leone encouraged her.

She boosted and got Patricia up on to the hay pile and helped her flounder along with her feet plunging into uncertain holes, and the long spears of hay scratching at her bare legs above the half socks, and the dust making her eyes smart. Then Patricia began to laugh. She liked it!

"Here they are!" the boys shouted.

A bevy of half-grown cats suddenly fled down the hay like shadows. "No, no!" Patricia screamed when the boys tried valiantly to catch a little black cat by its tail. Leone was assuring her, "Never mind, they won't hurt the kitties, Patricia."

"Look here! Come here!" the boys were calling.

Patricia was almost afraid to go. The boys had found the

nest of little kittens. They had got hold of the soft, mousy, wriggling things and were holding them up for her to see. Fascinated, she went nearer. The little kittens had pink skin fluffed over with the finest fur, big round heads, and little snubby ears, and blue eyes barely open.

"Oh! . . ." She looked up at Leone with her pink lips pursed. She loved the little kittens but she was afraid of them. "Oh, but they aren't kitties! They don't look like kitties."

The boys were highly amused. "What do they look like?" Marvin demanded. "What do you think they are? Cows? Horses?"

She said tremulously, "No, I *know* cows are big. But their heads look the way little baby cow heads do in the pictures. They do."

"I think they do, too," Leone asserted stoutly. She coaxed, "Touch them, Patricia. They won't hurt you."

The boys grinned at the way Patricia put out her fingers and drew them back. How could these little bits of kittens hurt her? Didn't she know they couldn't bite yet? Their little teeny teeth couldn't do anything but nibble. It was fun to feel them. Marvin caught up the white one and held it out to her, and they all kept urging her. He hoped her fingers would touch his. She cringed back, her mouth pursed in wonder.

"Oh, but they have such funny tails!"

"No, they ain't. They got tails like all cats got."

"Oh, no, Marvin. In the show the kitties have tails so big, and they waved them—just like the big plumes on men's hat's riding on horses."

The boys doubled up with laughter. "Who'd put cats in a show?"

"Oh, but they are!" Patricia looked at them in distress.

"Why shouldn't they be?" Leone demanded.

Of course she knew why, as well as the boys did. Nobody would pay to see a cat! Patricia had meant the tigers. She was so little she didn't know the difference. The boys were not to tease her though! Clyde was giggling. Gee, if she didn't have the funniest notions!

At last they got her to touch the kitten. She did it first with just the pink tip of one finger—then it felt so soft, so little and fluffy, with tiny whiskers like fine silk threads, that she reached out her hands. Marvin felt the brush of her fingers, as if a cobweb had blown across his hand, and a shiver of joy and pain went down his backbone. Patricia laughed in delight, and looked from one to the other of the children with her large shining eyes, to share her wonder.

"Take it!" Marvin urged.

"Oh, no, I wouldn't!"

"Why not? Go on and take it!"

She shook her head.

"She doesn't have to if she doesn't want to," Leone said warmly.

"Yes, she does!" Marvin thrust the kitten into her hands. She gave a little shriek and squeezed it by its soft belly, while the weak pinkish legs wavered and clawed out of her grasp.

"I'm going to drop it!"

"No, you won't!"

Its fluffiness filled her with ecstasy. "Oh, see its claws! They look like little bits of shavings from mother's pearl beads!" The boys grinned in amusement and delight at each other. Vila laughed happily. "Oh, and inside its little ears! Just the way shells look inside—only these are *silk* shells!" The boys grinned broadly. She caught the kitten to her cheek and held it wildly wriggling. "Oh, kitty, I love you! I want to have you to take home!"

"You can—you can have it," the children all urged her eagerly. Marvin said, "Gee, we got all kinds of cats, and that old gray one—" Clyde pinched him. "Shut up!" He grinned and blushed. Patricia laid the kitten gravely and reluctantly back in the rounded nest. She shook her head until the fluffy bell of shining hair trembled. She said solemnly, and as if she had forgotten that the others were there:

"No. I won't. Because all its other little sisters and brothers would be lonesome for it. And its mother would."

The boys stood grinning but they said nothing.

What were the kittens' names? Patricia asked. She was horrified that they had none. "Gee, we call 'em kitty," Marvin said; but Leone hastened to add, "Well, we call that one we have Old Gray."

Patricia said: "Oh, but they must have names! That's wicked. Nobody goes up to heaven to our Lord Jesus without a name!"

The boys just barely glanced at each other. They kept their red faces straight with agony. Then Marvin went pawing and rolling through the hay over to the other side of the pile, where he buried his flushed face and snorted.

"I'm going to give every one a name," Patricia asserted solemnly.

"What are you going to name 'em, Patricia?" Leone and Vila were impressed.

"I'm going to give them jewel names. Because the cats make me think about things like jewels. This is what I'm going to call them. I'm going to name this one Pearl because it's white, and this bluey one Sapphire, and the other bluey one Turquoise, and this little pinky one Coral, and this one . . . Jade!"

"Aren't you going to name one Di'mond, Patricia?" Leone asked eagerly. Vila thought that, too.

"No." Patricia was very decided. "Cats don't look like diamonds. They look like coloured jewels."

The boys giggled. Besides that one she had named *Pearl*—gee, they had already looked at these kittens and they knew very well that one was a he-cat! If she wasn't funny!

Vila was looking at Patricia so intently that she trembled.

Now she said, "Patricia's eyes are jewel eyes, too. They're—they're—" She didn't know how to say it, and yet she felt what she meant and wanted to say—felt it so that it hurt! The whites of Patricia's eyes gleamed, and a little blue spread out into them from the circles of the coloured parts, and in these there were all sorts of threads of colour woven together, the way they were inside the glass of marbles—bluish and violet-coloured and gray, and a sort of golden! All just as clear . . . Vila reached out and took Patricia's wrist quickly and with shy ardour, but then she only smiled and couldn't think of anything to say . . . she would have been afraid to say it, anyway.

"Now she must see all our places!"

They went through the big barn. "Look here, Patricia!" "Patricia can't. She's looking at this." She looked at everything, but when they urged her, "Touch it! Go ahead!" she wouldn't quite do that. When they went out of the barn they all took hands and ran pounding down the long slope of heavy boards and out into the farmyard. Patricia was afraid at first and then shrieked with laughter and wanted to do it over again.

"Now we mustn't do it any more," Leone said after the third time. "Her little face is all red. Let go her hand, Marvin! Now, darling, stand still, and Leone'll wipe off her little face."

They thought it was funny the way she ran when the chickens came near her. "Oh, gee, if we had time we'd go down to the pond and show her the geese. Wouldn't she run if that old goose got after her!" Leone said, "Marvin Sieverson! We shan't go there."

But the very best place was the orchard. Even the boys were not so wild and noisy there. Their feet made only soft swishing sounds when they went through the long grass. The boughs were loaded, some broken and sweeping the ground, and the sky was patterned with leaves.

"Patricia!" Marvin hinted, tempting her, holding out a little green apple.

Leone snatched it from his hand. "Why, Marvin Sieverson, shame on you! Do you want to make little Patricia sick?"

"Aw, gee!" He had just wanted to see if she would take it. He and Clyde had both been hunting through the grass for some apples that Patricia could really eat.

Only the yellow transparents were ripe. The large apples had a clear pale colour against the leaves that were only slightly darker—mellow and clear at the same time, a light pure yellow-green through which the August sunshine seemed to pass. Patricia took the big yellow apple that Marvin picked for her and carried it all around with her. "*Eat* it, Patricia, why don't you?" But she wanted to hold it. "Oh, thank you!" she said very earnestly for every single thing the children gave her—the red dahlia, and the tiny bunch of sweet peas, the bluebird's feather. Whenever she saw a bird she stopped. She put her little silky hand on Leone's wrist. "Look!" "It's just a bird." She stood and watched with fascinated eyes until the bird was lost in the sky and she had to turn away dazzled with blue and gold.

"Do you wish you could stay here and belong to us, Patricia?" Leone asked her wistfully. "We'd play you were my little girl, wouldn't we?"

Patricia wished that she could stay. There were streaks of dust down the shining linen dress and on the soft little arms, a damp parting in the lovely wave of the bangs, and around her mouth there was a faint stain of red from the juicy plums the boys had brought her to suck. Oh, yes, the country, she said, was *nice*! She looked about with shining innocent eyes of wonder. She loved the animals. In the city, she told them, animals weren't happy. There were the beautiful green birds in the shop—just the colour, almost, of these apple-tree leaves!— but her father wouldn't buy them for her because he didn't believe in keeping things in cages, and he wouldn't get her the big gray dog because it wasn't right to take dogs out on chains.

"Oh, if I lived in the country," she cried, "do you know what I'd do? I'd just run around and run around—"

"You'd play with *me*, wouldn't you, Patricia?" Marvin cut in jealously.

"I'd play—"

"Children!"

The grown people were calling them. Disaster showed on the children's faces. "Oh, we don't want Patricia to go home!" There were so many things still that they hadn't shown her. But Mr. Lindsay came into the orchard calling out jovially:

"Well! Here she is! Ready to go home now with Uncle Dave?" He took it for granted that she was. He took her reluctant little hand, and the other children trailed after them. When they reached the farmyard, he said, "See what's going with us!"

Patricia looked in awe and wonderment. "What is it?" she breathed.

"Don't you know what that is?"

Mr. and Mrs. Sieverson, standing back, both laughed. The children too were grinning.

Patricia ventured, "A baby cow!"

Then they all laughed to think that she had known.

"That's what it is, all right. But don't you know what baby cows are called? Calf! That's a calf! Well, sir, do you want this little calf to go with us?"

Patricia didn't know whether or not Uncle Dave meant that for a joke. But the little calf was so sweet—she loved it so terribly the instant she saw it—that she couldn't help risking that and begging, "Oh, yes!" Its head really was shaped like the tiny kittens'. But its eyes were very large and coloured a soft deep brown under a surface of rounded brightness, so gentle and so sad too, that it seemed to her as if the colour showed in each eye under a big tear. The calf turned its head toward her. Its frail legs bent inward, to prop it up. Its coat looked like cream spilled over with shining tar. There were curls, like the curly knots showing in freshly planed wood; and the shining ends of the hair looked as if they had curled because the whole coat had just been licked by the mother.

"Oh, yes, Uncle Dave! Is it going *with* us?"

"It's going to be our back-seat passenger. If the boss permits?"

It made Mr. Sieverson laugh—feel tickled—to see how the thought of riding to town with that calf pleased the little girl. But he said dutifully to Mr. Lindsay:

"Now, if that calf's going to be any nuisance to you—"

"No, no. As long as I've got the old car, put it in. Tie it up."

Patricia saw the rope then in Mr. Sieverson's hand. She cried, "Oh, not *tie* the little calf!"

"Sure," Mr. Sieverson said, grinning kindly at her. "You don't want it to jump out, do you?"

She looked at Uncle Dave for confirmation of that. He said: "Sure! Calves won't go riding any other way."

The two boys laughed.

Patricia stood back close to Leone but not saying anything more. She looked frightened. Mr. Sieverson said, with some feeling of reassuring her still more:

"You don't want to let this calf get loose or you won't get any of it!"

She didn't understand that.

"Get any of it to eat. This calf's going to make veal."

"Eat it?" she cried in horror; and she earnestly put him right. "Oh, no, I wouldn't *eat* it." Mr. Sieverson was joking.

"Why, sure!" he said. "Don't you eat good veal? You're going to take this calf to the butcher."

"Oh, no!" He meant that! Patricia was suddenly wild with crying. They all stood back, shocked, never expecting such a storm as this. "Oh, no! The little calf isn't going to be killed! I won't! I won't! No!" She put out her hands blindly and turned from one to the other for help. Mr. Sieverson didn't know what to do. She turned to him and beat the air with her little fists, shrieking, "Oh, you're *wicked*!"

He couldn't stand that. His face got red. Even if she was just a child, he demanded, "Don't you eat veal?"

"No! No!" Patricia shrieked.

"What, then?" he demanded.

She had to look at him. Her little pink mouth was open and her bright eyes drowned. She quavered, "Other kinds of meat . . . I'll eat chicken," and turned piteously to Uncle Dave.

Mr. Sieverson didn't like to be called "wicked" by anyone. The injustice, when he had just been trying to be nice to this little girl, too, hurt him. His wife murmured, "Well, now, Henry—" But he insisted, "Don't chicken have to be killed before you can eat it?"

But even Mr. Sieverson, although he was in the right of it, felt ashamed when he saw the little thing cry. Mrs. Sieverson gave him a look, stroked Patricia's hair, and said, "They won't take the calf." Mr. Lindsay hastened to promise, "No, no. Of course we won't take the calf." They were all trying now to reassure her. Vila was crying, too. The boys were pleading, "Patricia!" although they didn't know just what they would say to her in comfort if they got her to look at them. "No, no, it isn't going. It won't have to be tied up. See, he's put away the rope." The two men settled the thing with a look above her head. Patricia looked up at last, with piteous drowned eyes, as dark as wet violets. She broke away from all of them and, running to the calf—fearful of touching things as she was—she threw her arms in protection around its neck and stared fiercely at the shamefaced people.

"Oh, no, we couldn't take it!" Mr. Lindsay muttered. He cleared his throat.

The children surrounded Patricia again. They were begging her not to cry. Her cheek was laid against the little calf's silky ear, and she was telling it, in her own mind, "Don't you care, don't you mind, precious little calf, I've saved you." She let herself be drawn away but said "No!" when Mrs. Sieverson wanted to wipe the tears from her cheeks, and held up the little wet face trustingly for Leone to do it. That pleased all the Sieversons greatly.

"So now we can go! Hm?" Mr. Lindsay asked her.

She seemed to have forgiven them. She didn't want to look at Mr. Sieverson, but when she said good-bye to Mrs. Sieverson she touched her little skirts and made a curtsey. Clyde pinched Marvin to tell him to look. The children watched her with as great delight as they had watched the tightrope walker in the "show." Mr. Lindsay lifted her into the car. She smiled faintly at the children, but there were stains of tears on her pearly cheeks, and her eyes were still as dark as violets.

"You children go get her something—apples or something," Mrs. Sieverson whispered.

"We have, Mamma! We've got a whole lot of things for her."

They began piling presents into her lap. "Don't forget your little feather, Patricia!" Marvin ran off to find something else. The wilting flowers, the apple, the six rosy plums, the bluebird's feather she carefully took again. Marvin came panting back with his new game of "Round the World by Aëroplane." But Mr. Lindsay wouldn't let him give her that.

"No, no, my boy! You keep your game. She's got more things at home now than she can ever play with."

Now she seemed happy and appeased. The children crowded close to the side of the car and pleaded, "Come out again, won't you, Patricia?" Vila whispered in her shy voice, "I'll take care of Pearl and Samphire and those others, Patricia." Marvin said fiercely, "If any tomcat comes round, I'll—" and ground and gnashed his teeth and made fiercely appropriate motions. Leone gave him a look for making her think about the tomcat! But Patricia was still smiling and happy and hadn't understood. Now, in her relief and in the flurry of going, she was more eager and talkative than she had been all afternoon. She promised everything they asked.

"I will. I will, Leone. I will, Marvin. Thank you for all the beautiful things."

In the midst of it Mr. Lindsay leaned over to say in a low tone to Mr. Sieverson, a little ashamed, "Well, somebody else'll take that in for you, Henry, if you can't go."

"Sure. That's all right, Mr. Lindsay."

"Well, now, my little girl, tell them all good-bye."

"Good-bye." "Good-bye, Patricia!" They called and waved madly to her, all standing back together. She answered them. At the very last minute, just as the car was going out into the driveway, she leaned out with her shining hair mussed and blowing in the breeze, and cried:

"Good-bye, calf! I forgot to say good-bye to you."

Marvin laughed in delight, and then Clyde echoed him.

M r. Sieverson stood looking after the car. That "wicked" still rankled. He said, as if very much put out, "Well, now, I'll have to find another way of getting this calf in or else take it myself before night." Then he said, as if ashamed, "Gosh! I don't know. I almost hate to take it. That little thing put up such a fuss." He couldn't help adding, "She was a pretty little kid, wasn't she?"

Mrs. Sieverson did not answer at once. Then she said in an expressionless tone, "Well . . . maybe you better take the other one, then."

He looked at her and seemed to want to assent. Then he cried, "Oh, no! We can't do that. This is the one we'd picked on." He looked angry, and yet in his light-blue eyes under the shock of lightish hair there was a hurt, puzzled look. "Oh, well," he muttered. "Folks can't be foolish!" If ever folks were to start thinking of *such* things . . .

He went forward resolutely, saying "Hi! Stand still, there!" as he took hold of the calf. His wife stood back watching him and saying nothing. The calf turned, bolted a little way, and then let him take hold of it again. It did not seem to know whether to be afraid of him or not. Its eyes looked up into his. In the large eyes of dark mute brown and the smaller eyes of light blue there was much the same reluctant bewilderment in some far depths. But the man knew what he was after, and the calf did not know what was to come.

"Come on here!" Mr. Sieverson said sharply.

He put the rope around the calf's neck.

THE MAN OF

THE FAMILY

Floyd Oberholzer was just opening up the drug-store when Gerald came.

"Hello, Gerald. Want something?"

"I come to start in working."

"This morning?" Floyd was startled. "Why, school can't be over yet, is it? What is this—Wednesday?"

"Yes, but we got done with our tests yesterday, all but arithmetic, and I didn't have to take that."

"Oh, you didn't have to take that?" Floyd repeated vaguely. "Well, you come into the store and we'll see what there is for you to do."

Gerald followed him into the drug-store.

Floyd looked around somewhat helplessly. It was only a few months since he and Lois had bought this little business in Independenceville. They knew what to do themselves, but it was a different matter setting some one else to work. They hadn't expected Gerald so soon, or wanted him. Two or three months ago, he had come into the store to ask if he couldn't have a job, and because they hated to turn the kid away—it wasn't very long after the accident in which his father had been killed—Floyd had told him: "Well, you come around when school's out. Maybe we can find something then." And now he was here.

"Well, you're starting in early," Floyd said to him. "You've beat my wife—she isn't in the store yet. Well, I don't know, Gerald—I guess you might as well sweep out, the first thing."

He remembered then that Lois had swept the store before they closed last night; the boys had left so many cigarette stubs around. But he guessed it could stand it again. It would keep Gerald busy while Floyd decided what to have him do.

"All right," Gerald answered soberly. "Where do you keep your broom?"

"Right out there in the back, Gerald. See—I'll show you. Then you'll know where it is."

Gerald started in to sweep the wooden floor with awkward, scowling concentration. His back was stooped and intent. He took long hard strokes, trying to do a good job of it. Floyd looked at him, and then turned and went scuttling up the stairs.

"Hey—Lois!" he called softly.

" 'Smatter, pop?"

Lois, still in her bungalow apron, came to the door of the kitchen. The Oberholzers were living over the drug-store.

"Say, that kid's here."

"What kid?"

"Gerald Rayburn. He's come to start in working. Seems awful anxious to begin. What in the dickens shall I have him do?"

"You're a fine boss!" Lois began to laugh. "What's he doing now—standing in the middle of the floor and sucking his thumb?"

"I've got him sweeping."

"Why, I swept last night, you idiot!"

"Well, I know you did, but I forgot it. I didn't want to tell him to stand around. He goes at it like a little beaver. You ought to watch him. Oh, I suppose the kid *is* anxious to start in earning."

Lois didn't know what to say.

"You come down," said Floyd, "and tell him about the soda-fountain. That's your end of the business."

"Oh, it is, is it? All right, I'll come down and give the boss's orders since he doesn't know what they are himself," she replied with mock commiseration, and pinched Floyd's ear.

"Well, gosh, I didn't expect that kid the minute school let out! Most kids aren't that anxious to go to work. Isn't this the day they have the school picnic? Why, sure—that's why we got that pop."

He started down the stairs and then went back to the next-to-the-top step and stood frowning uncertainly.

"Think we can really use him, Lois?"

"Well, I guess we've got him, anyway!"

"I know we'll have to have somebody, but he's such a kid. I don't know—"

Lois said hastily: "Oh well, let's try him. You told him he could come. I feel so sorry for that family."

"Well, so do I. But then— Well, all right—"

Floyd left it at that, and scuttled down the stairs again. Lois went back to the kitchen which she herself had painted blue and white, with figured curtains, changing it from the gloomy old hole that the Tewkesburys had left it, to a gay new room. She hated to leave this beloved little place to go and help Floyd in the store. Now that they had hired just a little boy to help them for the summer, she supposed she would have to be downstairs most of the time. She almost wished she hadn't told Floyd to keep Gerald. Well, if Gerald couldn't do the work, he'd have to go, that was all.

"All right, Gerald," Floyd went into the store saying loudly and cheerfully. "Finished that? Well, then, I guess you'd better—" His eyes, quickly roving, caught sight of the magazine rack. "I guess you'd better straighten up those magazines. Folks take 'em out and read 'em all through and then put 'em back."

"All right."

Floyd whistled as he took the long gray cambric covers off

the tables in the middle of the room, where boxes of gilt-edged correspondence cards and leather-bound copies of the works of Edgar Guest had to be displayed until the graduating exercises were over. Gerald went at his work with such silent concentration that it almost embarrassed Floyd.

"What do you want I should do next?"

"Oh, well . . . Guess maybe I better show you about these cigarettes and tobacco. That's probably what they'll be after first. I'll show you how we've got things marked."

"All right."

Lois came down. Floyd gave her an expressive look and nodded toward Gerald.

"He's right at it!" Certainly the boy seemed to be trying hard. His freckled face with the crop of red hair was surly with concentration. Floyd couldn't help remembering that he was just a kid and too young to be starting in to work in earnest. He was quite willing to give up his charge and let Lois initiate him into the mysteries of the new white soda-fountain which they had installed in place of the cracked, lugubrious onyx splendor of the earlier day. Gerald stood silently beside Lois, bashfully aware of her bobbed hair and her plump white arms, answering dutifully: "Yes, ma'am."

"You can watch me this morning, Gerald, and run some errands, maybe. Wash up the glasses. Do the dirty work—how's that?"

"Yes, ma'am."

He was a little clumsy, partly out of bashfulness, but so serious and determined that Lois thought: "Goodness, I wonder if it'll last!" She wanted to give him all the help he needed, but she didn't quite know what to make of his surly little face. He hated to ask her questions, and several times she had to say, "Oh, not like that, Gerald!"

"Gee, that was an awful thing to happen to that family!" Floyd said to Lois in the back room of the store, where he had gone to look for a special package of hog medicine ordered by old Gus Reinbeck. "I think this kid kind of realizes, don't you?"

"Have they got anything, do you suppose?"

"A little insurance, they say, and that house, but not much more than to keep them until this boy can start earning."

"The mother can earn something herself, I should think," Lois said rather defiantly. *She* worked.

"Yes, but with three kids to look after. . . . And anyway, what is there for a woman to do in a burg like this except take in washing?"

"Well, maybe."

Back door and front of the store were open, and through the shimmery blackness of the back screen the garden was green and fresh. A tin cup hung on an old-fashioned pump under the vines. Gerald looked longingly at the boards of the platform, wet with spilled water. There was city water in the soda-fountain, but the pump looked so much cooler out there.

"Run out and get a drink if you want to, Gerald," Lois told him. "I always go out there for my water. It's fun to work the pump." Boys never could see a pump or a drinking fountain or even a hydrant without being consumed with thirst, she knew. Lois liked boys. Gerald made her think of her kid brother. It was a shame he had to go to work. She wanted to reassure him somehow, to rumple his red hair or pat his shoulder. But she must remember that they were hiring him. They couldn't afford to keep him out of pity. Besides, he seemed determined to evade all personal advances and stuck doggedly to work. Maybe the kid was miserable at missing that picnic.

It was getting hot in town. Cars began to rattle and whir down the street, and in a few moments Louie Grossman's big red truck drove up to the side door of the drug-store.

"Hey, Floyd! Got the pop?"

"Got the pop? You bet I've got the pop. You want it now?"

"Sure do, if it's goin' on this picnic."

"All right, sir! Want to come and help me take it out, Gerald?"

"All right."

Gerald went with Floyd into the back room of the store, bright and cool and scattered with light from the green leaves outside. He tugged at one end of the big pop case, and helped Floyd carry it outside and shove it into the truck.

"Now, another one, Gerald."

"All right."

"Well, the kids oughtn't to get thirsty to-day," Floyd said.

"No, they sure got plenty. What are you doing, Gerald?" Louie asked. "Ain't you going to the picnic?"

"I got to work," Gerald answered.

He went back into the store. The two men looked after him.

"He workin' for you now, Floyd?"

"Guess so. It looks like it. He came this morning."

"Goes at it pretty good, don't he?"

"Yes, he seems to be willing. He's pretty young, but then . . . Where they going for the picnic to-day, Louie?"

"Out to Bailey's Creek. You ever been there?"

"Not yet. Mighty pretty place, I guess," he added.

"Yes, but it ain't much of a road."

"Well, don't tip 'em out, Louie."

"No, I'll try and keep the old bus in her tracks."

Louie started the noisy engine of the big truck. It went roaring up the street between green lawns and white houses and pink peonies, to where the school children, boys in freshly ironed blouses and girls in summery dresses, waited in a flock under the elms of the school-yard . . . then out, spinning down the graveled highway between freshly planted fields, turning into the little woods road, narrow and rutted, where the children had to bend their heads under the switch of honey locusts that left small white petals in their sun-warmed hair . . . on into the depths of green woods through the heart of which the shining creek was flowing. . . .

Lois had come to the doorway to watch the truck leave.

"I wouldn't mind going to a picnic myself on a day like this," she murmured.

When she went back into the store, she looked curiously at Gerald. It gave her a guilty feeling, wholly unreasonable, to have him at work in their store to-day when it was a holiday for all the other children. But he had come of his own accord. They hadn't told him to do it.

"Did your sisters go on the picnic, Gerald?" she asked.

"Yes, *they* went," he answered, rather slightingly.

"How many have you, Gerald? Just Juanita and Betty?"

"Yes, ma'am."

"And you're the only boy?"

"Yes, ma'am."

"You could have started in to-morrow just as well, Gerald." He did not answer.

The bright morning grew hotter and hotter, until to enter the drug-store from the glaring cement outside was like going into a cool, clean-scented cavern. The regular set of loafers drifted in, asked for tobacco, and stayed, sitting on the white-topped stools at the soda-fountain and trying to be facetious with Gerald. "Well, you got a new clerk?" every one who came in demanded. It was a new joke every time. In an interval of no customers, Lois stooped down and drew out a pale green bottle frosted over with cold moisture from the case under the counter. It was still a treat to her to think she owned a store.

"I'm going to try some of this new lime stuff," she said. "See how it tastes. Don't you want the other straw, Gerald?"

"No, I guess not," he answered bashfully.

There was a glint of longing and reluctance in his eyes. But Lois thought: Maybe I oughtn't to start offering him things and being too easy with him. After all, Floyd was paying him to help them, and it wasn't her fault that his father had been killed. They were doing the best they could for him by letting him have a job. When, later, she decided to try one of those chocolates Floyd had ordered from a new traveling man, she turned her back while she nibbled it and wiped her fingers on the scrap of oiled paper in which it had been wrapped. Running the business all by themselves was still an adventure to the young Oberholzers; but even now they had run up against the fact more than once that it wasn't just a game. They had halfway discovered the meaning of that term—"If you want to do business—" Lois couldn't pick out from the traveling man's stock the delicately scented toilet waters that she herself liked, but had to choose the red and green brands with big gaudy flowers on the labels that the girls here in town would buy—the kind that "went." She had had to freeze out old Bart Bailey who came in every morning to read the paper and the detective magazines he had no money to buy, and left dirty thumb marks on all the pages.

Noon came with the shriek of the whistle from the power-house, with the noise of cars being started and of the men driving home to dinner.

"When does your mamma expect you home for dinner, Gerald?" Lois asked.

"Oh, I guess it don't matter," Gerald mumbled bashfully.

"Didn't you tell her when you'd come?"

"No, ma'am."

They let him go; but if they kept him in the store, he would have to go later and let them have their dinner at noon. That was one reason why they wanted help. He was back in good time. "Well, didn't take *you* long to eat your dinner!" Floyd said. But maybe it wasn't a good thing to act surprised at his promptness. It would wear off soon enough, if they could infer anything from their experiences with Marcelle Johnston, who had pretended to work for them for three weeks in the winter.

At intervals during the afternoon, Floyd and Lois reported to each other. "We're going to have an awful time teaching him to make a decent sundae. He doesn't catch on any too fast, but he seems to be willing to do whatever you tell him." Whether they wanted to keep him or not, it was evident that he meant to stay. He wanted the job. His surly little freckled face scarcely relaxed into a smile even when there was a dog fight outside and Miss Angie Robinson's little poodle sent that big hound of Ole Swanson's off yelping. He went at whatever he was told to do with dogged earnestness, although he didn't see things for himself. He said "Yes, ma'am" with sober respect; but he would ask: "What's the price of this here kind of tobacco, Lois?" and say to customers: "No, Floyd ain't in just now, he went over to the depot." As the afternoon wore along, his freckled face grew flushed.

"Does it seem like a long day, Gerald?" Lois asked him once. He admitted: "Kind of. Not so very."

Late in the afternoon, the picnic trucks came rattling into town with all the children disheveled and shouting. A few moments afterwards, a group of girls came bursting into the store. Their bright-colored summer dresses were wrinkled, their bobs were wildly rumpled, their tired eyes were shining.

"Oh gee, but we're thirsty! We're just dying! Oh, look at Gerald Rayburn! Are you working in here, Gerald?"

"Yes, didn't you know he was?" his young sister Juanita asked. "We want six bottles of pop, Gerald," she ordered airily.

"Have you got any money?"

"Yes, I have!"

"Where'd you get it then?" he demanded suspiciously.

"None of your business, Mr. Smarty! I guess it's not yours, is it?"

A bright pink flared up in Juanita's cheeks. Her eyes sparkled angrily. She was a pretty child, with red hair, like Gerald's, blazing out in a fuzzy aureole around her freckled face. She flounced down into one of the white chairs. "We want a table, don't we, kids? We don't want to sit at the fountain, like the boys." When Gerald brought the six cold red bottles carefully toppling on the tray, she lifted her little chin and disdained to look at him.

"You needn't think because I'm working here, you can come in and order what you want," he told her.

"Shut up!" she whispered furiously.

Her eyes were brighter still with tears. Mamma had given her the nickel for helping with the ironing yesterday afternoon instead of going off with the girls. She had given it to her for ironing Julie Bronson's pink chemise, with all the lace, so beautifully. It was none of Gerald's business what she did with it! She said to the other girls, with flashing eyes and quivering lips:

"He thinks he's so smart now just because he's starting in to work and Betty and I aren't. You'd just think he *owned* us to hear the way he talks. I don't care. I guess he isn't the only one who does anything. I guess I do lots of things. I'd like to see Gerald Rayburn ever wash the dishes!"

She stuck two straws into her bottle of strawberry pop and sucked it all up defiantly. Maybe she ought to have saved her nickel, but Gerald had no right trying to boss her in front of all the girls.

He told her, when she was leaving the store:

"You needn't go running around now, you can go home and help mamma."

"You keep still!" She threw her nickel down with a ring on the white counter of the soda-fountain. "I guess you aren't my boss *yet*!"

"That's all right, I know what I'm talking about."

"That's right, Gerald," old Hod Brumskill shouted, with humorous approval. "You make the women folks mind you. Ain't that so, boys?"

"You tell 'em it's so!"

They laughed loudly; and then, clustered together with their arms on the glass counter, that had a sign in red letters "Do not lean!", they tore open their packages of bitter-scented tobacco and began to talk in lowered voices about the Rayburn family: how it had been "left," how it got along, about the tragic death of Frank Rayburn, still disputing over the minutiae of that event which they had never yet been able to settle, although nearly a year had passed since the thing happened. "Well, I never could understand how a fella like that, that was used to climbin' all over everywhere, come to fall off that ladder like that . . ." "Why he just kinda stepped backwardlike—I s'pose he forgot maybe where he was at . . ." "Some says the ladder broke and let him down." "Naw, the ladder didn't *break*." "Well, was it true he'd been out drinkin' the night before? That's how I heard it." "Naw, he hadn't been out drinkin' the night before." "Well, I can't figger out . . ." "Why, he just kinda stepped backwards . . ." It was terrible, they all agreed with solemn faces, to think that poor little woman should have been left with those three children, although there was dispute again about how much they had been left with. Some said they "had something," some said they "had nothing." She was a nice woman. Yes, and she was a good-looking woman, too. . . . And then they drew closer together, and one of them said something about "Art Fox," and their voices broke into a laugh and a snicker.

Gerald was washing glasses at the soda-fountain. His freckled face flushed a dull red, and when they snickered he looked over at them furiously. He had a notion of what they were saying. When they passed him, leaving the store, they praised him loudly and self-consciously.

"Well, Gerald, you're all right, ain't you? Takin' right a-hold!"

"You bet he's all right."

"Well, Gerald's the man now, ain't that so, Gerald! He's the one."

"That's right."

The six o'clock whistle blew.

Gerald looked about hesitatingly for Floyd. Finally he went out to the back room of the store to find him.

"Shall I go now? The whistle blew."

"Yes, sure, you go along now, Gerald. I wasn't paying any attention."

Floyd was busy over some boxes on the floor. Gerald hesitated. His face was red. He wanted to ask if he had "done all right." But he was ashamed. Finally he blurted:

"Do you want I should come back to-morrow morning?"

Floyd was still busy over the boxes. Gerald waited.

"Yes, you come back in the morning, Gerald," Floyd answered cheerfully.

Gerald got out of the store as fast as he could. How bright the street seemed outside, and how fresh the air was! He felt as if he had been smelling camphor and perfumes all his life. He had a job! It seemed to him that every one must know. He wanted people to ask him what he had been doing, it made him feel proud and important; although when Mr. Baird, the minister, who had been in the store earlier in the day, greeted him with: "Well, is the day's work over, young man?" he was suddenly too bashful to do more than grunt in answer. He walked soberly down the main street, and broke into a run as he cut across the corner.

His feet burned. It was hard to stand all day like that, although he had told Lois he didn't mind it. He grew hot all over when he thought of the mistakes he had made. But the ache that had seemed lodged in his chest somewhere, ever since the day when his father was buried and all the relatives had told him: "Well, you'll have to look after your mamma now, Gerald, won't you?"—when his mother cried and clung to him that night—that ache was strangely eased. He was earning money. He could take care of his mother. It humiliated him that his mother should have to be doing the washing for other people, although it was only some of their neighbors; but she wouldn't have to do it always. He had not heard more than a few words of what those men in the drug-store were saying. But at the thought—the very suspicion of it—his mind felt hot and sore. If they'd been saying anything about his mother, they'd be sorry for it. He'd—he didn't know just what—but anyway, they'd better look out!

The new little semi-bungalow house looked bleak and desolate. It had been that way ever since his father died. No new flowers had been planted this spring, the clothes-line hadn't been fixed, the garage for the car they had been going to get this summer stood unpainted just as his father had left it last fall. But they would have things again. The relatives needn't say anything; he guessed he could take care of his own mother without their telling him. He loved her, but it was none of their business to know it.

She was standing in the doorway. Gerald evaded her kiss, ducked away from her and went tramping out to the kitchen. He was afraid she was going to make a fuss.

"I gotta wash my hands," he told her importantly.

She followed him and stood looking at him, pitiful and proud.

"Why don't you go up to the bathroom, sweetheart?"

"I druther wash down here."

It was what his father had done when he came home from work.

"Are you ready for supper?" she pleaded.

"You bet."

She touched his face, he couldn't avoid that. But he got into the dining room as fast as he could and sat down with satisfaction. There were all the things that he liked—hot biscuits, and jelly, and strawberries. He demanded coffee, and his mother gave it to him. Betty's little mouth puckered up and her eyes were round with amazement.

"You don't let *us* have coffee," she said.

"Well, brother's been working. He has to have it."

The two little girls chattered eagerly about the school picnic. Gerald stuck to the business of eating. He had never been so hungry; hot biscuits had never tasted so good. He replied briefly to his mother's fond questions about what he had been doing all day.

"Were Floyd and his wife good to you? Did they show you what to do?"

"Yeah, they were all right."

"Did you know how to wait on people?"

"Sure."

"Didn't it seem terribly long to you?"

"Naw."

"Well, you want to eat a good supper."

It was over now, and he didn't want to talk about it. He wished she'd let him alone.

The one cooky left on the plate was given to Gerald. Betty followed her mother into the kitchen, weeping and complaining. She was the baby, and the extra pieces of everything were for her.

"I don't see why you gave it to Gerald, mamma. You didn't even make him give me half."

"Well, darling, listen—when men have been working they get hungrier than women and little girls do, and then we have to let them have what they want to eat. We don't get so hungry."

"*I* was hungry."

"Were you, pet?" Her mother laughed, half commiseratingly. "Then you eat this strawberry mamma puts into your little mouth."

"I don't want a strawberry. I had enough strawberries. And I was working," Betty insisted. "I put on all the knives and forks. I *was* working, mamma."

"Were you? Well, you were helping. You're a nice little helper."

"Before I'd make a fuss about an old cooky!" Juanita said scornfully.

She flashed a quick indignant glance at Gerald, remembering how he had talked to her in the drug-store. Let him have everything in the house to eat if he wanted it, and if mamma wanted to give it to him! But there was an obscure justice that silenced her even while it made her resentful. Well, she wouldn't be here all her life. She'd get married some day— and then she'd do as she pleased.

Gerald went out and sat on the steps of the porch. This was the time of day when his father always used to come out here and look at the paper. Gerald was ashamed of having eaten the cooky. He thought it belonged to him, but let that baby Betty have it! He would after this. He didn't know when he had had such a good supper. He watched Bobbie Parker's yard across the street so that he could shout across at Bobby the instant he came outdoors. Maybe they could go over and see those turtles Bobbie's uncle had in his back-yard. It would be fun to see if they could really be taught tricks. He could hear the girls complaining about the dishes. "It's your turn to-night." "It isn't!" Gee whizz, if they couldn't even do a little thing like washing dishes!

The evening came on cool and bright. Gerald stayed on the porch steps, although Bobby didn't appear in the yard. What he had really meant to do was to ask Bobby about the picnic, and try to find out, without saying it in so many words, whether any other boy had hung around Arlene Fedderson. He didn't care, anyway. He had thought about it in the store all the time, but it didn't matter so much now. His mother was the one he had to look after. Again he felt a fine, tired glow of satisfaction. He had put in a good day's work, all right.

Then he blushed. He remembered those men at the drugstore. Here was that old Art Fox coming up the walk with a pailful of strawberries! Well, if he thought he was coming here with those berries, he could just go away again.

"H'lo, Gerald," Art Fox called out cheerfully. He was a good-natured man, a widower, with a red sunburned face and grayish hair and mustache. He lived about a block away from the Rayburns, in a good-sized house. Gerald had always thought he was a nice man, because he never said any more than "'Lo, boys!" when the boys ran across his lawn playing run-sheep-run.

"H'lo," Gerald answered briefly.

"Your ma around anywhere?"

"I don't know."

Art Fox halted. "Oh, well . . . She ain't gone out anywhere, has she?"

"I guess she has."

What did it matter whether that was true or not? Art Fox had no business coming here. He felt a sense of pain and outrage.

"That's too bad. I thought I'd drop around and see if you folks couldn't use a few strawberries. I got a bunch of 'em ripe—too many for an old fellow to eat by himself," he added with a mild attempt at jocularity. "Didn't know as you folks had any."

"We got some."

"That so? Well, I guess you can use a few more, can't you?"

"No, we got all we want."

"That so? Well, if you got all you need . . ." Art Fox stood there awkwardly for a moment. "Well, I guess I'll have to try to dump these on somebody else."

Gerald was silent.

"Your ma be home pretty soon, will she?"

"No, she ain't here."

"That so? Well . . . good-by, then."

Gerald said nothing. He could feel his heart thumping. He looked away. Art Fox was going down the walk with the strawberries newly washed and freshly red in the bright tin pail. Just as he turned the corner, Mrs. Rayburn came to the door.

"I thought I heard somebody. Have they gone? Was anybody here, Gerald?"

"Art Fox." Gerald did not turn around.

"Oh!" His mother seemed a little flustered. "What did he want? Has he gone away?" she asked.

"He brought some of his strawberries."

"Why, Gerald, why didn't you call me?"

"'Cause I told him we didn't want 'em. We got some of our own."

"Why, *Gerald* . . ."

"Well, we don't want him around here," Gerald said roughly.

He stared straight ahead at a little bird hopping about on the lawn, fighting down the childish tears that made his throat ache and his eyes burn. That sense of pain and outrage swelled in his heart. He thought of the unfinished garage standing bare and desolate in the back-yard—his father's old coat still hanging in the kitchen entry. If his mother couldn't take care of herself, he'd do it for her. He was the man of the house now. Art Fox could stay at home where he belonged. This was *their* home. She was *his* mother. Above that ache of unmanly tears he felt a hard exultance. They wouldn't laugh any more in the drug-store. They wouldn't talk about her.

She looked flushed and disconcerted. She stood in the doorway looking at Gerald. The back of his red head was like his father's. So was the set of his sturdy shoulders. She looked at them with an unwilling respect that turned slowly to resentment. All these last few weeks, a secret girlish pleasure had been growing up in her heart most surprisingly out of the blackness of her grief and loneliness. She knew that she was admired. She had thought it hidden from every one. At times she had laughed and called herself a fool; and at times her eyes were dreamy and a warmth settled softly about her. Now it was shamed and trampled. . . .

She started to say something to Gerald. But she stopped, as she had always stopped with Frank. She felt her anger melting helplessly away from her. He was so proud of working for her. He was so proud of his strength. He was only a little boy, after all—her little boy, sitting small and pitiful and unapproachable in the twilight.

She turned, her face suddenly quivering, went back into the hot darkness of the empty house, and sat down there alone.